FIRE DAMAG

Kate Medina has always been fascinated by the 'whys' of human behaviour, an interest that drove her to study Psychology at university and later to start a crime series featuring clinical psychologist, Dr Jessie Flynn. She has an MA in Creative Writing from Bath Spa University and her debut novel *White Crocodile* received widespread critical acclaim, as did *Fire Damage*, the first book in the Jessie Flynn series.

Before turning to writing full time, Kate spent five years in the Territorial Army and has lectured at the London Business School and the London School of Economics. She lives in London with her husband and three children.

www.katemedina.com
@KateTMedina

Also by Kate Medina

White Crocodile

KATE MEDINA

Fire Damage

HARPER

Harper
An imprint of HarperCollins*Publishers*
1 London Bridge Street
London SE1 9GF

www.harpercollins.co.uk

This paperback edition 2017

1

First published by HarperCollins*Publishers* 2016

A catalogue record for this book
is available from the British Library

ISBN: 9780008132279

Typeset in Sabon by Palimpsest Book Production Limited,
Falkirk, Stirlingshire

Printed and bound in Great Britain by
Clays Ltd, St Ives plc

*For Anthony Medina, with love
and thanks for everything*

1

The little boy inched through the doorway, arms and legs jerking like a marionette. Stopping just inside, he scanned the room with frightened eyes. In his hands, he gripped a torch. A huge, black metal Maglite, which swung slowly back and forth in front of him as if he was feeling his way through darkness. The beam traced along the walls, was swallowed for a moment by the sharp winter light cutting in through the sash window. It scoured each corner, drifted over the furniture, stopping to inspect the alcove under Jessie's desk, the corner where the filing cabinet housing her psychology books and journals cast shadow.

Kneeling down so that her face was level with his, but maintaining her distance, avoiding direct eye contact, Jessie smiled.

'Hello, Sami. I'm Jessie Flynn,' she said softly.

She had dressed in civvies this morning, a denim skirt, long-sleeved white shirt and simple, navy patent leather ballet pumps, ubiquitous clothes that communicated nothing about her, made no statement.

The little boy remained silent. He continued to rotate the torch, eyes twitching from side to side, nervously tracking its beam. Standing, Jessie stepped forward to close the door.

Sami shot back against the wall, his expression rigid with fear. A sob burst from his lips. Swinging the torch wildly, he made a harsh, throbbing noise deep in his throat, like the growl of a terrified dog.

Jessie moved away, hands spread calmingly.

'I'm sorry if I scared you, Sami. I didn't mean to.' She sat down slowly in one of the two leather armchairs by the window. 'I won't move from here. You explore my office. Take as long as you like.'

He remained where he was, pressed against the wall, ramrod straight. His chest hollowed and heaved from the effort of drawing in breath. Jessie stayed silent, waiting. Gradually, he moved from the wall, the heavy torch hugged close to his body like a loved teddy bear. One step. Another. The movements jerky, uncoordinated. His face, hauntingly pale, began to take on colour.

The torch's beam reflected off the patent leather of Jessie's ballet pumps, was dull on the denim of her skirt, tinged the white of her shirt citrus. The beam found her face. She smiled, compelled herself not to blink. Knew that beyond the light that fuzzed her vision, Sami was watching her intently, obsessively focused on every cue.

The torch dipped. Jessie raised her eyes, and for a fraction of a second their gazes met.

'The girl knows,' he whispered.

Sami's breath came fast and shallow; Jessie could feel it, hot and cold, damp against her cheek. Then came the soft touch of his fingers.

'Grrrrr. Grrrrr.'

That growling noise again, from the back of his throat. She sat completely motionless, staring ahead, making no sound. With lightning quickness, his fingers touched her neck and were gone. Jessie forced herself not to flinch. She could sense him only millimetres from her, the heat of the torch beam mapping a circle on her skin.

His fingers again, touching her hair this time, butterfly wings. She had tied her hair up in a ponytail to get it out of the way. Usually she wore it in the regulation bun when she was at work, but she had felt that it was too formal, too severe for today's patient. Reaching up, she tugged the elastic band from her hair. A jet-black curtain fell to her waist. The hair swallowed his arms, coating his hands and forearms to the elbows.

Sami froze.

'Sami, what's wrong.'

Without warning, he swung the heavy metal Maglite wildly at Jessie's head, slamming its metal edge into her temple. He swung again, smashing the torch against the side of her head. Raising her hands to fend him off, she ducked. Another blow caught her cheekbone, glanced off her shoulder. Dizziness. The floor rose, the ceiling dipped. She managed to snatch the Maglite from his grip as she fell to her hands and knees. Blood streamed from the gash in her head, into her eyes, blinding her.

He was screaming. Dragging her sleeve across her eyes, she spun on to her back, searching for the noise, searching for Sami. He had slid to the floor, hands pressed over his ears, body curled tight into a foetal position. He was wailing and sobbing, his chest heaving as if there was not enough air in the room. Crawling over, Jessie wrapped her arms around him. Held him tight. Felt him struggle and kick, writhe and scream. Felt his heart beating, almost punching its way out of his chest. Didn't let go.

Thought of another little boy, fifteen years ago, equally helpless and terrified. A little boy she had loved. Loved and failed.

'Burnt,' Sami sobbed. 'Arms burnt.'

'Nothing's burnt. You're safe.'

She could feel blood running down the side of her face, her cheek and neck slick with it.

'The girl is burnt. The man is burnt.' His voice was hoarse from screaming. 'Sami torch? *Sami torch?*'

Jessie found his torch, fumbled it back into his grip.

'Shadowman,' he whispered, clutching the torch to his heart. 'The Shadowman came. The girl knows.'

2

Jessie stood in the women's toilets and stared at herself in the mirror. She was shaking, her stomach churning. The cut on her forehead was a deep scarlet slash against the milky white of her skin, still bleeding. Her temple was throbbing, an egg-shaped bruise already forming under the skin. Tugging some paper from the dispenser, she soaked it under the hot tap, wiped it up her cheek and pressed it to the cut, wincing with the pain. She couldn't stop trembling. What the *hell* had just happened? She cast her mind back over the referral notes she had been given.

Sami Scott. Four-year-old boy.

Four years and four months old – a July birthday – young for his year. But although he had been due to start school in September, he hadn't, couldn't.

Father: Major Nicholas Scott, Intelligence Corps, badly burnt in Afghanistan three months previously.

Mother: Nooria Scott, Persian-English, born and raised in England.

Preliminary diagnosis: post-traumatic stress disorder.

But was it?

What was with the torch?

'The girl knows.'

Who was the girl? Was it Jessie? She was pretty sure it wasn't her. She was twenty-nine, and to a four-year-old she would seem ancient, a woman, not a girl. Semantics perhaps, but she thought not. She'd had the sense that he was referring to himself, but that couldn't be right. Despite the shoulder-length, curly dark hair, huge chocolate eyes, that chubby, cherubic appearance that could be either girl or boy, he was definitely a boy. The notes had clearly specified gender.

Referred to the Defence Psychology Service by his father who had been evacuated from Camp Bastion and repatriated to England in August, after suffering horrific burns in a petrol-bomb attack.

The face looking back at her in the mirror was ghostly, sallower even than usual, her eyes a blue so pale they were almost translucent. She looked wraithlike. Felt as though once she released her grip of the basin, there would be nothing to tether her to this earth; that she would float up into the chilly winter sky.

Looking at herself now, she was transported straight back fifteen years – a hospital mirror, the same ethereal being – just a traumatized girl then. So viscerally could she remember her helplessness, that she could taste it in her mouth. Acid vomit.

And now, another little boy who desperately needed her help. The last half an hour had stripped her raw. She felt completely out of her depth.

3

Jessie waited, engine idling, while the guards swung open the heavy metal gates. She gave them a brief, distracted wave as she drove out of Bradley Court Army Rehabilitation Centre, and joined the public road. The tension in her was so acute she could feel it physically: a skintight electric suit coating her body, clenched around her throat, the bare wires hissing and crackling against her skin.

There was no traffic on the narrow country road and her headlights cut twin beams through the gathering dusk, tracking the hedgerows, knotted with Elder and Dogwood, on one side, the dotted white line demarcating the oncoming lane on the other.

Winding down her window, she let the chill evening air funnel over her face and neck, cooling the heat from the electric suit, the rush of cold bringing tears to her eyes. She had felt like crying ever since the end of her session with Sami. She let them flow, needing the release.

Her mobile phone rang and she glanced at it. Gideon Duursema. She ignored it, couldn't face the 'how did it go?' conversation. Reaching across to the CD player, she cranked up the sound, let James Blunt, full volume, assault her eardrums. *Back to Bedlam*. Appropriate. It was the only CD she had in the car, a Secret Santa departmental gift last Christmas. Everyone had laughed when she unwrapped it, uniform groans of *Jesus, not him*. But there was something about his voice that took her somewhere better, whatever she had been doing. She had played it on a constant cycle for a year, knew all the songs by heart, felt opera-singer talented when she sang along, but knew that the reality was closer to a stray cat's chorus.

Slowing to twenty, she pulled into the single-track country lane that led to her cottage. It was windy, hemmed by high hedges, only a brief flash of open fields through the odd metal five-bar farm gate during the day. She'd had a close shave a few months before with the farmer and his herd of prize Friesians, and he'd promised to grind his tractor down the side of her beloved Mini if she ever drove that fast down *his* country lane again.

Rounding the final bend, her headlights picked out an unfamiliar car parked outside her cottage, a red Golf GTI, complete with spoiler and sports profiling. It looked like a pimp's ride. A man she didn't recognize was standing on her minute patch of lawn, arms folded across his chest, studying the leafless wisteria clogging the front wall. Behind him, her retired next-door-neighbour, Ahmose Rahotep, was standing on Jessie's doorstep, leaning on his stick, mouth pressed into a thin, tight line.

At the sound of her engine, the man turned. He was about thirty, broad shouldered and long limbed, dressed in grey jogging bottoms, and a navy-blue hooded sweatshirt.

She realized, suddenly, that there was something familiar about him. Something she couldn't quite place.

Pulling up behind the Golf, Jessie cut her engine. Her head was still throbbing, Sami's look of utter terror fixed in her mind. She had wanted to come home to a silent house and a glass of wine, space to think, to get a head start before she saw Sami again tomorrow and met his father, Major Nicholas Scott, for the first time.

No such luck.

With a sigh, she opened the car door. The man walked down the path as she climbed out and met her on the lane. Recognition dawned. Virtually all resemblance to his former self, the man she had last seen, a skeletal shadow, a hermit in his mother's house, confined to those unusual amber eyes. Her gaze found the scar from the bullet wound on his temple, damaged, stitched skin like the brown petals of a dead rose.

Captain Ben Callan, Military Police Special Investigation Branch. The only patient she had treated since she joined the Defence Psychology Service, two years previously, who she felt she'd completely and utterly failed.

'Ben . . . Captain Callan.' Her gaze dipped to the red-and-gold Royal Military Police insignia on his blue hoodie. 'You're—' She broke off.

'Yes,' he said quietly. 'I'm back.'

Pushing her hair from her face, wincing as her fingertips dragged against the cut Sami had inflicted with his torch, Jessie looked up at him. He was clean-shaven, his sandy-blond hair cut short. He looked as if he'd had a few proper meals since she'd last seen him in July, had added muscle at the gym. But vestiges of his Afghan experience, the last few months of the fight to reclaim his sanity, clung to him.

9

He was still ten kilos lighter than the photographs she had seen on his mother's mantelpiece. Black shadowed the skin beneath his eyes, which contained a watchfulness, a twitchy awareness of everything that was happening around him. She had seen that same look in many of the other veterans she had counselled, men and women who had survived long tours in a war zone – Afghanistan, Iraq – and frequent contact with a ubiquitous enemy. He clearly wasn't sleeping properly, was most likely having ongoing nightmares.

'How are you, Dr Flynn?' He grimaced at the cut on her head. 'Not good.'

She shrugged. 'I had a run-in with a small boy. As you can see, I lost.'

'Small boys can be dangerous.' He met her gaze, the ghost of a smile crossing his face. 'Big boys even more so.'

She cocked an eyebrow. 'So I've been told.'

'I'm glad to see your patients aren't letting you get the better of them, at least.'

'Round two tomorrow, so we'll see.'

She moved past him and he turned to follow her.

'What do you want?' she cast over her shoulder.

'I need your help.'

'My help? I thought you'd had enough of my help to last you a lifetime.'

'With a case.'

She pushed open her garden gate. 'As you can see from my war wound, I already have a case. In fact I have a five-centimetre-high stack of them sitting on my desk, begging for attention.'

'Gideon told me that you'd argue.'

'He was right.' She swung around to face him on the garden path. 'Look, it's good to see you back on your feet and I don't mean to be rude, but I've had a long and relatively shitty day. Couldn't we have had this conversation over the phone?'

His expression remained impassive. 'I would have been happy to. If you'd picked up.'

Sliding her mobile from her pocket, she checked the display. Five missed calls from an unknown number and three from her boss, Dr Gideon Duursema.

She pulled a face. 'Must have switched itself to silent.'

'Must have done. Though you'd have struggled to hear a grenade going off over the sound of that singer-soldier crap you were listening to.'

'How dare you. James Blunt is a god.'

He rolled his eyes. 'Let's not go there. I don't have a spare couple of hours to tell you how pitifully misguided you are.' Holding out a file, he glanced across at Ahmose who was in place on her doorstep, leaning heavily on his stick, a tired, bent St Peter valiantly guarding the gates to heaven. 'Look, I have a meeting tomorrow afternoon and I need a psychologist there. Gideon said to get you to call him if you want an argument.' He paused. 'Can we go inside to talk? It's confidential.'

Jessie sighed. 'Do I have a choice?'

His reply was curt. 'No.'

Turning, she laid a hand on Ahmose's arm. 'Thanks for looking out for me, Ahmose, but it's fine. Unfortunately it's work. Cup of tea tomorrow evening? I should be back by six.'

Ahmose nodded. 'I'll put the kettle on soon as I hear your car. My sister sent me some ghorayebah biscuits direct from Cairo.' Raising his hand to his mouth, he kissed the tips of his fingers. 'We can share those too.' He tilted towards

11

her, lowering his voice. 'He wasn't polite. I didn't want to leave him alone outside your place, just in case. You never know these days. He really wasn't polite.' Hooking his walking stick over his forearm, he reached for Jessie's hand, gave it a reassuring squeeze. 'I'll be able to hear if you shout.'

She gave Ahmose a quick peck on the cheek. 'I'll be fine. He's police. If you're not safe with the police then who are you safe with?'

'Police.' He almost spat out the word. 'Now don't you get me started.'

Jessie had chosen to buy her own house, rather than living in Army accommodation. As a single woman, even an officer, she would have got little more than one room and no privacy. And it made sense, given that her work took her to different parts of the UK and abroad, wherever a psychologist was required.

Her tiny farmworker's cottage was the middle in a row of three, down a single-track country lane in the Surrey Hills, an area of outstanding natural beauty, fifty square miles of rolling hills that cut east to west from the sprawling satellite villages bordering southwest London, to meet with the Sussex Downs in the south. It was picture-postcard England: narrow, winding lanes, thatched cottages, flint stone churches, cricket greens, village pubs garlanded with hanging baskets of busy Lizzies and lobelia, fields of hot yellow rape seed in summer, cabbages and sprouts in winter.

Her cottage put her five miles from the Army rehabilitation centre, a converted former manor house near Dorking and a short drive from the town of Aldershot, 'Home of the British Army', where many regiments had their base, and where much of her work took her.

Ahmose lived alone on one side. Over one of their many shared teas, he had told her that he'd bought the cottage to retire to with his wife, Alice. She had died of a stroke within four months of their moving in, and he had continued to live there alone, his sitting room a photographic shrine to the woman who had shared the English portion of his life for almost thirty years. The cottage on the other side was owned by a childless, professional London couple who came down once a month at the most and kept themselves to themselves when they did, which suited both her and Ahmose perfectly.

Callan had to duck to get through her front door, which opened directly into the living room. She hadn't noticed how tall he was, given that he had rarely been standing when she'd seen him at his mother's house, or if he was, he'd been hunched and folded in on himself, both physically and mentally. He was well over six foot, and in the cottage built to house farmworkers from the eighteenth century, average height five foot four, he looked huge, a vision of Gulliver. Slipping off her ballet pumps, Jessie lined them up side by side at the edge of the mat, shrugged off her jacket and hung it on the hook behind the door, straightening the sleeves until they hung parallel, creaseless, aware all the time that Callan was watching, the creaking of the floorboards as he shifted his weight from foot to foot telegraphing his impatience. When she had finished, he bent to untie his shoelaces, kick his trainers off carelessly.

He straightened and she watched him surveying her sitting room, the pristine cream carpet, minimal furnishings – two cream sofas and a reclaimed oak coffee table, free of clutter

– the fitted shelves empty of books and ornaments. Show-home spotless.

'What did you say to Ahmose?' she asked, when he joined her in the kitchen.

'We were having a conversation about gardening. I told him that your wisteria needed cutting right back. It will flower much better in spring with a decent prune.'

'Ah. That'll be why he was looking at you as if you were the devil. He does my garden. Takes a huge amount of pride in it. You've just driven an articulated lorry through his ego.'

Callan smiled and shrugged. 'I wasn't entirely idle for the past six months. At least my mother now has a flourishing garden, even if her nerves are shot to shit.'

For an unexpected moment, Jessie's mind flashed to Wimbledon, to the small sixties house she had grown up in. She had only seen her mother once since last Christmas, she realized, in March, when she had popped in with a present and cake to celebrate her mother's birthday, taken her for lunch at a local pub. Her own birthday this year spent at home with Ahmose, pleading pressure of work to duck a visit. Guilt at that decision still hanging over her like a shroud, adding to the other accumulated layers of guilt and self-recrimination. Even more reason not to get in touch.

'Coffee? Tea?' Tugging open the fridge, she pulled out a bottle of Sauvignon. 'Wine? I'm having wine – lots of it – if that helps your decision.'

He shook his head. 'I'm on duty.'

The words 'on duty' surprised her, though she realized that they shouldn't. He had, after all, come to ask for her help on a case. So he was back at work in the Military Police Special Investigation Branch then. Properly back. She was pleased for him. She glanced around, caught his eye and smiled.

'Dressed like that?'

He smiled, an easy smile that lit his amber eyes the colour of warm honey. Despite the watchfulness, he seemed relatively comfortable in his own skin, a state that three months ago she would have happily bet a sizeable sum he was too far gone ever to reach.

'I've been in the gym. I'm on call. I can work out and I can turn up to a crime scene looking like shit, but I can't drink. I'd love a coffee.'

While she put the kettle on, he wandered into the sitting room. Jessie poured herself a large glass of wine, returned the bottle to the fridge with the label facing outward, replaced the kettle on its stand, angling the handle so that it was parallel with the wall, wiped down the work surface, picked up his coffee and her glass and followed him.

He was standing by the fireplace, studying the pictures on her mantelpiece. Just two. The only personal things on display in her sitting room, the only clutter. One of her brother, the other of Jessie, Jamie and their mother at London Zoo, all three of them happy and healthy looking, an image of her family that seemed so unlikely given what followed, that sometimes she felt as if the photographs had been mocked up on Photoshop.

'Who's this?' He picked up the photograph of Jamie.

'My brother,' she said curtly. She willed him to put it back, leave it.

'Younger or older?'

'Younger by seven years.'

'A lot.'

She shrugged. 'He was a late addition.' *A Band-Aid baby.* She didn't say it.

'So he's . . . how old now?'

'Nothing.' She fought to keep her voice even, feeling the tension rise, the electric suit tingle against her skin. 'He's nothing. No age.'

Taking the picture from Callan, she put it back on the mantelpiece. It was her favourite picture of Jamie, taken when he was four, his mouth, ringed by a telltale brown smear of chocolate ice cream, wide open in a beautiful, innocent grin, his eyes clamped shut in the way that small children have of smiling with the whole of their faces. All teeth and gums. She remembered the occasion well. She had taken him down to watch the tourists queuing for entrance to Wimbledon tennis championships, the queue five thick and a kilometre long. Day 1. Back when Andre Agassi was limping out the last of his career. It had been punishingly hot and the atmosphere had felt like a street party, people handing around bottles of wine and juice, sharing golf umbrellas for shade.

She steadied herself against the mantelpiece, unprepared for the emotional vertigo of Jamie being so close, but not being there, feeling exposed in front of this virtual stranger.

The picture wasn't straight. The electric suit was hissing and snapping against her skin. Realigning the picture, she checked the distance between the two photographs. She could sense Callan watching her, knew she should move away and straighten things once he had gone, but couldn't. Just *couldn't.*

She spun around to face him.

'The case.' It came out more roughly than she had meant.

'Did you come to interfere with my things or did you come about a case?'

He held up his hands in a mock defensive gesture, but the expression on his face held no apology. Only query.

'Can I sit?'

'Sure.'

She indicated the sofa, curled herself into the chair opposite, folding her legs underneath her, wrapping her arms around her torso. Defensive body language, she knew, but too stressed now to unwrap herself. In the confined space of her living room his presence, those bright amber eyes fixed on her face, his easy confidence, so unexpected, made her feel gauche and claustrophobic in equal measures. The shift in the balance of confidence palpable, to her at least.

'Last week, one of our Intelligence Corps non-commissioned officers, a Sergeant Andy Jackson, died in Afghanistan.'

'He's not the first and I'm sure he won't be the last,' she replied.

'This was different. He was . . .' he paused, as if trying to find the right words. 'Being beasted, I suppose you'd call it, by one of the other Intelligence Corps sergeants, Colin Starkey. They were based at TAAC-South, headquartered in Kandahar Airfield, doing whatever secret squirrel stuff Intelligence Corps soldiers do. They went for a run in the desert around the airfield.' He paused. 'You've been to Afghanistan, haven't you?'

'Twice. The first time January to April 2014, to Camp Bastion, before our combat mission in Afghanistan ended and most of our troops were pulled out. The second time was for four weeks in February of this year. I was working with TAAC-Capital at Camp KAIA – Kabul International Airport.'

17

'So as you know, we still have a few troops out there training, advising and assisting the Afghan Army and Security Forces.'

Jessie nodded.

'What Starkey and Jackson did was insane given the security situation out there, more so given that it was the hottest time of the day, and even though it's autumn the temperature would have been hitting the mid-thirties, with fifty per cent humidity. They were both dressed in combat kit and had no water with them.' He sighed. 'Jackson ended up dead.'

'Dehydration?'

He shook his head. 'A bullet wound to the stomach.'

'From whose gun?'

'Starkey's.'

Jessie's eyes widened. 'And it isn't cut and dried? Murder or manslaughter?'

'The only viable print that was lifted from Starkey's gun was a partial of Jackson's on the trigger.'

'And Starkey's? There weren't any of his?'

'No. The gun was well oiled. It's almost impossible to lift prints from a well-oiled gun. Forensics said that they were lucky to get the sliver of Jackson's on the trigger.'

'What about Jackson's sidearm?'

'It was holstered when he was found. It had recently been cleaned and oiled. No prints.'

Jessie took a sip of wine, rolled the stem of the glass between her fingers, thinking. 'Who said that Jackson was being beasted? He could have gone voluntarily. There's not much else to do out there during downtime and many of the lads are obsessed with fitness.'

Callan nodded. 'So that's where the picture gets muddy.

A corporal who shared their quarters said that he walked in on them having an argument.'

'What about?'

'He didn't catch the subject, just the raised voices. They stopped when he came in and left straight after, to go for the run. But he said that Jackson looked . . .' He fell silent, searching for the right words. '. . . *off*. But not enough so as to make him step in.'

Jessie frowned. 'And he was a corporal, so he would have had to feel on very solid ground to question two sergeants.' Her legs were deadening, pins and needles. She shuffled them from under her, stretched out and put her feet on the coffee table. She saw Callan cast a quick look at her legs. Smoothing her skirt down below her knees, she continued: 'Starkey and Jackson were the same rank.'

He looked up and met her gaze, unembarrassed. 'Yes.'

'So . . . what's the psychology behind that?'

He shrugged. 'You're the shrink.'

Silence, which, after a moment, Callan broke. 'Starkey had a black eye forming when he was found and bruising to his torso when he was stripped and searched back at camp.'

'And Jackson?'

'His autopsy is booked for the day after tomorrow.'

'How did Starkey explain the black eye and bruising?'

'He didn't.'

'But he radioed the medics after Jackson was shot?'

Callan nodded. 'The shot was heard by the camp guards. Starkey radioed for help straight after.'

'Is Starkey under arrest?'

'He's back in the UK, relieved of duties and confined to barracks for the moment, but he hasn't been charged with

19

anything. We don't have enough evidence either way. I need to work out whether it's murder, manslaughter, suicide or an accident borne of plain fucking stupidity. As well as collecting physical evidence, I need to understand what Colin Starkey was thinking – what they were *both* thinking.'

'Motive,' Jessie murmured. She took another sip of wine and looked past him, to the window. It was dark now, the night so dense that it could have been made from liquid; the table lamp she had switched on a hot yellow sun reflected in the glass.

'Have you talked to Starkey yet?'

'Once today.'

'With a Ministry of Defence lawyer?'

'He didn't want one.'

'And . . .?' She looked back to him.

His amber eyes were fixed on her face, head on one side, as if he was studying her, sizing her up. Though his bald scrutiny put her on edge, she wasn't about to let him realize it. She met his gaze directly.

'Did you get anything from him?'

'Not much.'

'Name, rank and number?' Soldiers were notoriously tight-lipped; gave nothing away unless it was absolutely unavoidable.

He rolled his eyes. 'That's the polite way of saying it. Fuck-all is the less polite way.'

He'd finished his coffee, was looking around for somewhere to put the empty cup. Jessie jumped off the chair, took it from him and deposited it carefully in the kitchen sink, resisting the intense urge to wash it, dry it, stow it in the cupboard then and there.

'This has the potential to get properly out of hand,' he

said, when she returned to the living room. 'Jackson leaves a wife and two small children, under fives. His father is a troublemaker. He works as a shop steward at a factory in South London. Knows his rights – that kind of guy. He's already spoken to the *Daily Mail*. The newspapers are all over the cutbacks in defence spending, how it's putting lives at risk. They're gagging for anything that makes the Army look bad. I need to get to the bottom of this quickly, keep a lid on the negative publicity.'

'His son is dead. His grandchildren are fatherless. You can't blame him.'

Callan didn't hesitate. 'His son joined the Army. It goes with the territory.'

'But not to die like that, potentially at the hands of your own side.'

A grim smile pulled at the corners of his mouth. 'We don't get to choose how we die. Many people don't even get to choose how we live.' Tossing the file on to the coffee table, he pushed himself to his feet. 'I'll leave the file with you – not that there's much of use in it. I'm interviewing Colin Starkey tomorrow at Provost Barracks.' His will stretched out to her. 'I'll see you there at ten to four. Ask for me at the gate, they'll let you through. I'll meet you downstairs, main entrance.'

'Fine,' Jessie said simply. 'One interview and then we'll see.'

4

Jeanette Bass-Cooper stood on the narrow shingle beach and looked back up the wide stretch of lawn to the house. It was faux Greek, a huge and no doubt once grand villa, resplendent with fake colonnades, plastered and painted a sickly pale lemon, the paint peeling, plaster brittle and crumbling in places. It brought to mind one of the over made-up, ageing showgirls she had seen at a burlesque show in Paris a couple of weekends ago, gaudy and brazen against the sober Arts and Crafts on one side, the Georgian on the other. But it had potential. Six bedrooms, four bathrooms, three receptions, all with huge windows overlooking the water, décor that would have to be stripped back to its bare bones and redone, but its own private stretch of shingle beach and incredible views over the upper reaches of Chichester Harbour.

It had been empty for four months and the landline was disconnected. There was no mobile reception inside, which was why she had tottered in her heels through the garden – mobile held aloft, gaze fixed on the reception icon – and down on to the skinny stone beach to call the estate agent.

On one hand she was pleased there was no reception: no telephone masts to spoil this rural idyll she had set her heart on acquiring. But on the other, the inconvenience made her feel impotent. Getting away from it all was one thing, but with a commercial property business to run, being incommunicado was costly.

Signal. At last. Only two bars, but it would have to do. This wasn't going to be a long or complex conversation. All she needed from her estate agent was an explanation as to how – when she had bought a shopping centre in Liverpool for her business, the transaction complete from beginning to end in three days – it had taken five weeks and counting to fail even to exchange on this house. The owner was dead, for Chrissakes, so it clearly wasn't him holding up the deal.

She found Gavin Maxwell's number on speed dial. The frustration she felt at the prospect of speaking to him had already found its way to her shoulders, which had re-positioned themselves up around her ears.

'Come on, pick up,' she muttered, starting to pace. She glanced at her watch: 12 p.m. *Don't tell me he's gone to lunch.* Not that she would be surprised. Nothing would surprise her with this deal. 'Pick *up.*'

Seaweed caught in her heel and she bent to untangle it, still clutching the phone to her ear. In tight dress and heels, she felt like a hobbled calf, had to clench her abdominals to stop herself from toppling.

Mid-stoop, she stopped.

The first thing she noticed was the smell. Decomposing seaweed yes, but another overlaying it. Rotten and putrid. A dustbin full of refuse left fermenting in sun for a fortnight.

The second thing she noticed was the blackened stick,

tangled in the seaweed that had snagged her heel. Had someone held a fire on the beach? Teenagers making the most of the empty property to hold a party? She grasped the stick; her fingers sank into mush.

Jesus . . . her eyes bulged. Was that a hand?

She sucked in a choking breath.

A hand, the fingers, entwined with seaweed, bent into a tortured claw. She ran her eyes up the blackened stick and somewhere in the recesses of her chilled brain, she realized that it was an arm.

The third thing she noticed was that the torso attached to the arm was just that. A torso. Distended. *Bloated*. Her gaze tracked down. There were no legs. Nothing below waist level.

'Ohmygod!' she groaned.

The fourth thing she noticed was the empty eye sockets above the mouth, cavities of blackened bone, nothing soft remaining. The mouth itself, a lipless hole lined with yellow teeth, opened wide in a silent, agonized scream.

Skin. Did it have skin? Or was that only muscle, sinew and bone?

'Ms Bass-Cooper.' A distorted voice came out of the phone.

Terror was like tin foil in her mouth.

'Oh my God.' Her voice thick with tears. 'OH MY GOD.'

'MS BASS-COOPER. ARE YOU OK?'

The phone clattered from her hand.

5

The house was a mile outside the village of Crookham, a few miles northwest of Aldershot, standing alone in a shallow valley where the country lane dipped, before rising again and curving away over the next hill.

Jessie had taken the Farnham road from Aldershot, a map spread out on her passenger seat. She had never bought a sat nav, preferring to be in control of where she was going, even if that meant getting lost. What that said about her personality, she hadn't bothered to analyse.

She had passed a couple of other houses, but this one sat alone at the end of a short gravel drive, set back behind a column of clipped leylandii trees, planted tightly to form a hedge twenty feet high, shielding the house from the road. Unnecessary, Jessie thought, doubting that more than ten cars a day used this lane that came from nowhere important and led nowhere.

Her tyres crunched on gravel as she drove through the wooden five-bar gate, rotten, leaning drunkenly off its hinges, and parked in the circular drive behind a green mud-splattered Land Rover Defender. The house must have originally been three cottages that had been knocked into one. It was long and low, a couple of hundred years old at least: two storeys high, of red brick with wooden beams cutting through them, a clay-tiled roof which undulated like the surrounding hills. It looked to be – as was her own cottage, on a more modest scale – a money pit of maintenance. She passed two olive green painted front doors, the first with pot plants crowded around its base, the second, a rusting metal pig-trough filled with soil that looked as if it had been purchased as a garden feature and never planted out. The third door was clearly in use as the front door to the combined dwelling: a letterbox stuffed with an overlarge catalogue that prevented it from closing, and a hedgehog-shaped boot cleaner to one side, its bristles worn and caked in mud.

Jessie yanked out the catalogue, knocked and waited. The whole place had an air of isolation and neglect. The utter silence was oppressive; she couldn't even hear bird-song. Though she loved her own cottage, she also liked having Ahmose next door, within shouting distance, if she ever needed him. This place was too secluded, felt as if it could almost be alone on the planet. Being a psychologist hadn't anesthetized her to imaginary fears. It was actually the opposite. Accessing the dark side of other people's minds had made her imagination more feverish. She knew that if it were she out here alone, in darkness, every sound would be a window being cracked open from the outside. Shivering, she rubbed a hand over the back of her neck. It was cold today, the sky flinty-grey with clouds and she wished that she had put a thicker coat on.

A woman of around sixty opened the door. She wore an

26

apron, bearing the legend, *You must be confusing me with the maid we don't have,* accompanied by a photograph of a cone-breasted woman in a pencil skirt and twinset.

'I won't shake your hand,' she said, holding up a marigold-gloved hand coated with soapsuds. 'I was in the middle of washing up.' Jessie noticed a slight Midland twang underneath a voice that was brisk and efficient. 'I'm Wendy Chubb, and you must be Dr Flynn.'

Jessie smiled. 'Please call me Jessie.'

'Come in, won't you.' She closed the door behind Jessie, face wrinkling at the cold air that blew with them into the room. 'Sami's upstairs in his bedroom playing with his toys. Major Scott's in the sitting room. He asked me to tell you to pop in and see him first before your session with Sami.' Wendy smiled. 'Must be interesting being a psychologist. Satisfying too, sorting out people's minds for them. I could do with a bit of that myself.'

Jessie laughed. 'If only it was that easy. Sometimes I think that we psychologists create more problems than we solve.'

'Well, I hope you can help Sami. He's a delightful little boy, he is. Intelligent too. He helped me make a cake the other day. Managed to weigh all the ingredients out with hardly any help.' She met Jessie's gaze, pale eyelashes blinking. 'What do you think is the matter with him?'

Jessie shrugged. She wasn't about to break patient confidentiality, even if she did have a clue at this early stage, which she didn't.

'I've only seen him once.' Subconsciously, she touched a hand to the scar on her head. 'He seems scared and very troubled.'

Wendy nodded. 'Been in the wars?'

'A brief scuffle with my car door,' Jessie lied.

'Car doors can be dangerous. *Any* doors can be dangerous. I got my thumb jammed in one of Nooria's kitchen cabinets. Some of them were damaged and she asked me to help her replace them, make it nice for when Major Scott got back from Afghanistan. I thought I'd taken my thumb clean off it was so painful. Luckily it was only bruising, but even so.' She gave quick bright laugh, canted towards Jessie and lowered her voice. 'Shocking thing, what happened to the Major. Affected Sami terribly badly. Scared of being burnt, he is. While we were making that cake, he was fine, but as soon as I lit the gas on the cooker he got awfully frightened. Ran up to his room crying and wouldn't come back down.'

Jessie's face remained impassive, but she was now listening intently. Patient confidentiality and her own moral code prevented her from giving out information, but she could gain some. Everything she learnt about a patient helped her construct a picture of causation and of what intervention they would need to help heal them. Some sources were more reliable than others, but every bit of information was a segment in the ten-million-piece, incredibly complex, opaque jigsaw that made up the human mind.

'He was talking about being burnt when I saw him yesterday.'

Wendy frowned. 'Can't blame the little lad. It was terribly traumatic for him when his father got back from Afghanistan. He was already in a bit of a state, frightened like, when his mum brought him to the hospital. Probably because they'd been alone out here every night for the six months his father was on tour. Major Scott prefers it to family accommodation on base, but I wouldn't want to be

28

out here at night without a man around.' A shadow crossed her face. 'When he saw his father in the hospital, he started wailing, screaming and crying. Wouldn't go near him. He hasn't been right since. Eight weeks or so ago that was now.'

'So you've worked here a while?'

She nodded. 'Nooria employed me nine months ago. Late February it was, shortly after Major Scott left for Afghanistan. I do a bit of housework and help out with Sami. Nooria loves to paint. She's doing a foundation course in fine art at the Royal College of Art in London.' Wendy pointed to a framed graphite sketch on the wall, Sami as a baby, with that trademark curly hair and huge dark eyes.

'It's wonderful.'

'She certainly is talented. That's where she is now. She goes to college on Tuesday, Wednesday and Thursday.'

Wendy continued to talk about Nooria's painting, but Jessie tuned out. She glanced surreptitiously at her watch. She had agreed to meet Ben Callan at ten to four for the session with Starkey, wanted to have a good look through the file Callan had given her before the meeting. It was half-past twelve now.

'Is the Major . . .?' She let the words hang.

'Oh course, yes. Sorry. I'm a talker. Always have been, always will be. In there, the sitting room.'

Jessie had never met Major Nicholas Scott, but she had heard about him when she was working with PsyOps – 15 Psychological Operations Group – in Camp KAIA, the second of her two tours of duty in Afghanistan. PsyOps was a tri-service, 'purple' military unit, parented by 1 Military Intelligence Brigade, of which Major Scott was part, but they drafted in psychologists from the Medical Corps to advise.

She and Scott had not overlapped in Afghanistan, but she had probably passed him somewhere in the air over Europe last February, her coming back, him going out to the tour which would cost him so much. Scott was in his early forties, well respected, no nonsense, someone who got the job done, and well. He had seemed to command respect among senior Afghan figures, had achieved some successes where others, who came before, had failed.

The heavy sky cast little light and the low-ceilinged room, with its twin box sash windows, was dim. It was an austere room, masculine, a dark leather chesterfield sofa and two matching leather bucket chairs opposite, a plasma television on an oak stand in one corner, no books or photographs. Jessie had expected something more modern and feminine, but, except for a simple watercolour – a toddler Sami asleep in his cot, dressed in a pale yellow sleep-suit that made him look like a beautiful baby girl – Nooria's influence seemed minimal. Major Scott was sitting by the window, in one of the bucket chairs, which he had turned to face the garden.

Approaching from his right side, Jessie caught a glimpse of the handsome man he would have been before the attack: blond-haired, well defined cheekbones and a square jaw, softened now with stubble a few days old, tall and well built, she could tell, even though he was sitting. The beige carpet muffled her footsteps; he seemed unaware of her presence. Halfway across the room, she stopped.

'Major Scott.'

Jessie's first, strong impulse when he stood and turned to face her was to recoil. Forcing her expression impassive, she held the gaze of his one good eye through the tinted lens of his sunglasses. The left side of his face was so badly burnt that the skin had melted, slid away from the bones underneath, leaving threads of brown, tortured tissue. Batman's Joker dropped into a vat of acid. His nose resembled that of a skeleton: cartilage all that was left to form shape, scarred skin stretched over the nub and grafted into place. A pair of gold-framed aviator sunglasses covered his eyes. As he stood, Jessie caught the glimpse of his left eye through the side of their frame: an empty socket, the skin around it patchwork, only a glistening burgundy cavity remaining. He wore a blue polo neck jumper and jeans. The skin down the left side of his neck was like liquid, disappearing under the dark wool.

Jessie held out her right hand. 'I'm Dr Jessie Flynn.'

He nodded, shook it briefly. 'Thank you for taking on Sami.' His voice was clipped, strained, at odds with his words.

'It's my job, and one I'm very happy to do. He's a cute boy.'

'But you probably signed on for adults, not for children.'

'I did a master's in Child Psychology before my Clinical PhD so it's one of my areas of expertise.' She attempted a joke. 'Helpful for dealing with many of the adults I see too.'

Scott didn't smile. He had already turned back to the chair, which he angled a little into the room, but not entirely, so that Jessie could see the good side of his face, but not make direct eye contact. She felt foolish for trying to lighten the moment – it had been inappropriate. She took a seat on the sofa where he had indicated.

'Actually, Major Scott, I need to see the whole family, not just Sami.'

'What?' His voice was incredulous.

'For a child like Sami, if I'm to understand what's going on and to help treat him, I need to see all of you – individually.'

The animosity in his voice shocked her. 'I didn't refer him to an Army psychologist because I wanted someone poking around in our lives. I referred him because I had no choice. He was supposed to start school in September, and instead he's raving. Your job is to sort him out. The rest of us are fine.' The last sentence said bitterly. Scott was clearly anything but fine.

Jessie persisted. 'His problems haven't arisen in isolation and you and your wife need to deal with them. You're the ones who are with him twenty-four hours a day.'

'He has post-traumatic stress disorder. It's bloody obvious. I've seen it in the field countless times and that's with grown men.' He spoke through gritted teeth, barely suppressed fury in his voice. There was an undercurrent of something else too, making his voice tremble. Fear? Fear and helplessness. Emotions Jessie knew well. 'His mother's always been overprotective, made him too sensitive. Seeing me in the hospital tipped him over the edge. Other kids might have been able to handle it, he couldn't.'

'It may be post-traumatic stress disorder – probably is – but it's complex and very intense. He will be having nightmares, terrors, be imagining frightening images, while he's awake and while he's asleep. As you said, it's hard enough for grown men and women to handle, terrifying for a little boy.' Her mind flashed to Sami, writhing and sobbing in her arms. *The man is burnt. The girl is burnt.*

She wasn't about to quote statistics to Scott, but she knew them by heart. *For every hundred veterans of operations in*

Afghanistan, around twenty will have post-traumatic stress disorder. Disorder characterized by alcoholism, drug addiction and suicide. 'He needs his parents to understand exactly what he's going through, be there to help him appropriately when he needs it. Which is now. All the time, in fact, twenty-four/seven, until he's over it.'

He sneered and curled his lip. 'You can see Nooria. She's the kid's mother. She's the one who cares for him day-to-day. Now do your job and leave me alone.'

He had turned back to the window – conversation clearly over – his gaze almost stretching out through the glass, as if he wanted to smash through it, run away across the fields and take possession of someone else's life. Jessie couldn't blame him. Standing silently, she made her way to the door. There was a macho cult in the military, one she had come across many times before, that forbade asking for help. She was surprised that he had referred Sami, but having seen the child, he had clearly had no choice. She'd go and see Sami now, but she wasn't finished with Major Nicholas bloody Scott.

6

The second door on the right was closed. Jessie stood outside for a moment, her ear pressed to the cold wood to see if she could hear any noises. There were none. She knocked and when she received no reply, pushed the door open.

Her first glimpse of Sami's bedroom revealed the polar opposite of what she had expected for a little boy, the only child, in a relatively affluent family. It was a good size, a decent double, with a single oak-framed bed pushed against the wall to her right, a window opposite and a large oak chest of drawers to her left. Beneath the window were four coloured plastic toy buckets, filled with toys. The walls were a soft sunshine yellow, the same shade as Sami's sleep-suit in the watercolour Nooria had painted of him. That was the limit of where the room met with her expectation.

The curtain was drawn across the window, recessed overhead electric lights on full, giving the room a harsh, office-like glow. The yellow floral curtain must have been backed with blackout material, because not a single ray of natural light penetrated its folds. On his bed were a sheet and pillow, but no covers: no duvet or blanket. No Thomas the Tank Engine or Bob the Builder bed linen. There were no cuddly toys, not a single teddy bear, on the bed. It was bare, the whole room cold and institutional, similar to the Military Police holding cells she had seen last year while assessing a soldier who had broken his girlfriend's jaw in four places with his fist and was on suicide watch.

Sami was sitting underneath the window playing with some toys, his back to her. Next to him on the floor was the huge, black metal Maglite torch. Even though the room was flooded with light, the torch was switched on, its beam cutting a pale cylinder to the wall, lighting floating motes of dust.

Jessie remained in the doorway. If she had learnt anything from her experience yesterday it was to maintain her distance until he was entirely comfortable with her presence. The dull thud from her temple reminded her of that.

'Sami, it's Jessie Flynn. I've come to see you.'

For a moment, she thought that he hadn't heard her: he made no movement, no sound, no indication that he had done so. Then, slowly an arm reached out, a hand closed around the shaft of the torch. Shuffling around on his bottom, dragging the torch with him, the little boy half-turned towards her.

Jessie smiled. 'Hi, Sami.'

His face showed no expression. He didn't smile back. He didn't frown.

'Can I come in?'

No expression still, his huge dark eyes fixed on her face.

35

The scrutiny intense, unwavering. Then a barely perceptible nod.

'Thank you.'

Stepping through the doorway, Jessie pushed the door closed behind her. She wanted privacy, a physical barrier to the sounds of their interaction floating down the stairs. Though she knew that she was putting her reputation at risk shutting herself into a room with a child, she had a strong sense it was important they weren't overheard. For his freedom of mind; for her own.

'What are you playing with?'

'Dolly.'

'Can I play with your toys too?'

Severe or not, she had secured her hair in a bun this time, but had softened her look with a pale blue V-neck jumper, white jeans and trainers.

Again, an almost imperceptible inclination of his head. Jessie crossed the room, lowered herself on to the carpet next to him.

One of the four plastic tubs lined in front of him was full of dolls: four or five of various sizes, plus their accessories: a pink potty, a couple of milk bottles, plates, bowls and spoons, bibs, a few changes of sleep-suits in pastel colours. Sami, cradling one of the dolls in his lap, was halfway through changing her clothes.

'Could I play with one too?'

No verbal reply, but another tiny nod.

Jessie reached into the bucket and retrieved a doll. It was large, the size of a real newborn, dressed in a baby pink sleep-suit with a fairy castle embroidered on the front in lilac, underneath the castle the words 'Baby Isabel' stitched in gold cursive script. A glittery pink plastic dummy was jammed in her mouth; glassy pale blue eyes stared fixedly back at Jessie. She had not been a 'dolly' girl, or into princesses either, preferring Scalextric, or arranging her cuddly toys into intergalactic battle groups based on snatched episodes of *Dr Who*, lying behind the sofa, watching through her father's feet, when she was supposed to be in bed.

'Do you like dolls?'

He nodded. 'Sami like dolls.'

He had finished changing the doll, was looking longingly at Baby Isabel. Jessie passed the doll to him.

'The girl likes dolls.'

The girl.

'Which doll is the girl's favourite?' Jessie asked softly.

Without hesitation, he held up Baby Isabel.

'Why does the girl like Baby Isabel best?'

He shrugged.

'Is it because she's got beautiful blue eyes?'

Another shrug.

'What about her sleep-suit? The castle? It's very pretty.'

He ran his fingertips gently over the silky castle, but still didn't reply.

'Sami, who is the girl?'

He looked up, his brow furrowing. 'The girl,' he said matter-of-factly. 'The girl likes dolls.'

'Is the girl you?'

He met her gaze blankly. She resisted the instinctive temptation to repeat the question with her hands spread, palms upwards, body language that would have tapped into an adult's subconscious, urging them to respond.

'Are you the girl, Sami?'

'Grrrrr.' The growling sound, deep in his throat, a faint rumble.

Reaching out, he started gathering together his doll things, shoving them back into the plastic bucket, tossing each one in quickly as if it had become too hot to handle. A deep furrow had entrenched itself in his brow.

'Sami, are you feeling frightened? There's no need to be.'

'The dolls are the girl's.' There was a quiver in his voice.

Hugging Baby Isabel tight to his chest, he stroked her hair, dipped his head and gave her a gentle kiss on the cheek, and then tucked her carefully back inside the plastic tub.

For a long time, Sami remained silent, the torch clutched to his chest, light radiating out from him like a lighthouse beam. His gaze was hooded, turned inwards on itself. Jessie had no idea what he was thinking, what emotions were churning through his fragile mind. But at least she had the sense that he felt more comfortable with her, was beginning to trust her.

Psychology with children was like watching a toddler learning to walk: a few baby steps forward, a totter backwards, a fall. Endless frustration. It couldn't be rushed. Children's minds were not robust enough to be actively delved into, forced, in the way that many adults' could. Play was the only way to access the trauma a child of this age had experienced. Play enabled the child to reveal themselves at their own pace, as and when they felt comfortable to do so. It required extreme patience, not one of Jessie's strongest points despite her chosen profession, and she sometimes wondered how she had ended up doing a master's in Child Psychology at all.

No. She knew why.

7

'What would you like to do now, Sami?'

He didn't respond. Clutching the torch to his chest, he stared rigidly at the floor.

In one of the buckets was a plastic play-mat with fields and fences, winding lanes printed on it. There was also a farmhouse, and a collection of plastic farm animals.

'How about we play farms?' Jessie suggested.

'Yes,' Sami murmured. 'Play farms.'

Jessie hefted the bucket over and set it in front of him. Pulling out the play-mat, she spread it on the floor between them. She placed the farmhouse in the centre of the printed cobblestone farmyard and sat back on her haunches.

'Why don't you get out some animals, Sami?'

He nodded, aped in a monotone, 'Sami get animals.'

Both hands gripping the shaft of the torch, he hoisted it over the edge of the bucket, spotlighting each animal in turn.

'Here is a sheep.'

Balancing the torch on the edge of the bucket with one

hand, he reached in with the other and picked out the sheep. Placing the sheep in one of the fields on the play-mat, he reached back into the bucket.

'Here is another sheep.'

He stood it next to the first.

'Here is a cow.'

He repeated the process, his torch beam picking out a brown cow, a group of chickens, a dapple-grey carthorse, two pink pigs. Each animal was arranged carefully on the play-mat, the chickens in the cobbled farmyard by the farmhouse, the pigs in the sty, the cow and the horse in different fields. He seemed to be enjoying the game. For the first time since Jessie had met him, she heard animation in his voice, saw a flicker of light in his eyes.

'You like the farm animals?' Jessie asked.

Sami met her gaze and smiled a tiny, tight smile – the first hint of a smile that she had seen.

'Sami like animals,' he murmured. He looked back to the play-mat. 'All the animals are in the farm. The sheeps, the cow, the chickens, the horse, the pigs, are all in the farm.'

Jessie glanced into the bucket; there was a dark shape at the bottom.

'Hold on,' she said. 'Here, look, you've missed one.'

At the bottom of the bucket was a donkey. A black plastic donkey. Reaching in, she retrieved it, held the donkey out to Sami.

He cringed away, his face a mask of terror. Only his shoulders moved, their rise and fall exaggerated, as though he was struggling to catch his breath.

'The donkey is dead,' he whispered, through pale lips.

He stared at the donkey, unblinking. Shadows ringed his eyes, dark smudges in the pallor of his face.

'The donkey is fine,' Jessie said, her voice deliberately higher in pitch, jolly. She placed the donkey on the playmat, in the same field as the carthorse. 'Look he's fine. He's in the field with the carthorse.' She turned the donkey ninety degrees so that it and the carthorse were nose to nose. 'They're having a chat. What do you think they're talking about, Sami?'

He had started to tremble, his breath coming in quick, shallow bursts.

'The donkey is burnt.' Reaching out, he pushed the donkey on to its side with the tip of one finger. 'The donkey is dead.'

'No, Sami. The donkey is made from black plastic. It's just a black plastic donkey.'

Sami shook his head. He rocked backwards and forwards on his haunches.

'The donkey is burnt. The donkey is dead.' He started searching frantically around him, eyes wide with fear. 'Where is the blanket?'

Jessie wanted to touch him, to reach out and wrap her arms around him, keep him safe. But she couldn't. Wasn't allowed to. Modern political correctness made cuddling children – even distressed ones – forbidden. She had already taken a risk shutting the door.

'Blanket? Why do you need a blanket, Sami?'

Ignoring the question, he delved into the dolls' container, tossing dolls and pieces of equipment out on the carpet behind him.

'Where is the blanket, where is the blanket, where is the blanket?' he chanted in a singsong voice, almost under his breath. He found a pink doll's blanket, a silky rabbit embroidered in one corner.

41

'The girl knows.'

'What does the girl know?' Jessie asked softly.

'Here is the blanket,' Sami muttered.

Shuffling back across the carpet on his knees, he reached the play-mat. He laid the doll's blanket over the donkey. Carefully, he tucked the blanket under the donkey, flipping it over so that the animal didn't touch his skin, rolling the donkey up. He laid the roll of blanket containing the donkey on the carpet next to Jessie. Picking up the Maglite, he shone it on the roll.

'The donkey is burnt. The donkey is dead.'

'You think the donkey has been burnt? And the donkey is now dead?'

The little boy's face looked suddenly old, lined with fear and sadness. 'The donkey is dead.'

'So you've covered it with the blanket?'

'The torch can see. The donkey is burnt. The donkey is dead.' Tears welled up in his eyes and a barely audible croak came from somewhere at the back of his throat. 'The Shadowman came. The girl knows.'

8

Jessie found a parking space at the far end of Aldershot high street, shoved a couple of pounds in the machine and tacked the ticket to her windscreen. For a Tuesday afternoon, the high street was unexpectedly busy: shoppers, trussed up in padded coats, scarves and hats, gloved hands clutching bulging plastic bags, scurrying along, heads down against the chill wind cutting between the buildings.

She popped into Pret A Manger to grab a sandwich, ate it, sitting at a stool in the window, chewing but not tasting the malted granary bread, tuna and rocket – fuel rather than enjoyment. Back on the high street, she scanned the shops on either side of her, caught sight of the green triangular Early Learning Centre sign a hundred yards to her left.

There had been something about the animals in that farm that had resonated with Sami, both good and bad. In the two sessions she'd had with him, he hadn't smiled once. The animals had achieved the hint of a smile at least, if only a fleeting one. They had also delivered the opposite: abject terror. From today's observations, she believed that they might provide her with a way to access his mind; a door, ajar a fraction now, that she could perhaps push open. Particularly if she could recreate the farm, the timing and sequence in which he received the animals in the more controlled environment of her office at Bradley Court.

The Early Learning Centre was empty: the rush to stock up on large multicoloured plastic objects for kiddies' Christmas presents had clearly not yet begun. A blonde sales girl, early twenties, was standing behind the counter, texting on her iPhone.

She glanced up and smiled. 'Let me know if I can help you.'

Jessie returned the smile. 'Thank you.'

The shelves bore a bewildering array of toys in all shapes, sizes and colours: dressing-up and pretend play, dolls and doll houses, vehicles and construction, art, music and creative play, a whole range of beach toys, incongruous given the single-digit temperatures outside and the chill rain that had begun hammering the shop's plate-glass window.

'The baby toys are on special, if you're interested.' The shop assistant had finished her text.

'Oh, no, thank you. Actually, I'm looking for a farm.'

'Action figures and play-sets . . . at the back,' she continued, when Jessie couldn't catch sight of the sign. 'Follow me.'

At the back of the store were boxes of every conceivable kind of play-set: dinosaurs, pony club, police, army – tiny green plastic warriors in jungle camouflage – schools, hospitals and farms.

'This farm is wonderful.' The sales girl held up a large vinyl box. 'The actual box unzips down the sides . . . look . . . and flattens out to become the play-mat.' She rotated it so that Jessie could see. 'It's got a farmyard, fields and even a pond, printed on both sides. There are ducks inside to go on the pond. And it comes with a plastic farmhouse, a tractor and all the other farm animals.'

But were any of the animals black? Could she ask the question without sounding committable? Did she have a choice?

'It looks perfect.' Jessie paused. 'Are, uh, are any of the animals black?' she asked in a voice so quiet that even she could barely hear herself over the patter of rain against the plate-glass window.

'Excuse me?' The sales girl eyed her, unsure whether to take the question seriously.

'Are any of the animals black?' she repeated. 'I, uh . . .' How to explain this so she didn't sound insane. The truth was far too complex. 'My nephew likes black animals. His . . . his cousin – my sister's boy, not my brother's . . . this farm is for my brother's son. He has a black plastic donkey that Sami . . . that Sam loves, so I wanted to make sure that at least one of the animals was black. He, uh, he likes black animals . . .' she tailed off.

The sales girl didn't look convinced, not that Jessie could blame her.

'I don't know,' she said. 'But you can always buy extra.' With a tilt of her head, she indicated a row of narrow shelves, stacked one on top of each other, bearing small plastic toy animals of every description. 'I know they're a bit expensive, but they're Schleich.' She paused. 'Hand-painted in Germany,' she continued, 'each one unique,' when it was obvious that Jessie had never heard of Schleich.

'Perfect, thank you. I'll take the farm set and I'll have a look at the Schleich animals.'

While the sales girl wandered back to the cash desk and her mobile, Jessie chose two from the Schleich set, a jet-black cow and a black-and-white collie dog, looking carefully through the dogs until she found one that had just a couple of small white patches on its body. How would Sami react to an animal that was mostly, but not entirely black? Would it engender the same horror in him as a wholly black animal?

She put the rest of the dogs back, ordering them one behind the other, so that, from the front of the shelf where customers stood to choose, they were perfectly aligned. She glanced at the other animals. They were in disarray, as if a tribe of kids had come in and trashed them, which they probably had. Looking at the mess in front of her, she felt the familiar crackle of electricity travel across her skin, a tightness around her throat.

Laying the cow and the collie on the floor beside her, she rearranged the horses, one behind the other in the same manner as the dogs, the foals, the goats, the sheep. She was so absorbed in the task that she didn't hear the sales girl approach.

'I can do that.'

Jessie started. 'Oh, hi. It's OK, I'm nearly finished.'

'I can do that,' she repeated, an edge to her tone. 'It's my job.'

'I've only got the ducks to do and then I'm finished,' Jessie said firmly. The electric suit was spitting against her skin, a pulsing tension that she had to assuage. She was aware that the sales girl must think she was a nutter. Would give anything to be able to walk away, leaving the ducks in a mess. Perhaps she should tell the sales girl that she was a psychologist.

'I'll leave you to it then.' The sales girl retreated in angry, clicking steps, casting back over her shoulder, 'As you've only got the ducks left to do.'

Jessie rested her head against the wall. She felt close to tears. *I'm a psychologist who could give most of my patients a run for their money in the fucked-up stakes.* Finishing quickly, she stood back and surveyed her handiwork. The animals were lined in perfect rows, parade ground squared-away. She felt calm; her pulse back to normal. Collecting the Schleichs from the floor beside her, she carried them to the cash desk, laid them on top of the farm box.

'They didn't look tidy,' Jessie murmured.

The sales girl wouldn't meet her eye. 'Gift wrap?'

'No. No, thank you.'

The rain had turned to damp sleet and the sky had darkened to charcoal, as if, while she'd been in the shop, someone had dimmed the ceiling light. Thunder grumbled on the edge of town. Pulling her hood up, Jessie stepped on to the pavement. She was pretty sure that the sales girl would be on her mobile phone the second she was out of sight, texting, 'You'd never guess what . . .' to a friend.

Head down, she jogged up the street, wet sleet sloshing against her hood. She was nearly back to her own car when she caught sight of a red Golf GTI parked crookedly, half on the pavement, a hand-scrawled 'Military Police' notice propped on the dashboard. Stopping, she looked around. She was beyond the shops, where they petered to small office buildings. Behind her was a modern brick building with a large black front door bearing a brass lion's head knocker that would have looked more in place gracing the entrance to a stately home. A rectangular plaque beside the door bore engravings that she couldn't read from this distance. Turning back to the Golf, she was debating whether to leave a note tucked under the wiper.

'Are you checking my car for neatness?'

She started, turned. Callan was right behind her, a look of amusement in those watchful amber eyes. He was wearing jeans and the same navy hoodie she'd seen him in yesterday, a black waterproof, undone, covering the hoodie.

'You failed miserably,' she said. 'The coke can and crisp packets in the footwell aren't going to win you any prizes.'

'I'll try harder next time, Doctor.' His tone was teasing. Pulling the keys from his pocket, he unlocked the car. 'Do you want a lift somewhere?'

'Don't I need to be a hooker to travel in a car like this?' The ghost of a smile on his lips.

Jessie smiled back sweetly. 'No, thank you. I've got my own car. Parked legally. Paid for.' She indicated the sticker in his window. 'Isn't that called abuse of position?'

'I was late for an appointment.' He caught her questioning look. 'Admin. Nothing exciting.' His gaze slid away from hers. 'I couldn't find a space. There have to be some perks to the job.' He walked around to the driver's side, pulled open the door. 'Four p.m. I'll meet you at ten to, Provost Barracks main entrance.'

She nodded. 'I remember. I'll be there.'

'Don't be late.' A shift in his voice – humour to tension. 'I won't.'

Standing on the pavement, she watched him pull on to the road and accelerate away, tyres churning up a plume of wet sleet from the tarmac. She started to walk back to her own car, then stopped. On impulse, she crossed the pavement to the brass plaque. A small business accounting firm occupied the ground and first floor, an IT business the second. At the bottom of the list, third floor, Mr John Rushton-Booth, Consultant Neurologist.

9

Jeanette Bass-Cooper looked hard at the detective inspector. She prided herself on being open-minded, but even she had limits. He looked as if he had been dragged out of some Soho rock club at 4 a.m., beer still in hand, and teleported down here to the seaside, kicking and screaming, blinking those disconcerting mismatched eyes against the daylight, smoky and feeble as it was.

His partner, on the other hand, the detective sergeant – Workman, Jeanette thought she'd said – was his antithesis. Shapeless black wash-and-wear trousers skimming solid ankles, chunky lace-ups that wouldn't be out of place on a 1930s nanny, mousy hair cut into a low-maintenance bob. But she seemed sensible at least. *Reliable*.

Detective Inspector Bobby 'Marilyn' Simmons – Marilyn after Manson, he would hasten to add if questioned on the nickname his colleagues had bestowed on him the first day he joined the force, a nickname that had dogged him ever since – looked at the short, boxy woman in front of him in her black dress and high-heeled patent boots and felt the beginnings of a headache. The words 'mutton' and 'lamb' flashed into his mind. But at least she seemed intelligent, could string a sentence together that contained no swear words, a rare skill in the world he occupied.

A wind had picked up, whipping the water of the harbour into a frothy, gunmetal soup, cutting straight through his leather jacket. Hauling up his collar, he hunkered down, wishing that he'd brought a scarf, put on a windproof fleece, anything more sensible than his battered biker.

'DS Workman. Take Ms Bass-Cooper to the Command Vehicle to get her out of the cold. Switch the engine on to get the blowers going. I don't want our one witness freezing to death before we've drained her of information. Take a written statement while you're there.'

As DS Workman led Jeanette Bass-Cooper back up the garden towards the gaggle of police vehicles haphazardly parked on the gravel drive, Marilyn turned and strode across the crispy, frostbitten grass towards the narrow strip of pebbles that Bass-Cooper had termed a beach. Not one he fancied sunbathing on.

Looking out across the water to Itchenor, he felt a shot of déjà vu. He had worked on another murder last spring, around the bay in Bosham, a small village of expensive detached houses like the one behind him. Murder in this part of West Sussex was so rare that it had made the national newspapers. A house-sitter, stabbed to death in her bedroom in the middle of the night; her sister, brother-in-law and elderly father in adjacent bedrooms who had heard nothing. It had him stumped for close to a fortnight, until he had found out that the sixty-year-old owner of the house, who had been on holiday with his wife at the time, had a penchant for swinging. Over the telephone from Florida he had explained to Marilyn that he had 'absolutely no idea' how photographs of himself, posing naked on a sandy beach, came to be posted on a swingers' website under the moniker, 'The Director of Fun'. It turned out that the murderer was a fellow swinger, a fifty-five-year-old woman who thought she was dispatching the director's wife.

This case, Marilyn feared, would be tougher to crack.

The forensics teams, dressed in their identical navy-blue waterproof onesies, looked, on fleeting glance, like a group of harbour day-trippers – only the masks covering their mouths and noses dispelling that image. They had got here quickly and erected a forensic tent over the body – what remained of it at least. Marilyn didn't fancy the tent's chances if this wind picked up. The occasional white flash of the forensics' camera crew lit it up from the inside, giving him some uncomfortable memories of last night. A nightclub in Portsmouth. He was too old to stay out until 3 a.m., should get sensible, get himself a girlfriend knocking forty, rather than Cindy, virtually half his age and beautiful, but sharp as a blunt instrument.

'So what have we got?'

Tony Burrows, the lead Crime Scene Investigator pulled his hood back, slid a latex-gloved hand over his bald spot, fingertips grazing the dark hair that ringed his scalp. He reminded Marilyn of a Benedictine monk, the impression emphasized by his short legs and softly rounded stomach. 'Male.'

Marilyn waited. When no more information was forth-coming, 'Yup. And . . .?'

'That's about it, at the moment. The body is not what could be termed fresh kill, and we only have half of it.'

Marilyn winced. Despite his chosen profession, he didn't

have a strong stomach, had failed, even after nearly twenty years in Surrey and Sussex Major Crimes, to fully acclimatize to the visceral assault on the senses that dead bodies rendered.

'Where is the other half?'

'Anybody's guess. But the cut is clean, if messy. Chops—' Burrows made a vertical hacking motion with his hand – 'rather than tears or rips. An axe, perhaps? A butcher's chopper, maybe. The body is very badly decomposed, most of the skin and a good part of the flesh missing, as you can see, so identifying the cause may be difficult.'

Marilyn's eyes hung closed for a moment. 'Do you think he was dumped here?'

'Could have been. There'd be no traces left if someone had carried the body down the garden and tossed it on to the beach. Not given how long this Doe has been dead for. Unless he was stored somewhere else and then dumped recently.' He paused, massaged the dome of his head, eyes raised to the grey sky in thought. 'But that's unlikely. Our victim has been exposed to the elements for some time, I think, by the looks of him. Dr Ghoshal will be able to tell you more once he gets him on the slab.'

Marilyn nodded. Cupping his hands in front of his face, he blew into them, stomped his feet to get the circulation going. The house had been vacant for four months, Ms Bass-Cooper had said. His mind turning inwards in thought, he moved away from Tony Burrows and his team, buzzing like flies around the corpse, followed the curve of shingle to the rotten wooden fence that signalled the extent of the garden. Leaning against a wooden upright, he gazed out across the water. Yachts and motor cruisers bobbed at anchor, straining against their moorings in the swell. Though he'd lived in Chichester for almost all of his working life, the best part of twenty years, he wasn't a sailor – struggled to envision anything less appealing than squatting in a damp little boat being pushed around by the wind. But having lived and worked near the sea for so long, he knew something about tides.

Where was the other half of that body? Had it been dumped in another part of the harbour and taken in a different direction by the tide? Or was it being stored in the killer's freezer, a sick kind of trophy? Trophy-taking was a common feature when the victim and murderer were strangers: the killer wanting to keep the victim, the moment of death, clear in his or her memory, the trophy a physical tool to aid that process.

The cut was clean – *chopped*, Burrows had said. *An axe? A butcher's cleaver?* For sure, a killer who meant business.

Shrugging his jacket sleeves down over his frozen hands, Marilyn sighed. A killer who meant business was all he needed right now.

10

He looked so different in his Military Police uniform –
olive-green trousers, shirt and tie, a knife crease running
down the front of each leg, the shirt buttoned up and
starched resolutely, the red beret of the Military Police that
gave them the nickname Redcaps, pulled low over his eyes
– that Jessie almost walked straight past him.

'Dr Flynn.'

She stopped, did a double take. 'Oh, God, you scrub up
. . . different.'

Callan smiled, but there was tension in the smile and it
was gone almost before she'd registered it.

'Ready?' he asked.

'Absolutely.'

They walked side by side up the grey vinyl-tiled stairs
to the second floor, their twin footfall emphasizing the
silence that had settled after their initial greeting, and
the tension that crackled from him. Removing his beret, he
held the door at the top of the stairs open for her, and then
pulled up, turning to face her in the corridor. At the far end,

she could see a room crowded with desks, hear the ambient hum of conversation drifting down the corridor towards them, the tap of fingers on computer keys, the ring of a telephone, a sudden burst of laughter.

'You've read the file?' He was all business now.

'Yes.'

'Give me a rundown.'

She met his gaze. 'You are joking?'

'I want to be sure that you've got the background.'

'I've got the background and I'm not ten, so I'm not doing any damn test. You're going to have to trust me.'

His tie wasn't straight.

He sighed. 'Fine. So the bit the file doesn't include. Starkey was raised on a council estate in West London. Before his sixteenth birthday he had racked up a couple of minor criminal convictions, for stealing cars and selling cannabis. He was put under the control of social services, given the option of remaining with his family and seeing a psychologist rather than going to a young offenders' institution.'

'Don't tell me,' Jessie interrupted. 'Gideon Duursema?'

'Your boss has a lot to answer for.'

She rolled her eyes. 'You don't know the half of it.'

His tie was driving her mad; the electric suit was hissing against her skin.

'Callan, your tie's, uh, your tie is crooked.'

'What?' His voice was incredulous.

'The knot of your tie is crooked.'

He reached up and straightened it distractedly. 'OK?'

Jessie grimaced; he'd made it worse.

'As I was saying, reports from his commanding officer in Afghanistan, in fact every commanding officer he's had since he joined up, have been exemplary. He seems to be

55

highly regarded by everyone he's worked with. The Army seemed to have straightened him out, though the man I met yesterday didn't fit so well with what I've read.'

Jessie shuffled closer. 'Here, let me straighten it.'

She reached up. She could sense him humming with impatience, but he stood unmoving, gaze fixed on some point down the corridor behind her, while she fiddled with the knot. Knew suddenly that he had realized – realized it wasn't merely perfectionism that drove her to straighten his tie.

'Did you listen to anything I said?' he asked curtly, when she had dropped her hand.

'Yes, all of it. Has he had any injuries? Was he involved in heavy action in Afghanistan?'

'No. But—' he broke off.

'But it's not easy out there for anybody.'

He shook his head. 'It's not.'

A laden pause; Jessie broke it.

'What was your sense of him?'

'My sense?' He shrugged. 'Negative.'

'You didn't like him?'

'It's not about *like*. It's about . . .' Another shrug.

'A bad feeling?'

He frowned. 'Feelings shouldn't come into it, right? Not in my job.'

'We're all human.'

'We are that.' He dipped his gaze, breaking eye contact. 'Shall we go and see Starkey now?'

Sergeant Colin Starkey was standing by the window, watching something in the car park below, lights from one of the Military Police cruisers washing his face alternately blue, then red. The room was spartan, utilitarian: plain white walls, scuffed in places from the scrapes of tables and chairs, the odd black vertical streak of shoe rubber where occupants had rested their soles against the wall. Two overhead strip lights lit a single rectangular wooden table and three chairs, two on the near side, one on the far side nearest to the window and Starkey. One of the strip lights flickered on, off, on again, as if it was tapping out its own Morse code.

If Jessie had any expectations of what Colin Starkey would look like, they had not coalesced into specifics. Only a vague stereotype, which had rarely been matched by any of the sergeants or staff sergeants she had met since she'd joined the Army. Crew cut, tattoos, barrel chest, a voice that sounded as if the owner was broadcasting through a loud hailer.

Starkey turned from the window, his gaze locking with Jessie's. He flashed a sharp-toothed grin.

'Things are looking up for me.'

Ignoring his comment, Jessie sat down on one of the chairs on the near side of the table, laid her hands calmly on the tabletop. She was used to being baited in that way, had made the mistake of rising to the lure a few times early on in her Army career and had felt stripped naked because of it. She wasn't planning on making that mistake with Starkey.

Looking past her to Callan, Starkey gave a sloppy salute, which Callan returned smartly.

Starkey was only a few years older than she was, early thirties, Jessie guessed, so he was doing well to have earned the three chevrons already. He was tall, almost as tall as Callan, and well built, with dark hair that curled over his collar, longer than regulation, dark brown eyes and a square jaw shadowed with dark stubble. A faint bruise shaded the skin under his right eye. He was hard looking, but very handsome. For some reason, she hadn't expected him to be.

'So you must be Jessie Flynn,' Starkey said, with another grin.

'Doctor to you, Sergeant Starkey.'

'Come and sit down please,' Callan cut in, indicating the chair opposite, waiting until Starkey had joined them at the table before he sat down next to Jessie. Pulling a digital recorder from his pocket, he laid it on the table and flicked the switch. It purred softly in the silence.

'As we discussed yesterday, this meeting is a psychological evaluation. Sergeant Starkey, you have said that you do not want a Ministry of Defence lawyer appointed on your behalf. Is that correct?'

Starkey nodded. Callan indicated the tape recorder. 'Say it out loud please, Sergeant.'

'I agree that I do not want a lawyer appointed on my behalf,' he replied in an American drawl, Clint Eastwood in *Dirty Harry*.

Jessie noticed a muscle twitch in Callan's jaw, but when he spoke his voice was measured, controlled.

'Whatever you say between these walls may be used against you in any court martial that may follow.'

'Why the hell would I say no to spending half an hour talking to a beautiful girl.' A gleam had come into his feral eyes. 'Even if it gets me banged up.'

'So talk me through what happened.' Callan had a hand on the file, but didn't open it. He had clearly memorized the contents. 'On the afternoon of Wednesday, 28th October – six days ago.'

'I believe I did that yesterday, Captain Callan.' Still the American drawl.

58

'Go through it again.'

Starkey shrugged, glanced at Jessie. An instinct for self-preservation, establishing ground rules at the outset, made her hold his gaze across the tabletop; hold it until he looked away.

'I suggested we go for a run and he agreed.' His eyes rolled around the room, drifting up the walls, across the ceiling.

'Who is "he"?'

'He. Him. Are you trying to trick me, Captain Callan?'

Callan sighed, glanced at the tape recorder again. 'Jackson. You are referring to Sergeant Andy Jackson.'

'Right, Jackson. We'd both had a busy day, needed to run off the cobwebs.'

'In 35 degree heat, in full combat kit.'

'More heat, more sweat, releases more toxins. You should know that, Captain. You look like a bit of a fitness freak.'

'What were you doing in Afghanistan?' Jessie cut in.

'I'm with the Intelligence Corps.'

'Working on what, specifically?'

Starkey sighed. He tilted his head back and his gaze, under hooded eyelids, drifted to Callan. 'You must have talked to my superiors, Captain Callan.'

'I have.'

'And what did they say?'

Callan didn't answer.

Starkey laughed softly to himself. 'Not much, I'm guessing.' He raised his right hand, putting the tips of his index finger and thumb together to form a circle. 'Need to be in the know. In the circle.'

'Training ANSF? Drugs? Terrorism? Warlords and tribal loyalties?' Callan said.

Starkey smirked. 'You're not in the circle, Captain.'

His eyes skipped off around the room again, came to rest on the window. It had started to rain. Lights from the courtyard reflected in globules of water on the glass, thousands of tiny bulbs. The strip light above continued to flicker, coating their faces white-grey-white and grey again, when the frail afternoon light was left to cope on its own for a fraction of a second. Callan glanced up at it, his brow furrowing in irritation. He looked back to Starkey.

'Answer the question, Starkey.'

Starkey's eyes snapped back from the window to rest on Jessie's.

'Do you know what frightens people, Dr Flynn?'

'I'd say that real fear is different for everyone. We all have our secret demons. Isn't real fear about tapping into that person's individual demons?' Jessie said. 'Pressing their buttons.'

Starkey grinned. He seemed to like her answer.

'So what was Andy Jackson's demon?' she asked.

'You're asking the wrong questions, Doctor.'

'Am I?'

'He was too stupid to have demons. He was a follower, plain and simple.'

'Is that how you got him into the desert? Because he liked to follow?'

'This isn't about me,' Starkey replied.

She could feel Callan shifting uncomfortably beside her, sense his impatience at this play of words.

'So what is it about? Drugs? Terrorism? Warlords and tribal loyalties? Where do your loyalties lie, Starkey?'

Starkey crossed his arms over his chest. 'Do you know what Afghanistan's nickname is, Dr Flynn? The Graveyard of Empires.' He smirked. 'Have you ever been there? To the Graveyard?'

'Twice,' she said. 'Both with PsyOps.'

He raised his eyebrows, clearly surprised. 'I'm impressed.'

'You needn't be. It's my job.'

'So you know what a complete shit show it is out there then, ever since we demobbed to keep the politicians' ratings up, keep Joe Public happy. But we're still there, aren't we – some of us suckers?' He laughed, a bitter sound. 'PsyOps? We're fucking amateurs compared to them. We think we're playing them, but we're the ones being played.'

He started singing, softly, under his breath, *'I'm a puppet just a puppet on a string.'*

Jessie could sense that Callan was getting frustrated. His hands were clenched into fists on the tabletop, his legs jiggering underneath it. Out of the corner of her eye, she saw the tense set of his jaw. It would be easier for him if Starkey refused to talk at all. At least he could then assemble evidence from other avenues, without having the water muddied like this. But it wasn't so strange to Jessie. She had seen it a number of times – both before joining the Army and after. Patients who loved the wordplay, saw it as a game. Didn't want to be tied down, or couldn't be. Their heads a jumble of disassociated ideas, memories drifting loose, thoughts they couldn't straighten into anything intelligible. Which was Starkey?

Callan stood suddenly, strode over to the light switch. Flicked it off, waited a couple of beats, flicked it on again. The strip light above them continued to flicker.

'For fuck's sake,' he snapped, returning to the table.

'Is that what you and Jackson were working on?' Jessie asked. 'PsyOps?'

61

Starkey smirked. 'I thought you were PsyOps.'

'But you were working on something with Jackson?'

'There's a lot of intelligence to be gathered in Afghanistan. Some things I worked on with Jackson, other things not.' A muscle in his jaw twitched. In anguish? With stress? 'Fucking amateurs, and that's how we get burnt,' he muttered.

'Burnt.' Her mind flitted to Major Nicholas Scott, his skin like melted treacle. Scott was attacked in Afghanistan. A long shot, she realized. 'Did you work with Major Scott?'

'We only overlapped for a few days,' Starkey said.

She felt Callan shift beside her, tilt forward in the chair.

'I heard he was a good guy, though, Scott,' Starkey said. 'Committed to the cause.'

'And he got burnt.'

Starkey's fingers were tapping out a frantic tune on the tabletop. 'Maybe he was too committed, did too much for the cause.' He found her gaze across the table. *Just a puppet on a string.*

'Do you have nightmares, Sergeant Starkey?'

'Nightmares. My life's turned into a nightmare.'

He leaned forward, stretching his hands across the table towards her, palms upwards, fingers cupped slightly as if he was holding them out to God. She resisted the urge to lean back, put distance between them. She could sense Callan next to her, muscles taut, tuned to make a move if Starkey did.

'You know what really frightens me, Dr Flynn?' Starkey's voice was barely more than a whisper. 'Injustice.'

'Are you the subject of an injustice?'

'Why don't you ask Captain Stiff-as-a-fucking-board Redcap here, Doctor? Because I sure as hell don't know what he's thinking.'

Anger rippled across Callan's shoulders. 'Stop playing games and tell me the truth. Why did Andy Jackson die?'

'The truth will set you free, Captain Callan.'

'Jesus Christ.' Callan slammed both hands flat on the tabletop, making the voice recorder rattle.

Starkey grinned. 'Temper temper.'

Shoving his chair back, Callan strode to the door. 'What the fuck is wrong with the lights.' He slammed his hand on the switch a couple of times, flicking the lights on and off. On again. Off. The frail afternoon light seeping through the window coated their faces in sepia, the colour of old photographs.

Jessie remained where she was at the table. Her gaze sought out Starkey's; she looked him straight in the eye. She thought that his gaze might flicker, wander. It didn't. The eyes that met hers were intelligent, astute.

'If you continue in My word, then you are truly disciples of Mine; and you will know the truth, and the truth will set you free,' she said quietly. 'John 8:32.'

Starkey raised his hands, clapped them together, a slow, deliberate handclap.

'Very good, Dr Flynn. I didn't have you down as the religious type.' He lowered his voice. 'Though I'd like to see you in a nun's habit.'

Jessie stared back, unflinching. 'Convent education does wonders for religious knowledge. Sadly, we wore drab grey uniforms, calf-length, but you can dream, Starkey. So what is the truth?'

Callan was leaning against the wall by the door. 'This evaluation is terminated, Sergeant Starkey.'

Jessie glanced over at him. What the hell was he playing at? Something seemed to have ignited in his eyes: they shone, icy white, from the slits in his face. Icy white, but unfocused.

'I have a few more questions, Callan.'

The muscles along his jaw bulged.

She turned back to Starkey.

Callan was suddenly beside the table. Grabbing Starkey by the collar, he hauled him off the chair, slammed him back against the wall and jammed his forearm into Starkey's throat.

'You're a fucking little shit, Starkey, and if you have done something wrong, I will find out and I will hang you for it.'

Jessie jumped to her feet. 'Let him go, Captain Callan. *Now*.'

He let go of Starkey, stepping back, raising his hands in front of him in a defensive gesture. He looked almost as shocked as Starkey. Starkey backed away, straightening out his uniform.

'I could fucking hang you for *that*, Captain.'

Callan was shaking his head, but it didn't look as if he was shaking it in denial of what Starkey had said. The movement was jerky, uncoordinated, as if he was trying to dislodge something from his brain.

'Are you OK, Captain Callan?' Jessie asked.

'I'm fine,' he said, through gritted teeth.

A hand caught her arm. Turning, she found Starkey right behind her.

'The answer to your question about the truth, Jessie, is – I don't know.' His voice was quiet, a caress in her ear. She could feel his breath, hot against her cheek. She yanked her arm away, suddenly aware that she and Starkey were alone in the room, that Callan had left. 'I never found out. But if you could ask a dead man, say please – nicely, mind – he might tell you the answer.'

11

'What the fuck was that all about?' She was so angry that she didn't try to keep her voice down.

She had found Callan in the room at the end of the corridor, a Special Investigation Branch team room it seemed from the white boards bearing crime scene photographs, the hubbub of conversation, the manic clicking of computer keys. He was sitting behind a desk in the far corner, elbows on the desktop, cradling his head in his hands.

Looking up, he met her gaze. He looked wrecked. Utterly wrung out. His eyes were bloodshot and she wasn't sure if it was a product of the sickly grey light seeping through the blinds from the window above his desk, but his skin looked greyish pale, his face drawn.

He shrugged. 'It was about the fact that I don't have time for cunts any more.'

'Unfortunately dealing with cunts is always going to be part of your job. If you can't handle it, perhaps you should do something else.'

'Like what? Become a banker or a lawyer? I've probably

left it a bit late, and I'm not sure the personality fit would be seamless.'

'He could have you on a charge.'

'He won't.'

'What makes you so sure?'

'He's not the type. He may be a murdering bastard, but I don't think he's a petty one.'

Jessie slumped down in the chair across the desk from Callan. 'And he may actually be innocent.'

Silence. She let it stretch. Dropping his head to his hands again, Callan ground his fingers into his eyes sockets, grated them through his hair.

'You're right, I was out of order.' His tone was sheepish. 'And I do not have any preconceptions about Starkey's guilt or innocence. He wound me up. After I . . . after what I went through in Afghanistan, I find that much harder to handle than I used to. Where is he?'

'He's left. Our conversation finished a short while after you disappeared. He said he'd see himself out. He's not under arrest, after all.'

'What do you think?'

'I think you should be straight with me.'

He ignored the inference. 'About Starkey?'

'About you.'

'I just was straight with you.'

'I think there's more. I think there's something you're not telling me.' Her gaze found the scar from the bullet wound on his temple.

'And I think my life is no longer any of your business.'

'*You* asked *me* here.'

'To help with a case.'

She watched him in silence for a moment, caught between

two conflicting desires – the first to tell him to go *fuck himself* for walking out and leaving her with Starkey, and the second, to press him for the truth. But he was right. It wasn't her business. He was no longer her patient.

Crossing her arms across her chest, she sat back. 'You said that the impression Starkey gives doesn't reconcile with the glowing reports from his commanding officers, and I agree. But then he is Intelligence Corps.'

'What do you mean?'

'It's not mainline Army, is it? What they do, what they're after, the methods they use.'

'Is he sane?'

Jessie dropped her gaze to the floor, drawing a picture of Starkey to mind. The look in his eyes: intelligence definitely, but was there complete sentience? *You know what really frightens me. . . . injustice.* His fingers frantically tapping on the tabletop. *Fucking amateurs and that's how we get burnt.*

'He's clever, but is he aware of what he's doing? Yes, I believe he is.'

'So he was playing with us?'

'I don't think it's that simple.' She sat forward. 'If he's deliberately playing a game, then he's doing it for a reason. It's not for fun. No one was having fun in that room, even him, whatever it looked like.'

'So what's his upside?'

'He's hiding something. Probably a whole range of some-things.'

'The fact that he killed Jackson?'

'I think it's more complex than that. Why would he want Jackson dead? Because he didn't like him? Everyone works with people they don't like. And he has been in the Army

67

long enough to have learnt self-control in the face of extreme provocation.' She looked up. 'Is there any history between them?'

'Nothing formal. No disciplinary. Their commanding officer said that they got on fine. He also said that they were both based at TAAC-South, but weren't working together at the time of Jackson's death.'

'What else did the commanding officer say?'

Callan put the tips of his index finger and thumb together to form a circle, aping the gesture that Starkey had made.

Jessie rolled her eyes. 'Need to know.'

'Right.'

'Jesus. They're certainly into protecting their own.' She sighed. 'I don't think you're going to get anything else out of Starkey. He clearly believes that he has too much to lose.'

'So to move forward I need to find factual evidence.'

'Yes. And if you find factual evidence, even if it's not enough to charge Starkey, you can use it to put the thumb-screws on him. Force him to talk.'

'What was that bit about "the truth will set you free"?' The corners of his mouth twitched. 'I didn't know that you went to a convent school.'

'There's a lot that you don't know about me, Callan.'

Their eyes locked across his desk. Jessie felt colour rise in her cheeks. Glancing at her watch, an excuse to look away, she slid her chair back.

'If there's nothing more you need, I'm off. I said I'd have tea with Ahmose at six. I have some smoothing over to do after your insults regarding his gardening prowess.'

Callan looked at his watch, too. 'It's only five. How about a—' He broke off, seemed to be weighing up saying something, then changed his mind. 'I'll call you if I need anything else.'

Leaning over the desk she shook his hand, the gesture feeling strangely over formal, but too late now to retract.

'I'm not sure that there will be much more I can help you with.'

He smiled, held her hand for a fraction of a second longer. 'Perhaps. Perhaps not.'

Jessie withdrew her hand. 'Goodbye, Captain Callan.'

It was dark outside, a strong wind gusting clouds over a sliver of moon. Provost Barracks' car park was deserted. Lights on inside the building cast yellow rectangles on to the tarmac next to it, but beyond was only blackness. Jessie wished she'd parked closer to the main door, if only so that she wouldn't trip over or sink into a freezing puddle in her blind trog to her car.

Tugging her collar up around her neck, she dipped her head and crossed the tarmac at a jog. Pausing, she scanned the rows of cars ahead, found her Mini a couple further on from where she was standing, half the size of the other cars in the row, the only one that wasn't black, white or silver. Its sunshine yellow paintwork made her smile.

She was about to walk towards it when something caught her eye. Movement? Was there something moving by the car a couple down from hers? She stared hard through the darkness, continuing to walk, but slowly, relaxing as she walked. No, she'd been wrong. The car park was silent and deserted. She was alone.

Reaching her Mini, she fished in her handbag for her car keys. Her fingers fumbled over object after object, none of them the keys. She should have got them out of her handbag inside the building where there was light.

A sudden noise behind her. Pressing herself against the driver's door, she twisted around. As before, dark rows of cars. No lights, nothing moving. The only noise, her own breathing, the sound harsh and leathery in the chill evening air. In the distance, she could see the gate and guardhouse. Lights on, but all the guards inside – who could blame them? She couldn't find her keys – they weren't in the compartment where she usually put them. Her fingers, numb with cold, filtered through the contents again – lipstick, wallet, hairbrush, a collection of coins for parking clanking around at the bottom of her bag – wishing, not for the first time, that she had a sensible handbag with a compartment for everything, rather than this holdall leather rucksack that her mum had bought her for Christmas two years ago, that she only used out of a sense of duty. Her heart rate was raised and she was angry with herself for it.

She breathed out slowly; her fingers had closed around the cold, heavy bunch of keys.

'Doctor Flynn.'

'Jesus!' She spun around.

He was right behind her. How the hell had he got so close without her realizing? He smiled, his gaze tracking down her body, lingering on her breasts. Not that he was getting much of a look, she figured, small as they were at the best of times, now camouflaged under a shirt, jumper and coat.

'Is there anything that you want, Sergeant Starkey?'

'Lots of things, but perhaps we shouldn't go there now.'

'If that's a "no", I'm leaving. I've got someone to see.'

Clicking the lock, she tugged open the driver's door. He leant his forearm on its top.

'It will be interesting to see if you can break me. I've been Intelligence Corps for twelve years. If there's a psychological game in town, I know how to play it.'

'I'm not trying to break you.' She was about to add, *I'm trying to help you,* but realized that would go down like a lead balloon with someone like Starkey. 'What do you want?'

He tilted towards her. 'I think that the devil offered Jackson a deal and I think he took it,' he hissed.

'We're off the record here, Starkey. No tape recorder. No witnesses. I looked into your eyes in that room and I know that you're entirely sane. Why don't you drop the act.'

Starkey's tongue moved around inside his mouth. 'You're a tough lady, Dr Flynn.'

Jessie didn't reply. She didn't trust her voice not to betray her lack of confidence. She looked past him to the guardhouse: the guards still inside, playing poker or swapping dirty jokes.

'Jackson and some other Int. Corps were working with an Afghan government official who runs the water board – don't know his name,' Starkey began. 'Americans gave them a shitload of money to dam the Helmand river so they could manage their water supply, irrigate the land. Farmers not fighters. Make them richer and they'd have the independence to make their own decisions as to whom they supported. And then of course, they'd support the puppet government of Hamid Karzai, not those Taliban scumbags.' He laughed softly to himself. 'Problem with all this shit is that money never gets used for what it's supposed to.'

'What do you mean?'

He shrugged, grinned. 'That's the end of the fairy story, young lady.'

'The truth will set you free, Starkey. Isn't that what you said?'

His gaze swung away from hers; she noticed a muscle above his eye twitch.

'You think if I tell you what happened – everything – I'll be free,' he continued, suddenly nervous. He tapped a finger to his temple. 'Free of a mental burden, at least. But I won't.'

'Explain. I don't understand.'

Shoving his hands inside his pockets, he shrugged, refusing to meet her eye. 'There's nothing more to tell. I don't know shit.' He almost spat out that last word. 'I didn't find out shit.'

Jessie stared back at him. She was freezing cold and tired. She'd had enough of the word games. 'I think we're done here, Starkey.'

Tossing her rucksack into the car, she slid into the driver's seat, reached to pull the door closed. It wouldn't budge; he was holding it open with his foot.

'Excuse me,' she said.

He didn't move. Swinging her leg out, she kicked his foot away, slammed the door shut. She was tempted to lock it, but didn't want to give him the satisfaction of seeing that he'd rattled her. As she started the engine and pulled away, she glanced in the rear-view mirror, and their gazes locked in reflection. He lifted his hand in a slow, regal wave, smiled a faint, knowing smile.

12

The light was on in Ahmose's cottage, and she could see him inside, sitting in his stiff wing-backed chair – the one he favoured because he didn't have to lower himself too far to get into it – by a roaring log fire, reading the paper.

Ahmose had obviously spent the day gardening because some of the plants in her tiny front garden, across the low flint wall dividing the properties, were wrapped in what looked like white woollen coats, protecting them from the winter freeze.

He pulled open the door, a wide smile spreading across his face.

'Perfect timing. I put the kettle on when I heard your engine. It should be boiled.'

She gave him a kiss on the cheek and stepped into the hallway, immediately felt herself relax as the warmth of the little cottage enveloped her, the woody charcoal smell of the open fire filled her nostrils.

While Ahmose busied himself filling the china teapot,

getting the cups and saucers from the cupboard, arranging them all on the floral tray that had been Alice's favourite, Jessie found a plate and fanned out the biscuits his sister had sent him from Cairo in a neat semicircle. She spent a moment adjusting them, so that an exact portion of each biscuit showed from under the next.

Their weekly tea was a ritual that they had developed over the five years they'd been neighbours. Jessie's heart had sunk the first time Ahmose had appeared on her doorstep the day after she moved in – clutching a miniature indoor rose, full of advice on how to keep it flowering – imagining a nosy old man who'd never give her any peace. The reality, she quickly found, was the opposite. She sought him out more often than he sought her, had learnt to value his calm, sensible views, his clear-headed take on her problems, his stories and his humour. Their weekly tea was now a sacred part of her calendar: civilized, to be savoured, a deeply companionable, uncompetitive couple of hours. Ahmose felt more like family now than her blood relatives, certainly far more than the father she had only seen five times in the past ten years.

Curling on the sofa, Jessie wrapped both hands around the piping cup. With the open fire the cottage was warm, but she felt chilled to the bone from standing too long in the car park playing verbal games with Starkey. She reached for a biscuit.

'You must let me pay for the plant warmers, Ahmose.'

'Most certainly not. A nice garden makes both our cottages look beautiful, adds value.'

She smiled. 'You sound like a Home Counties estate agent.'

'And it gives an old man something to do, some exercise,'

he replied. 'Oh, and before I forget, your mother dropped by a couple of hours ago.'

'My mother?' Jessie was surprised. She couldn't remember the last time her mother had popped around. Years ago, it was – three at least.

She rolled her eyes. 'She seems to think that I don't actually have a job. That I'll be here in the middle of the afternoon.'

'It's a mother's job to believe that their child is forever too young to be gainfully employed and to worry about them constantly. I offered for her to wait in your house – I thought that you wouldn't mind – but she said that she needed to get home for six.'

Jessie nodded, took a sip of tea. 'Did she want anything specific?'

'I don't think so. I think that she just wanted to see you. She said that it has been a long time.'

Jessie bit her lip. It had been a long time, eight months – her mother's birthday. The weather had been unseasonally hot and she'd been wearing a T-shirt and jeans. She remembered her mother asking if she couldn't have *dressed up a bit for lunch* – even though they were only going to a pub on Wimbledon Common. Chafing against each other even now, fifteen years later. None of the life-changing events they had lived through talked about in detail. Nothing resolved.

'You should go and see her, Jessie, whatever has gone under the bridge.' And when she didn't reply, he continued: 'The mother–daughter relationship is . . .' A pause as he searched for the right world. 'Irreplaceable. Difficult, challenging, of course, but irreplaceable.'

Jessie shrugged. 'It was always more mother–son for my mother.'

Ahmose took a biscuit from the plate, chewed in silence. Jessie watched him warily over the lip of her cup.

'Alice and I never had the chance to have children,' he murmured, dropping the half-finished biscuit into his saucer. 'It was before all that IVF was widely available.' He waved his hand towards the window, as if encompassing all the modern inventions of the last thirty years. 'It broke Alice's heart. She never got over it. I saw it in her eyes most when she smiled, when she was happy . . .' A pause. 'There was always something missing, as if sadness was sitting right behind her eyes, taking some of the light from them, even when she was smiling.' Reaching across, Ahmose laid a hand on Jessie's arm. 'Losing a child must be worse than never having had one at all, because you know what a fantastic human being they would have made, how incredibly unique and wonderful they would have been. That is what your mother lives with every day.'

Jessie felt tears prick her eyes. 'It's not so great losing a brother.'

She had spent fifteen years dodging memories. How much longer could she maintain it?

'Go and see her,' Ahmose said gently. 'Please. If only because I have asked you to.'

13

The morning of Jamie's funeral, she had risen at 4.30 a.m. – pitch-black outside, even though it was nearly mid-summer – and tiptoed downstairs. She had expected to be alone with her thoughts of Jamie, the burden of her guilt, but her mother was already awake, sitting at the kitchen table in her towelling robe, clutching a cup of coffee that had grown a milky film it had sat so long, untouched.

She was holding Jamie's school jumper, pressing it to her face, drinking in his smell. Jessie was surprised how small it was. The images she retained of Jamie, despite his illness, were larger than life, a personality that occupied a vast, fizzing space. Looking at her mum clutching his jumper, fingers stroking the balled wall, she realized how young he was, how little. Seven years, gone in a heartbeat. A life snuffed out before it had properly begun.

'I thought you were asleep,' Jessie murmured. She couldn't meet her mother's gaze.

'How could I?' The words barely audible.

Distractedly, her mother took a sip of coffee, her face

wrinkling in surprise at its coldness. How long had she sat here, cradling the cup?

'I'll make you another,' Jessie said.

She padded over to the kettle. While she was waiting for it to boil, she pulled back the kitchen curtain expecting, for some reason, to see dawn breaking; startled when all she saw was her own pallid reflection. Though she had been in the kitchen for barely two minutes, each second had elongated until it was nanometre thin, filling an hour of memories, of self-recrimination. The ticking of the kitchen clock sounded like a hammer on steel, the dim overhead lights, half the bulbs missing, interrogation-chamber bright. She was hypersensitive to every movement, her mother's every tic.

Filling two cups, Jessie moved back to the table.

'I've been trying to remember Jamie before the illness.' Her mother's voice wavered. 'But all I can remember is him without colour, pale and sickly. He used to have the most beautiful complexion, the most vibrant look about him.' She plucked at her own sallow, papery skin. 'You both did . . . do. Perfect Irish roses. Your father's look.'

Leaning over, she cupped Jessie's chin in her fingers, their first physical contact since Jamie's death. 'You're so like your father. Beautiful, like him. He was . . . is beautiful . . . on the outside, at least.'

'Will he . . . will he be there?'

'What?'

'Dad? Will Dad be at . . .' Jessie's tongue felt like a wad of cotton wool in her mouth. 'At the funeral?'

A vague shrug. 'How would I know?' Her mother's hand moved to stroke her cheek. Her touch like a chill breeze. 'Yesterday, in the supermarket, I imagined holding Jamie when he was just an hour old. I was in bed, in hospital, my knees

78

bent, and he was lying in the dent between my thighs. I closed my eyes, standing in the middle of the aisle, and I could feel him. Actually *feel* the warmth of him. The shape of his skull under my fingers, that duck's fluff of baby hair. He clutched my hand with his tiny fingers. I remember studying his nails in wonderment. They were so perfect, every nail a perfect crescent. It always amazes me that something so small, a baby's hand, can work at all.' Her words ran out, her face closed down. A single tear squeezed from her eye and ran down her cheek.

'Mum?' Jessie bit her lip to stop herself from crying. 'It'll be all right.'

'No. It won't be all right.' Her mum rose, turned towards the door. 'I'm going to get dressed.'

'Mum. Please.'

To stop talking meant that time would start ticking again, the unstoppable slide towards the inevitable: a black car at the front door, the slow journey down the A3 to the crematorium, the impatient flow of traffic cutting around them, brake lights flashing as drivers caught sight of the little coffin smothered in flowers and slowed to stare, the black-garbed crowd waiting outside the crematorium, children and parents from school, children who had teased and taunted Jamie when he couldn't run any more, couldn't play football – *Thought your sister was the Jessie, jessie.*

Jamie's body being interred in fire.

'*Mum.*'

Her mother paused at the door; her dead eyes found Jessie's. 'When your dad left us, I thought that the unrequited love I had for him was the hardest I'd ever experience.' Her voice cracked. 'But I was wrong. When someone dies they can't love us back. However hard we love them, they can never, ever love us back.'

14

Wendy Chubb rubbed a hand against the window. Steam from the washing-up bowl had clouded the glass, but even so she was sure that she had seen a flash of light in the garden. She stared hard through the smeared circle she had rubbed clear. Only darkness now.

The light from the house washed the patio next to it with a feeble glow, but beyond that the night was thick and black, the hills that rose up on either side of the house seeming to suck whatever moonlight there was from the garden.

What had made her look out the window anyway? A noise? Had it been a noise? Tilting her head, she listened. She heard the old house creaking, the walls murmuring to each other, the knock of air in the pipes, the gurgle of hot water filling the radiators. Wind bristled the trees in the garden. Her gaze swept left to right through the glass, straining to make out the line of leylandii shielding the house from the road, the knot of apple trees in the centre of the garden, the pots lined up at the edge of the patio, plants in them dead from cold and neglect.

Suddenly she leapt back, her hand flying to her mouth, smothering a gasp of surprise and fear. A bright flash. Right up close to the house, barely five metres from where she was standing. She breathed hard, trying to settle the hammering of her heart. What on earth was there to be afraid of? Now that she thought for a moment, fear felt ridiculous. She was inside a locked house, Major Scott in the sitting room across the hallway. And there was clearly a rational explanation for the light.

Sami? Was he outside with his torch? She hurried to the bottom of the stairs.

'Sami.' No answer. She leaned against the banister, shouted, '*Sami.*'

Silence.

'*Sami.*'

Light hurried footsteps, the boards creaking above her head.

'Yes.' His voice sounding timid.

Poor kid.

'Oh. I wondered if you'd . . .' she broke off. 'Don't worry, darling. You carry on playing. I'll be up in five minutes to put you to bed.' *Stupid woman.* Of course he hadn't gone outside. He couldn't reach the lock and the Yale was far too stiff for him, even if he could. She stuck her head into the sitting room. Major Scott was in the leather chair, asleep he looked to be, breathing heavily, mouth open, a globule of saliva gathered on his bottom lip. Wendy glanced at her watch. Nooria's train wasn't due into Aldershot for another half-hour.

Back in the kitchen, she hung by the door, not wanting to approach the window, feeling ridiculous at the tight knot of fear in her stomach. Stepping firmly across the kitchen, she pressed her face to the glass.

No lights. Nobody out there. Just the soupy darkness, wind moving the trees, black outlines shifting and twitching, but purely due to the wind. And transposed over it all, the pale, frightened moon of her own face.

15

Back in her own cottage, Jessie took off her shoes, lined them up in the shoe rack by the door, removed her coat and hung it on the hook, straightening the sleeves. Taking a step back, she checked their alignment, straightened again, millimetre by millimetre, until they were exactly level.

She was hungry, in need of something more than biscuits to eat. Padding into the kitchen in her socks, she tugged open the fridge. Rows of clear plastic Klip-It boxes faced her on the shelves, each one labelled with its contents, the labels hand-printed in neat, black capitals. Cheese, salad, eggs, beans, apples, red peppers . . . The product of her weekly shop debagged and decanted, nothing entering the fridge in its original packaging. No foreign dirt, no mess, no uneven shapes to knock her sense of order off kilter. Everything organized and in its place.

Her gaze ranged along the uniform black capitals, nothing taking her fancy, her heart sagging under the weight of the disorder spelled out by the codified containers. Reaching out, she picked one up and reversed it, grabbed the bottle of

Sauvignon and poured herself a glass. Returning the bottle without bothering to line up the label, she slammed the fridge door.

She was halfway across the kitchen when she stopped. She could feel the electric suit hiss. Ignoring the rising tension, she forced herself to keep walking, into the lounge. Jamie's photo caught her eye – that chocolate-ringed smile. Her limbs felt on fire, her throat so constricted that breathing was a struggle. She felt as if she would explode with the tension building inside her.

Fighting back tears, she retraced her steps to the fridge. Hauling the door open, shivering at the blast of cold air that enveloped her, she realigned the box, turned the wine bottle until the label faced exactly outwards, exactly – to the millimetre – and pushed the door closed. Sliding down the fridge, she folded herself into a ball on the kitchen floor and burst into tears.

OCD. Obsessive-compulsive disorder. She knew all about it. Had studied it at university, read case after case in her spare time. She knew everything there was to know and still she was helpless to fight the disorder in herself. A disorder that was now as much a part of who she was as her black hair or blue eyes, it had inhabited her for so long. She was a character in a sick and twisted play. Knew exactly how the performance would play out and wanted no part of it, but had no ability to resist. She was consumed by the need for order, for control, even as she had no control over her own mind.

When she was all cried out, she pushed herself up from the floor and went over to the sink. Letting the cold tap gush until the water was freezing, she doused her face, let the water run down her neck and chest. As the water numbed her skin, her brain spun with thoughts, memories, memories on memories. Love. Guilt. Helplessness. Self-hatred.

She had never realized that so much love could exist for another person until she had seen her mother grieving for Jamie.

16

Downstairs Mummy and Daddy were arguing – he could hear their raised voices. Wendy had put him to bed, put him in his woolly sheep pyjamas and dressing gown, put socks on his feet. *Keep you warm.* Told him that Mummy and Daddy were tired tonight, stressed. *Be a good boy. Go to sleep.*

He had gone to sleep, like Wendy had asked him, but the shouting had woken him. He liked Wendy, felt safe when she was here. Now she was gone. He had seen her from his bedroom window, hurrying to her car, head down, glancing around her as she walked. He had heard her engine puttering out of the drive.

It was only him, Mummy and Daddy in the house. Him upstairs alone, and their raised voices coming up through the floor.

Daddy was shouting: *I don't want people interfering in our lives.*

Sitting up in bed, he looked towards the window. Wendy hadn't pulled the curtains all the way across – they didn't join in the middle. A sliver of moonlight cut through the gap, glinting across his room like a knife. He wanted them closed, wanted the knife gone. But he didn't want to go near the window, to pull them closed himself. He was scared of what might be outside the glass. He had seen the light in the garden, flashing close to the house, had asked Wendy about the light. *Light? I didn't see a light. You must have imagined it. Go to sleep now, like a good boy.*

Sami swallowed. A lump was stuck in his throat and it wouldn't go up or down. Inching silently to the end of his bed, dragging his torch with him, he slid on to the floor. He sat for a second, panting, his chest tight with fear. Was he alone? The darkness in his bedroom seemed to be moving.

On hands and knees, he crawled silently into the corner, squeezing himself behind the toy buckets, curling himself into a tiny ball. He could see nothing but the smooth coloured plastic of the buckets. Red. Blue. Yellow. Green. He couldn't see the void of darkness beyond; the darkness couldn't find him.

Mummy and Daddy were arguing. He pressed his hands over his ears, could still hear them.

Mummy was shouting. Daddy was angry.

He wanted to curl up in Mummy's arms, like he used to before Mummy got sad.

Quietly, he tugged Baby Isabel out of the dolls' toy bucket, shrunk back into the corner, clutching her tight to his chest.

'The boy is bad,' he whispered into Baby Isabel's ear. 'The girl . . . the girl is good. The boy is bad.'

He felt for his torch. It was next to him. Having it there made him feel safer. He wanted to switch it on, but he was too frightened to move again.

'The bad girl has got out of bed.' His lips moved silently

against Baby Isabel's ear. 'Stay in bed. Don't get out. Bad girl.'

He breathed in – a deep, sucking breath – trying to make his heart stop drumming in his chest. The noise of his heart was too loud. Someone would hear. The darkness would hear. Shadowman would hear. Pressing his hand to his chest, he tried to hold his heart to stop it from thumping. He couldn't. Jamming his eyes shut, he started to cry.

Daddy was shouting. Mummy was sobbing.

He had to switch his torch on, had to keep himself safe.

'Go away, Shadowman,' he whispered. 'Go away, Shadow-man, goway, Shadowman, goway, goway, goway.' Chanting under his breath, clutching Baby Isabel tight with one hand, he swung the beam of his torch back and forth across the room with the other. 'Stay in bed. Gowayshadowman, goway, goway, goway.'

17

Nineties bubble-gum music pumped from the doors as Jessie pushed them open. Britney Spears. Was she still knocking out tunes?

It was a typical Mc-bar in a side street in Aldershot, one that could be lifted and replanted in any small-town high street in England and look as if it belonged. Modern brushed gold fittings, pale wooden bar, mushroom-coloured walls, pairs of fat leather sofas for chilling arranged either side of low wooden coffee tables, booths heaving with twenty-somethings clutching alcopops and bottles of Becks, eyeing each other up.

Jessie pushed her way over to the bar and slid on to a stool, ordered herself a vodka and tonic. She had dressed with intent: wore a thigh-length red dress and nude stilettos, a slash of Ruby Tuesday lipstick and statement eyes. A jet-black curtain of hair hung almost to her waist. It was a tried-and-tested outfit, though one she rarely wore, dragged from the back of her wardrobe and dusted down when cleaning the house had failed to keep her demons at bay. She knew that she looked hot. Hot and available.

Crossing her legs, she spun the stool, tilted back against the bar and scanned the crowd. In less than a minute, she had locked eyes with a man standing near the door with a few of his mates. He looked a couple of years younger than her – twenty-six or -seven, perhaps. He wore a tight white long-sleeved T-shirt that hugged his abdominals and navy-blue jeans. He was tall, dark-haired, dark-eyed, good looking enough, with a nice smile. Nice enough. She didn't intend to marry him.

Dropping her gaze, she twisted a lock of hair around her finger. Looking up, she found his gaze again. The corners of her mouth tilted in a tiny smile. She took another sip of her vodka and tonic, eyes locked with his, then twisted back to the bar.

Thirty seconds later, a voice in her ear. 'Can I get you another?'

Turning, she laid a hand on his chest. 'Why not.'

Jessie ran her hands up the man's torso under his T-shirt, feeling the hard ridges of his abdominals, the muscles of his chest warm and solid under her fingers. He worked out three times a week, he had told her proudly. She could tell.

They had left the bar, walked down a side street to the car park at the back. The air was freezing, a light layer of frost coating the tarmac, silvery in the moonlight, the car park, unsurprisingly, deserted.

She could feel him, already hard, pressing against her thigh. Sliding her hand to the back of his neck, Jessie moulded her body to his and slid her tongue into his mouth. With her other hand, she found his belt buckle.

The rough brick sandpapered her back through her leather jacket as he shoved up inside her. She closed her eyes and her mind locked on to the feel of him, the rhythmic movement, the sensation. Nothing else mattered. Only the pure, uncomplicated, animal feeling. She bit her lip, felt heat building. For a second her mind filled with an image of Callan, looking at her across his desk, looking wrecked. Pushing the image away, she blanked her mind, focused only on the man, the feeling of him inside her. Closing her eyes, she clung to him as the orgasm came, tucking her face into the crook of his neck, drawing in his smell, feeling his warmth, the twin manic beats of their hearts.

For a brief, incredibly intense moment, she wished that she were in a normal relationship, could lie back now, feel strong arms around her as she drifted into sleep. Wake up to someone who gave a shit. Wished that she could make the commitment, gain that level of trust with another human being. Knew that it was impossible.

The man slid out of her, turned sideways to tuck himself back inside his trousers, zip himself up.

'Can I see you again?'

Jessie smiled. She could feel his semen dribbling down her leg. 'Sure.'

He leaned forward to kiss her, but she raised a hand to his chest, held him at arm's length, T-shirt bunched teasingly in her fist. She was done.

'Give me your number and I'll text you mine.' She pretended to key his number into her phone as he recited it. 'Great.' She smiled. 'I'll see you soon.'

He held her wrist. 'This weekend? Dinner?'

'That would be lovely.' Twisting her wrist gently to free it, she touched her lips to his cheek. 'I'll call you.'

She didn't look back as she walked away, her brain stilled from its obsessions, for the moment at least, by the hormonal surge. She knew that by the time she got home the hormones would have dissipated. Knew that she would step straight into a scalding shower, scrub his liquids from her skin feeling dirty and stupid, fighting the rush of negative emotion that would engulf her. Shame, loss, emptiness and guilt – always guilt.

You were with your boyfriend? Why weren't you with him?

Every time it felt a bit shallower, sadder. Worked a little less.

You promised me you'd look after him. You promised me.

Darren. She knew the man's name. Virtually nothing else about him.

He died because of you. Jamie died because of you.

18

'I've got netball practice after school.'

'Can't you miss it this once? I'm working late.'

Jessie shook her head, the lie sliding smoothly off her tongue. 'It's team selection. I need to be there.'

Her mum sighed, already on the edge of her patience, nerves frayed from digging two kids out of bed, getting them uniformed and fed, herself ready for work, all by 7.30 a.m. 'I don't like Jamie being alone in the house. He's only seven.'

'Ask Felix's mum to drop him home. He can watch TV or play with his PlayStation. I'll be back by five. He'll only be on his own for half an hour.' Jessie ran out of the house, not bothering to take her netball kit.

It was getting dark when she got home. The sun dipping below the pitched roofs of the sixties detached houses lining the end of their cul-de-sac. Someone's music pounded from an open window, down the street, 'YMCA', *happy music*. She smiled. She had spent longer with Adam than she had planned, hanging out on the common and smoking, lying in the grass, fumbling and kissing, making plans. Her first boyfriend, the one. She was fourteen and sure of it. She glanced at her watch – it was nearly six thirty. Jamie had been alone for two hours. *Shit.* Her mum would kill her if she ever found out.

The light was on in the sitting room and upstairs in Jamie's bedroom. She could see a lumpy shadow against the curtain in his room. She stood on the pavement frowning up at his window, then pushed the gate open. He must be playing some weird game, acting out a dumb scene from 'Diary of a Wimpy Kid'. It wouldn't be the first time.

The front garden was a mass of yellow. Early spring daffodils, mixed with weeds, clogging the beds that lined the garden path, the pathway itself studded with moss, more weeds forcing their way up through the cracked concrete between the paving stones. Her mother no longer had the time to garden, something she used to love back when they were a proper family and she was a homemaker. Jessie remembered trailing her around the garden when she was four or five, Jamie not yet even thought of – aeons ago it felt now, lifetimes. They had planted these daffodils together. Happy flowers, her mum used to say. *Happy music. Happy flowers.*

Her key twisted in the lock and she opened the front door. Silence.

'Jamie?' She stood in the hall and called up the stairs. 'Jamie, it's Jessie. I'm home.'

No reply. Only the sound of her pulse, slightly raised from the fast walk home, throbbing in the silence. She stepped into the lounge. The television was off, the PlayStation tucked on the shelf under the television stand, the wire coiled around the handset, far too tidy for Jamie to have done it himself. Jessie was surprised. Usually, any chance he got, he'd have it out, be playing, oblivious to anything else.

The kitchen was also empty and there was no sign that he had helped himself to a snack. Returning to the hallway, she kicked off her school shoes and called up the stairs again, louder.

'Come down, Jamie. I'll make you something to eat.'

Still no reply.

Odd.

He wasn't playing music, so he could definitely hear her. She sighed, hands on hips.

'*Jamie*. I *really* can't be bothered to come up and get you.'

She felt anger rising. Anger mixed with tension. A fluttering in her stomach that made her feel slightly queasy. What kind of game was he playing?

She started up the stairs, moving slowly – unsure why – the soft carpet giving under her socked feet. On the landing, she stopped. All the doors were open save Jamie's, but she could see light shining from the crack under his closed door. As she walked past her mother's room, she caught sight of the unmade bed, pyjamas strewn on the floor, make-up, hairbrush, cleansers and face creams, scattered on top of the dressing table, abstract shapes framed in the twilight cutting through the window. Her mother: naturally orderly, but with so little time these days to do anything except lurch from one crisis to the next.

Jessie stopped outside Jamie's bedroom door and panic gripped her without warning. Quite what she was afraid of, she didn't know. Staring blankly ahead at the white-painted wood in front of her, she turned the handle.

As the door swung open, her gaze caught the poster on the wall above his bed, an Athena poster of a litter of choc-olate Labrador puppies squashed into a wicker shopping basket. Too old to keep it, he'd said, but he hadn't taken it down. The bed below, unmade – nothing strange in that – his school bag dumped beside it – so he *was* home – the tension in her stomach so acute she could taste bile in her mouth.

'Jamie.' Hearing the sob straining her vocal cords.

The door swung fully open. And she saw.

The blue Batman curtains first.

And then Jamie. Hanging by his neck from the curtain rail by his red-and-grey striped school tie.

Somewhere someone was screaming. A scream so raw that it could only mean pain. Jessie fought upwards towards it, through dense, hot layers of unconsciousness. The taste of vomit, rich and acid, filled her mouth. She was lying on the carpet, a part of her brain realized, head resting on the soft wool, the stain of vomit forming a halo around her head, clotted in her hair, damp and sticky against her cheek.

If she turned her head, just a fraction, opened her eyes, she would see him hanging there. She kept her eyes jammed shut, but the image filled the insides of her eyelids with microscopic detail. His face, puffy where the circulation had been cut off, purplish-blue around the lips. The chair from his desk over-turned beneath him, the papers he mustn't have bothered moving off the desk itself before he clambered on to it, scattered on the floor. The absolute gaping, yawing void of silence.

A car swished down the street, Westlife thumping from its speakers. Shoving herself to her feet, Jessie barrelled out of Jamie's bedroom and into her mother's.

Clutching the phone to her ear, she punched at the keys. Couldn't see through the hot tears streaming from her eyes. 999. A dial tone. 9 . . . Sobbing now. 99 . . . Sobbing, choking, howling in utter desperation.

19

Clearly nothing of much excitement occurred in this corner of West Sussex, as the crime scene tape strung across the front of the Art Deco house was now home to a line of onlookers, dressed for endurance in wellies and all-weather gear. Many, from the red, pinched look of their faces, had been there for some considerable time, even though it was barely eight thirty in the morning. Marilyn remembered the same from the murder in Smuggler's Lane last year: the constant stream of 'near neighbours', some of whom came from as far afield as Bognor Regis thirty miles to the east, or Petersfield, twenty north, every one of them professing concern at a murder on their own doorstep lest they be the next victim, every one all ears for the tiniest, goriest detail.

He watched from a distance – having no intention of getting close enough to be buttonholed by any of them – as the uniformed constable guarding the integrity of the tape waved them out of the way to let the 'Police Dogs' van through. From the rigidity of his stance to the way his hands were cutting staccato arcs through the air, Marilyn could tell that his patience was fraying. He chuckled. Manning the line was part of the police initiation ceremony: the police equivalent of downing a yard of ale or walking around for the day with one trouser leg rolled up to the knee and a sign saying 'please kick me' stuck on your back. The constable would be a better officer for it – more cynical, less patient, more able to cut through the crap and zero in on the details that mattered.

The specialist search team had arrived yesterday afternoon, spent the hours until sundown dredging ditches, going through the drains, searching culverts. Nothing had been found. They would be back soon to continue – more chattering fodder for the 'neighbours'. Police divers would spend the morning searching the water close to the house, and then fan out into adjacent fingers of the harbour. Search conditions promised to be miserable for those on land and in the water: freezing cold, a chill twenty-knot wind cutting across the sea, thick grey clouds massed above their heads promising yet another downpour.

Tugging up the collar of his jacket, Marilyn crossed the gravel drive to meet the dog handlers. There were two, each with a springer spaniel. An experienced sergeant in his mid-thirties who had been handling dogs for fifteen years and a constable with eight years under her belt. Marilyn had worked with both of them before, rated them, trusted them to deliver the best that could be delivered under difficult circumstances, knew of no one on his or neighbouring forces who would do better. He shook hands with each, stepped back and waited while they struggled into their forensic overalls.

From the back of the van the dogs were whining and yapping, scratching to get out. The van had stopped, their handlers disembarked. They knew that something was up, were keen to get on with the job.

These were not ordinary search-and-rescue dogs that Marilyn had called in. These were cadaver dogs. Trained to find a corpse, irrespective of its state of decomposition. These two spaniels were 'air-scenting dogs', able to pick up the scent of rotting flesh carried on the breeze. Their sense of smell was so acute that they could follow a microscopic trail of flesh and bone fallen from the skin or clothes of a person who had carried a body to where they had dumped it a month before.

Through the open car door, Marilyn caught sight of a Treagust and Sons' plastic bag in the passenger footwell, rotten lamb shanks or pigs' trotters to call the dogs from the body once it had been found – prevent them from scoffing what was left of the corpse – or to quench their hunger when the search was called off if it wasn't found. Treagust was his favourite local butcher, a family-run business based in Emsworth, a quaint fishing village on the harbour a few miles west, which sold fantastic local produce, most of it organic, grass-fed, free-range, traceable. Only the best for the cadaver dogs, he thought grimly.

The handlers opened the back doors of their van, opened the cages within and slipped leashes around their dogs' necks.

'So what are we after?' the male sergeant asked.

'Legs,' Marilyn replied frankly.

'Right.' They nodded in unison, entirely unfazed; they'd heard and seen far worse.

'A man's legs,' Marilyn added. Rubbing his nose, which he suspected had succumbed to frostbite a couple of hours ago, feeling nothing but faint pins and needles pricking in its tip, he looked across the sloping grass to the water. The autopsy was booked for two thirty this afternoon and he would like to present Dr Ghoshal, the pathologist, with a whole body, rather than the ravaged half that he currently had. 'We have a torso. The legs are missing. I'd like to have the other half by the autopsy this afternoon if possible. The legs may be in some serial killer's freezer, but my sense is that's unlikely.'

Whatever the general public thought from the plethora of police series and novels featuring serial killers, they were actually a rare beast and the likelihood that one was practising in this idyllic corner of West Sussex was remote. Then again, that was exactly what the Gloucestershire Constabulary had told themselves when Fred and Rosemary West's first victim had escaped, reported them and been summarily dismissed as a hysteric. Complacency was the policeman's worst enemy and playing statistics a dangerous game.

'My sense is that the propeller of a gin palace or big yacht took this body apart. Tony Burrows is so convinced that an axe or butcher's cleaver is responsible that out of sheer bloody-mindedness I have bet him a hundred quid that I'm right. Drinks on me if you find the legs.'

The dog handlers nodded again, well accustomed to the games that the coppers from the Surrey and Sussex Major Crimes Unit played to stop the brutal reality of the beatings, rapes and murders they dealt with from sinking too far under the skin.

'We'll do our best, sir, but this wind isn't going to help,' the sergeant said.

There were so many smells by the harbour's edge – rotting seaweed; dead fish and seabirds washed up on the shore; the contents of yachts' bilges, human excrement pumped into the water – a smorgasbord to excite a dog's senses, that the smell of decomposition would be incredibly hard for the spaniels to detect.

'The torso has been here for some time. Weeks rather than days, Tony Burrows reckoned, from the bloating and deterioration to the skin and flesh, though obviously until Dr Ghoshal confirms, that's guesswork. It was covered with seaweed and in an advanced state of decomposition. If it was summer we'd have been left with a steaming puddle of God knows what, but at least the cold weather has some bonuses.' He shivered in his leather biker jacket. 'I imagine that the torso was dumped in the water, either from a boat or from a vehicle and then washed up here. There's a number of places in the harbour where you can back a car right up to the water, particularly at high tide.'

The handlers nodded. The spaniels were straining at their leashes, noses to the air, fidgety to get on with the job. 'What are you thinking?' the constable asked. 'Where shall we start?'

Marilyn sighed. Chichester Harbour was ten thousand acres of deep water, tidal mudflats and saltings, shaped like a giant hand, a village at the end of each finger, used by thousands of craft each year, visited by tens of thousands of people.

He sighed. 'I'm thinking that we've got more chance of finding a needle in a haystack, but we need to give it a go. The more I have of the body, the greater chance I've got of finding out who he is, and then, of course, what happened to him. One of you goes one way along the shore, the other goes the other way. We've got five hours before I have to leave for the autopsy, in possession of the legs or not. I'm afraid I can't be more helpful than that.'

They nodded in unison. The constable hauled her spaniel back to her side. 'We'll do our best, sir.'

20

The sky was battleship grey, clouds so low that Jessie felt if she stretched up her arm the tips of her fingers would be swallowed in thick, grey cotton. Rain was beginning to spit against her windscreen. Parking a hundred metres down the road from her mother's house, beyond the line of sight, she switched off her headlights. Mothers in Volvos ferrying kids to school swished by on the wet road; a dog walker passed her, dragging a fat black Labrador on a lead, all sagging tongue and wagging tail, happy to be heading for the common whatever the weather.

Her mother still lived in the house Jessie had grown up in, a small, sixties detached house in a cul-du-sac in Wimbledon. Two doors down was a smart new white-washed concrete and glass modernist box that towered over its neighbours, a 'For Sale' sign outside; a couple on from that, a huge hole in the ground, a yellow JCB, its tracks clotted with mud, parked beside it. Wimbledon desirable now, all the older, smaller houses like her mother's being bought up by developers, bulldozed and replaced with looming new monoliths far too big for their modest plots.

She walked down the road, pulling her hood up against the rain that was falling solidly. Reaching the gate, she stopped, shifting so that her body was shielded by the trunk of the flowering cherry tree in her mother's front garden, a tangle of conflicting emotions stopping her from walking straight up the garden path and hammering on the front door. She could see her mother in the kitchen, leaning back against the counter, a cup of tea or coffee in her hand. She was wearing a new dressing gown, pink and fluffy. Jessie swung the gate open. She was about to step through when she stopped. A man had come into the kitchen. Wrapping his arms around Jessie's mother, he dipped his head and kissed her neck. Tipping her head back, she pushed him away laughing. Laying her cup on the sideboard, she grabbed a tea towel and brushed it down the front of her gown. He must have jogged her cup, spilt some tea or coffee, when he'd hugged her. The mother Jessie knew would have snapped to anger, fixating fifteen years of anguish on to every tiny misdemeanour. This mother just laughed. Twisting the tea towel into a rope, she playfully whipped the man with it. Tossing the tea towel back on the sideboard, she glanced at her watch. Giving him another hug and a kiss, she left the kitchen.

The man was late fifties, Jessie guessed, grey-haired, tall and thin. He had a kind face, deep laughter lines etched around his eyes and the corners of his mouth that made him look as if he didn't take life too seriously.

Stepping quietly back on to the pavement, Jessie pulled the gate closed. Intruding on this scene felt impossible: blundering into a scenario she didn't recognize, one that

103

she felt entirely unprepared for. It was the first time she'd seen her mum genuinely happy in fifteen years. She couldn't barge in there with all the memories that were attached to her.

Another time. She would come and see her mum another time, catch her alone.

21

Jessie drove to Wimbledon station and parked in the underground car park. She had arranged to meet Nooria Scott, Sami's mother, at the Royal College of Art, in Battersea, at ten o'clock this morning. Nooria was studying for a two-year master's in Fine Art and had said that she was only a few days away from her first exhibition in the college galleries, was working flat out.

As the train rattled along the cutting, Jessie leaned her head against the headrest and gazed out of the window. London always felt like a city of two halves. Endless rows of terraced houses, dull and grey in the rain, postage-stamp back gardens studded with rusting climbing frames and trampolines, plastic children's toys shiny with damp. Then, as the train got closer into central London, the terraces segueing into glass-and-steel apartment blocks, a studio flat costing over a quarter of a million pounds, the Fords and Vauxhalls of Greater London replaced by Porsches and Mercedes.

She got off at Battersea Park station and walked across

the park, taking her time, unable to recall when she had last come up to central London, making a mental note to visit more often, though she knew she wouldn't. She cut along the edge of the park to the Thames and followed the river path. Across the river, on the opposite bank, were the fine red-brick mansion blocks of Chelsea, directly in front of her was Albert Bridge, its pastel colours – pale yellow, baby pink, sky blue – incongruous in the slushy sleet, making her smile. This felt like London proper, a wide straight cut of the Thames, barges straining at their moorings, beautiful, historic buildings, the odd tourist with a camera, despite the weather, valiantly trudging through the park.

The Royal College of Art, Fine Art Department, was located inside the new Dyson building by Battersea Bridge, a modernist triumph of concrete and glass, square and utilitarian. Inside, the space was huge, more concrete and glass, the foyer, four storeys high, light and air filled, a concrete staircase snaking up to metal walkways suspended on cables. Students in black jeans and polo necks, baggy, paint-splashed dungarees, shirts and trousers in clashing primary colours, carrying huge black folios, jostled past Jessie.

She had sent Nooria a text as she left Battersea Park station, received one back asking her to wait in the foyer.

'You must be Dr Flynn.'

Jessie turned to face a stunning woman, her skin the same olive as Sami's, her face a perfect oval, deep green eyes under a heavy fringe, thick dark hair which she had pulled up into an untidy chignon.

'Call me Jessie, please.' She extended her hand. 'Dr Flynn sounds way too formal in these surroundings.' She smiled. 'Am I so easy to spot?'

Nooria gave a slight shrug. 'Nooria Scott. And yes, you are easy to spot. You're the only one who has polished shoes.'

She wore navy-blue paint-splashed dungarees and a baggy white shirt, sleeves rolled up to her elbows. She was twenty-eight, Jessie knew, though her clothes gave her a casual, college-girl freshness, which made her look years younger. Jessie couldn't imagine her as a mother, let alone the mother of that deeply disturbed little boy, or shut in that damp old house in the country. As if she was an exotic bird that had been stolen from its native rainforest and trapped in a tiny, dark cage.

Nooria indicated the café, on one side of the entrance hall. They ordered two coffees, Nooria insisting that she pay for Jessie's as some compensation for dragging her all the way up to central London. They found a table by the window and sat down facing each other.

'I'm sorry, but I don't have long,' Nooria said. 'As I mentioned when we spoke, I have my first exhibition which starts on Friday. We get a chance to exhibit in college galleries twice over our two-year master's course and it's during the exhibitions that artists get talent-spotted, so, as you can imagine, it's very important.'

Jessie indicated her folio. 'Could I have a look?'

'I'd rather you didn't. They're only rough sketches – ideas.' Her gaze skipped off to the window, the cars on Battersea Bridge Road streaming silently past, barely three metres away on the other side of the glass. 'It's a bit like baring your soul, showing someone paintings. Unfinished paintings even more so.'

'What do you paint?'

'Still-lifes mainly. People,' she added. 'Do you like art?'

'Not modern art, like Tracy Emin's. I'm probably being completely ignorant, but I don't see the point or the skill in it. But fine art, yes, purely as an observer. It was never one of my great talents at school.'

'But people were?'

'I'm not sure that anything was. I just found my way into psychology.' Jessie didn't want to go there, to explain why. She reached for her cup, took a sip of coffee to give herself a natural reason to break eye contact. A little boy, about Sami's age, trotted past the window, clutching tight to his mother's hand. It reminded Jessie that Nooria hadn't yet mentioned her son.

'As you don't have long, could we start?' she said.

Nooria glanced away, chewing at a fingernail. 'I have to be honest, I'm not very comfortable with the concept of being analysed. I don't think it's up to someone else to define what "normal" means.' Tilting sideways, she pulled an electronic cigarette from her pocket and held it up, wrinkling her nose. 'I have this thing, which I hate. It tastes disgusting.' She had a faint East London accent; discordant, given her exotic looks. 'If it wasn't so utterly freezing I'd ask you to come outside so I could smoke properly.'

Jessie waited until Nooria had taken a couple of puffs of the electronic cigarette, seemed more settled, before she replied.

'I'm not planning on telling you how to think. There is no normal.' *I certainly know that.* 'Psychology is about repairing things that have broken. A part of Sami is broken. He's not being silly, or fanciful. His mind has been damaged by an experience—'

'By seeing his father,' Nooria cut in. Her brow furrowed as she took another suck of the cigarette. 'It's not surprising.

108

It was horrible, absolutely horrible, seeing him in that hospital. Burnt. So . . . badly burnt.' She took another tense puff, dragged on it for longer this time. 'He was completely . . .' she paused, searching for the right words. 'Changed. Not just what he looks like, though God, that's bad enough.' Her gaze dipped. 'He was strong, confident before. A real man, if you know what I mean. An alpha male. And now—' She broke off, shaking her head. 'That fucking place. I hate that fucking place. You have no idea how much.'

'Afghanistan?'

She nodded. 'Have you ever been there?'

'Twice,' Jessie said.

A pause. Nooria took another suck, the tip lighting red briefly.

'Do you know that I'm half Persian?' she murmured.

Jessie nodded; that information had been in Sami's referral file.

'My father,' Nooria continued. 'I never actually met him, at least not when I was old enough to remember.'

'Was he Afghan?'

'Yes, originally. My mother told me that he came to the UK with his parents when he was thirteen. Evidently Afghanistan suffered a terrible drought in 1971 and '72 which destroyed the economy and his family decided to seek a better life in the West. He lived in England from then on. Still does, I presume. He walked out when I was nine months old, broke off all contact and left my mother without a penny, even though he was wealthy, an engineer.'

'How did Sami react when he first saw his father in hospital?'

Nooria sighed. She looked exhausted, emotionally drained. 'He started screaming. He was completely hysterical. I couldn't calm him down. I had to take him out of the hospital. But then obviously when Nick got home, Sami had to face him. Face the reality of what he had become . . . what he looked like.'

'And Sami was fine before that?'

'He was a bit quiet. Nick had been away for six months and he missed him. Sami loved . . . loves his dad. But apart from that he was fine. Normal.' She gave a slight smile. 'Even though there is no "normal".'

Jessie's mind cast back to her conversation with Wendy. *When he saw his father in hospital he started wailing, screaming and crying. Wouldn't go near him.* She made a mental note to seek her out again, get her talking.

'Sami keeps mentioning a girl. I can't work out whether he's referring to himself or to someone else, but I do have the sense that he's talking about himself.'

Nooria shrugged. 'He's four. I insisted that I was a boy when I was four. I wanted to be a train driver. Nobody gave a hoot. We take things too seriously these days, what children say, too seriously.'

Jessie tried and failed to catch Nooria's eye. She was surprised at her cavalier comment. As Sami's mum, she needed to take the time to understand his psychological problems, to engage with what he was feeling. Jessie approached the issue another way.

'I saw him yesterday, at your house. I was playing with him in his room, playing with his dolls. He loves them.'

'He does.' Dropping the electronic cigarette with a clatter on the table, Nooria looked up. Her gaze was direct, challenging. 'You're going to tell me that's odd too now, aren't you? A boy playing with dolls.'

Jessie shook her head. 'When I was his age, I lined all

my cuddly toys up and killed them with laser beams because I'd watched too many episodes of *Dr Who*,' she said. 'I used to love playing with Scalextric because I could make the cars spin off and crash at the corner. My brother on the other hand . . .' Jessie paused, a catch in her voice. 'My brother asked the Father Christmas at our local shopping centre for a doll when he was five because he loved mine so much. Father Christmas said, "You're a boy. You shouldn't be asking for dolls." It made me so sad for him, being shoved in some stereotypical box. I think children should be able to play with whatever they want to play with. But that's not the issue here, is it? Sami kept telling me that the dolls were "the girl's". Who is the girl, Nooria?'

Nooria shrugged. Her fingers found the electronic cigarette on the table, but she didn't pick it up, just fiddled with it on the tabletop. 'I've already said that I don't know.' She gave a brittle laugh. 'Don't tell me, your brother is now a transvestite.'

Jessie glanced out of the window. She wished that she hadn't mentioned Jamie. She swallowed, eased the words out around the lump that had formed in her throat.

'No, he's not.'

Silence. Several moments slipped by while neither of them spoke. Nooria glanced at her watch.

'How is your relationship with Sami?' Jessie asked.

'Mine?' She sounded surprised.

'You are his mother.'

'Yes, but I'm not the issue. My husband is.'

Jessie's mind went back to her first meeting with Major Scott. *Speak to Nooria. She's the boy's mother. She's the one who looks after him.*

'Sami is in a relationship with both of you and you are

111

in a relationship with your husband. They're all interrelated. You can't isolate one and ignore all the others. Not if you want Sami to get better.'

Nooria's shoulders sagged. 'Wendy is more of a mother to him than I am at the moment.'

'Young children are hard work. Even ones without the issues that Sami currently has. It's not a crime to get some extra help, and Wendy seems calm and loving.'

Tears had come into Nooria's eyes and she brushed them roughly away.

'To be honest, I can't really cope with him – not at the moment. I love him. I love him to pieces, more than anything else in the world, but a large part of me struggles to cope with where he is.'

Jessie sensed a rare chink in her armour, dived for it.

'Both times I've met him, he talks about the Shadowman.'

Nooria pushed her chair back so suddenly that it clattered to the floor. She scooped it up, ducking her head self-consciously from the looks cast her way by the other diners.

'The Shadowman? That's Nick. He started saying it when he saw Nick.' She raised a hand to her mouth. 'Look, I'm sorry, but I do need to go.' Fresh tears glistened in her eyes.

'Nooria.'

She tucked her folio under her arm. 'Send me a text to arrange our next meeting, if you want. Might not be for a couple of weeks though.' She shrugged. 'The exhibition.'

Jessie stood. 'I need to see you sooner than that.'

But Nooria had turned away, was lost in the artsy crowd crossing the foyer and channelling up the stairs.

22

When Callan saw the body on the aluminium dissecting table, he had the impulse to drive straight up the M1 to the Defence Intelligence and Security Centre in Chicksands, walk into Starkey's room, take him by his hair and slam his face into the wall. Do it properly this time. Cause some real damage.

Andy Jackson – what was left of him – didn't look more than eighteen, though Callan knew he was ten years older than that. Death softened the hard lines of people's faces, turned men back into boys. The only thing that Callan could think of, looking at him – laid out on the slab, skin the colour of curdled milk, eyes filmy with death – was that a young woman was now a widow and that two little children would grow up with only celluloid memories of their father. What a waste of a life. A young man who worked out in the gym, paid his bills, called his family once a week from Afghanistan. Callan wasn't looking forward to the discussion he knew he would need to have with Andy Jackson's wife and parents.

His eyes strayed lower. The body had been cut from

shoulder bones to pubis, skin peeled back, the ribs, marbled with fat, sawn through and cleaved open to reveal the intestinal cavity. A neat hole was punched through the stomach, the bullet wound, like an eyeless socket, blood clotted around the hole. It was disturbing how similar a human body looked to the animal carcasses he'd seen laid out on the market stalls in Afghanistan, the stench of death rising off them in the heat, alive with humming, feasting flies.

Senior Medical Officer, Major Val Monks, the coroner, walked around the table, galoshes squeaking as their soles grasped and released the damp floor. Holding her gloved hands out from the side of her body like a scarecrow, she gave Callan an air kiss on each cheek. Hardly an orthodox Army way of greeting, but he'd always thought that she was a square peg in a round hole. Having said that, all majors were not created equal. A major in the infantry was responsible for the day-to-day lives of scores of men. Val was responsible for a mortuary containing a score of dead ones.

She was early fifties, mother to one son in his twenties, 'who had no intention of following his old mum into the Army', she'd told him last time they worked together, over a year ago now. *Before.* Without the peppermint green scrubs, she could have been mistaken for any ordinary middle-aged mum shopping in Tesco's, dark hair cut easy-care short, body gone a little soft around the middle, deep crow's feet radiating from her gentle brown eyes, skin loose around the jawline. But she was professional, her mind as sharp as a tack.

'Captain Callan. Good to see you again.' Her smile was genuine. 'I wasn't sure you'd be coming back, Ben.'

He shrugged. 'How could I stay away from all this?'

She returned his smile, but hers didn't quite reach her

eyes. He noticed her gaze flash fleetingly to the scar on his temple.

'Don't push yourself too hard.'

'I won't. And I'm fine.'

'You don't look a hundred per cent.'

'You have one son. You don't need to mother me too.'

'I'm not so sure about that.'

Callan edged past her, uncomfortable with the scrutiny. 'You've made a start.'

Val took the hint. 'Yes, I've done the external examination, taken blood and urine samples, and oral and anal swabs, fingernail scrapes, hair follicle samples, the works. Better to be safe than sorry.'

Callan listened, eyes scanning the opened corpse on the slab in front of him. He was wearing identical scrubs to Val, a mask over his face. The air circulating in the mask was tightening his chest; he felt as if he was struggling for oxygen. Pulling the mask down, he took a couple of deep breaths. The air in the room was refrigerator chilled, but the cold couldn't freeze out the smell of death, of viscera. He slid his mask back into place.

'Give me the background to the case.' Val had moved back to the dissecting table, was hovering over the body.

'You've read the report,' Callan replied.

'Of course. But I want to hear it from you. Your opinion.'

Callan shrugged. 'I don't have much of an opinion at the moment. Two sergeants go for a run in the Afghan desert seven days ago. One of them ends up dead with a bullet wound from the other's gun in his stomach.'

'He shot himself? That's what the report intimated.'

'The very meagre fingerprint evidence that we have points to that.'

'In what way?'

'The only fingerprint forensics lifted from the gun was a partial of Jackson's on the trigger.'

'Could Starkey have shot Jackson, wiped the prints clean and then pressed his gun into Jackson's hands?'

Callan smiled. 'You've been watching too many bad cop shows, Val. No. The gun was well oiled. They need to be, in the desert with all that sand, to prevent stoppages. Starkey took good care of his personal weapon, which is great news for him and the armourer, terrible news for forensics.'

Val nodded. 'Why was Starkey armed?'

'They were both armed. There've been so many green-on-blue attacks – so called friendly Afghans killing UK and US forces – that everyone carries their personal weapon at all times, even within NATO camps.'

'Fortunately, I've never had the privilege of going to Afghanistan. The Army prefers to ship the dead bodies to me, rather than to ship the live me to the bodies.'

Callan had forgotten how forthright she was, at odds with her appearance. It reminded him of why he liked working with her.

He looked down again at the splayed corpse on the dissecting table in front of him, skin waxy as a shop dummy's, blotchy with black and blue post-mortem lividity, a couple of other purple marks visible to his eye, blooming over the skin of the shoulder and torso. Taking a step back, he pulled the mask from his face again, took another couple of deep breaths, through his mouth this time, sucking the chill air into his lungs without the smell accompanying it down his airways. Snapping his mask back into place, he turned to Val.

'Starkey had a black eye and bruising to his torso. There look to be bruises on Jackson.'

'Yes, there are. Significant bruising to the torso, indicative of a physical assault, and very severe bruising to the knuckles of his right hand, indicating, I would say, that he gave as good as he got, which would stack up, given what you have told me about Starkey.'

Callan's gaze followed the latex-clad index finger of her right hand as it moved to Jackson's left shoulder.

'Here,' she continued. 'A large bruise, with faint finger marks.' Her finger tracked upwards. 'See, here. Curling over Jackson's collarbone. That indicates to me that he was shoved hard on the shoulder with a flat hand, perhaps more than once.'

Callan nodded.

'And there are a couple more bruises here and here,' Val continued, moving her finger down Jackson's left side, until it was hovering to the left of his sternum. 'Fist marks, rather than the flat hand you saw on the shoulder.' Her finger continued down on to his stomach. 'And another on his abdomen, to the left of his umbilicus.' She straightened, with a sigh. 'It certainly looks as if they had a fight before Jackson was shot.'

Callan rubbed a hand across his eyes, left his fingers there for a moment, pressing into his eye sockets. His head was aching: a dull, monotonous thud.

'You OK, Callan?'

'Of course. Just a headache. I'm not used to working for a living.' Giving Val a brief smile, he dropped his hand back to his side. 'What else?'

'Horizontal abrasions to the lower back.'

Callan bent forward, looking where she indicated. 'Grazes?'

'Yes. From sand, I would say, as they were in the desert. So at some point, Jackson was lying on the ground – moving though, twisting from side to side, definitely still alive. His shirt must have ridden up, leaving the skin of his waist and lower back exposed, which is why we have grazes there and nowhere else.'

Straightening, Callan nodded. 'Starkey had grazes on his elbows and forearms. Does Jackson have any defensive wounds?'

'Skin cells under the fingernails. I've taken swabs and sent them off for DNA analysis but, from what you say, we can assume that the DNA will be Starkey's.' Val gave a grim smile. 'They had a physical fight, for sure, before Jackson was shot.' Folding her arms, she tilted back on her heels. 'I would say that they started off standing – the shove mark to the shoulder would indicate that – and finished up wrestling in the dirt.'

'Adult,' Callan muttered.

Val raised an eyebrow and smiled. 'You can always rely on male soldiers to be adult.'

Callan shivered. It was colder in this room than outside in the car park; he wished he'd kept his coat on.

'How long did the medics take to arrive after the shot was fired?' she asked.

'Four or five minutes.'

Val frowned. 'And Jackson died within that time?' Her voice sounded incredulous.

Stomach wounds, where the victim received medical attention quickly, were rarely fatal – Callan had seen enough in combat to know that. Bleeding to death from a stomach wound was protracted, lengthy, particularly one caused by a 9 mm handgun bullet, relative small fry in the world of ballistics. The stomach wasn't a vital organ, at least not in terms of keeping someone alive in the short term. So death from a stomach wound came when the victim had lost so much blood that their body couldn't function any more. It was a slow and painful way to die.

'Seems like you've got yourself a puzzle here, Callan.'

'A puzzle I'm hoping you're going to help me solve.'

'I think you may be putting too much faith in my abilities.' She beckoned him forward, indicating the bullet wound, the clotted blood surrounding it.

'Notice anything strange, Callan?'

'Not a lot of bleeding.'

'Right.' A pause. 'Jackson's Army medicals – did they flag any problems?'

Callan was suddenly freezing cold and his head hurt. Hurt more than ached, a sharp, stabbing pain.

'The medicals, Callan? Any congenital problems?'

What was she talking about?

Pulling the mask off, he sucked in a deep breath. 'Medicals. My medicals? No. No problems.'

'His medicals. *His*. Andy Jackson's.' Her voice was heavy with concern. 'Did they flag any problems? Congenital defects?'

'None. He wouldn't have been allowed to join the Army if they had.'

The smell was getting to him – that smell he'd erased from his brain over the past six months, antiseptic and death, so thick in the room he could taste it on his tongue – raw meat, methane from intestinal gases, the metallic stench of clotted blood. Gripping on to the edge of the autopsy table, he steadied himself.

'Do you want to step out for a minute, Callan?'

'I'm fine.' His voice was slurred, even to his ears.

119

'I don't think you are.'

He was losing focus. *Shit*. Why hadn't he recognized the signs? He had a few seconds, maybe less. 'Yes. I need a minute.'

Black spots in front of his eyes, vision around that blurred. Turning, he stumbled for the door. Slammed out into the anteroom, banks of lockers to store corpses to his left and right. Bouncing off a couple of the lockers, he staggered towards the door, banged into it, grappled for the handle – *where's the fucking handle?* – found it, shoved it down, fell into the corridor. Mercifully, it was deserted.

His legs gave way and though he grasped for the wall, his fingertips screeched on smooth paint and he slid straight down it, crumpling to the floor. His head was jerking from side to side, he couldn't control it. His legs were cycling against the vinyl tiles, arms thrashing, his whole body writhing and spasming. His head felt as if it would explode from the pressure.

Slowly, the fit receded. Swallowing the vomit in his mouth, he lay for a minute, curled up on the cold vinyl, shaking and panting. He felt as if someone had banged an icicle through his skull, straight into his brain. Shaking, he dragged himself around on to his stomach, hauled himself on to his hands and knees. The air conditioning was blowing cold air; he could feel the sweat running down between his shoulder blades. He felt sick and he still couldn't see properly.

Footsteps approaching. *Fuck*. He couldn't be seen like this. He'd lose his job. Lose everything. Jamming his hands against the corridor walls, he levered himself to his feet. He felt weak, shaky, like a newborn fucking calf, struggling to walk. The inside of his mouth was coated in bile and he knew that he must stink of it.

A lieutenant from the Military Police rounded the corner carrying a sheaf of papers, an officer who'd joined the Special Investigation Branch after Callan left for his most recent tour in Afghanistan. He saluted. Callan nodded, couldn't yet coordinate a salute, not a convincing one anyway. The lieutenant paused by the door into the anteroom, hand resting on the handle. He looked as if he was about to say something.

Pushing himself away from the wall, Callan stepped forward, indicating the door. 'After you,' he said.

'First time autopsy?' the lieutenant asked, his lip curling.

'It's been a while.'

'So I heard, Captain Callan.' He was using all the right terminology so Callan couldn't pull him up on it, but his tone was clearly insubordinate.

Head dipped to avoid further eye contact, Callan pushed through the door into the anteroom, then through to the dissecting room. Val Monks glanced up from Jackson's body when she heard the door open.

'We're done here for the moment, Callan.'

'What?' he muttered.

He wouldn't meet her eye. He was as pale as the corpse on her slab, his amber eyes twitching, radiating nerves. Her heart went out to him. Her son was a conveyancing solicitor in Guildford. A safe, cosy job, the only danger it entailed, grappling with spoilt middle-class housewives who wanted their houses bought yesterday. This boy, only a couple of years older, had a bullet buried in his brain.

Epilepsy.

She'd seen it before, as a junior doctor. She knew that she should report him to his superiors, would be disciplined and rightly so, if it was found that she had known and

121

said nothing. But she had no intention of doing that. The Army let kids like this down every day; used them up and spat them out. If discovered, he'd be invalided out, given a small payoff and left to sort himself out, sink or swim in civilian life with no support. Too many of them were sinking, committing suicide, ending up as drug addicts living under cardboard in some faceless city. Someone else could find out and report him. It wasn't going to be her.

'Let's go grab a coffee in my office and I'll talk you through the findings.'

'The smell.' He forced a weak smile. 'Not used to it any more.'

'Come on.'

She put a hand on his arm, a motherly pat, which turned into a grip to support him when she realized that he was struggling to walk straight. In her office, she made him a coffee – decaf. Adding caffeine to the mix wouldn't be helpful.

'I'm pretty sure that the gunshot wound was not the cause of death.' She sat herself across the desk from him, all business. He met her gaze, briefly, and a flash of under-standing passed between them. A brief smile of gratitude crossed his face and was gone.

'My money is on acute myocardial infarction.'

The term felt familiar, but his sluggish brain refused to respond, to enlighten him. 'Right.'

'Heart failure, in other words,' Val continued, reading his mind. 'Sudden death triggered by chronic heart failure. He was technically dead when he was shot. His heart had stopped beating when the bullet entered his stomach.'

'Are you sure?'

She nodded. 'You saw yourself – the blood. There wasn't enough. If his heart had been fully pumping when the bullet passed through his stomach, there would have been significantly more. All the indications point to heart failure, though I am going to send his heart off to a specialist for a second opinion.' She folded her arms across her chest, tipped back on her heels. 'I know that I've already asked the question, but are you sure there was nothing in his medical records indicating heart problems?'

'I've read his medical notes three times. There's nothing. No medical problems. There is no way he would have been allowed to join the Army with a pre-existing heart condition, and if it developed after he joined and his superiors were aware of it, he would have been invalided out, no question.'

'Smoking? Alcohol? Drugs? I've taken samples for toxicology, but we'll have to wait a couple of days for the results.'

'He was a smoker. And I imagine he also drank a bit. Drugs? I don't think so. No one I've spoken to about him has mentioned drugs and it's highly unlikely, given his job and where he was at the time.'

'Smoking and alcohol are risk factors in heart disease, but in someone of this age it would be very unusual for them to be causal.' Sighing, she glanced towards the window. It had started snowing lightly.

'Could he have been pushed so hard during the run, by Starkey, beyond the point of absolute exhaustion, with the high temperature, that his heart just gave out?' Callan asked.

Elbows on the desk, Val steepled her fingers, rested the tips against her lips and frowned. 'It's possible. Yes, it is possible. People have different tolerances to physical exertion, high temperatures, etc. Even fit young men. I assume that Starkey is also a fit young man, a similar age to Jackson?'

Callan nodded.

'And he was fine.'

'Yes.'

Val dropped her hands to the desktop. 'The other option, of course, is shock.'

'Shock?'

'Such total and absolute fear that the heart gives out.'

'Is that likely?' Callan asked.

'I've seen it. I have seen it.' She frowned. 'But admittedly only once, in a very young soldier, a private, who was serving in Iraq. He died of a heart attack brought on by pure fear.' She paused, tapped a finger to her lips, thinking. 'My money is on Jackson having a pre-existing heart condition.'

Callan folded his arms and leaned back in the chair. 'That he knew about?'

Val shrugged. 'My name's not Mystic Meg, Callan, so, no, I can't read minds. Especially not the mind of a corpse. Bodies, yes. Minds, sadly not.' Shuffling some papers into a pile and moving them to the edge of her desk, she pulled her keyboard over. 'Give me a minute.'

Callan's eyes drifted around the room while he waited. It was small, white-walled, grey vinyl tiling on the floor – the ubiquitous military decoration, cheap and functional – made infinitesimally homely by the addition of a vase bearing a spray of lilac tulips, clearly not picked in the UK, given the weather outside.

'Right, here we go.' Val twisted the monitor so that Callan could see the screen. 'It's a report written by the American Heart Association. A study.'

Callan read the big black type at the top of the article out loud. '"Acute coronary findings at autopsy in heart failure patients with sudden death." Riveting title.'

She looked up, catching his gaze. 'Sarcasm. I like it. Feeling a bit more like your old self?'

'I'm not sure my old self is the way to go.'

He had managed the title, but couldn't focus on the rest. The type was tiny, jumping around in front of his eyes. 'So what are the findings?'

'Have you lost the ability to read, Callan?' She broke off, could have kicked herself.

'Reading was never my strong point. Why do you think I joined the Army?'

'So what it says, if I gloss over all the tedious bits, is . . .' She hummed as her eyes skimmed the lines of type, as much to cover her embarrassment as anything else. 'Here.' She placed a finger on the screen. 'Forty per cent of patients with myocardial failure did not have the MI diagnosed during their lifetime. So basically, of the autopsied bodies in the study, four out of ten died suddenly of heart failure, having no idea, when they were alive, that they had heart problems.'

'So it's feasible that he had a pre-existing heart condition without realizing.'

'It is. It certainly is. Now, does any of that help you, Callan?'

Sliding his chair back, he stood. 'I'm sure it will when I get it straight in my mind. Thanks, Val, you're invaluable as always.'

'And you're a charmer.'

'Call me when you get the toxicology reports and DNA.'

She stood too, rounded the desk and laid a hand on his arm. 'Get some help, Callan. A neurologist. I can find a good one for you.'

'I'm seeing a neurologist,' he muttered, refusing to meet her gaze. 'But I think there's fuck-all that anyone can do to help me.'

23

Standing at her office window, looking out across the mani-
cured lawn to the car park, Jessie watched the snowflakes
spiralling down. Though it meant a drop in temperature,
snow was preferable to the continual bouts of cold rain
and slushy sleet that had dogged the past few days. The
snow looked as if it wasn't going to settle though, the flakes
too flimsy, melting into the wet tarmac as soon as they
touched.

A knock at the door. She turned from the window. She
was expecting Major Scott and Sami, had brought her iPad
from home to keep Sami entertained with a film, under the
watchful eye of the Defence Psychology Service's secretary,
Jenny Chappell, while she spoke to Scott.

Wendy Chubb stuck her head in through the door. 'I've
brought Sami for his session.'

'Oh, hi. I thought—'

'I know, you were expecting Major Scott. He called to
say that he's been held up at the hospital, asked me to bring
Sami in and send his apologies.' She walked into the room

guiding a timid-looking Sami – head down, gaze hugging the floor – in front of her. 'He'll collect Sami in half an hour and you can have your conversation then.'

Unzipping Sami's coat, she slid it from his shoulders. Taking it from her, Jessie hung it on the hook on the back of her door, smoothing down the sleeves quickly, levelling the hem with her fingers.

She turned back to the room. 'Great, thank you, Wendy.'

Wendy didn't appear to have heard her – she made no move to leave. She was staring towards the window, a pensive look on her face. Beyond the glass, the snowflakes were phosphorescent in the electric light from Jessie's office, daylight now only a brief interlude between the curtains of winter darkness.

'Wendy.'

Wendy started, glancing back from the window, brow furrowing as she met Jessie's gaze.

'I hate the winter,' she murmured. 'It makes me feel so . . .' Pulling her scarf tight around her neck, she tailed off with a shrug.

'So . . . what?'

A brief smile, the lines of concern etched in her forehead and around her eyes unchanged by it. 'Oh . . . cold. Just cold.'

Jessie looked hard at her. Her posture was so rigid that it appeared every one of her muscles were tensed. *Fight or flight.*

'Are you OK, Wendy?'

Another smile, unconvincing in its fleetingness. 'Yes, of course.'

'I can ask Jenny to walk you to your car.'

'Why on earth would you do that?'

'Well . . . if . . .' Jessie waved her hand vaguely towards the window. 'It's getting dark—'

'What? And you think that I'm afraid of the dark?' Wendy cut in with a sharp, bright laugh. 'A great lump like me?'

Scooping up her handbag from the floor and hooking it over her shoulder, she strode towards the door. But at the threshold, she stopped, turned back slowly.

'You can help him, can't you?' she said in a low voice, glancing towards Sami, who had found his way to the toy corner, was sitting there motionless, gaze fixed on the farm box that Jessie had bought. 'You can help him?'

'I'll do everything that I can.'

Stepping back into the room, reaching out, she grasped Jessie's arm with a firmness, an urgency that took Jessie by surprise.

'Please. Promise me. He needs help, that little boy. He really needs help.'

'I can't promise anything, but I will do the best I can. Nothing happens overnight with severely disturbed children.' Jessie pulled her arm gently from Wendy's grip. She didn't want to leave Sami too long without attending to him, needed to manage his first encounter with the farm. 'I'd better start his session now.'

Brow furrowing, Wendy nodded. 'Yes, of course. Sorry. I'll go.'

'Hey, Sami.' Jessie knelt down.

He was sitting in front of the farm box – it had clearly piqued his interest – but he hadn't yet tried to open it. His body was statue-still, his gaze fixed on the box, the torch cradled in his lap. His face, his expression, was a closed book.

'I bought myself a farm, like your farm,' Jessie said. 'Shall we open it?'

Without looking up at her, he gave a slight nod.

She had opened the farm herself earlier, sorted through the animals. None were black, so she was glad that she had bought the two Schleichs, even if it had led the sales girl to believe that she was committable. She had put all the animals in a separate box, left only the plastic farmhouse and tractor inside the original one.

'Do you want to open it, Sami?'

Another nod, infinitesimally more certain than the first.

Jessie indicated the zips on the four corners. 'The box unzips and lays out flat,' she said. 'Go ahead. Open it.'

Hesitantly, he unzipped each corner and the heavy-duty printed vinyl fell open, revealing the plastic farmhouse and tractor.

'Tractor,' he cried, with uncharacteristic delight, rolling the torch off his lap. He picked the tractor up, turned it around in his hands, testing that the wheels moved, opening and closing each of the doors. Placing the tractor carefully back in the cobbled farmyard, he shifted it backwards and forwards until it was lined up exactly next to the farmhouse, which Jessie had positioned on its grey printed concrete foundation.

Leaning forward, he pointed at the play-mat. 'There's the farmyard.'

'That's right. There's the farmyard.' Jessie reflected back what he had said. She wanted to engage him without, at this stage, leading the conversation, or his thoughts, in any particular direction.

'There's a field.'

'Yes. A big field,' Jessie echoed.

'Another field.' He dragged his finger down the muddy track separating the two fields. The track led to a wood. 'Here's a wood.

'Yes, there are lots of trees in the wood.'

His finger continued tracking across the play-mat.

'Here's a pond.' Sami stopped, his finger at the edge of the pond. He looked up at Jessie, his brow furrowing. 'Where are the waves?'

'Waves? What do you mean, Sami?'

'Waves on the pond.' Leaning forward, he ran his flat hand over the smooth blue printed surface of the vinyl pond. 'Where are the waves?'

'It's probably a sunny day. You only get waves when it's windy.'

He glanced over to the window. It was snowing, the flakes heavier now; perhaps they would settle. Eyebrows raised in query, he looked back to Jessie.

'Snow.' His voice quivered.

Jessie kept hers even. 'Yes, but we're playing a game. We can pretend that it's summer on our farm, that it's sunny, even though it's snowing outside.'

He sat for a moment, in silence, his body absolutely still. Only his hands and eyes moved. His hands tensed around the handle of his torch; his eyes flickered backwards and forwards across the play-mat, his brain, behind the mask of stillness that was his face, clearly working feverishly. Hauling the torch back on to his lap, his fingers found the switch, but he didn't slide it into the 'on' position.

'Waves on the pond,' he muttered. 'Waves on the pond. Sunny. It's sunny. Waves on—' He stopped muttering, a sudden look of surprise crossing his face. 'Where are the animals?'

130

'Here.' Jessie reached behind her. 'I put them in a separate box. An animal box.' She pushed the box over to him.

She had kept the Schleich black cow aside, but had put the black-and-white collie dog in the box, tucking it at the bottom, under the other animals.

As before, when he had been playing with the farm in his own house, Sami switched on his torch and dipped it into the cardboard box, highlighting the tangle of plastic bodies. One by one, he picked out the animals, holding each in the beam of light, studying it with a focus uncharacteristic in someone of his age, before placing it on the play-mat.

'Here is the sheep . . .' He placed the sheep in the small field.

'Here is the horse . . .' The large field.

'Here is a pig . . .' The sty.

'Here are the ducks . . .' The pond. He took longer over the ducks, placing them in the centre of the pond and retrieving them, running a flat hand over the surface of the pond, that same quizzically concerned expression on his face as earlier. 'Waves,' he murmured. Hesitantly, he withdrew his hand.

Reaching back into the box, his fingers closed around the collie dog. Jessie sat quietly next to him, her hands folded into her lap, trying to keep the tension she felt from creeping into her muscles. Though she was watching him intently – every facial cue, every tic – she couldn't afford to betray the anxiety she felt with her own body language. It was imperative that she remain neutral.

Lifting the collie dog from the bucket, he held it at arm's length, highlighted in the beam of his torch. The hand holding the collie shook.

'Do you like dogs, Sami?' Jessie asked softly.

He didn't answer; he was biting his lip.

'Is the dog burnt?' His voice barely a whisper.

'Of course not. It's just a black-and-white collie dog. You must have seen them on the farm near where you live. Or maybe on television? The farmers use them to round up their sheep.'

'The dog isn't burnt?'

His words so quiet that Jessie strained to hear them.

'No. The dog isn't burnt,' she answered. 'The dog is fine.'

Holding the collie close to the torch – so close that it was pressed hard against the glass lens – Sami studied it. Jessie remained silent, watching him turn the dog over and over in his fingers. He had to be the first to speak, to reveal his train of thought without prompting.

Finally, he placed the dog on the play-mat, in the same field as the sheep.

'The girl likes dogs,' he murmured.

The girl. Again.

'Are you the girl, Sami?'

'Grrrr.' The growling sound from deep in his throat.

Reaching out, Jessie touched her fingers to his arm. He flinched away.

'Sami. Are you the girl?'

'Mummy says Sami is the girl.' His voice was robotic, as if the words had been pre-programmed inside him. 'Daddy says Sami is not the girl.'

Jessie's mind cast back to her conversation with Nooria at the RCA this morning. *He's four. I insisted that I was a boy when I was four. Nobody gave a hoot.*

'So you are the girl, Sami?'

He shook his head, tears welling in his eyes. 'Daddy says Sami is a boy.'

132

Jessie knew that she should pull back, but she felt as if she was on the cusp of something important, that she was finally making headway. She could feel the adrenalin rush, the feeling that always came when she broke a barrier with a patient. She had to push a little further.

'Why does Mummy say that Sami is the girl?'

'Sami not the girl.' His voice cracked on the words. 'Daddy says . . . Daddy says Sami not the girl.'

'Is the Shadowman your father, Sami?'

Sami looked up, his tear-filled eyes wide with fear. 'Shadowman under the covers,' he whispered.

'What do you mean, Sami?'

'Mummy and Daddy fighting. Mummy says my fault. Daddy says my fault.'

'What were they arguing about?'

'Grrrr.' Louder this time. Dragging his torch with him, he shuffled on his bottom across the carpet until his back was pressed against the wall. Swinging the torch from side to side in front of him like a watchtower light, eyes fixed on Jessie, he muttered, 'Go back to bed. Stay in bed.' His head bent to his chest as if it had become too heavy to hold upright. 'You're bad, Sami. Stay in bed or the Shadowman will come.'

24

As Marilyn walked back down the corridor clutching the autopsy report, he tried to push from his mind the sad, sagging pile of flesh and bone that was his murder victim. Having your life forcibly taken was bad enough, but being sliced up and microscopically examined by perfect strangers felt to him like the ultimate violation.

He was still smarting over the fact that the cadaver dogs had failed to find the legs. Not that he had been surprised. They would, by now, be indistinguishable by sight from the mess of driftwood and seaweed clogging the shoreline, the faint scent of decomposition remaining so infused with other harbour smells that it would have taken the dog equivalent of Sherlock Holmes to find them. Given the tides, the constant movement of boats, the wildlife – seagulls, foxes, rats, to name a few – that liked to pick at foreign bodies, whatever their origin, the legs could be virtually anywhere on the thirty miles of harbour shoreline. But, mitigating circumstances aside, it felt like failure and however laid-back he appeared to others to be, he hated to fail.

The silver lining to that particular cloud was that he was now a hundred pounds richer. Dr Ghoshal had agreed with him: the propeller of a motor cruiser or large yacht was responsible for hacking the body in two, not an axe or butcher's cleaver, as the lead CSI, Tony Burrows had surmised. He felt relief that he could at least rule out a sick ghoul keeping trophy legs in his freezer, even if he couldn't rule out the involvement of a sick ghoul in this murder full stop. He scanned the pages of the autopsy report as he walked, absorbing the pathologist's conclusions.

Full-grown male. Aged thirty-five to forty from the teeth, which were well looked after. Probably not a UK national – the dental work didn't look British. So either the victim was a British national who lived abroad, or he was a foreign national. No sign of previous serious trauma to the body, no healed fractures. Cause of death: severe blunt trauma to the back of the head. The body was too badly decomposed to find any trace evidence indicating the material composition of the murder weapon. Death had occurred approximately two months previously. A best guess, but accurate within a couple of weeks either way.

He had been dumped elsewhere in the harbour and floated, face down, for a number of days, meeting a propeller along the way, before the torso beached itself where the unfortunate Ms Bass-Cooper had found it. There was no way of identifying the disposal site. The direction in which a body floated would depend on whether the tide was coming in or going out of the harbour at the time, but wind direction and strength also played a part, as did nautical activity. This long after the body had been dumped, there was no way of determining any of those things.

Marilyn would contact the local boatyards, see if anyone

owning a motor cruiser or yacht had reported damage to their propeller, but again the enquiry was unlikely to be fruitful. A large propeller would cut through a corpse like butter, the collision hardly spilling a drop from the cocktails on the sundeck.

Dr Ghoshal hadn't yet completed microscopic examinations of the tissues or fluids, or toxicology, all of which needed to be sent to a specialist lab. Results would take a few days to come back.

'I'm afraid that the only way you're identifying this unfortunate man is through his dental records,' Dr Ghoshal had told Marilyn, peeling off his gloves, bending over the sink to scrub his hands with Hibiscrub. Marilyn noticed a frown shifting the glasses on the bridge of his nose as he towelled his hands dry.

'Looks like something's bothering you, Doctor,' Marilyn said, raising his eyebrows in query.

Dr Ghoshal tugged off his glasses, slid them into his pocket.

'Severe blunt trauma to the back of the head is the cause of death,' he murmured. 'No doubt about that . . .'

'But?'

A frown had entrenched itself in Dr Ghoshal's brow. 'But some of the flesh doesn't look quite right. Not just decomposition and salt-water damage.'

Marilyn glanced at the body, stifling a shudder. *Jesus Christ.* None of the flesh looked right. 'What do you mean?'

Dr Ghoshal shook his head. 'I don't like jumping to conclusions. Let's wait for the results from the microscopic examinations and toxicology.' He held out a scrubbed hand. 'I'll be in touch as soon as I get the results, Detective Inspector.'

25

Jessie had spent half an hour picking a suitable television programme for Sami before leaving her cottage this morning, mentally scanning through the films available from Amazon Prime to weed out violence, ghosts, shadows, anything that could likely be construed by a severely disturbed four-year-old as frightening. Tom and Jerry – too violent. Scooby-Doo – too scary. Pingu – creepy. God knows why kids loved a Plasticine penguin that didn't even speak.

She had finally settled on Dora the Explorer, uploaded five episodes to her iPad. Now, she sat Sami on a chair in Jenny Chappell's office and switched on the iPad, thanking God for technology and for modern children who were content to be glued to it.

It was a couple of minutes after she returned to her office that she heard heavy steps making their way down the hall. She had switched the overhead light off, put on only her desk lamp and another freestanding sidelight, angling them both so that they reflected off the dark wood-panelled walls and cast a mellow yellow hue. Outside her window, daylight had departed, even though it was barely 4.30 p.m.

'Thank you for coming, Major Scott.'

She held out her hand. After a moment's delay, he shook it. He was wearing navy jeans and a blue-and-white checked collared shirt under a navy-blue V-necked jumper. His eyes were hidden behind the same mirrored aviator sunglasses he had been wearing yesterday. All she could see when she looked at him were twin reflections of her own distorted face. His appalling injuries stood out less starkly here at Bradley Court than they had in his own home. Here, he was one of many men who had been grievously injured in battle: some not as severely, many significantly worse.

He stood in the middle of the room, feet splayed, hands resting on his hips, rigid body language that reminded her of Sami. He clearly didn't want to be here, had fought a battle with his own conscience and lost to it.

'I don't have long.' His tone was pure provocation.

Jessie didn't rise to it. She stared straight back into his pale, haunted face.

'This won't take long. Please, have a seat.'

Closing the door behind him, she indicated the two battered leather chairs set either side of a low coffee table by the window that she used for her sessions, so that she could sit opposite her patients without the physical barrier of her desk between them. Communication between two people was eighty per cent body language and tone of voice. What was actually said – the words spoken – only twenty per cent of the message the listener received. Every posture, every movement, every minute tic, helped her to form an impression of the whole: the way a patient jiggled their feet, the tension in their muscles, whether they crossed their legs,

138

their arms, leant back, sat forward, wouldn't make eye contact, tried to stare her out. Vital information, before a single word had been exchanged. She needed to see the whole of Scott, particularly as those mirrored sunglasses negated a vital source of information, the eyes. It was disconcerting and she felt as if she was only getting half the story: one page text, the next blank.

'Would you like a tea or coffee?'

'No.' He paused. 'Thank you.' The last words clearly hard to speak.

Grabbing a file from her desk, not one relevant to the case, but something to hold on her knee, a small barrier between them to give her confidence, she sat across from him. This man unnerved her.

'Thank you for coming in, Major Scott.'

'I won't say it's a pleasure.'

There was nothing relaxed about him, even when sitting. He perched stiffly on the edge of the chair, feet planted wide apart, knees splayed, expression surly.

'I don't think it's much of a pleasure for Sami either,' Jessie replied.

'I still don't understand why the hell you need to see all of us. Why you can't—' He broke off, shaking his head. 'Forget it. I'm here now. Let's get started.'

Dipping her gaze to the file, she took a breath.

'In the sessions I've had with Sami he refers to "the girl". At first, I couldn't understand who the girl was, but I now get the impression that he's referring to himself.'

A heavy sigh. 'Nooria had a child, before I met her. A daughter.'

'She was married before?'

'No. A boyfriend. She got pregnant and ended up having

139

the baby. The boyfriend didn't stick around. He dumped her before the baby was born.' His tone was confrontational, as if he was challenging her to disapprove. She smiled inwardly. If he knew what she did in a bid to assuage her own demons, he wouldn't have been so concerned with her moral compass.

'The baby died, cot death, at three months old. Nooria had given so much to have the child, on her own, with no support, not even from her own mother, who Nooria said was horrified. When the baby died, she was devastated. She's never fully recovered.' He steadied himself. 'She was desperate for Sami to be a girl. Absolutely desperate. She bought girls' clothes, dolls, painted the room pale yellow . . .' He tailed off, shaking his head.

'You didn't find out Sami's sex before he was born?'

'I was away – in Afghanistan – for most of the pregnancy and I didn't want her to. I wanted it to be a surprise. Sami came a month early, at thirty-six weeks. I'd only been back a few days, just made it.'

'How did she react when she saw he was a boy?'

Scott's gaze dropped. 'She cried and cried.' He shrugged. 'I was delighted. Typical man, I suppose – I wanted a son.'

'Did she get postnatal depression?'

His brow creased, as if the thought had never occurred to him.

'She was upset for the first few days. Upset. Tense. Everything made her cry. But that's down to hormones, isn't it?' His voice wavered; he wasn't on solid ground. He didn't strike Jessie as the type who would be in tune with female emotions, imagined him as a 1950s father, sitting in the pub cradling his pint, waiting for news of whether his wife had pushed out a boy or girl. 'She settled down after a few days. And she loves Sami deeply. Once she'd got over the shock of having a boy, she fell in love with him.'

'So the girl that Sami talks about . . .?' Jessie nudged.

Sighing wearily, he looked towards the window. It was dark now, the night closed in. It had stopped snowing, the black sky moonless, empty of stars.

'I let Nooria treat Sami like a girl. Dress him in the girls' clothes she'd bought, call him "her". Even the name – Sami. She's always called him Sami. It's Samuel, after my father, but when you shorten it to Sami, it could equally be Samantha.' Tilting forward, he put his head in his hands. 'You're going to think I'm crazy, aren't you? But I didn't see the harm, when he was a baby. Who cared if he wore yellow or blue?' His voice cracked. 'Who cared?'

'But it got out of hand?'

'You've seen him. He thinks that he's a girl, for Christ's sake. He's soft. His mum has doted on him and now he's soft. He's got all those bloody dolls.' He laughed, a bitter sound. 'I lost it with him last week, took the bucket of dolls and tipped the whole lot of them into a bin bag. He became hysterical, and I mean *hysterical*. He was screaming and wailing, throwing himself against the walls, beating his head on the floor. I thought he was going to hurt himself badly.' He faltered.

'You gave the dolls back to him?'

He shook his head. 'I stormed out, went to the fucking pub. Left Wendy to sort out the mess. The dolls were back in their bucket when I got home.'

'How did you meet Nooria?' Jessie asked, changing the subject to defuse the tension in the room, so thick she could almost have cleaved it in two with a knife.

'I was married before. I have two daughters, ten and twelve now. Nooria was a teaching assistant at my daughters' school, a posh private school, full of stiff upper-class twats. White knickers and good behaviour. Good behaviour until I got there, at least.' He pulled a face. 'I met her when my youngest daughter started in Reception. Nooria was new to the school that year, the Reception class teaching assistant. I left my wife, Jacqui, a year later, for her.'

At his words, an image rose, unbidden, in Jessie's mind: watching from under her fringe – an angry, disenfranchised twelve-year-old – as Jamie, a little boy of only five, strode up the aisle, clutching a pillow bearing the wedding rings, too young to fully understand that he was giving his father away permanently to someone else, to another life. Diane, a beautiful young bride in apricot silk and lace, the picture Jessie still retained of her, even though Diane and her father had been married for seventeen years. No kids at least, a small bonus for her mother, a hold, however negligible, over her ex-husband.

'How do your daughters get on with Sami?'

'They've never met him. I don't see much of them. Their mother hates me, not surprisingly.'

He fell silent. Jessie waited, sensing that he would continue.

'The first time I met Nooria, I couldn't take my eyes off her. She was so beautiful.' He laughed acerbically. 'I'm the ultimate fucking stereotype, aren't I? It doesn't get much more tacky than that. The husband who couldn't keep it in his pants. I made a complete fool of Jacqui in public, in front of all the other officers' wives and the middle-class social climbers who send their kids to that kind of school. She didn't deserve it.'

'The wife rarely does deserve it. But you didn't do it to hurt her, did you?'

Jessie's mind calculated. Scott must be in his early forties, Nooria fifteen years younger. So she had been early twenties when they met. That would have made her a teenager when she'd had her first baby, the little girl who died. A teenager dealing with all that alone. She would have had to build a carapace around herself to cope. No wonder she was evasive, hard to pin down.

'It's my fault.' The unburnt side of his face sagged, as if the strings holding his features in place had snapped. 'This whole fucking thing . . . Sami . . . I shouldn't have left them for so long. I should have been there to support Nooria, to look after her . . . to look after them both.'

'It's your job. You had no choice.'

His reply was bitter. 'Perhaps I should have made a better choice of profession. I wouldn't have fucking ended up looking like this, if I had done.' Raising his hands, he tugged his sunglasses off, dropped them on to his knee. The wet burgundy cavity of his missing eye glistened in the lamplight. Darts of steely light glinted in his good eye; Jessie kept her gaze focused on it. 'And now I don't have any choices, because the Army doesn't want me. I can't do the job any more, so I'm out.'

'You have transferable skills.' She tried to force conviction into her voice, heard it waver. 'A lot of companies . . . civilian companies will appreciate your skills.'

A naked expression of torment crossed his face. 'I've fucked everything up. My life, Nooria's life, Sami's.'

Jessie was about to say – 'It'll all work out' – but she stopped herself. She was sick of platitudes. Sick of hearing them and even sicker of saying them. She would do her best for Sami, for all of them. Though she doubted that, in this case, her best was going to be good enough. Scott was living the nightmare.

'I've just got one more question. Who is the Shadowman?'

'The Shadowman?' he murmured, his brow furrowing. He glanced towards the window. It was snowing again, the flakes fluttering close to the glass glowing in the light from Jessie's window; total darkness beyond.

'The Shadowman? Surely the Shadowman is me?'

26

Jessie's boss, Dr Gideon Duursema, head of the Defence Psychology Service, was sitting behind his desk, squinting through bifocals at a psychology research paper. He looked up when he heard her knock.

'Ah, the wanderer returns.'

'I've been working.' She slumped into the chair across the desk from him. 'You should try it occasionally.'

Tossing the research paper on the desktop, he pulled off his glasses and folded them on top of the paper.

'I've been trying to track you down. You should check your messages occasionally.' There was censure in his quietly spoken voice, which Jessie ignored.

'As I said, I've been working.'

Duursema was a black Zimbabwean, in his late fifties. He had arrived in England from Zimbabwe thirty years ago, the son of a wealthy farming family, sent by his parents to study Psychology at Oxford when Robert Mugabe and his ZANU party came to power. He had always planned to go back after doing a PhD, but by then

Mugabe had begun to show his true colours and Gideon remained in England, found a job, a wife, became almost more English than the English. He reminded Jessie of a younger Nelson Mandela, small in stature, but big in thought and heart, calm and measured. But the soft exterior masked an uncompromising pragmatism, which in his job, a tricky one by any standards, was vital.

'You've been working on the Sami Scott case?' The merest hint of his Zimbabwean accent remained.

Jessie nodded. 'Among others, yes.'

'I gave you three sessions with the child. No more.'

'Three won't be enough. And I need to see his mother and father.' She didn't mention that she had already seen them both. 'I can't help Sami without understanding more about his home life, his relationship with his parents, their relationship with each other . . .' she tailed off, catching the look that Gideon shot her.

'You seem to have forgotten that I also have a PhD in Clinical Psychology.'

'You hide it well,' she muttered under her breath.

'Don't be flippant with me, Dr Flynn.'

She smiled. 'No, sir.'

Tilting sideways, he retrieved a stack of files ten inches thick from the floor behind his desk, fifty of them at least. He dumped them on the desk in front of her.

'This is our current caseload. You, me, Susanne, John and Gordon, need to divide these up between us. These are the soldiers, sailors and airmen – serving military personnel – who need our help, *right now*. I'm sorry, but we don't have the resources to focus on children of soldiers, spouses of soldiers, mothers or fathers of soldiers, and so the list goes on. His parents need to go to their

GP and get him referred to a National Health Service psychologist.'

'He's a deeply troubled little boy. He needs help now, not some time in the next millennia – which is what would happen on the NHS.'

'It's the best I can do.'

'I can't just abandon him.'

'He's not Army.'

'His father is.'

'Not for much longer.'

'Oh, for Christ's sake!' She threw up her hands in exasperation. 'Don't play the hard-arse, Gideon, it doesn't suit you.'

Duursema stroked a hand through his greying beard, fixing Jessie with a steady gaze, but he didn't credit her comment with a reply.

'Can't we get more funding. More resources?' she asked.

He pushed the telephone over to her. 'Be my guest. Give Mr Cameron a call and say that we need a bit more cash, because although most of our soldiers have been pulled out of Afghanistan now, unfortunately the fallout from that crappy bloody war goes on in the minds of a huge number of them. And while you're at it, would you mention that my niece's school is rubbish, that I'd like my bins emptied more than once a fortnight, please, because we now have rats trotting happily along my garden wall as if they're sightseeing on the Great Wall of China.' He indicated the stack of files in front of her. 'The government has driven a coach and horses through military funding, which is why we have ten inches of cases needing treatment and not enough resources to tackle a quarter of them in a decent timeframe.'

'I'll see him in my spare time.'

'Spare time?' He widened his eyes in mock shock. 'You have spare time? I'm clearly not working you hard enough.' Sitting back in his chair, he puffed a balloon of air from his lungs, a long, heavy sigh. 'What's your conclusion?'

'On the Sami Scott case or the David Cameron case?'

'Don't be a smart arse, it suits you too well.'

Jessie hunched her shoulders. 'I don't have one yet.'

'Post-traumatic stress disorder?'

'That's what his father thinks.'

'And you don't agree?'

'I don't know. I saw his mum this morning and she was very defensive.' She paused. 'Actually, defensive isn't quite the right word. She was evasive. I think she just wants it all to go away.'

'Wave the magic wand and lo and behold the child is cured.'

'Right.'

He glanced sideways at the stack of cases. 'That would be ideal for all of us.'

Spreading her hands, Jessie shrugged helplessly. 'The parents insist that all his problems are due to the trauma of seeing his father so badly burnt.'

'What do you think?'

'I think that it doesn't quite add up.'

'Why?'

'It's nothing concrete. But there is an undercurrent running through the whole family that's making me nervous.'

Duursema leaned forward, steepling his fingers. 'You don't think he's being sexually abused? Anything like that?'

'He's not sexually precocious.'

'Sexual abuse doesn't always manifest itself like that. Particularly in such a young child.'

Go back to bed. Stay in bed. You're a naughty boy, Sami.
Jessie bit her lip. 'I know, I know.'

'If you suspect sexual abuse you have to call in the Redcaps' Special Investigation Branch, immediately.'

She nodded. 'But I can't start tossing out accusations. I don't know enough yet.'

'Brief Captain Callan about your suspicions. He knows Scott. You're working with him on the Starkey case already, aren't you?'

'I met with him and Starkey yesterday. I think my involvement is probably over now.'

'Call and brief him anyway, to cover our arses if nothing else. And keep me updated. If you suspect – really suspect – that Sami Scott is being abused, we hand this case to the Redcaps immediately. *Immediately.* Do I make myself clear?'

Jessie nodded. Duursema sat back, crossed his arms. When he spoke again his voice was softer.

'Let me help you, Jessie.'

She looked up. 'Help me with what?'

She had gathered up all the stray pens on his desk, put them back in the penholder, tidied the loose papers into a pile, was lining his blotter up flush with the edge of his desk. She hadn't even realized she'd been doing it.

'Tidy desk tidy mind.' Sliding her chair back, she stood. 'I'll keep in touch.'

'Jessie.'

Turning, she pushed through the door.

'You can't keep running from it.' His raised voice tracked her down the corridor. 'It won't go away on its own. You need to deal with it.' A pause. 'Oh, and a bit of respect would be nice.'

27

Head down, scarf pulled up around her face in a vain attempt to stave off the cold, Jessie crunched down the gravel path to the car park. As she'd predicted, the snow hadn't settled, only transformed into a mushy soup which was seeping through the stitching of her ill-chosen suede boots. At least the snow hadn't turned to sleet or rain.

As she walked, she revisited her conversation with Gideon. *Sexual abuse.* She didn't even want to acknowledge it as a possibility, though she knew the thought had been fluttering on the periphery of her mind. A thought she had, so far, flinched away from.

'Dr Flynn.'

She spun around, heart jumping into her mouth.

'Sorry. Sorry if I scared you.'

'I wasn't scared.' Her muscles relaxed slightly; heart still thumping hard against her ribcage.

Callan gave the suggestion of a smile. 'That's why you look like a ghost.'

'I always look like a ghost. Benefit of Irish colouring.

Great on dark nights like this. My skin is so luminous that I don't need a torch.'

'Who were you expecting?' His tone suddenly serious.

Should she tell him about Starkey ambushing her in the car park last night? *No.* It wouldn't be fair. He hadn't actually done anything wrong, just creeped her out.

'No one. I'm a little on edge.' She hunched her shoulders. 'Work, as usual.'

She met his gaze. He looked dreadful: his amber eyes washed out and bloodshot, perpetually flitting, missing nothing, the black rings under them even more pronounced than yesterday, as if he had been face-painted as a panda.

'I need a favour,' he said.

'What?'

'Come and see Jackson's wife and kids with me.'

'When are you planning to go?'

'This evening.' He shuffled his feet in the slush. 'Now.'

'Why now?'

'The autopsy was earlier today. There are a few questions I need to ask his family, potentially uncomfortable questions. His wife and kids have moved in with his parents, in Wandsworth, for the moment. Andy Jackson's father works days and can't afford to take time off. He insisted on being there when I come.' He paused. 'An extra pair of hands, particularly a psychologist, would be useful with, uh, with the kids there.'

She indicated the cut on her head. 'I'm not sure that I'm so great with kids.'

He didn't smile, was jittering from foot to foot as if trying to get warm. But Jessie realized that nerves rather than cold were responsible, could sense he was on the edge, couldn't face the discussion alone.

'Of course I'll come.' A smile lifted the corners of her mouth. 'I wanted a ride in the pimp-mobile anyway.'

He'd cleaned it out since yesterday: the passenger footwell was clear of crisp packets and Coke cans and the car had that waxy alkaline smell of shampoo and car polish. Flipping the heaters to maximum, he started the engine.

After a few dark miles of undulating country lanes, they joined the A3, heading into southwest London. Cutting straight across to the fast lane, Callan put his foot down. The needle rose smoothly to ninety. As he drove, he gave her a rundown of the autopsy findings and what he wanted to achieve from the visit to Andy Jackson's wife, besides tea and sympathy.

'I'm pretty sure that Steve, Jackson's father, will try to dominate the discussion, but one of us needs to talk to his wife – alone, ideally. Get some information as to whether Jackson had any medical problems. Also his state of mind and other intangibles: his personality, impressions of how he was coping in Afghanistan.'

Jessie nodded. 'Why medical problems? Is it looking as if he died of natural causes?'

Callan shrugged. 'The autopsy wasn't conclusive, but the pathologist, Val Monks, thinks that his heart had stopped beating before the bullet entered his stomach. I'm expecting a call from Val when she has more.'

She looked across at him, biting her lip. 'Mrs Jackson will be forced to give up her Army house now that Andy Jackson is dead, find somewhere else permanent to live.'

'She'll get a widow's pension.'

'And then she'll be tossed out into civilian life with no support.'

'The Army isn't a charity or a babysitting service.'

'You're damn right there.' Her tone was harsh. 'Eat 'em up and spit 'em out.'

'It can be a great life when it's going well and a shit one when it isn't,' Callan replied evenly. 'Unfortunately, Jackson's family have been handed the shit end of the stick.'

Despite feeling anger rise at the injustice of it all, she knew that what Callan said was true. Yin and Yang. The Army life could be hard to beat when it was going well – the flip side, horrific. But with Afghanistan and Iraq, the continuing turmoil in the Middle East, the death toll among young service personnel was considerably higher than in the preceding decades. When a soldier died, their dependants were given a pension, a few months to find alternative accommodation and then left to fend for themselves. Many soldiers married young, and it could be incredibly hard for wives who had spent the whole of their adult lives as Army dependants to cope alone. Life on the outside was isolating. The issue was constantly top of mind for the Psychology Service.

They had reached the end of the A3, where three lanes merged to two, then narrowed soon after to one, the traffic backed up in front of them, a mass of flashing tail-lights. Neither Callan nor Jessie spoke. There wasn't much to say. As they got closer to Wandsworth, the tension she felt at the prospect of seeing Jackson's wife and children had grown. She knew that Callan felt it even more acutely.

Cutting across two lanes of the Wandsworth one-way system, he took a left turn and they entered a maze of streets, three-storey terraced houses. He turned into another street, this one narrower, the pavement studded every twenty metres with birch trees.

'Forty-six,' he said.

Jessie pointed. 'There.'

Callan parked fifty metres further down the street, the only available space, and shut off the engine. The Jacksons' lived in a neat, red-brick terrace house at the end of the street, anchored on one side by a newsagent, metal shutters pulled down over its plate-glass window, on the other by another architecturally identical house, its brickwork painted a pale cream. The street was a mix of houses: a few obviously occupied by people who had lived there for many years, bought them when they were cheap, before Wandsworth's gentrification, net curtains hanging in the windows, paint peeling from facades. Others had clearly been snapped up by professional couples. White plantation shutters and dove grey silk curtains replacing net, Land Rover Freelanders parked on the kerb. The suburban normality felt miles from the Army, from Afghanistan, from death, and Jessie wondered how Jackson had found his way into the Intelligence Corps from this quiet West London street.

The Jacksons' house was one of the former, slightly shabby now, a thin layer of city grime coating its brickwork but, other than that, it was tidy and well kept. A path of pale yellow and pink crazy paving led from the gate to the yellow front door, a six-inch high hedge of evergreen box lining either side of the path. A circular pattern, like a wagon wheel, was laid out in the same stone in the tiny front garden, the patches of earth between each spoke filled with more evergreen box bushes. Tidy, low maintenance. The light was on in the front downstairs room, but thick, dark curtains pulled across the window prevented them from seeing inside.

Callan had dressed in a dark grey suit and a red-and-black striped tie. Only the highly polished shoes hinted that he might be something other than a City worker returning home from a day in the office. Army habits hard to extinguish even when out of uniform. It had been a problem with the Army in Northern Ireland, Jessie remembered from her training, soldiers undercover as vagrants giving themselves away by the shine on their shoes.

She and Callan exchanged tense glances on the doorstep.

'I'm not expecting this to be easy,' he said in a low voice, reaching for the doorbell. 'Jackson's father, Steve, didn't sound like the type of man to take anything lying down.'

The bell sounded like a bee in a jam jar. For a few moments their twin breaths, clouding the cold air in the porch, were the only sound. Then light footsteps on wooden boards approaching.

The woman who opened the door couldn't have been more than fifty, but she looked ten years older, shrunken and faded, as if she had been washed on a hot cycle too many times. Her brown hair, streaked with grey, was pulled back into a tight ponytail and she was wearing a shapeless grey jumper and grey trousers, elasticated at the waist. Her feet were shoved into backless slippers. The only colour on her was a bright red poppy pinned to her jumper. *Remembrance Day*. Every day was Remembrance Day now for Jackson's parents, his wife and children.

Callan held up his identification with his left hand, extended his right. She didn't shake it.

'Captain Ben Callan, Military Police, Special Investigation Branch.'

She looked scared. 'Steve,' she called back over her shoulder. 'Steve. That policeman is here.'

155

Jessie stepped past Callan.

'Mrs Jackson. I'm Jessie Flynn, one of Captain Callan's . . . colleagues. May we come in?'

Almost reluctantly, as if by keeping them on the doorstep she was keeping reality at bay, Mrs Jackson inched the door open. Jessie and Callan stepped over the threshold, into the narrow hallway, as Steve Jackson pounded down the stairs, two at a time. He was a short, stocky man with a grey crew cut. Piercing blue eyes were the only colour in his face, the skin around them heavily lined, grey and wan. Callan held out his hand.

'Mr Jackson, I'm Captain Ben Callan. This is Dr Jessie Flynn, one of my colleagues. She's a clinical psychologist.'

Ignoring Callan's outstretched hand, a frowning Steve Jackson looked from Jessie to Callan and back.

'A psychologist?' He blew air out of his nose. 'What the hell do we want with a bloody psychologist? We need justice, not counselling.'

'She's helping me with the case. It's not clear-cut.'

'It's bloody clear-cut to me. My son was shot, murdered, by one of his colleagues. Not by a bloody Afghan. I would have expected that. I would have been able to *live* with that. But, Jesus, one of his own comrades—'

Choking off the rest of his sentence, he turned and strode into the sitting room: the room at the front of the house they had seen, lit behind brown curtains, from the pavement. Callan followed. Jessie hung back by the door.

Rachel Jackson had already been visited by men from the Intelligence Corps who had broken the news of her husband's death. The family were putting themselves through this visit for Andy Jackson – to get justice – and Jessie knew that

156

what they really wanted was for her and Callan to go, leave them alone, never come back.

The living room smelt of air freshener and smoke. An artificial coal fire burned in the fireplace, the only furniture two slightly shabby-looking flower-patterned sofas set at right angles to each other around an old wooden coffee table. There were four used mugs on the coffee table and a couple of plates with biscuit crumbs on them. A half-empty packet of Superkings lay next to a full ashtray. A red Henry vacuum cleaner sat in the corner of the room, plugged in, as if someone had started vacuuming and then lost interest halfway through the job.

A huge framed photograph of Jackson, in his dress uniform, hung over the fireplace. Other photographs lined the mantelpiece and the oak sideboard next to it, every milestone in his progression from toddler, to gap-toothed little boy clutching a football, to young man dressed in his best shirt for a night out, faithfully captured on celluloid. Steve Jackson indicated the sofa.

'Have a seat, Captain.'

Reaching for the packet of Superkings, he shook one out and lit it.

Callan sat down. He looked huge and awkward on the little flower-patterned sofa. Mrs Jackson hovered in the doorway behind Jessie.

'Would you like a tea or coffee?' she asked.

Callan shook his head. 'I'm fine, thank you, Mrs Jackson.'

'Dr Flynn?'

'Yes, a coffee please,' Jessie said. She didn't particularly want a coffee, but she did want to get Jackson's mother alone, knew that she'd have a better chance of getting under the woman's skin without his father there, bristling with

157

aggression. He was clearly the boss in their relationship and, while they were in the same room, Mrs Jackson would defer to him. 'I'll help you make it.'

She followed Mrs Jackson down the narrow hallway. The kitchen was small, the surfaces cluttered with unwashed mugs and plates. Jessie could feel crumbs grinding into the soles of her shoes as she shuffled her feet, embarrassed, uncomfortable, torn between an almost overwhelming urge to roll her sleeves up, get to work cleaning, and an opposing one, to walk out of the front door, never come back. The weight of grief in this house felt too familiar, too much like stepping back fifteen years into her own personal nightmare. The mundanities of life meaningless in the face of such overwhelming loss. Everything meaningless.

'I'm sorry about my husband. He doesn't mean to be rude. It's just—'

'My brother died unexpectedly when I was fourteen. Please don't apologize. You have nothing to apologize for.'

Mrs Jackson met her gaze and gave a small, grateful nod. Her eyes looked dead, Jessie realized, the way her mother's had after Jamie's death.

A young girl's voice suddenly from upstairs, quickly shushed.

Raised men's voices from the sitting room, Steve Jackson shouting, *'Accidental death? Are you fucking kidding me? He was murdered, for Christ's sake.'*

Mrs Jackson flinched. 'Milk? Sugar?'

Callan's reply, his voice steady, controlled: *'I have to keep an open mind at this stage.'*

'Milk please, Mrs Jackson.'

The girl again, her pitch higher this time, laced with tension. Jessie wished that Steve Jackson would keep his

158

voice down, control his temper, if only for his grand-children's sake.

Taking the cup from Mrs Jackson, she took a few sips, set it back on the worktop. 'Is your daughter-in-law here, Mrs Jackson? I'd like to talk to her, just briefly, if possible.'

Mrs Jackson looked uncertain. 'She's putting the children to bed.' A laden pause. 'She's very upset.'

Jessie nodded. 'I won't ask her anything that makes her uncomfortable, and talking to someone outside the family can be useful. I know the Army way of life well, but I'm not a soldier.'

Mrs Jackson rubbed a hand over her eyes; she looked as if she was about to cry.

'Please sit down,' she managed, indicating the kitchen table. 'I'll go and speak to her.' Hurriedly, she left the kitchen.

Jessie waited, sipping her coffee, hearing Mrs Jackson's footsteps receding down the hall, her soft tread on the carpeted stairs, cut through by Steve Jackson's voice.

'*He wouldn't have been allowed to join the Army if he had any medical problems, would he?*'

Callan: '*Are you sure?*'

'*Of course I'm bloody sure. He was my son. He didn't have any medical problems.*'

Jessie sensed, rather than heard, someone join her in the room. She turned. The woman in the doorway, who was about her own age, looked exhausted, emotionally wrung out and then wrung a few turns tighter. Her blonde hair was lank and greasy, her eye make-up applied – perhaps for their visit – hastily, a large smudge of mascara under one eye. She looked as if she had been crying constantly for the past week: the whites of her brown eyes red veined, sunk deep within their sockets. She was

159

wearing a shapeless yellow hooded sweatshirt and jeans. Jessie stood, but didn't hold out her hand. She wanted to establish their relationship on an informal footing from the outset, if she could.

'I'm Jessie Flynn. I'm a clinical psychologist.'

Rachel gave a dull nod.

'I wanted to have a chat with you,' Jessie continued. 'Nothing formal. Just a . . . a chat. And you can, of course, ask me anything. Any questions you have. Anything that you think might help.'

Rachel sat down across the table from Jessie, but didn't meet her eye.

'I'm not sure if your mother-in-law told you, but I lost my brother a few years ago.'

Rachel's gaze was fixed resolutely at an invisible spot in the middle of the kitchen table. She began to pick at the skin around her thumbnail. Jessie noticed that the skin on both hands around the edges of the nails was red raw, smudged with blood.

Jessie continued, 'It was a long time ago, but I wanted you to know that I can understand a tiny bit of what you're going through—' She broke off as a memory surfaced violently. A memory of sitting helplessly at the kitchen table while her mother thumped her fists against the kitchen wall and sobbed her heart out for Jamie.

'I saw a big black car coming down our cul-de-sac,' Rachel said quietly, concentrating on her breathing, each word forced out between sucking breaths; 'driven by a man in Army uniform, and my heart stopped. My first thought was that Andy had been hurt, but when they got out and the driver asked if I was Sergeant Jackson's wife and I said, "Yes", and he said, "Can you hand your baby

160

to my colleague," I knew. I *knew* that he was dead.' She dug her nail deeper into the skin of her thumb. 'I had to break the news to my five-year-old daughter the next morning. I sat her down and told her that she wasn't going to school. She was so happy.' Her face twisted with anguish. 'And then I had to tell her why – that Daddy can't ever come home from Afghanistan now because he's gone to heaven. She didn't say anything, didn't ask any questions. It was only the next day, when we came here, that I heard her asking her grandpa what heaven was. Steve told her that it's an amazing place up in the sky, way above the clouds, and that Daddy had gone up there on a rocket ship. She's such a girly-girl. She hates rocket ships, space men, anything like that. But that night, before bed, I found her searching through Steve's toolbox in the under-stairs cupboard. I asked her what she was doing and she said that she was looking for some tools to take to bed with her in case Daddy's rocket ship needed fixing.' Jessie heard the sob straining her vocal cords. 'The baby will never remember him. He'll look at photographs and know that the man in the photographs was his father, but he'll never have any real sense of him. At least Roxy will have that.' She wiped the streak of tears roughly from her cheeks. 'I hope Bobby never wants to join the fucking Army.' Blood dripped from her thumb where she had dug a raw hole with her nail. Reaching across the table, Jessie laid her hand on hers, grasped it tight.

'Please don't hurt yourself like that.'

Another memory. Her mother thumping her head against the kitchen table, trying to blunt the emotional hurt with physical pain.

'He was . . . he was making a difference in Afghanistan,

wasn't he? My Andrew.' His name dragged a little jerk out of her, as if the effort hurt her.

Jessie hesitated. She had no idea what Andy Jackson was working on in Afghanistan. And a cynic would say that none of them were making a difference. That it was a pointless war driven by dishonest politicians who would never put their own sons or daughters in the firing line.

'Yes, he was. He was making a big difference.' What else could she say?

'He was so proud. Said he had some important contacts, Afghans. Right in with them, he was . . .'

'Did he say who they were?' Jessie asked softly.

Rachel shook her head. 'No, he never did. He never told me much. Said it was all top secret.' She gave a sad smile. 'We only had one call a week from Afghanistan and he wanted to hear me talk mainly, wanted to know how the kids were doing—'

'Mummy.'

A tiny voice behind Jessie. Twisting around in the chair, she saw a little girl, dressed in pink Hello Kitty pyjamas, standing in the doorway. She was clutching a sheaf of A4 papers to her chest with one arm, a fistful of felt-tip pens in the other hand.

Rachel scrubbed her sleeve quickly across her eyes, stretched out her arms. 'Roxy, sweetheart. I just put you into bed.'

'I could hear Granddaddy shouting.' Her face creased into a frown. 'It's too loud.'

Rachel forced a smile. 'He's shouting at the television, sweetheart, like you do when Dora's on.'

Roxy looked confused. 'Who's the other man?'

Rachel smoothed her hair. 'The television. Just the telly, sweetheart, voices on the telly.'

162

Rachel wiped her sleeve across her eyes again: she looked as if she was about to burst into tears. Jessie met her gaze and a look passed between them.

Jessie put her hand out and touched the little girl's arm. 'I love your drawings, Roxy. They're so colourful. Can you tell me what they're about?'

Roxy looked at Jessie for a moment, her brow creased into a tight frown. Appraisal concluded, she shuffled sideways, laid the drawings on the tabletop in front of Jessie.

The first picture was of a family of four walking in the park, father, mother, daughter and a baby in a pram. The sun was out and the grass was studded with huge, brightly coloured flowers.

'This was when we went to Wandsworth Common, with Daddy.'

'It's beautiful. I love your flowers.' Jessie pointed. 'And what's this?'

Roxy smiled hesitantly. 'A squirrel. There were lots of squirrels. I wanted to feed them, but Daddy wouldn't let me. He said they're dirty.'

The next picture showed Roxy, Rachel and the baby standing, a male figure in camouflage clothing lying, prone, in front of them. The figure was holding a box in one hand, the box almost as big as his whole body. Roxy had written the letters PAN on the box.

'This one is Daddy. He's hurt. His leg hurts.'

'What's this?' Jessie indicated the box.

'It's medicine to take his hurtie leg away.'

The last picture was similar, but in this one Andy Jackson's eyes were closed and he wasn't holding a box. Tears ran down the faces of Rachel, Roxy and her baby brother. Huge, bright blue tears that had formed puddles around their feet. In the sky, which she had coloured black, Roxy had drawn a space ship, its fiery tail trailing up to the sky, as if it was coming down to land.

'I asked him to leave the Army,' Rachel murmured.

Jessie looked from the child to her mother. Rachel's dull gaze was fixed on the last picture.

'Once the government sent troops to Afghanistan. It's a stupid bloody war . . . stupid and needless . . .' Her voice rose, as if the effort to get the words out was affecting her ability to control the volume. 'I asked him to leave so many times, but he wouldn't. *Couldn't.* He had been dreaming of being a Spook since he was eight years old. It was his life – the Intelligence Corps was my Andy's life. It would have killed him to—' She slammed a hand over her mouth, realizing what she had said. 'I just want him back.' A sob erupted from under her hand.

Jessie pulled Roxy on to her knee, hugged her tight. Roxy tucked her face into Jessie's neck; Jessie could feel her little body trembling. She cursed herself for not keeping a better eye on Rachel, for not realizing how the pictures were affecting her.

'What the hell have you said to her?' Steve Jackson was in the doorway.

'I'm sorry, we were talking about—' Jessie gestured helplessly to Roxy's pictures. 'About your son.'

Crossing the room in two steps, he wrapped his arm around his granddaughter, pulled her off Jessie's knee. The muscles along his jaw bulged.

'I think it's time that you left,' he snarled. 'Now. Both of you. Get out of my bloody house *now.*'

28

A heavy blackness swept over Jessie as she and Callan walked, in silence, back to the car. He held the passenger door open for her. She met his gaze across its top.

'I can't stand seeing pain like that. It's such a fucking waste.'

Callan didn't reply. Jessie got in and he shut the door, went around to the driver's side and climbed in. Starting the car, he flicked the radio on – Magic FM, easy listening music – turned up the volume. Jessie reached over and switched it off.

'Sorry to be a miserable shit but I'm not in the mood for cheery music.'

'I don't have any James Blunt, though if you rummage in the glovebox you might find some "slit your wrists music" from the Manic Street Preachers to cheer us up,' he said.

Leaning forward, she reached for the glovebox, paused, her hand on the catch.

'Seeing the photographs of Jackson as that smiling blond boy, looking at him back then and knowing what was coming to him, what his future was going to be – that's what hit me the hardest. Because that's the memory his mum has of him, isn't it? A little boy with skinny legs and that gap-toothed smile. Her little son. Not a grown man with his own children.'

Pulling out the stack of CDs, she flicked through them half-heartedly, holding each one to the window so that the orange glow from the sodium streetlamps lit the titles.

'I never believed in the wars in Iraq or Afghanistan,' she continued, slumping back in the seat, the CDs in her hand, none chosen. 'It's easy to be a politician, to put your hand up for a vote and send thousands of young men and women to a country you've never visited, into a political situation that you don't understand, and a war that can't be won. They don't get it. The number of lives that have been torn apart by those wars. Children like Roxy and her baby brother who are fatherless, mums and dads like the Jacksons who have lost their children.'

They joined West Hill, taking them from Wandsworth back up to the A3, heading southwest out of London, the late rush-hour stream of tail-lights a red fog ahead of them.

'It's all been for nothing, was for nothing,' she finished.

'Is that what you believe?' Callan asked quietly.

As she looked across, her gaze caught the scar from the bullet wound on his temple and she faltered. She had never aired her view to another soldier, only to Ahmose, ranting over their weekly teas. It felt like the ultimate betrayal, telling patients of hers who had lost limbs and worse in Afghanistan that she believed it was all for nothing. It was easier to pretend that the war had been worth the lost lives, even though she knew that many of them – most of them, probably – felt as she did.

'I support the soldiers, of course I do, but no, I never believed that we were right to interfere in the Middle East. It's a multi-headed monster. Chop one head off and another grows, worse than the first. Look at the Islamic State now – the butchers that they've brought with them, the hatred. And the warlords in Afghanistan. Are they really better than the Taliban? Are people's lives – normal people's lives, women's lives – any better? When I treat the young men and women who've been so badly scarred – mentally and physically – I'm furious at the Army and at the politicians for sending them out there in the first place, to fight an unwinnable war.' She paused. 'So yes, it is what I believe. And I also believe that in a couple of years' time, not even that long, Afghanistan will be the same as it was before, or worse. The Taliban are resurging. About the only sensible thing Starkey said in our interview was that Afghanistan is the graveyard of empires. He's right, and he'll soon be proved right again . . .' she tailed off. 'Sorry for the rant. You've probably had enough ranting from Steve Jackson to last you a lifetime and then you get an hour locked in a small space with me.'

They had reached Tibbet's Corner, the roundabout where West Hill segued into the A3. A mile to the left, down Parkside, was her childhood home, where her mother lived.

'I grew up near here.'

'In Wandsworth?'

'Wimbledon. My mum still lives there, in the house I grew up in.'

'Do you see her much?'

'No.' The familiar feeling of guilt rising with her answer.

'Tell me about your brother,' he asked softly. 'The one in the photograph.'

The noise of the Golf's V8 engine roared in the silence that followed his question. She was tempted to tell him that her story was none of his business, but that response felt unnecessarily aggressive, pointless, particularly after what they had gone through together this evening. And she had seen him at his lowest.

'There's not much to tell. He died when he was seven. I was fourteen.'

'What did he die of?'

She hesitated, glanced out of the window. Wimbledon Common was spinning past, the black silhouettes of trees framed by the starlit sky beyond. Trees that hemmed in a thousand acres of wild grass and woodland, ponds and streams where she would take Jamie sledging in winter, tadpoling in the spring, sit him down and make daisy chains in summer, cycle and kick footballs.

'He got run over by a car.'

'I'm sorry.'

'It was a long time ago. Sounds harsh, but I don't think about him much any more.'

She glanced across at the same moment he did and their gazes met for a fraction of a second. Jessie's eyes slid away. The car sped on, the false ring of her words hanging in the air.

'How did your mother take it?'

'How do you think she took it?'

'Badly?'

Looking out of the window, she felt tears welling. Truth and lies. By acknowledging how Jamie had died, saying it out loud, she would have to acknowledge her role in his death. Her culpability. Bring that culpability into her new life – the one she had manufactured away from her mother, the living reminder of her past.

'Jamie was the sweet one. He was lovely,' she murmured. 'A truly lovely little boy.'

Callan braked sharply to avoid hitting a van that had just swung wildly in front of him, the sudden deceleration jerking Jessie forward in her seat, sending the CDs clattering from her lap. Bending forward, she scooped them from the footwell, stacked them up, put them back neatly in the glovebox, had a quick tidy of the other contents before closing it.

'Happy?' Callan asked.

'Huh?'

'With the arrangement of my glovebox.'

'Oh . . . I . . .' She sat back and sighed. 'After he died, I used to sneak out of school during my lunch hour, run home and clean the house. Make it nice for my mum when she got back from work. It was the only thing that seemed to make her happy. The only thing *I* could do to make her happy.'

She had never told anyone that, not even Ahmose.

'Is that where it came from?'

'Where what came from?'

'The OCD.'

'I don't have—' She broke off. She was sick of saying it, sick of the mantra. Who was she convincing? Not even herself any more. 'Yes, that is where it came from. I've had it for years now.'

He flicked the indicator, swung the Golf across three lanes and on to the exit slip road. Left at the roundabout and they joined a country road, a couple of miles later another, narrower, high hedges on either side more densely black than the night sky above them.

'What about you, Callan?'

169

He seemed unsurprised that she would turn the question around on him, but he didn't respond.

'What's your story? What are you hiding?'

'You know my story and you've seen all there is to see of me.' A brief half-smile. 'Of my brain at least.'

They had reached Bradley Court. Pulling up in the car park next to her Mini, he switched off the engine and turned to face her. Now that they had stopped, and the darkness had closed around them, he seemed claustrophobically close, his proximity suddenly uncomfortably intimate in the small car. Shifting sideways until her left arm was pressed against the passenger door, she looked across. Her heart rate was slightly raised and she knew that her cheeks were flushed, hoped that he couldn't tell in the darkness of the car.

'The truth, soldier,' she said. 'Tell me the truth.'

'The truth will set you free, Dr Flynn,' he murmured, with another brief smile. 'When you tell me the truth – the whole truth – I'll tell you the truth.' Leaning over, he gave her a quick, soft kiss on the cheek. 'Thank you for coming with me. Goodnight. Sweet dreams.'

29

Wendy walked to the end of the road and turned right into Birch Close, a short cul-de-sac of eight modern semi-detached houses. The last house in the row was owned by Pauline, a friend she had met dog walking. Wendy slowed; Pauline's lights were off. She must be out at bridge or perhaps asleep.

Continuing to walk, Wendy reached the end of the tarmac where it petered to sand, a narrow trail leading away from the houses, before it branched left and right to run alongside the vast space of Paschal Wood and the Royal Military Academy Sandhurst training grounds.

On cold, clear winter days when the deciduous trees had lost their leaves, she could hear the gunfire from the ranges, the mixed explosions of blank rounds and thunder flashes from the night-training exercises. When she had first moved into Saddleback Close, gardens backing close up to the Ministry of Defence boundary fence, the noises had kept her awake at night. Now, the sound was like an old friend, as comforting to her as leaving the radio on low while she slept.

Tonight the gorse scrub and woods beyond the fence were silent, deserted. Finding the space between her leather gloves and the thick sleeve of her Puffa jacket, Wendy glanced at her watch. It was nearly midnight. She hadn't realized that it was so late. Rusty would have to make do with a short walk this evening. She'd make it up to him tomorrow, tell Nooria that she'd have to leave by five.

She started to sing, making the cocker spaniel glance up at her, his tail wagging. Reaching the sandy trail that cut off left and right from the end of the track she was on, Wendy bent and unhooked his leash. Darting across the trail, Rusty nosed under the Sandhurst boundary fence and streaked into the darkness. By the time Wendy had reached the wooden fence, he had disappeared completely. She couldn't even hear him shoving his way through the tangled gorse, or the excited yaps that usually accompanied his runs.

Shivering, she pulled the Puffa's collar up around her cheeks. She felt freezing suddenly and she really didn't want to climb over the fence and search for him. It was MoD property after all, out of bounds to the public, and it wasn't in her nature to break rules. Besides, tonight, the dark space of Paschal Wood and Sandhurst felt vast and watchful. A cold wind was making the pines emit an odd, high-pitched wail, barely audible, but there all the same.

'Rusty,' she called quietly. She couldn't bring herself to shout, standing there, all alone on the track.

She waited. No sign of him.

'Rusty.'

No answering bark. She felt vulnerable enough walking alone along pavements at this time of night and wished now that she had taken him for a lead walk around the housing estate instead. She had felt on edge since last night, when she thought she'd seen light in the Scotts' garden. Though she had told herself that the flash had been a figment of her imagination, there was a tiny corner of her mind that remained unconvinced. The edginess she felt transported her straight back to when she was a girl. She'd always been nervous of the dark, had checked under her bed and in her bedroom cupboards before switching out the light at night, a habit that had endured right into her teenage years.

'As if a murderer is going to bother to sit in your cupboard for hours waiting for you to switch out the light and go to bed before jumping out!' her dad used to joke.

And even though her rational mind told her that her father would say the same in this situation – that no mugger or rapist in their right mind would be hanging around out here on a freezing November night on the off-chance that some crazy woman would walk by with her dog – something about the absolute impenetrability of the darkness made her heart rate quicken.

'Rusty. *Rusty.*'

Hauling herself over the fence, snagging her sleeve on a nail head sticking out from the *Danger — MoD Property* sign, she dropped heavily on to the ground the other side. Something cut into her ankle, and she cursed under her breath.

'*Rusty,*' she yelled.

Pushing her way forward, hands in front of her face to prevent the branches from scratching at her skin, she forced her way through the pines. Her eyes had accustomed to the gloom out there on the track, but here in the woods she could see nothing concrete on either side of her, just a sense of the trees and bushes layering into the distance, everything disfigured by the darkness. A branch raked across her cheek and she jumped back, pressing her gloved hand to her face, feeling a sting where the wood must have torn her skin. *This is madness.* If Rusty wouldn't come when she called, he could find his own way home.

She stiffened. Was that a twig she'd heard breaking? Was something moving out there among the trees? Her heart pounded as she stared hard into the dense murk.

And there he was suddenly. Just Rusty. A wiggle of brown and white squeezing his way through the gorse, tongue lolling, eyes bright.

A balloon of air emptied from her lungs.

'Rusty! Where have you been?'

And she realized now, as Rusty pressed himself against her leg, tired, shivering, obviously as keen as she was to get warm, as she felt the tension drain from her leaden limbs, that she had been more frightened than she cared to admit. Bending, she dragged a hand through Rusty's matted fur.

'Come on, boy. Let's go home.'

Turning, she pushed her way back through the trees to the boundary fence, gloved hands up in front of her face so that she didn't get scratched again. It was a relief to be out of the wood, the lights from the windows of the houses on Saddleback Close – the few that were on at this time of night – a welcoming beacon.

But as she hooked her foot on to the bottom rail and turned to make sure that Rusty was still behind her, something caught her eye.

A shape? Discrete from the swaying trees? A few metres away from her.

She stopped. 'Hello?'

No response.

Nothing moving.

Nothing concrete. Just a sense. But something about the change in feel of the darkness told her that she and Rusty were no longer alone.

30

A chill shook Jessie, as if the temperature in her bedroom had suddenly dropped. Pulling her duvet up to her chin, she rolled on to her side and closed her eyes, trying to push the memories away. But they came anyway, forcing through the cracks and filling her mind. She saw the drawing that Roxy had done, her dead father at her feet, the family standing in those bright blue puddles of tears. And out of nowhere she smelled the cool spring morning, grass damp with dew, ash on the breeze. She wiped her eyes with the back of her hand, felt her cheeks dampen again immediately with tears. Burying her face in her pillow, she let the memories flood over her, the tears flow, helpless to prevent either.

Six months after Jamie's death, she had woken in the middle of the night. Her pony alarm clock read 4.30 a.m. Her curtains were closed, but slightly too short for the window: moonlight cast a wavy pattern on to the wall below them. Sitting up in bed, she let her gaze accustom to the pale light. Her room looked tidy, unnaturally so. The efforts of a fourteen-year-old girl who had a notice board littered with Post-its bearing the phone numbers of school counsellors, child psychologists, child bereavement support groups, but hadn't talked to any of them.

She's a fighter, her form teacher had told her mother. She turned up to school on time every day, played cat games with her friends at break, joined in all the games sessions with enthusiasm, got straight A's. *She's making excellent progress.* Ran home after school to manically clean the house, while her friends were heading to tennis or swimming lessons. *She's winning.* Taking the days one at a time, sometimes hour by hour, she got through them somehow, with a smile on her face.

Inside, though, she was drowning.

Climbing out of bed, she found her dressing gown and wrapped it around herself. Quietly, so as not to wake her mother, she padded down the hallway to Jamie's room. She stood in the doorway and everything in her soul told her to close the door and go back to bed.

The room was exactly as it had been before he died. Her mother had changed nothing, packed away nothing. Jessie had not been in here since his death, the memory of finding him hanging too sharp and cruel.

But standing here now, looking around the room in the pale moonlight, she had never felt such clarity before – it was blinding. She was lost and empty and the only thing that made sense to her was that she needed her mother back. Needed to shock her out of the mire. Nothing else mattered: not the perfect, tidy house or the straight A's. All she wanted was her mum.

Tiptoeing down to the kitchen, she pulled a roll of bin bags from the cupboard under the sink. Returning to Jamie's room, she began to fill the bags. She pulled his clothes from their hangers, opened his drawers and methodically emptied each one, took the duvet from his bed, and pressed it and his pillow on top of the clothes. Standing on his desk, she unhooked one end of the curtain rail and shunted the Batman curtains off the pole. She emptied the toy chest, the bookshelf, cleared the desk of its contents.

One, two, three, four, five full bin bags.

The only things she didn't take were the Athena poster of the chocolate Labrador puppies – she couldn't bring herself to – and Pandy, his favourite cuddly bear, one of the plethora of presents that had arrived to celebrate his birth, the giver long since forgotten. Leaving the poster on the wall, she carried Pandy back to her own bed and tucked him under her covers.

Out in the garden, the horizon was tinted pink with the promise of dawn, but the air was nighttime chill, the grass damp and cold on her bare soles. She piled the bin bags in the middle of the lawn, away from the house, the shed and the wooden fences, and went back to the kitchen for some cooking oil and a box of matches.

It was fifteen minutes before she heard the kitchen door creak open, footsteps running down the garden.

'What the hell are you doing?' her mother shouted. 'What are you burning?'

'The past,' Jessie murmured. 'I'm burning the past.'

With a wail of agony, her mother ran to the smouldering pile, tried to snatch a few scraps from it. She jumped back, the heat too strong, nothing left to salvage.

'What have you done, Jessie?' she moaned. '*What have you done?*'

'He's not coming back.' Despite the heat from the fire, Jessie felt cold, bloodless, a tremor running through her body. 'He's never coming back. There was no point keeping all his things. They just reminded us—'

Her mother spun around, her face twisted in fury. '*Reminded us?* REMINDED US? He was my son. He was my *baby*.'

She turned back to the fire, stood there sobbing, the flames lighting her face, wet and screwed up, lips and chin stringy with slime from her running nose. Jessie's insides constricted in agony. It wasn't supposed to have worked like this. Everything was slipping away.

'I want you back, Mum,' Jessie said, her voice breaking on a sob. Sidling over, she slid her arm around her mother's waist, rested her head on her shoulder. 'I want my mum back.'

'You're fifteen in a few months. Almost an adult.' Her mother's body was rigid, her voice distant. 'You don't need a mother any more.' Disentangling herself from Jessie's embrace, she turned and walked back up the garden to the house without another word or a backward glance.

For weeks afterwards, if Jessie woke at night she would tiptoe to the landing window, which overlooked the garden, and see her mother standing by the pile of burnt grass and ashes, a statue made of stone.

Callan ejected the magazine from his Browning and filled the cartridge with 9 mm rounds. Raising the gun, hands wrapped around the butt, feet spread shoulder width apart, he took aim at the man-shaped target at the far end of the concrete range. His index finger found the trigger. Slowing his breathing until it was light and regular, he squeezed until he felt the trigger resist, waited for an out breath and pumped five rounds into the target, ripping out a neat circle at its heart.

He had to come clean with Jessie, particularly after she'd come to the Jacksons' with him, something she hadn't needed to do. He couldn't keep stringing her along without giving her the whole picture. He realized that now.

His mobile rang – Val Monks on her office phone. Sliding on the safety, reholstering his weapon, he answered.

'Working late, Val?'

He heard her smother a yawn. 'No rest for the wicked, Callan.'

'You can't work twenty-four hours a day and be wicked, Val.'

She laughed, but the laugh was half-hearted, and Callan could tell that she had something on her mind.

'I'll make this quick, as I presume you're tucked up. Either that or you have a hot date and I'm getting in the way.'

Callan looked down the range at the black cutout of a man charging towards him, clutching a rifle. *A hot date.*

'I've been waiting for you to call me back.' She sounded irritated.

'Call you back?'

'Did you get the message?'

'What message?'

'I left a message late this afternoon with one of your Special Investigation Branch colleagues, a Lieutenant Gold. Did he pass it on?'

'No.'

'Ah. I thought you were just getting slack in your old age.'

Callan didn't reply. Ed Gold – the new guy – what was he playing at?

Val continued: 'I've had the tox reports back. The tox reports on Jackson. I pulled some strings to get them processed quickly.'

180

Callan shifted closer to the range's exit doors so that his signal acquired another bar. 'I'm listening.'

'Well, we found opiates in a sample of his urine and in a sample of his blood. In analysis of his hair follicles, we found both opiates and acetaminophen.'

'Opiates?'

'Yes. From opium. As in opium from poppies – and I won't insult your intelligence by reminding you where lots of poppies are grown.'

Afghanistan. One of the coalition forces' big headaches. All this reconstruction money being pumped in by coalition governments, much of it diverted to purposes for which it was never intended. Western governments unintentionally funding the flood of narcotics into their own countries with taxpayers' money. A very un-virtuous circle and naive in the extreme.

A sudden image of Starkey rose in his mind, leaning across the table, fists clenched, eyes wild: *We're fucking amateurs compared to them. We think we're playing them, but we're the ones being played.*

'Opium in urine takes around twenty-four hours to be metabolized to a level where it is no longer detectable in tests, the exact time obviously depending on the individual's metabolism. Opium in blood takes around three days to do the same.'

'Jesus.' Callan whistled between his teeth. 'So he took opium within twenty-four hours of his death, while he was on duty in Afghanistan.'

'Right.'

'And the hair follicle?'

'Opium in hair follicles is detectable for a minimum of four months, often up to six.'

181

'So from the hair follicle analysis, you're saying that he was a habitual user – that he's had opiates in his system for months.' Callan massaged his temple. He could feel the beginnings of another headache, right behind his eyes.

'Yes, but it's not quite so simple. Because we also found acetaminophen in the hair follicles, but not in the urine or blood samples.'

'What the hell is acetaminophen?'

'Acetaminophen, more commonly known as Tylenol, is a drug that pharmaceutical companies add to prescription-only opiate-based painkillers, to discourage users from abusing them and becoming addicted.'

'How does that work?'

A sigh came down the phone. 'Opiate-based painkillers available on prescription are very effective at dampening pain, but they are also highly addictive – opiates are highly addictive – and so drug companies add Tylenol, a drug which damages the user's liver, in a morally questionable attempt to stop users from abusing their prescription painkillers.'

'Abuse these and you screw up your liver.'

'Right.'

'Nice.'

'That's big business for you. They tick the "we're doing all we can to minimize this prescription drug's potential for abuse" box while, in fact, it's a very cruel solution.'

Callan pinched the bridge of his nose. 'So give me the summary, Val.'

'What the tox results say is that Jackson took opium – pure opium – recently, in Afghanistan, multiple times – and before that, stretching back months, he was most probably on an opiate-based prescription painkiller.'

'Jesus. So he was in a real mess.'

'Took the words right out of my mouth, Callan.' Another yawn. 'Now have a lovely evening with that hot date. I'm locking up here. I'll call you as soon as I hear from my heart specialist, but once again I don't need to insult your intelligence by telling you that habitual drug use places a considerable strain on the heart.'

The phone clicked off. Callan shoved his mobile back in his pocket.

Opiate-based prescription painkillers. Opium.

Pulling the Browning from his holster, he slid off the safety and shot five more rounds at the target, carving out another perfect circle right in the middle of its forehead.

31

Pauline braked so hard that her handbag catapulted from the passenger seat, landing upside down in the Micra's footwell, keys, lipstick, compact, wallet spreading themselves over the mat. A dog had just shot across the road in front of her.

Thank God she had only been driving at fifteen miles an hour – slowing in approach to her own drive – or she would have run it over. Her reactions were not what they used to be. Pulling over to the kerb outside her house, she switched off the engine, her hand shaking as she pulled the key from the ignition. She felt a bit tipsy. She'd had no cards all night, no luck at all, and her partner had been a pedant who had driven her mad quoting the rule book, when the only reason she went to the bridge club was to get herself out of the house one night a week and meet some pleasant people. She had drunk more than she should have done and realized now that she was probably over the limit. All she wanted to do was to crawl into bed with a hot cup of tea.

But the dog – Rusty? Was it Rusty?

She glanced at the illuminated clock on her dashboard. One a.m. *Heavens, it can't have been Rusty.* Wendy had been at work all day – she wouldn't be out walking him at this time, surely? But even so, the dog *had* looked very much like him: the size, the blaze of beige and white as it streaked past.

Pauline's automatic security light flashed on as she climbed out of the car and crossed the lawn to her front door. The night felt colder, windier, than it had when she'd left the bridge club in the centre of Camberley – the jam of buildings in town cutting off the wind and sharing some of their heat with the street. Something loose was slamming rhythmically – a gate left open, maybe – and a curious low humming was coming from the trees in the Sandhurst training ground. Something about the sound set her teeth on edge. It wasn't a night to be trudging around in the dark searching for stray dogs.

As she opened the door, she heard a noise behind her, which nearly made her jump out of her skin. The dog was back – on the lawn – and now she saw that it was, without question, Rusty. Crouching, clicking with her tongue, she held her hand out.

'Rusty. Good boy. Come. Rusty, come.'

He seemed agitated, darting from side to side across her front lawn, edging towards the start of the sandy path that led to the training area, and then running back toward her. The movement, his behaviour, set a tiny alarm bell off in her brain. It was almost as if he was trying to get her to follow him. She looked beyond him, up and down the road, unable to see anyone, anything but the dense night. She had the unsettling sense that beyond the wall of darkness in front of her, the trees in Paschal Wood and the training area were alive in the wind. Shivering, she drew back into her hallway. Where on earth was Wendy?

'Rusty. Rusty, come.'

Darting into her kitchen, she fetched a handful of dog treats. Squatting on the doorstep, making that clicking noise she had learnt from watching dog whisperer programmes on the television, holding out the handful of treats, she was finally able to tempt him close enough to catch. Holding him by the collar, she pulled him inside. He was panting and shaking, pulling, trying to wrench himself free.

'Oh heavens, what on earth have you been up to?' She stroked her hand over his back to calm him. His fur was wet, clumped and sticky. As she looked at the colour of the liquid on his pale fur, on her own lined palm, she felt naked fear dawn.

32

Standing in her back garden, gown wrapped tight around her, slippers soaking up the morning dew, Jessie took a sip of coffee. A milky mist hung low over the fields, and beyond them the sky was tinged ochre with the light of the rising sun.

She had slept fitfully, her mind lurching from one disturbing image to the next, all of them to do with burning: *the trail of Roxy's rocket taking her dad to heaven; the black plastic donkey wrapped in Baby Isabel's blanket; the girl is burnt, the man is burnt, the bonfire she had lit in her mother's garden, to extinguish the past. Always back to Jamie and to her mother.*

At one in the morning, she thought she'd heard a noise downstairs, had slipped out of bed – grabbing one half of a pair of stone bookends from her bedside table – and tiptoed down the carpeted stairs, clutching the bookend like a mallet, unsure of whether she could bring herself to crack it against someone's skull if there was anyone there. But when she reached the kitchen, she realized that she must have left the back door unlocked; the sound was the door twitching against its frame in the wind. The farm cat – stretched out, soaking up the under-floor heating – must somehow have managed to prise it open and slip inside. Scooping him up, she put him outside, closed and locked the door, feeling guilty for disturbing his comfortable slumber.

Back in bed, sleep continued to elude her. At 5 a.m. she had admitted defeat and risen. She'd tidied the house: brushing away imagined dust with a damp cloth, rearranging cupboards that had been rearranged the week before, hoovering the spotless carpets, taking the cups from the cupboard and inspecting each one in turn, washing the few that bore illusory stains.

In the field beyond the fence, a flock of sheep grazed, rose-tinted in the dawn light. Though she tried only to focus on the beauty of the dawn, a beauty that the grey clouds gathering to the west told her wouldn't last, her mind kept circling back to Sami.

Was Nooria having an affair? The Army lifestyle put huge strain on relationships and divorce rates were high. Service before self, the Army before everything, constant moves, forced absences for months at a time. Nooria was fifteen years younger than Scott, stuck out in that farmhouse in the middle of nowhere, alone. Had she hooked up with someone at art college perhaps, someone who hadn't taken a shine to Sami?

And what about sexual abuse? – the beast that dare not speak its name. She'd told Gideon that she thought it unlikely, but why had she said that? What evidence did she have to back up her statement? One in twenty children in the United Kingdom were the victim of sexual abuse and of those, over 90 per cent were abused by someone they knew. Was Sami one of those children?

Go back to bed. Stay in bed. You're bad. The Shadowman will come.

The thought made her sick to her stomach, but she had to acknowledge that it did happen, and often. People exploited innocence for money, for power and control over the child or over their parent, the mother usually, and purely for their own, sick enjoyment.

She could meet with Sami's parents again, but she felt as if she was merely going around in circles. Did she have time to eke out the truth from Sami himself? She was making progress in their sessions, but it was slow and time was running out. If he was the victim of sexual abuse, he needed to be removed and quickly.

What about Scott's ex-wife? Wendy had mentioned meeting her a few times in Aldershot. She had been a fitness instructor before marrying Scott, had been forced by financial circumstances to return to the profession when Scott left her for Nooria. Humiliation piled upon humiliation. She was linked to Scott by blood – two daughters. Would Jacqui be able to give any insights as to Scott's psychology and what might be going on in his current family?

And what about on Nooria's side? She had no siblings, an absent father and an estranged mother. The closest people to her, perhaps, the teachers at the school she was working in when she met Scott. A stretch, Jessie realized – clutching at straws.

But she had hit a wall. To move forward, she had to branch out. She would see Sami again this morning and then make a decision as to where she went from there.

33

They were back in the same spartan, utilitarian interview room as for the first interview, Starkey waiting for Callan, again, by the window, a rain-heavy early morning sky beyond the glass.

'Sergeant Starkey.'

Starkey turned. He fixed Callan with a cool stare before he came slowly, reluctantly to attention. Callan returned the salute.

'Captain Callan. I won't say that it's nice to see you because that would be dishonest and I hate dishonesty.'

'Do you now?' Callan muttered, sitting down at the table, laying the digital recorder on the metal tabletop and switching it on. 'Have a seat, Sergeant Starkey.'

Starkey pulled out the chair and sat down. They faced each other across the table, Callan's amber eyes looking straight into Starkey's dark ones, neither having any intention of looking away first. The tension between them palpable.

'You have said twice before that you do not want a

Ministry of Defence lawyer appointed on your behalf. Is that still the case, Sergeant Starkey?'

'It is, Captain Callan. I have done nothing wrong, so I do not need defending.'

Callan laid both hands flat on the desktop either side of the recorder. The forensic evidence from Starkey's well-oiled gun had given him nothing concrete to work with, only the partial print of Jackson's on the trigger, and forensics had been lucky to find that. So Jackson could have shot himself accidently while they fought or Starkey could have shot him deliberately. Callan also had no independent witnesses. The only live participant, sitting across the table from him, looking belligerent. He knew that he was playing this game from a huge disadvantage.

'Why did you shoot Jackson, Starkey?' he began.

'I didn't shoot him. He shot himself.'

'With your sidearm?' His tone was combative, deliberately so. He had nothing to lose in goading Starkey, seeing if Starkey cracked and told him some truth – any truth.

'Yes.'

'Why did Jackson have your sidearm?'

'He took it off me.'

'And you let him take it?'

Starkey flashed that sharp-toothed grin, unruffled. But Callan noticed that the whites of his eyes were bloodshot. For all his bravado, he clearly wasn't sleeping properly. Callan knew that feeling well.

'He had his own, so I wasn't expecting him to want mine too. That's greedy.'

'I could have you disciplined for not taking due care of your personal weapon.'

Starkey smirked. 'Sounds to me like you have jack shit, Captain.'

Callan sat back, scratched a leisurely hand through his stubble. He wasn't going to give Starkey the satisfaction of losing his temper and at least someone had fixed the bloody strip light.

'You had a fight.'

'Soldiers fight all the time. So what?'

'This fight ended in a death.'

Starkey shrugged. 'He was being an arsehole. Trying to take my gun. Not my fault if the idiot shot himself accidently in the process.'

'You coerced Jackson into going for that run and you had a reason for doing so.'

'Coerced. You swallowed a dictionary, Captain?'

Callan ignored the comment. 'What did you want from him, Starkey?'

No reply.

'What was Jackson hiding?'

Silence.

Leaning back in his chair, Callan sighed. 'I've been going through the list of British Army Intelligence Corps. Officers who were based at TAAC-South, Kandahar, at any point during the past three months. The list wasn't long – only three names. You, Jackson and Major Scott.' He paused. 'The petrol bomb attack on Major Scott – it sounded planned to me.'

Still no reply, but a minute tensing of Starkey's jaw. Callan was merely fishing, verbalizing ideas, tossing out tenuous links, seeing if any of them hit a nerve. It looked as if that one just had.

'You were driving Scott at the time and you were lucky to come out of it unharmed,' he continued.

Starkey's lip curled. 'Quit ferreting, Captain. It's getting you nowhere.'

'Did Jackson set you and Scott up? Did he have a deal with the enemy?'

'Patrols in Kandahar are being attacked all the time. Shit happens.'

'You weren't on patrol. You're Intelligence Corps and you were going to meet with an Afghan governmental official. Who were you going to meet with and why?'

'It was only my fourth day in Afghanistan, Captain Callan. I was the new boy. I knew shit.'

'Did someone tip them off as to the route you were taking? Did Jackson? Is that what you thought?'

Starkey shrugged.

'Did Jackson betray you and Scott?'

'Why don't you ask Scott? They were working together long before I arrived in Kandahar.'

'Funnily enough, Scott doesn't remember much.'

'And neither do I. Must be the shock – wiped my memory clean.' Leaning back in his chair, he put his hands behind his head and yawned.

Callan felt hot. Despite the cold outside, the room was warm. Unbuttoning his jacket, he shrugged it off and hung it on the back of the chair.

'Feeling the heat, Captain?'

Callan bit down on his temper, kept his voice even. 'Jackson didn't die of that gunshot wound. He died of a heart attack.'

Starkey's eyebrows rose.

'Did Jackson have a heart problem, Starkey?'

Fingers tapping a rhythm on the tabletop, Starkey's gaze slid away from Callan's. 'How the hell would I know?' He

193

paused, something changing in his face, a dawning recognition. Eyes finding Callan's again, he smiled. 'A heart attack? So that's the murder charge off the table.'

'There's manslaughter,' Callan said coolly. 'Ten years plus in the can, cosying up to Bubba every night. So why don't you start being straight with me.'

Starkey stretched out both hands, hunched his shoulders. 'I know nothing.' Spanish accent, Manuel in *Fawlty Towers*. An improvement on Clint Eastwood, and at least he had dropped the insane act. Perhaps he'd put it on for Dr Flynn's benefit, couldn't be bothered when it was only Callan. Or perhaps he didn't give enough of a shit any more to pretend. He'd had two days since that first interview to sit and think, work out the best strategy for coming out of this mess as well as he could. And he was Intelligence Corps. He was smart and cunning, no doubt about it.

'We found opium in his system. What can you tell me about that?'

'I can't tell you anything about that.' Starkey's dark eyes were hooded, unreadable. 'But if you could ask a dead man—' He broke off. Callan watched the light come on in his brain, as if someone had flicked a switch; light that reflected through his eyes, suddenly bright and knowing. 'Opium? He was on opium? Now if I'm not mistaken, Captain, aren't drugs bad for the heart?'

'He shouldn't have been out there, running with you.'

Starkey shrugged. 'He shouldn't have been in the Army at all. Fucking druggie.'

'Watch your mouth, Starkey. That's a fellow soldier you're talking about.'

'Was. *Was* a fellow solider.' He smirked. 'When is the funeral?'

A picture of Jackson's wife, his kids, filled Callan's mind.

Sliding his hands from the table, he balled them into fists in his lap. The urge to lean across the table and punch Starkey in the face was almost overwhelming, but he wasn't going to lose it this time, whatever the provocation.

'Don't worry about it. I don't think you're invited,' he said.

Pushing his chair back, Starkey stood up.

'What the fuck are you doing?' Callan snapped.

'If I'm not mistaken, you have nothing on me, Captain Callan. That means I'm free to go.'

'You are not a civilian, Starkey, and you are free to go only when I tell you.'

Jesus Christ. He had nothing. Knew that he had nothing. He could posture all he liked, pull rank, be an arsehole, but both he and Starkey knew that he had jack shit. Callan pushed himself to his feet. They faced each other across the table, Callan an inch or so taller, but both big men, barely suppressed aggression radiating from them like heat.

'I will find out what happened, Starkey.'

'Good luck with that, Captain. You can interview me as many times as you like, but you'll get nowhere. I was taught by the British Army to be the best of the best when it comes to intelligence, half truths, lies, taking interviewers for twenty-rounds in the ring and then KO'ing them. You can't break me and you can't make me talk.'

Starkey walked towards the door. Callan followed, stood behind him, right in his personal space.

'The truth will set you free, Starkey. Isn't that what you said?'

Starkey paused, his hand on the door, but he didn't turn.

'The truth never set anyone free, Captain Callan. Only the fucking stupid believe that. And whatever I am, I'm not stupid.'

195

34

Marilyn had dressed in a pair of black jeans, torn at the knee, so faded now that they were a mottled shade of the same grey as the clouds massed above him. On top, he wore a black hooded Def Leppard sweatshirt that was stretched in all the wrong places, and his battered black leather biker. He knew that he looked like Ronnie Wood on an off-day. But there was something in his DNA, a dogged bloody-mindedness, he realized, when his rational brain was engaged that he should have grown out of in his teens that had made him put on his grottiest clothes, purely because they were Army, spit-shined within an inch of their lives and then some.

The young military policeman facing him had to be one of the worst he'd met: little more than mid-twenties but with an attitude befitting someone twice his age, and a broomstick shoved so far up his arse, Marilyn fancied he would see the top of it nestling behind his tongue if he opened his mouth to speak.

Smiling, Marilyn held out his hand. 'Bobby Simmons.'

The lieutenant didn't return his handshake.

'*Detective Inspector* Bobby Simmons, Surrey and Sussex Major Crimes.'

He caught the warning look that DS Workman cast him, ignored it.

The lieutenant waited a beat before shaking his hand. 'Lieutenant Edward – Ed – Gold. I'm running this crime scene.'

We'll see about that, Marilyn thought. He didn't say it. Wasn't about to give Gold the satisfaction of getting a rise out of him this early in the game.

The female victim was clearly a civilian. Her clothes, her age, her shape for God's sake, all attested to that fact. Not to mention the few words her friend had told the uniformed officers who had answered the 999 call, before she was shunted into the ambulance and taken to Royal Surrey County Hospital, where she was currently under sedation, being treated for shock.

The body of the murdered woman was on military ground – he was happy to concede that fact – lying in the Sandhurst scrub, tight up against the boundary fence. There was a torn piece of black material caught on a nail head sticking out from the fence, matching a missing chunk from the sleeve of her Puffa jacket. Had she caught her arm while climbing the fence – trying to escape, perhaps?

She had been stabbed in the left side, once, a neat, clean hole from a knife that was nowhere in evidence, a knife that must have found her heart. From the dried blood coating her hands, it was clear that she had pressed them to her side, desperately clutching on for the few minutes the blood took to pump from the wound, knowing that her life was bleeding out, that no one was coming to save her. *Jesus.*

Blowing air out of his nostrils, Marilyn stamped his feet to get his circulation going. Rain dribbled down his neck; he pulled the hood of his sweatshirt up, knowing that in a couple of minutes it would be sopping. He needed to get an incident-tent over the body and fast, if he was going to preserve any trace evidence. Where the hell were his crime scene investigators?

DS Workman was at his shoulder. 'Call the CSIs,' he snapped. 'We need them here now.' Turning to Gold, he continued, 'Get that body covered. This rain will annihilate any trace evidence.'

Gold shucked down his jacket sleeves, reached up to rearrange his red beret.

'Now, Gold.'

Gold still didn't move.

Raising his voice so that the Military Police Scenes of Crime Officers, the Corporal jiggling nervously behind Ed Gold could hear him, clear as a bell, Marilyn said, 'You've just told me that you're in charge of this scene. I'll buy front-row tickets to listen to you explain to your Special Investigation Branch chief, Colonel Holden-Hough, why all the evidence was washed away in Noah's flood.'

Gold's mouth tightened into a thin line. 'Corporal Kiddie, get this scene watertight. Now,' he barked. 'Right now.'

Marilyn turned away, shaking his head. He didn't want another murder to investigate – was struggling to make headway with the first – but there was no way that this was a military matter. It was pure coincidence that she had died on military soil. If it wasn't for the fact that the poor woman deserved justice, deserved to have her killer caught, tried and convicted, he would let this clown fuck up the crime scene. But his conscience wouldn't allow it.

'I'd like to see Captain Ben Callan. I've worked with him before on a case. Can you give him a call?'

Gold stood his ground. 'I've been assigned this case.' His gaze narrowed. 'And Callan isn't going to be around much longer.'

Marilyn was momentarily thrown. It had been well over a year since he'd last seen Callan, but he had seemed career military: tough, dedicated, excellent at his job, going places. 'He's leaving the Army?'

'He'll be invalided out shortly.'

'Why?'

Gold hesitated, raised a hand to cover his mouth, as if he realized he'd already said too much. 'He was injured in Afghanistan. Shot in the head. He has . . . ongoing health issues associated with that injury.'

'Detective Inspector.' Sarah's voice behind him. Marilyn swung around.

'DS Workman.'

'I've just heard from the hospital that they're bringing Pauline Lewis out of sedation. It will take half an hour to get there. Shall I go?'

Marilyn didn't respond immediately. He wasn't sure which he'd prefer to do less. Stand here and measure dick size with this Gold prick or spend a few hours in a hospital trying to get salient information out of some old biddy who'd had the shock of her life.

He sighed. 'Yes, you take the hospital. I'll stay here. I have a phone call to make.'

Turning away, he pulled out his iPhone, jammed a thumb on the contact list. Did he have Callan's mobile number? *Thankfully, yes.* He dialled, pacing while he waited.

A distorted voice came down the phone. 'Callan speaking.'

'Captain Callan, it's Detective Inspector Bobby Simmons.'

On the other end of the line, Callan smiled. 'Marilyn, what can I do for you?'

'I could do with your help and quickly, if you can manage it.'

'Manage it?'

'I've been told that you're being invalided out of the Army.'

A pause, Callan's voice when he spoke again flint hard. 'Where did you get that from, Detective Inspector?'

'One of your fellow MPs, here at the crime scene. A Lieutenant Ed Gold. He tells me that you're leaving the Army. I'm sorry. I didn't know you'd been injured in Afghanistan.'

Silence. Marilyn felt it stretch uncomfortably. He had the uncharacteristic urge to fill it, said with false cheer, 'But please don't leave before you come and prise this joker off my crime scene.'

35

Nooria was agitated. She strode into Jessie's office, pulling Sami along by the hand, a skittish energy radiating from her.

'Wendy didn't turn up this morning and Nick is in hospital having a checkup. They need to do more operations, more skin grafts. I'm supposed to be in college. It's my exhibition the day after tomorrow.' Her voice was high and brittle. 'Nick was going to pick Sami up after your session, but he texted me a couple of minutes ago to say that he won't be free for another hour.'

'It's fine, Nooria. Sami can stay here until Major Scott collects him. I have some kids' cartoons on my iPad and Jenny, the department secretary, can keep an eye on him while he's watching. We did that yesterday – it's not a problem.'

Nooria's eyes hung closed for a moment. 'I don't mean to be rude, but I don't feel that these sessions are doing Sami any good.' The words rushed out of her; she wouldn't meet Jessie's gaze. 'I don't want him to see you again after today.'

'He's only had three sessions. It takes time.'

'Nick doesn't want him to continue either.'

She was standing, feet planted wide apart, hands on her hips. Wearing sky-blue combat trousers and a white cotton jerkin, her hair braided and hanging over her left shoulder, she looked fifteen. A beautiful, petulant fifteen-year-old.

Jessie stood her ground. 'Nick . . . Major Scott referred him.' She kept her voice down, wished that Nooria would do the same. Sami was in the corner of her office laying out the farm mat, but Jessie could tell from the tilt of his head that he was listening. She held a finger to her lips, indicated with the other hand for Nooria to step outside the door.

Out in the corridor, Nooria turned to face her again.

'It was a mistake. We made a mistake. The sessions are not doing any good,' she hissed. 'He's getting worse, more withdrawn, more frightened. I can't deal with him at all now.'

'As he starts to revisit the trauma, he will seem more withdrawn and frightened, but it's a process he needs to go through so that he can come out the other side. You need to be patient.'

'I can't take it much longer. Honestly, I can't.' Tears welled in her eyes. 'We're in a living hell at home.' Pulling a tissue from the pocket of her combats, she jammed it to her eyes, blotting the tears. 'I'll take him to our GP, get him referred somewhere else, somewhere that only deals with children.'

'That would be a disaster right now. He trusts me and he's opening up. It's a difficult process but the results *are* positive.' She couldn't afford to lose Sami, let him be taken elsewhere. Not now. Not while she had so many unanswered questions as to what lay behind his trauma, so many doubts, so many

202

concerns. She had a duty to protect him – a moral duty as well as a professional one. 'Is there anything you want to tell me, Nooria? Anything you haven't mentioned so far?'

'What on earth are you talking about?'

Jessie took a breath. 'Scott told me that you had a daughter a few years ago, with an ex-boyfriend. A daughter who died.'

Nooria looked shocked. 'He shouldn't have done that. It's my business, my private business and it's *not* relevant.' She pursed pale lips.

'Every past experience is relevant, especially something that traumatic.'

'What? So I'm the problem now?' The tissue was shredding in her fingers.

'That's not what I'm saying. I'm trying to help.'

'By interrogating me?' she hissed. 'By insinuating that I'm damaging my own child.' The intensity of her fury surprised Jessie.

'I don't mean to interrogate you, but as I said at the beginning, Sami's problems have to be tackled in the context of the family's dynamics.' *The whole family's problems –* she didn't say it. Could sense that she was treading on very thin ice.

Nooria put a hand over her mouth. She looked as if she was about to burst into a flood of tears.

'Sami refers to himself as "the girl",' Jessie said. 'Scott told me that you dressed him in girls' clothes when he was little, let his hair grow long, called him Sami. Why?'

'Sami is his name.'

'Samuel is his name.'

'Sami is the Afghan variant of Samuel. Samuel, Sam, Sammy, Sami. Is there really any difference?'

'You're avoiding the issue. Why? Why don't you want to talk about it?'

'You tell me. You're the psychologist. You seem to have all the answers.' She gave a careless shrug and with that small reaction something hardened in Jessie's chest.

'Unfortunately for Sami I don't have any answers yet,' she snapped. 'And your behaviour isn't helping.'

Stepping forward suddenly, Nooria shoved her index finger right in Jessie's face. Her eyes flashed with fury.

'That's because I'm sick of the bloody Army, sick of you people, sick of the interference in my life. I would never have married Nick if I'd known my life would be taken over like this.'

'Unfortunately, the Army tends to do that.'

'I thought it would help, that he would help.' Her head jerked and her chin dropped to her chest. 'But he didn't, couldn't.'

'What do you mean, Nooria?'

She put a hand over her mouth, holding back a sob. 'You're so naive. You. All of you. You don't understand. You'll never understand anything.'

Jessie laid a hand on her arm, expected her to snatch it away, but she didn't. She just stood there in the middle of the corridor, trembling, a naked expression of torment on her face.

'What don't I understand, Nooria? Explain it to me?'

'Afghanistan. Afghans. You Westerners can never hope to understand the psychology of people out there. You think that you can dictate how they live, how they run their countries, their politics and you have . . . you have no idea how their psychology works.'

'What has this got to do with Sami?'

204

'Nick.' Tears were streaming down her face now. 'It's my fault. It's all my fault.'

Pulling away, she ran off down the corridor.

Sitting cross-legged in front of the farm like a little Buddha, Sami was stroking his hand rhythmically across the pond.

'Waves on the pond,' he muttered. 'Waves on the pond.'

'Hey, Sami.'

He glanced up at Jessie, a quizzical look on his face. His gaze slid past her to the window. It was a stormy morning, heavy grey clouds sitting low over the trees, wind frothing their leaves and branches.

'Why do you want waves on the pond, Sami?'

'It's windy.'

'Yes, it's windy today. Cold and windy.'

His brow furrowed. 'Not sunny?'

Jessie lowered herself down next to him.

'We pretended that it was sunny last time, didn't we, even though it was snowing. How about today we use the weather outside? Make it cold and windy on our farm too.'

He nodded, his eyes bright. 'Windy makes waves.'

Jessie smiled. 'You're right, Sami. Windy does make waves.'

She sensed a rigidity in his posture that hadn't been there a few moments before. A changing roll call of expressions moved across his face, as if reflecting the thoughts careening around inside his skull.

'But it's not dark,' he murmured.

'No, it's not dark. It's morning, so the sun only came up a couple of hours ago, even though it's now hidden by the clouds.'

'Waves,' he muttered again. 'Waves in the dark.' Stretching

out his hand, he pulled his torch close. The tip of his index finger found the switch and slid it on.

'It doesn't need to be dark to make waves, Sami. It only has to be windy.'

Brow wrinkling, he nodded silently. 'Where is the man?'

'The man?'

'The man,' he echoed.

'The farmer? You mean the farmer?'

Sami hadn't shown any interest in the farmer before, so Jessie had left him and his wife at the bottom of the animal box. Pulling them both out, she handed them to him. Holding one in each hand, Sami turned them over and over, studying them. Dropping the farmer's wife back into the box, he bent forward and slid the farmer under the play-mat, positioning him so that he was directly under the pond.

'The man is in the pond.' His voice trembled.

'Why have you put the man in the pond?' Jessie asked softly.

Sami chewed on his lip. 'Windy. Waves on the pond.'

'Yes.' She kept her voice gentle, even. 'It's windy outside and we're pretending that it's windy in our game too, so there are waves on the pond. But why have you put the farmer under the pond, Sami?'

Sami looked up at Jessie, his eyes so wide that his pupils were entirely ringed with white. He looked like a frightened rabbit, as if he might bolt at any sound.

'The man is in the pond. The Shadowman is in the pond.'

The Shadowman.

'The Shadowman? Do you see the Shadowman, Sami?'

Sami gave a rigid nod.

'The Shadowman,' he echoed. He was clasping the torch

206

so tightly that his fingers were bleached of colour. 'Shadowman, whispering, whispering.'

'Who is the Shadowman, Sami?'

He didn't answer her. 'Whispering, whispering,' he muttered under his breath. 'Make Mummy sad.'

Surely the Shadowman is me?

'Is the Shadowman your daddy?'

'Mummy and Daddy fighting. Daddy make Mummy sad.' His face was mottled and pale as marble. A single tear squeezed from his eye and ran down his cheek. 'The torch can find the Shadowman.' Sliding the torch under the play-mat, he muttered: 'The Shadowman is here. Under the covers.'

'Sami.'

Jessie touched his arm gently; he leapt as if she'd branded him with a red-hot iron. He looked up at her, his eyes wild and full of fear.

'Stay in bed,' he muttered. 'The girl is good. The boy is bad. Stay in bed, Mummy says.'

He hugged the torch, chest heaving in great, shuddering sobs.

'The Shadowman is burnt. The torch keeps the boy safe.'

Jessie put her hand out, closed it around his, on the shaft of the torch, wrapped her other arm around his tiny, trembling body.

'I won't let anyone hurt you, Sami. I promise.'

Curling into her, he hid his face in her shoulder.

'Sami is safe with the woman,' he whispered. 'Sami is safe with you.'

36

Raised voices, the scuffle of feet, a man shouting and a child screaming, right outside her office door.

Jessie was counselling a twenty-four-year-old corporal who had lost both legs to the thigh when the lightly armoured Snatch Land Rover – mobile coffins, the troops called them – he had been travelling in had hit IED while on routine patrol in Helmand Province. He was the only survivor, spending two hours trapped under the overturned Land Rover, playing dead, before he was rescued, listening to the young men who he had worked and lived with for the past three years dying slowly and painfully around him.

Her office door slammed open and Sami rocketed into the room. Charging across the carpet, he launched himself at her, wrapping his arms around her legs. Scott strode into the room after him – barely suppressed fury on his face – Jenny, the department secretary, behind him, looking pale and tense. Scott stopped when he saw Corporal Jones.

'Sami!' Jessie heard the metallic tone, the anger lacing his voice.

'Do you mind if we finish the session here, Corporal Jones?' Jessie asked.

The corporal glanced at Major Scott, double-digit ranks above him in the Army hierarchy. 'Of course not.' Reaching for his crutches, he levered himself upright. He made slow progress across the office on his crutches and prosthetics. Scott stood aside, eye burning. When Corporal Jones had crossed the threshold, he slammed the door closed.

Jessie levered Sami away from her. Holding him at arm's length, she knelt in front of him so that she could look him in the eye.

'Your daddy is here, Sami. It's time to go home, but I'll see you again tomorrow.'

'*No!*' Sami cried, his voice thick with anguish. He clutched the torch tight to his chest with one hand, clung to Jessie's hand with the other. 'Don't want to go home. The girl is safe with the woman. Sami is safe with you.'

Scott crossed the room and put his hands on Sami's shoulders.

'Sami, for God's sake, you're being ridiculous.'

Sami screamed. Scrabbling from his father's grip, he shot around to the back of Jessie's desk and buried himself in the space below it.

'Shall I bring him home?' Jessie said. 'I can delay my next appointment.'

'No,' Scott replied through gritted teeth. 'He's coming home with me now.'

He was struggling for control. He leaned down to retrieve Sami, but Sami howled and kicked at his hand. Catching one of Sami's ankles, he hauled him out from under the desk. Sami swung at his dad with his torch, but Scott saw it coming, caught his arm and held it. Sami screamed and

209

struggled wildly, like a furious, trapped animal, as Scott pulled him across the room.

'He's not coming here again, not after this performance. *Nothing* you are doing is helping.'

'I had this conversation with Nooria earlier. There's always a tough period before it gets better.'

'A tough period? Is that what you call *this*? A tough bloody period,' he shouted. 'You are *not* seeing him again.'

He walked towards the door, towing a howling, writhing Sami after him.

'Major Scott, my boss is concerned for Sami's safety. He believes that he might . . . might have suffered abuse.' Her voice shook as she spoke and she hated herself for it. 'He wants to call in the Military Police. I am trying to ensure that doesn't happen, but if you stop me from seeing Sami I will call them in myself.'

Scott spun around. 'Jesus Christ, you bitch. You are supposed to be helping us.'

'I'm trying to help you, but neither of you is telling me the truth.'

'Look at me,' he snarled. '*Just . . .*' His voice faltered; his head dipped and he paused. 'Just look at me. This is the fucking truth. This is all there is.'

Jessie held the gaze of his one good eye across the room. A lump had formed in her throat. She felt that if she spoke another word – one word – the floodgates would open. She swallowed, breathed.

'I'm seeing him tomorrow, ten a.m. He had better be here.'

Scott didn't answer. Holding Sami tight by the hand, he pulled him out of the room, still struggling and sobbing. Pushing the door shut, twisting the key in the lock to ensure her privacy, Jessie leaned back against it and burst into tears.

37

Pulling into Birch Close, Callan parked his Golf halfway across someone's drive, the only place he could find among the civilian and Army police vehicles clogging the tiny cul-de-sac. Jogging down the sandy path that led from the end of the close to the Sandhurst boundary fence, he saw Detective Inspector Bobby Simmons pacing backwards and forwards, a cigarette hanging from his lips, mobile phone clamped to his ear. He looked a wreck. An ageing, alcoholic rocker: grubby black clothes hanging off his skinny frame, deep lines cutting vertically through the skin of his face, black hair too long and those odd, mismatched eyes, one blue, one brown, absorbing everything going on around him, even as he was engaged in conversation with whoever was on the other end of the line.

They had worked together on another case last year. The twenty-one-year-old, six months pregnant wife of a corporal serving in Afghanistan who Callan had cut down from the banister of her stairwell, the body four days old, bloated and yellowing, the smell so visceral that he could taste it on his tongue days later. The couple had lived off base, so Surrey and Sussex Major Crimes had led the investigation; a formality, as it had become clear, very early on, that she had taken her own life. He remembered Marilyn back then, full of preconceptions about Army officers, bristling before they'd exchanged a word, and later, standing at the bottom of the stairs, a green pallor colouring his face, clearly grateful that Callan had volunteered to do the honours with the kitchen knife. They had ended up in the pub together that evening, got drunk, realized that they actually liked each other despite their surface differences.

Two lines of police *Do Not Cross* tape were strung across the pathway, which ran alongside the boundary fence, sectioning off two hundred metres of it.

Beyond Marilyn, Lieutenant Ed Gold was standing stiffly inside the tape, talking to Corporal Kiddie. Neither of them appeared to be doing much. Further inside the tape, a group of uniformed police officers were being given instructions. The unlucky ones would end up combing the pathway, on all fours, searching the sodden earth and puddles for clues. Others would go on the knock, from house to house, trying to find someone who had seen something, anything useful late last night. At least they might get offered a cup of tea. On the other side of the boundary fence, within Sandhurst, a white forensic tent had been erected, obviously covering the body of Wendy Chubb. A couple of figures in white Tyvek overalls hummed around the tent. It had stopped raining at last, but the ground under Callan's feet was boggy and huge puddles, reflecting the stormy grey sky, swamped the path. Search conditions were far from optimal.

Marilyn finished his call and they shook hands.

'Good to see you, Callan.' He laid a hand on Callan's shoulder, a stretch as Callan was a good twenty centimetres taller than he was. 'Look, I'm sorry about what I said earlier, on the phone, about you leaving the Army. I obviously got the wrong end of the stick.'

A shadow crossed Callan's face and Marilyn realized that he'd got closer to the truth than was comfortable. His eyes grazed across the scar on Callan's temple – clearly a bullet wound; he'd seen a few in his time. So Gold had been right about that, at least.

'Don't worry about it,' Callan murmured, unsmiling.

'Right then.' Marilyn rubbed his hands together, raised them, cupped, to his face and blew into them. 'I can't tell you how good it is to see you here. My tolerance for fuckwits appears to be running on empty today. This is clearly a case for our unit and as you can see I've brought in my teams, but your friend Gold isn't having any of it.'

'The victim is definitely civvy?'

'Without a doubt.' Marilyn pulled out his notebook, flicked to the first page. The phone call had been from DS Workman who was at the hospital, had just spent half an hour interviewing Pauline.

'Wendy Chubb, a fifty-six-year-old housekeeper. Lived at 25 Saddleback Close.' He jerked his thumb over his left shoulder. 'Over there – one of the houses with a garden backing on to these woods.' Frowning, he looked up, meeting Callan's searching gaze.

'What is it, Marilyn?'

'There is an Army connection, so I think we're going to need to work together on this one after all.'

'What's the connection?'

'She's a housekeeper for an Army family. The Scotts – Major Scott.'

'Scott?' Callan frowned. 'Are you sure of the name?'

'Yes. I've got it written here, straight from my DS who has interviewed Wendy Chubb's friend. Major Nicholas Scott. We'll need to verify it, but I doubt we'll find that the information is wrong.' Marilyn folded his arms across his chest, tipped back on his heels, looking hard at Callan. 'Do I sense a motive?'

'I don't know, but I'm dealing with another case in which Scott is involved.'

'A murder?'

'Someone died in suspicious circumstances, yes, but it wasn't a murder per se.'

'Cryptic.'

'Not deliberately. That's as far as I've got.'

Marilyn nodded. 'Well let me give you a guided tour of our body and we can take it from there.'

'Give me a minute,' Callan said, moving past Marilyn.

Gold was still standing together with Corporal Kiddie. They were laughing about something. Gold looked over as Callan approached, let the laugh fade to a small, knowing smile. When Callan was comfortably within earshot he turned to Kiddie and said, 'How can you tell when a drug addict is lying?'

Kiddie looked surprised. 'What? A drug addict? I don't know.'

'Come on. A drug addict. How can you tell when he's lying?'

'I don't know. Tell me.'

'He opens his mouth.'

'Jesus, you're at a crime scene,' Callan hissed. 'Have a bit of respect.'

Shoulders shaking, Gold shrugged. 'I wasn't joking about the victim,' he muttered, in a 'fuck you' tone.

'Get out of here now,' Callan snapped.

Gold walked off sniggering and Callan realized that the rise had given him even more satisfaction. *Fuck*. He thought he'd been careful with his epilepsy medication, but obviously not careful enough. He'd clearly have to watch his back.

38

A knock on the door. Jessie didn't move.

'Jessie, it's Gideon. Unlock the door.'

She took a couple of breaths, sucking air deep into her lungs. The lump was still fixed firmly in her throat, making it hard to breathe, even harder to speak.

'I'll try again. It's Gideon, your boss. Unlock the door, now.'

Scrubbing her sleeve fiercely over her face to wipe away the tears, she flapped both hands in front of her cheeks, cooling her skin. She didn't care what she looked like, as long as she didn't look as if she had been crying. She felt way out of her depth with the Sami Scott case and admitting that she had cried would only compound her failure. Untucking her hair from behind her ears so that it hung half over her face, she unlocked the door.

'Dr Duursema.' Her voice cracked, too high, too loud. 'What can I do for you?'

'You can let me in for starters and we can go from there.' He strode past her, sat himself in one of the leather chairs by the window.

'I have another session starting in five minutes,' Jessie said, hovering by the door.

'They can wait. Close the door, then come and sit.'

Jessie did as she was told: closed the door, sat down opposite him, hands gripping the worn leather arms of the chair to stop their obvious trembling. Gideon crossed his legs, folded his hands into his lap. 'I want to tell you a story,' he said. 'No interruptions. Just listen.'

His voice was calm, unaccusing, not what she had expected. She had expected a bollocking. She was full of jittery energy, the electric suit hissing against her skin. But she forced herself to sit and meet his gaze, nod, go through the motions of being professional, in control. The charade.

'Before I joined the Defence Psychology Service I worked in West London – Fulham, to be precise. When people hear the word Fulham, they think of two-million-pound houses, banker families who couldn't quite afford Chelsea or Kensington. But actually it's a surprisingly mixed area, huge swathes of council estates, very deprived in parts.' He stroked a hand through his beard. 'I spent day after day dealing with the scum of society, rescuing children from drug-addicted parents, from conditions so squalid you wouldn't let a pig or goat live like that. So when the Welches were referred to me for assessment after their GP became concerned at injuries their toddler daughter had suffered, I was thrilled. The dad was a lawyer with one of the big London firms. He'd studied law at Oxford – he was in his final year when I was in my first, not that I ever met him there. The little girl's mum was a housewife, a beautiful blonde woman, perfect mum, baked cakes, kept a tidy house, dressed the child in pretty outfits and walked her to

217

nursery, entertained other City folk. It was such a pleasure to have those parents after the scum I'd been dealing with. I was enchanted with them.'

'What happened?' Jessie asked.

'The mum drowned the little girl in a bath full of freezing cold water one evening. The father was at work, but he'd been on the phone to her the whole time. One of his colleagues had come into his office, caught him telling his wife to 'hold the little cow under, teach her a lesson'. I'm not sure that they meant to drown her. I think it was a punishment that went too far. The mother called an ambulance, said she'd left her daughter in the bath to answer the phone and had found her floating, unconscious, when she got back. The little girl never regained consciousness. She died the next day, a week before her third birthday.'

'Were they convicted of murder?'

Gideon rolled his eyes. 'Of course not. Just like Baby P's mother and her boyfriend, they were convicted of "causing or allowing her death", that weird, nondescript category of crime the law has conjured up for parents who abuse and kill their children, that results in them being sentenced to seven or eight years, out in three or four for good behaviour. It was a travesty. They'll have been out for a good ten years now, enjoying their lives, while that little girl rots.' His expression was neutral, hadn't changed with the telling, but Jessie was aware of the exaggerated rise and fall of his chest. 'That's what I found so hard to tell the trial afterwards. I *had* seen the child's bruises. I had noticed the weight loss. But abuse – torture, it was, to give it its proper name – I couldn't bring myself to believe it. The parents were too nice, too middle class, too *normal*. They had made her eat salt and chilli powder, bound her arms and legs for hours to cut off the circulation, locked her in the under-stairs cupboard in the dark all night. All the horrific details came out in the trial – and there I was, trying to defend my position. A position that, looking back, was completely indefensible.' His eyes hung closed for a moment. 'But at the time it *hadn't* been obvious. They always had a plausible explanation for her injuries and though I knew it didn't quite add up, I wasn't brave enough to challenge them because they didn't fit my profile of abusive parents. They could string a sentence together. They were friends with doctors and bankers. Their daughter went to one of the most expensive private nurseries in Fulham. I was young, like you, reasonably new to the game and I didn't want to lose credibility by causing a big fuss over nothing.' He gave a heavy sigh. 'It was my fault that the poor little girl lived like she did and died like she did, and it's something I've had to live with every day of my life since. My own personal ghost.' He tapped his right hand on his left shoulder. 'Sitting right here. Not one day has gone by since that little girl died that I don't think of her, don't see her face, don't curse myself for being so naive.' He sat forward, elbows on his knees, steepling his fingers. 'You have to give the child the benefit of the doubt, Jessie. The *child*. Not the parents. Because if you are wrong about abuse, then the parents will hate you, the family will get monitored too closely by social services for a couple of years, the parents will argue and blame each other and they might even break up and that's all shit. But if you're right and you do nothing, the consequences will be far, far worse.'

He stood up.

'Forty-eight hours, Jessie. That's it. After that I call Colonel Holden-Hough, hand the Scotts over to the Special Investigation Branch.'

'What do you think I should do in those forty-eight hours?'

He shrugged. 'I don't know, Jessie. But whatever you do, make it count.'

39

She used to take Jamie for walks on Wimbledon Common when he was feeling frustrated, confused, schoolwork spinning around in his brain, getting nowhere. Wrap him up and take him out – whatever the weather – to brush off the cobwebs with fresh air, climb trees, fish for frogs' spawn in the ponds, make a camp in the trees, pull wet bark off fallen logs to find woodlice and tiny red spiders. For as long as she could remember, nature had been escape, space for Jamie's brain, and hers, to work themselves out.

Leaving Bradley Court, she drove fast up to Farley Heath, right in the centre of the Surrey Hills, and parked her Mini at the side of the road, shoved her mobile in her coat pocket – though she wasn't sure she'd answer it if anyone called – pulled on a woollen hat and set off through the trees. The forest closed around her as she walked, shutting out the grey sky, dampening the wind, cocooning her in semi-darkness, the smell of leaf mulch, moss and pine needles filling her nostrils. She took a left and then a right, found a narrow track that snaked through the trees and followed it, walking from memory; the last time she had been here, a couple of weeks before Christmas – when she'd been wrestling with guilt about not spending the holiday with her mother – the ground had been frosted white.

In the denseness of the trees everything looked and felt the same and there was something comforting about that: the unchallenging uniformity. She strode on without hesitation, making no sound on the dirt path, feeling as if she could be the only person left alive in the world, and comfortable with that thought.

After twenty minutes of fast walking, she reached the edge of the forest, where the trees opened out and the land fell away from her towards Jelley's Copse. Tiny vehicles inched along the country lanes below her, houses looked shoebox-sized, cows and sheep miniature plastic replicas.

A toy land – Sami's farm.

Finding a fallen tree, at the edge of the wood, she sat down. *Sami.*

Looking at the toy land below her, she pictured his face, the abject terror written on it when his father had come to take him home. *I'm safe with you. Sami is safe with you.*

Forty-eight hours.

Her only hope now was that past behaviour was a good indicator of future behaviour. Skeletons in cupboards, haunting the now. What skeletons did Scott and Nooria have?

Forty-eight hours. It would be gone in the blink of an eye.

Pushing herself up from the log, she turned and retraced her steps through the forest to her car and reality.

Just look at me. This is the truth. This is all there is.

Was it?

She had forty-eight hours to find out.

222

40

A blonde woman was jogging down the stairs. She pushed through the turnstile, into the fitness centre foyer. Her body, encased in tight black Lycra trousers that finished mid-calf and a lime-green racer-backed Lycra vest, was lean and muscled, tanned a rich, nut brown.

'Jacqui,' the woman behind the reception desk called out. 'This lady wants to speak with you.'

Jacqui spun around on one toned leg like a ballerina, eyes finding Jessie's.

'I've got a five-minute break. I need a blast of fresh air before my next class. If you're looking for some personal training, speak to Marion at the desk. They've got my diary. They can book you in for an introductory.'

She made to move past Jessie, reaching for the door handle. She would once have been a very beautiful woman – still was, but for the expression on her face. Her mouth turned down at the corners and a hard light shone in her pale blue eyes. Her blonde hair was scraped back into a tight ponytail, half a centimetre of mouse-coloured roots showing.

'Mrs Scott, my name is Dr Jessie Flynn. I'm an Army psychologist. I want to talk to you about Nick Scott.'

Jacqui stopped, her hand on the door handle. A shadow crossed her face.

'We're not married any more.'

'I know.'

'So what do you want with me?' she snapped.

'Did you hear that he's been injured in Afghanistan?'

Her body remained rigidly facing the door, but her head swivelled. She met Jessie's gaze and her free hand went to her ear. Jessie watched her formulating the lie.

'So you have heard,' Jessie interrupted. 'Who told you?'

Jacqui sighed. 'Jesus, are you a psychologist or a bloody mind reader?'

Jessie gave a brief smile. 'A bit of both, maybe. Who told you?'

Jacqui's hand fell from the door, both hands found her hips and she sighed again, heavily. 'A friend, OK. One of my friends told me. I have a few, though most of the bitches dropped me like a hot brick once he left.'

'Can we talk? Please. I'll brave the rain.'

Hands on her hips, she took a moment to answer. 'Fine,' she muttered wearily. 'I hope you don't mind the smell of smoke, because I'm having a cigarette whether you do or not.'

Pushing through the door from the foyer, they jogged across the grass, through the sheeting rain, to a group of white painted metal tables and chairs set on a small patio area under a dirty white free-standing awning with the name of the health club, 'Start Fitness', printed in navy-blue swirly writing across it. They sat at a table in the middle, the tables and chairs closer to the edge soaking wet. Pulling a packet of Silk Cut and a lighter from her handbag, Jacqui lit a cigarette and took a few long drags. The hand holding the cigarette shook.

'So, Nicholas.' Both her voice and her gaze were hard. 'What do you want to know?'

'I'm working with his son, Sami. He's having some psychological problems, probably related to seeing his father badly burnt.' Jessie was struggling to make the explanation sound convincing. The swerve to suspicion about child abuse had knocked her off kilter – made this visit necessary, but unorthodox – a blunt attempt to find out what the hell was going on in that family without calling in the Redcaps, blowing their lives apart irreparably, whether they were innocent or guilty. She would be hung, drawn and quartered if Scott ever found out that she had tracked his ex-wife down and interviewed her. 'I want to . . . to understand him . . . Scott. Them. To understand them.'

Jacqui threw her head back and gave a bitter laugh. 'What? And you come to me?'

'You were married to him for twelve years.'

'Twelve long years, two daughters, and then I get tossed out like a bag of trash, for that woman.' She laughed again, acerbically. 'I assume that he told you he left me? For her?'

'Nooria. Yes.'

Jacqui nodded. 'That woman.' Then she added, 'That Paki bitch,' almost, but not quite, under her breath. She took a drag of her cigarette, blew the smoke through pursed lips. 'Are your mum and dad together, Miss, sorry, *Dr* Flynn?'

'Jessie. Please call me Jessie, and, no, they're not together.'

Jacqui sneered nastily. 'Don't tell me, your father ran off with someone ten years younger?'

'Twenty,' Jessie said plainly. And in that one word, she felt a crack in the tough carapace Jacqui had cocooned herself in, a slight breaking down of the barrier between them.

'Did he have any kids with her?'

Jessie shook her head. 'I think they tried, but it didn't happen.'

Jacqui nodded, but didn't say anything. Tilting her head back, she blew another cloud of smoke up into the canopy above them.

'That was the bit that killed me . . . fucking killed me,' she said, after a moment. 'That he had a child with her. I could have taken the leaving – humiliating as it was – but I could have taken it.' Her nails, polished shell pink, drummed on the tabletop, an attempt, Jessie thought, to hide the stress she was feeling. Stress that the cigarette couldn't quite calm. 'But the fact that he then merrily created another family for himself, like my daughters were . . . like *our* two daughters were disposable – it made me furious. So angry. So . . . fucking *angry*.' She broke off, took another fierce drag of her cigarette. 'I know I shouldn't say this to you, but I hope that little boy is fucked up. And I mean *fucked up*. I wish nothing but ill on him and that stupid little Paki bitch my Nick married.' Anger pulsed off her like a living thing. She met Jessie's gaze again, defiantly. 'I don't care what you think of me. I don't fucking care.'

'Are you still in touch with Scott?'

'Not bloody likely,' she hissed.

'What about your daughters?'

'He's seen them five times in the six years since he left us. Five times and he lives three miles down the road.'

'Have your daughters ever met Sami?'

'Over my dead bloody body.'

'And you?'

She shrugged. 'I've seen him a few times.' Her eyes rose to the canopy again, following another wispy trail of smoke. 'I saw him a couple of times in Aldershot, with that fat, loud woman – the housekeeper.'

'Wendy.'

Jacqui hunched her shoulders again. 'Whatever.'

'How did you feel when he left?'

'How do you think I felt?' she snapped. 'Ask your mum if you're unsure how it fucking feels when your husband runs off with some teenage whore.'

Sucking another draught of smoke deep into her lungs, she closed her eyes, savouring the sensation. 'That's the problem with men in general and it's magnified a thousand times in the Army. It's all about posturing, isn't it? Macho shit. Who's got the biggest dick and who can stick that dick in the youngest . . .' She paused. 'Youngest . . . see you next Tuesday.'

Jessie took a moment. *See you next* . . . C U N . . . She got it finally, realized Jacqui had been watching her compute, a tiny smile on her face.

'I'm a bit slow,' Jessie said.

'Better brought up than me.' Jacqui crushed the cigarette out on the metal stem of the umbrella, had a quick glance around her before she tossed the butt under the table. 'He was always a handsome bastard. That's what did it for me. His looks. His looks and his self-confidence – he had that in spades. Too much, perhaps.' She reached for the packet of Silk Cut and lighter, tucked the lighter back inside the packet. 'I should have finished it myself. Should have had the guts. But by then I was kind of, *in it*, you know? Right

227

in it. It's a bit like being in prison, being an Army wife. You get used to having every part of your life regimented for you. No need to think, to make your own friends, to organize a social life. It's all there on a plate.'

'Why?'

Jacqui's brow furrowed. 'Why what?'

'Why should you have ended it?'

Jacqui looked down at her hands, laid flat on the tabletop. Her nail polish, catching what little light there was, looked like ten pink pearls against the drab white tabletop.

'Because he had two affairs before Nooria,' she murmured.

A brief smile crossed her face at the look of surprise on Jessie's.

'You couldn't read his mind, then.' Her shoulders shook as she chuckled. 'One of them was the wife of a private in his platoon – Nick was a captain, the poor sod's platoon commander. She was only seventeen, for Christ's sake.'

'Did the Army know?'

'The husband found out, but it was all hushed up. Poor kid was nineteen, married his childhood sweetheart and found her spreading her legs for his boss. There wasn't much he could do about it. And the Army brass don't care about that kind of thing. Integrity is supposed to matter, but they're all men at the end of the day, aren't they?' Scooping up her handbag, she tucked the cigarettes in a side pocket and zipped it up. 'I suppose I should thank my lucky stars that he didn't run off with one of my daughters' friends.' She didn't smile when she said it. 'Bit young back then, even for Nick. But now . . .'

Ten and twelve.

'He thinks I hate him,' she murmured.

'Do you?'

'Love and hate.' She sighed. 'Aren't they two sides of the same coin?' Looking across the tables under the canopy to the sheet of rain beyond them, she fiddled with the catch on her handbag. 'Is he badly injured?'

Jessie nodded. 'Yes, I'm afraid he is.'

'I tried to see him. I went to the hospital, but they wouldn't let me in because we're not related any more. I'm nothing in his life now. A nobody.' She paused, looked as if she was about to continue, but changed her mind.

'So you went to the house,' Jessie said quietly.

'You are a mind reader.'

'When?'

She shrugged, evasively. 'A few times.'

'When? When was the last time?'

A heavy sigh. 'A couple of evenings ago. I was on my way back from work. Thought I'd pass by on the off chance.'

'Did you see him?'

She shook her head. 'I saw that silly fat housekeeper at the kitchen window. And the boy . . . Sami . . . peeping out from upstairs. The curtains are always drawn. And well . . . I didn't want to be seen there, did I? Not by *her* or the housekeeper.' Her eyes locked with Jessie's. 'Tell me what happened to him. Please.'

'It was a petrol bomb attack. He was a passenger in a car. He's burnt down the left side of his face, missing his left eye. His arm – his left hand and arm – were also badly burnt.'

'He'll have to leave the Army then.' Her voice was laced with sadness. 'They only look after their own so long as their own can deliver.'

'Yes, he will.'

For a moment, she looked as if she might cry. Lifting a

hand she wiped the back of it across her eyes. Then the shutter fell back over her face, and the hard, brittle cheer came on to it, as if Jessie was watching two halves of different plays, a tragedy and a comedy.

'What goes around comes around,' she said. Pulling a mint spray from her pocket, she held it to her open mouth and depressed the top a couple of times, shooting a minty haze on to her tongue. 'The clients would be horrified if they knew I smoked. All about the image, like most things these days. All about the image.' She pushed the chair back and stood. 'I've another class starting now. Got to go.' She hooked her handbag on to her shoulder and then paused. 'Oh, one thing I forgot to mention – Nick's conviction.'

'Conviction?'

'Yes. He has a criminal conviction. Is it not in his Army file?'

Jessie shook her head. 'No.' She frowned. 'What was it for?'

Jacqui smirked. 'The mind reader's at a loss.'

'Come on, Jacqui, don't play games.'

'Oh fuck . . .' Jacqui's eye had caught the clock on the wall above the entrance. 'Fuck, *fuck*, *FUCK*.' Spinning around, she shoved through the tables.

'*Jacqui*,' Jessie shouted, but Jacqui didn't turn.

'My class started five minutes ago,' she yelled back over her shoulder. 'They'll all be waiting. I'll be strung up if management find out. I can't afford to lose this job.'

Jessie watched her make the short dash through the rain and slam through the door into the foyer, the dark glass swinging closed behind her.

230

41

Bearwood School was a huge day and boarding school set in magnificent grounds in the heart of the Surrey Hills, close to Wokingham.

Jessie couldn't imagine Jacqui fitting in here, even before Scott's affair, could see why she had died a social death when her husband had seduced the Reception class teaching assistant. The facade, the facilities, said bankers, lawyers, the odd self-made entrepreneur, middle- and upper-class English with their stiff upper lips, a few American oil billionaires and Russian oligarchs thrown in for good measure; the Army families who could afford to send their children here, even with the benefit of service educational allowances, only higher ranking officers.

It reminded her of Highclere Castle, the stately home used in the filming of *Downton Abbey*, resplendent with turrets and gables, gargoyles grimacing down from corners, surrounded by sweeping parkland, woods and a lake. Above the front door was a stained glass window, depicting an old man sailing in a tiny boat on a rough sea, his white sail bearing the red George Cross, a sea serpent rising from the water underneath the boat. The experience at a school like this, Jessie imagined, would be entirely binary for both pupils and parents: love it or hate it, fit in or be a square peg in a gold-plated round hole.

After meeting Jacqui, she had gone back to Bradley Court and telephoned the school pretending to be an interested parent and booked herself an after-school appointment with the Reception class teacher, Miss Flora Appleby. Before she left the office, she had scoured the website for photographs and found a plump woman in her mid-thirties, with a mass of curly brown hair that did nothing to slim her face. But her expression was open and friendly, her body language, standing on the edge of a running track cheering on her pupils, encouraging and supportive. From the photograph, at least, she seemed the perfect type to teach a class of four-year-olds, who in most other countries would still be playing in sandpits and climbing trees. Underneath the photograph, a caption stated that Miss Appleby had taught the Reception class for the past nine years, which meant that she would have been here at the same time as Nooria.

Parking her Mini in the visitor's car park at the back of the school, Jessie climbed out, straightening out the creases from her black Marks and Spencer's trouser suit, regretting now that she had worn it. She was pretty sure, having seen the school, that most pupils' mothers would spend their days lunching, shopping in designer boutiques and playing tennis, and that any suit they owned would be a pale blue Chanel number reserved purely for ladies day at Ascot.

She was buzzed in the great oak front door and met in

the hallway by an efficient-looking grey-haired woman in a suit not unlike Jessie's own.

'Mrs Flynn, I presume?'

'Yes.' Jessie held out her hand.

'And your husband . . .?'

'Unfortunately, he wasn't able to get away from work in time. We looked around at open day,' she lied, hoping the woman wouldn't question her on exactly when that was, 'and loved the school, but I wanted to meet the Reception teacher, to see who would be teaching, uh, Sarah, teaching Sarah if she came here.' Her smile had a nervous tilt to it. 'I really was just hoping for a very informal chat.'

Now, standing in the panelled reception, the great oak staircase winding three floors above her, light cutting through the huge stained glass window over the door, casting multi-coloured patterns on her drab, black suit, she doubted her sense at having come. What was she hoping to gain from the visit anyway? A window into Nooria's mind from someone who had worked with her five years ago? Now she was here, it felt a ridiculous stretch, a flight of fantasy.

'Mrs Flynn.' The receptionist interrupted her thoughts. 'Miss Appleby is waiting for you in the library. Please, come this way.'

Miss Appleby looked very similar to her photograph, though she had lost a little weight since it had been taken last summer. She was wearing a black dress, black cardigan and black woollen tights, and her hair was pulled back into a high ponytail, which accentuated her English rose colouring and her huge blue eyes, and minimized the fact that she would still be medically termed obese.

233

She was sitting on one of two cream linen sofas set opposite each other by the window. A low frosted-glass coffee table between them was laid with a silver tray bearing a white china teapot, a milk jug, two matching teacups and a plate of biscuits. Next to the tray was a centimetre-thick, glossy, full-colour brochure with an aerial shot of Bearwood School on the front. Jessie's heart sank even further when she saw the arrangement.

Miss Appleby stood and held out her hand. 'Mrs Flynn, lovely to meet you. Please come and sit down.'

Jessie shook her hand and sat opposite.

'Tea?' Miss Appleby asked.

'Please.'

'Milk? Sugar?'

'Milk, no sugar, thank you.'

She poured Jessie tea, and then reached for the brochure. 'This is our updated brochure, new for 2016.'

Jessie held up her hands. 'Miss Appleby. Before you begin, I have a confession to make.'

'A confession?' Her brow wrinkled. 'What on earth do you mean?' Her language, her diction, would have been at home on a woman decades older – the product of working in such a rarefied atmosphere for an entire career, Jessie thought.

'I wasn't completely honest when I set up this meeting with you.'

Laying the brochure back on the table, she pursed her lips. 'Oh, well . . . I, uh, I am very busy.'

'Please give me a minute to explain.' Jessie pulled out her Army identification and passed it across the table. 'I'm a clinical psychologist.'

'A psychologist?'

234

'Yes, with the Army.'

Miss Appleby raised a hand to her mouth. 'What on earth do you want with me?'

'I'm counselling a child, a little boy called Sami Scott. His mother is Nooria Scott. His father is Major Nicholas Scott. You worked with Nooria for a few years.'

Miss Appleby's pale blue eyes widened. 'Nooria?'

Jessie gave a silent nod, letting her work through her surprise.

'Yes, but she left four and a half years ago.' Raising her gaze to the ceiling, her lips moved as she mentally calculated. 'In the middle of the summer term – May 2011. She was seven months pregnant with Scott's child when she left.'

'I know.'

'So . . . what . . .?' Folding her hands into her lap, Miss Appleby let the words hang in the air.

'Do you feel you know . . . knew her?' Jessie asked.

'Well I don't keep in touch with Nooria much, just Christmas cards, but I know her . . . knew her . . . pretty well back then, I suppose.' She paused, fingertips picking at a loose thread on her skirt. 'Better than anyone else, at least. She doesn't have any brothers or sisters, or a father, and she fell out with her mother when she was sixteen.' She hunched her shoulders. 'She seemed so alone. I think that's probably why she confided in me.'

'What was she like when she worked here? Was she good at her job?'

Miss Appleby nodded. 'She was clever and hardworking. She could have done much better than be a teaching assistant, could have been a teacher, but I think she never had the opportunity. She stayed at school until the end of her

A-levels, working to support herself, but then I think she couldn't do it any more, so she got the job here as teaching assistant. She had it tough before she came here.'

'Was she good with the kids?'

'They all loved her.' She smiled as a memory rose. 'Especially the boys. She was so beautiful, so nice and kind, the boys loved her. Even though they were only four and five, they were drawn to her. It made me laugh. Men, they're born not made.'

Jessie used the mention of men to move on to the subject of Nooria's boyfriend.

'Did Nooria have a boyfriend when she was here?'

Miss Appleby frowned; she took a moment to reply. 'On and off. Her boyfriend wasn't around much. She said that he worked abroad.'

'Was he English? British?'

Miss Appleby reached for her tea and a biscuit, dunked the biscuit and took a bite. 'No,' she said, her mouth half-full. 'He was from the Middle East.'

'The Middle East?' Jessie tried to hide her surprise. It hadn't occurred to her, for some reason, that Nooria's boyfriend – the father of her first child – would be Middle Eastern. She had pictured some spotty-faced British teenager who had turned on his heels and run at the first sign of pregnancy. 'Where was he from?'

Miss Appleby hesitated. 'I know this sounds a bit ridiculous coming from a teacher, but all I remember is that it was a country that was in conflict, because Nooria kept talking about him changing sides.'

'Iraq?'

'Maybe.' She shrugged. 'I'm sorry, I have a terrible memory for names, which is bit of a challenge in my job, to say the least.' She wrinkled her nose, cast her gaze to the ceiling.

Tyres crunched on gravel outside the window. Jessie glanced sideways, saw a sleek black Bentley gliding past, a peaked-capped chauffeur in the driver's seat. She looked back to Miss Appleby; her expression had changed, a light switched on. 'No, no, I remember now,' she said. 'Of course, how stupid of me. Afghanistan, he was from Afghanistan.'

'Afghanistan?' Jessie asked. 'Are you sure?'

'Yes. Quite sure now . . . now that I remember.'

'Did you meet him?' Jessie asked.

Miss Appleby nodded.

'What was he like?'

'I only saw him a couple of times from a distance, when he came to collect her from school. He was good looking, I suppose, if a bit serious, severe even. It's hard to tell with darker-skinned people, but he looked a good few years older than Nooria. Mid-thirties maybe. She was only eighteen when she started here – she'd just finished school herself. She was already seeing him, had been for some time.'

'Did she talk about him much?'

'No. That was the funny thing. She never called him her boyfriend and she didn't even see him that often. He lived in Afghanistan most of the time, so she only saw him when he was over here.'

'So what was in it for her?'

Miss Appleby hunched her shoulders. 'To be honest, I have no idea. But I think . . . I think that she was frightened of him, that she didn't have the guts to break it off.'

'Do you remember what he was called?'

'Nightmare,' Miss Appleby said, popping the rest of the damp biscuit into her mouth.

'*What?*' Jessie waited, jiggling her foot impatiently, while Miss Appleby chewed and swallowed, washed the biscuit down with a sip of tea, patted her mouth with the white linen napkin.

'I can't remember how to pronounce his name, but Nooria said that it meant "nightmare" in Dari.' Folding the napkin, she laid it carefully on the table. 'She also said that he lived up to his name. I remember that she laughed when she said it, but it was hollow, you know, one of those laughs that don't reach the eyes.'

'What about her affair with Scott?'

'Oh, God, that was a huge scandal. I still can't believe that Nooria did that. I was so surprised.'

Jessie sat forward. 'Why? Why were you so surprised?'

Miss Appleby's brow wrinkled. 'Because lots of the dads flirted with her, at sports day and parents evening, but she never showed any interest, always kept her distance, was respectful of their wives. She knew that they all fancied her – who wouldn't – but she was always professional.'

'And with Major Scott?'

'It was completely different with him. It was as if she had decided that he was the one, virtually from the first time that she met him. She knew that he was married, but she didn't seem to care. She wanted him.'

'And she got him.'

She pulled a face. 'For better or worse.'

'You didn't like him?'

'Well, I . . . God, I don't want to sound bitchy, but no, not really. He was incredibly handsome, but also just as incredibly arrogant. A real alpha male type.' A man who would never look twice at Miss Appleby. 'You've met him, I suppose?' she continued.

Jessie nodded. She thought of the man in her office this morning, the fury in his one good eye, the wet burgundy cavity of the other, the skin of his face like boiled treacle. There was no point opening up that Pandora's Box here.

'Yes, he is very good looking.'

'You must be surrounded by them in the Army, aren't you? Hot alpha males.'

Jessie smiled, thought fleetingly, for some reason, of Callan, and then immediately after of the man she had . . . fucked – there was no other word for it – in the pub car park two nights ago, another in a long line of men whose faces and names she could no longer remember. Sex without commitment. Satisfaction without guilt. *You were with your boyfriend. It's your fault that he died.*

She dipped her head, blushing with the memories. 'It's one of the few perks of the job.' Her gaze caught the face of her watch; she'd taken up enough of Miss Appleby's time. 'I just have one more question. Did Nooria ever talk to you about the death of her first baby, the little girl?'

Miss Appleby looked shocked. 'Death?'

The door opened suddenly and a teenage girl, school skirt hitched up micro short, marched into the room clutching a stack of books. She stopped short when she saw them.

'Sorry, Miss Appleby.'

'Two minutes, Tilly, then you can have your library back.' The door closed. Miss Appleby turned back to Jessie. 'Tilly's the Year 9 library monitor. Now, where were we? Oh yes.' She tilted forward, lowering her voice. 'No, the little girl didn't die.'

'But that's what—' Jessie broke off.

'What Nooria told you?

239

'No. Scott. It's what he told me.'

Miss Appleby wrinkled her nose. 'He probably doesn't even know.'

'So what happened to the baby?'

The clanging of a bell. Miss Appleby looked flustered. She gathered up the school brochure from the table, grabbed her handbag from the floor beside her. 'That's the boarders' dinner bell. I'm a house mistress as well as the Reception class teacher. I'm sorry, I have to go.'

Jessie put a hand on her arm. 'What happened to the baby, Miss Appleby?'

'She . . . she was born severely disabled,' she replied quietly. '*Severely* disabled, both physically and mentally. Nooria tried to keep her, she really tried, but she was on her own and only seventeen when the baby was born. She couldn't cope.'

'What about her boyfriend? The baby's father?'

'She said that he didn't care about the baby at all.' Miss Appleby paused, glanced over to the door, as if she wanted to run straight through it.

'Miss Appleby.'

'He told her that they should drown it. "That's what we'd do in my country," he said.'

'Where is the baby now?'

'Girl. She'd be a girl now . . . nine or ten. I don't know to be honest, but I assume she's in the same home as before.'

'Do you have the name by any chance?'

'No, sorry, I don't. Nooria never told me. All she said was that it was in a town on the south coast somewhere. It wouldn't be too far from here, because she used to drive there and back every Sunday to see her daughter.' She stood. 'I'm sorry, but I really do have to go now.'

Jessie stood and held out her hand. 'Thank you for seeing me. You've been very helpful.'

Miss Appleby gave a sad smile. 'I won't tell the dragon in reception that you lied.'

'Not until I'm safely off the premises anyway.'

They walked together to the door.

'Actually . . .' Miss Appleby laid a hand on Jessie's arm, '. . . I do remember Nooria complaining about the journey. She always said that she got stuck behind old people out for their Sunday drive because it was a single-track road, touristy and impossible to pass. I hate it, she used to say.'

'Right,' Jessie said.

'The hate . . .' A pause. Miss Appleby was looking hard at her. 'Instead of eight.'

Jessie shook her head. 'Sorry, I still don't get what you mean.'

'Eight. The road. It was the A-something-something-eight. Or something-eight-something. There was an eight in it, at least. Eight – hate.'

Jessie nodded. 'Oh, OK. I get it now.' She smiled. 'I'm a bit slow sometimes. So do you remember any of the other numbers?'

Miss Appleby looked apologetic. 'Sorry, no. It was so long ago. I'm surprised I even remembered that.' She smiled. 'Funny the kinds of things that stick in your mind.'

42

Jessie coasted to a stop outside the pub and cut her engine. Callan was already there – his red Golf parked on the other side of the narrow country lane, two wheels on the muddy grass verge. The night was silent and calm, the only noise the faint murmur of voices from inside the pub. Above her, dark clouds brushed across a sliver of moon, only a few stars tonight, sparsely dotted in a sea of jet black.

The pub was a small whitewashed country inn, with a red front door and red painted window frames. Baskets of red and white flowers hung from the eaves, and a low flintstone wall hemmed in a tiny garden. Though Jessie was only five foot six, the top of her head brushed against the top of the doorframe as she stepped through it. Callan must have had to shuffle through the door on his knees.

Inside, she was faced with a long wooden bar barely two arm's lengths away, studded with taps bearing the names of local beers and bitters: Baldy, Surrey Hills Ranmore Ale, Old Speckled Hen, Sussex Best Bitter. A bench upholstered in worn burgundy velvet ran the length of the pub on the nearside wall, either side of the door, and tables were pushed up against it. The cream-painted walls were hanging with horse brasses and grainy black-and-white farm photographs from decades ago, the farmers working with horse-drawn ploughs. It was warm and cosy, the perfect winter pub.

Callan was sitting in the corner at a table for two close to the log fire. He was wearing jeans and a blue-and-white checked shirt, a pint of bitter in his hand, relaxed, off duty. Looking at him now, Jessie remembered the warmth of his lips on her cheek and felt colour infuse her face.

'I'll just get a drink, Callan,' she called over to him. 'Do you want another?'

'Come and sit down, I'll get one for you.' He walked over, ducking so that he didn't bang his head on the gnarled wooden beams holding up the ceiling. 'What would you like?'

'Sauvignon please.'

He smiled, an easy, familiar smile. 'I should have known.'

'All hail the resident wino.'

She slid on to the bench at the table while he bought her glass of wine. Setting it in front of her, he sat down opposite, stretching his long legs out beside the table to get comfortable.

'Perhaps you should call me Ben as we're having dinner together, Jessie. Shouting Callan across the pub makes it sound as if we're work colleagues.'

She raised an eyebrow. 'We are work colleagues.'

'It's evening, after work hours, so how about we relax the formalities.' His mouth tilted in a quizzical smile.

'I thought you Redcaps never stopped working,' she said coolly, holding his gaze, even though her stomach was constricting with nerves. She hadn't had a relationship for fifteen years, since Adam, and she'd only been a girl back

243

then. Sitting here, having dinner with a man, particularly one as attractive as him, was uncharted territory. Callan kept things strictly professional; Ben ventured into personal territory. Territory that she didn't feel equipped to handle.

'For this one night only then, Ben,' she murmured, shifting sideways, putting a few more centimetres between them.

'Great.' He took a swig of bitter. 'How was your day?'

She was momentarily thrown. 'My day?'

'Yes. Your day.'

'Well, it was, uh . . .' she tailed off with a shrug.

'It's called making conversation, Jessie. It's what normal people do. Particularly when they're having dinner together in a romantic country pub.' She caught the slight lift at the corners of his mouth.

'Sadly, I don't think either of us can be classed as normal.'

'We can try.'

She took a sip of Sauvignon. It was cold and light and she savoured the taste on her tongue.

'My day was . . . disturbing. But asking me about my day will lead straight on to why I wanted to see you.'

He sighed, held up both hands. 'I give up. Why did you want to see me?'

'I need your help.' Unlacing her fingers from the glass, she found the stem, twisted it in the tips of her fingers, looking down at the little whirl she had made in the pale gold liquid. 'I need your help with the little boy I'm working with, Sami Scott. He's Major Scott's son.' She looked up. 'You know Scott, don't you?'

'I've heard of him, yes.'

She gave him a rundown on her sessions with Sami: his utter terror at being burnt; the Shadowman; the girl; her suspicions that there was more than Scott's injuries to blame for Sami's condition; the criminal conviction his ex-wife had mentioned; Nooria's ex-boyfriend and the little girl who Jessie thought had died, but who had been born severely disabled and was alive, in a home somewhere near the south coast.

'I'm worried that he might be being abused.'

Callan sat forward. 'Why?'

'Because who is the Shadowman?'

'His father.'

'Perhaps. That's certainly what both his parents say.'

'You don't agree?

'I have a feeling that there's more going on, that what the parents tell me doesn't quite add up.'

'Scott was severely burnt in Afghanistan. Put yourself in the little boy's position – imagine if that was your father. You see him leaving and he's fine. Six months later, he's in hospital, burnt beyond recognition. It's a classic driver for post-traumatic stress disorder.'

A shadow crossed her face. 'I put myself in Sami's position, try to get inside his head, every time I see him.'

'But you don't buy it,' Callan murmured.

'I don't know what I buy. I'm stuck. The parents are stonewalling me. We had a horrible session today. Sami is terrified. Terrified of being burnt, terrified of the Shadowman. And *terrified* of going home. He was clinging to me and sobbing, just sobbing.' She swallowed, feeling tears well in her own eyes, his desperation as he clung to her raw in her mind. 'Sobbing and screaming that he's safe with me. I wanted to bundle him up and run out with him, hide him somewhere, protect him.'

Reaching across the table, Callan laid a hand on hers. Jessie pulled hers away, angry at herself for becoming emotional. Callan dipped his gaze, looked embarrassed.

'I need to find out what Scott was convicted for and I can't do that on my own. I also want to find out where Nooria's daughter is, who the ex-boyfriend is, the child's father . . .' she tailed off. 'Because traumatic history like that can't be contained, put in some box labelled "The Past". It must continue to affect Nooria and that means it affects the whole family. As a psychologist, I don't have access to any of that information, and that's why I need your help.'

Callan looked away, across the bar, fixing for a moment on one of the photographs which showed a carthorse dragging a plough across a muddy field.

'Scott's housekeeper, Wendy Chubb, was murdered last night.'

'*What?*' Jessie sat quite still, staring at him.

'That's where I've been all day. At the crime scene.'

'Oh, God, no.' She put a hand over her mouth, an image filling her mind: Wendy Chubb opening the door to her two days ago, soap suds on a marigold glove, such mundane normality that the thought of her lying somewhere with her head bashed in or her throat cut was incomprehensible.

'It could have been a random attack,' Callan said.

'But you don't believe that, do you?'

Eyes fixed on the pint of bitter in his hands, he didn't reply. Jessie nudged his arm. 'Callan.'

He sighed. 'It didn't seem random, but it could have been.' He didn't sound convinced, or convincing.

'How was she murdered?'

'She was stabbed.'

'Where? Where was she found?'

'Close to her home. She lives . . . lived in a housing estate that backs on to Paschal Wood and the Sandhurst training ground. She was found by the boundary fence, inside

246

Sandhurst. It's close to the houses, but remote all the same, pretty much only used by dog walkers and cyclists during the day, families with kids at the weekends.'

'What happened?'

'She was walking her dog last night, around midnight.'

'Do you have any idea who killed her?'

'No. We've found no significant evidence so far.'

'Druggies? Could she have disturbed someone criminal? A burglar?'

He shook his head. 'It's a middle-class housing estate, elderly people and families with small children. No way it's a druggy hangout. Surrey and Sussex Major Crimes told me that there have been no burglaries on the estate for over a year. It's secure. One road in, one road out, people keeping an eye on their neighbours, no major wealth. It's not a good target for burglars.' He looked down at his hands. 'It was pouring and the crime scene was pretty much drenched by the time I got there. No footprints, no trace evidence.'

'Why wasn't the scene preserved?'

He gave a grim smile. 'Because some fucking idiot . . . sorry, Jessie.'

She touched his arm. 'It's fine.'

'Some idiot lieutenant was given the case. I've taken it back off him.'

Sighing, he took a long draught of bitter, and his gaze drifted back to the far wall, fixing again on that photograph of horse and plough.

'What is it Callan, uh, Ben?'

'Nothing,' he murmured. But he wouldn't meet her eye.

'There's something else, isn't there?'

A pause before Callan shook his head, the movement

slight, unconvincing. 'It could still have been a random attack. Wrong place wrong time.'

'You don't believe that.'

Silence.

'Tell me, Ben. Tell me what's bothering you.'

The dim ceiling light cast shadows across his face as he looked back and met her gaze. His amber eyes were dark, hooded. 'I haven't been entirely honest with you, Jessie.'

'What do you mean?'

A sigh. 'Colin Starkey was driving the car Scott was in when he was attacked. They were on their way to some rendezvous with an Afghan government official. The car was flagged down in a street in Kandahar – there was a body in the road and they thought that the Afghans needed help, so they pulled over. Scott wound down his window. One of the Afghans threw a petrol bomb into the car.'

'What?' She stared back at him, incredulous. 'Why the *hell* didn't you tell me that Starkey and Scott were so closely connected?'

He opened his mouth to reply, but Jessie cut in. Holding her hand up, thumb and index finger meeting to form a circle, she said, 'And don't you fucking dare say, "need to know".'

'I didn't tell you because I didn't think it was relevant. What can possibly be the connection between a case you are working on with Scott's son and the why's of a petrol bomb attack on him three months ago?'

'That's not the point. You asked me to interview Starkey with you. You—' She broke off, her mind whirring. 'You think there's a connection between Jackson's death and the attack on Scott, don't you?'

Callan shrugged. 'I don't know what I think, which is why I wanted you to meet Starkey with no preconceptions.'

'You think that Starkey is the link.'

'There may be no link. They may be . . . probably are
. . . totally unrelated events.'

'And that would mean that Gideon Duursema also knows,
because you would have given him the whole picture,
wouldn't you? Before asking him to assign me to interview
Starkey with you.'

He didn't answer.

She stood up. 'I don't work with people who lie.'

Callan gave a harsh half-laugh. 'You work with people
who lie all the time.'

'*Patients*. Patients who can't help themselves. You're not
my patient.'

'I was your patient.' Reaching across the table, he grabbed
her hand.

'Let go of me,' she said through gritted teeth.

He held on. 'There's something else.'

'I don't want to hear it.' She wriggled her hand free.

'I've got the tox reports back on Jackson.'

'I don't think you heard me.' Her voice rose; other
customers looked over. 'I'm not interested.'

'Jessie, listen.'

Standing, she made her way down the pub without looking
back, walked out of the front door and into the night.

Rising to follow her, Callan banged his head hard against
one of the beams. 'Fuck.'

'The feisty ones can be a nightmare.'

'What?'

The barman was grinning at him over the bar. 'Beautiful,
though.'

Ignoring him, rubbing his head, Callan left the pub.

'Jessie. Wait.' He jogged up the lane towards where she

was fumbling in her handbag, trying to find her car keys. He reached her just as she slid into the driver's seat and yanked the door closed.

His head was killing him; thumping like a bass drum.

'OK. I was wrong.' He mouthed, pulling the handle. She'd locked it. *Fuck*. 'I should have told you.'

He stepped back, but there must have been something on the road behind him, a bump or pothole in the tarmac because he stumbled, fell hard on to the kerb. His head was spinning, his heart rate was through the roof, and he was suddenly ice cold.

He knew what was coming, realized an instant before sentience went. His vision clouded: he couldn't see the moon or the stars above him any more, couldn't see anything, only a kaleidoscope of grey and black checks, swirls, lines crisscrossing, swimming in front of his eyes. His body was jerking, slamming against the rough tarmac. He felt arms close around him.

'Jesus Christ, Callan . . . Ben . . . *Ben*.'

He could hear her voice, as if through deep water.

'Ben, can you hear me?'

Slowly, the fit subsided. He lay still for a moment, panting, trying to catch his breath. Rolling on to his stomach, he retched into the gutter.

'Why didn't you tell me?' she asked, laying her coat on top of him. He felt her hand, stroking through his hair. He was sweating, shaking and icy cold, stinking of vomit.

'I'm not your patient any more,' he muttered, laying his head on the rough tarmac. 'It's none of your fucking business. I'm not your patient.'

250

43

'I could have driven back to the barracks.'

'You couldn't even walk across the street.'

'Why didn't you drive me in your car?'

'Because I don't want it smelling of puke.'

He laughed. 'I didn't need to ask, did I?'

Callan had had a shower, his blond hair was damp and he smelled faintly of Jessie's lavender shampoo. He was wearing an old brown V-neck jumper of her dad's that she'd kept in the back of her wardrobe for years – she couldn't even remember why now, but probably teenage nostalgia – and his own jeans, which she had sponged down as best she could. She didn't want to think about what they were doing to her cream chair. The jumper was too small for him, pulled tight across his chest and abs, a gaping hole under his left arm where the stitching had given way as it stretched over his bicep. But at least it didn't smell of vomit.

She had driven his Golf back to her cottage, ignoring his complaints about the damage her gear changes were doing to his sport's gearbox; insisted that he relax for an hour or two, have something to eat, before he went back to Wendy Chubb's crime scene. Jessie passed him a beer and laid a plate of buttered toast on the coffee table, tucked herself in one corner of her sofa, facing him.

'So what are you going to do?'

'Now?' There was an amused glint in his amber eyes. 'Sit here, drink beer and get dirt and vomit from my jeans all over your spotless white chair.'

Jessie gave him a wry half-smile. She realized that she should feel the hiss of the electric suit across her skin, the obsessive-compulsive tension grow until it was too strong to ignore – the need to clean overwhelming – but instead all she felt, looking back at him, was a deep ache in the pit of her stomach. Something to do with no food and too much wine? But she knew that wasn't it.

'About your problem,' she murmured.

He looked straight back, all innocence. 'My problem?'

'So you were play-acting in the gutter outside the pub then – a cry for attention. Didn't you get enough as a boy?' She raised an eyebrow. 'Either that, or I assume that you have epilepsy?'

'Seizures, my neurologist says.'

'Isn't that called splitting hairs?'

Callan shrugged. 'Frontal lobe seizures is the official diagnosis.' He tapped the scar on his temple. 'Caused by the bullet that the Army surgeons decided was too risky to remove. A permanent gift from the Taliban.'

The ring of a mobile. Tilting sideways, Callan tugged his phone from his trouser pocket, glanced down at the name flashing on its screen. Without answering, he slid it back into his pocket.

'And . . . so?' Jessie asked, meeting his gaze once again.

'And so I carry on – business as usual. I'm not about to tell the Army, if that's what you're asking. If they find out, they'll kick me out, obviously, but I'm not going to hand it to them on a plate.' He glared back at her and even as he glared his eyes looked thoughtful. 'Do you remember when you came around to my mother's house the last time?'

She nodded. 'Of course.'

'When you blew me out.'

Jessie laughed. 'I didn't blow you out. I terminated our professional relationship because you were refusing to be helped. I had a ton of other patients who were all willing to at least try. Your intransigence put you to the bottom of my list.'

She remembered clearly: he was the first patient she had treated since joining the Defence Psychology Service who she felt she'd entirely failed. She had been seeing him for four months, fortnightly visits to his mother's house, where he was living – if it could be called living – after being discharged from Frimley Park Hospital in Surrey, where he'd been transferred to recover after a failed operation to remove a Taliban bullet from his brain at Camp Bastion's field hospital. The surgeons had decided that removal was too risky, that leaving it in place was a safer option. The only lasting effects would be psychological, they had told him. They couldn't have been more wrong.

'Have you ever been to Afghanistan?' his mother had asked her, that last time. The tiny sitting room they were standing in was dark, even though it was mid-summer, net curtains hanging across the windows filtering the bright July sunlight. The last time Jessie had been there – two weeks before – Callan's mother had been well dressed, her hair brushed, had offered Jessie tea and biscuits. Now, dressed in a saggy drip-dry summer dress and plastic flip-flops, hair unwashed and unbrushed, she met Jessie's gaze with barely concealed contempt in her eyes. She was in the place where nightmares came from. Couldn't keep up the pretence any more that she could keep the show on the road while her twenty-eight-year-old son – her only child – shattered.

'Yes, I have.' Jessie nodded. 'Twice.'

'And it didn't affect you?' She sounded as if her insides were all sharp edges.

'I don't think anyone who goes out there comes back unaffected.'

Her eyes were damp with welling tears. 'But not like Ben.'

'I didn't go through what Ben went through. I wasn't out there working with Afghans day in day out, not knowing if one of them was an insurgent waiting to kill me. And then realizing, one day, that my worst nightmare had come true. That one of the Afghans I had worked with day in day out, trusted, *helped*, was that insurgent.'

'I want my son back.' Her voice broke.

'You'll get him back.' Jessie's words sounded hollow, even to her own ears. 'He needs time.'

'He's had time,' she cried out. '*You've* had time.'

Silence swallowed them. Jessie bit her lip. What could she tell this woman? That she suspected there was something broken in her son's brain that a psychologist couldn't fix?

Callan had been standing in the sun-drenched garden, she remembered, wearing, despite the heat, an old navy jumper and shapeless navy cords. He was holding a spade, but didn't seem to be doing anything with it, just clutching the handle, gazing, unfocused, into the distance. Despite everything though – the hunched body, skin the hue of dirty snow, eyes sunk so deep in their sockets that she could barely make out their colour – there was still something compellingly physical about him.

'Captain Callan.'

He saw who it was, looked away.

'You're wasting your time.' His voice was thick, the words uneven. 'You can't help me.'

'I'm not sure that I want to try to any more,' Jessie said quietly.

He glanced over again, his brow furrowing. The dull light in his eyes remained unchanged. 'Aren't you supposed to stick with me until the bitter end?'

'Perhaps. But you know what? I can't be bothered any more. I remember, a few weeks ago, talking with your mother about what an amazing man you are.'

'Were.'

'*Are*. She said are.'

He didn't reply; wouldn't meet her gaze.

'The first from your family to get into a grammar school, the first to go to university. The first man from your family for – how many generations? – who hasn't ended up working on the shop floor. So many firsts. Do you really want to be the first to flush your life down the can, all because you prefer to wallow in self-pity rather than get a grip?'

'You don't understand.'

'So tell me. I can't help you if you won't talk to me.'

He bowed his head. 'What good does talking do?'

'You won't know until you try.'

Jessie waited. No reply. Only the weight of the hot July day pressing down on them both, the air liquid with heat, the sound of a lawnmower chewing through grass a few houses down the street, a telephone ringing through an open window next door.

He started to talk, almost under his breath, so quietly that Jessie had to tilt forward to catch the words.

'I lay on the concrete floor in that fucking Afghan police station with a bullet in my brain and the weight of my best friend on top of me and I thought that was it – the end. I could feel the coil of his guts in my hand. I was trying to hold them inside his stomach, while I lay there playing dead, wondering whether they were going to realize that I was alive and slit my throat or drag me outside and parade me to the world's media, a bloody piece of pulp.' The rise and fall of his shoulders was exaggerated, as if he was having trouble catching his breath. 'I thought that if I held them in his body long enough, someone would rescue us before he died. It took an hour for him to die, and that hour felt like ten lifetimes. They were there all that time, the Afghans we had worked with for the past three months. Worked with and trusted. Rifling through our pockets, ripping off his wedding ring. He was moaning and talking about his daughter. She was six months old when he left for Afghanistan.' He paused and his eyes hung closed. 'I couldn't speak, couldn't comfort him because I was supposed to be dead.'

'He wasn't alone. You were there. He would have been able to sense that.'

'Bullshit.' Raising a fist to his head, he smacked it against his forehead. 'I can't get it out of my head. He died alone, in agony, because I was a fucking coward.'

Jessie's gaze found the bullet wound; tortured skin, an unforgiving reminder of what he had been through.

'Committing suicide isn't bravery.'

His fingers whitened on the handle of the spade. 'I should have died too,' he muttered.

'Where would that have got you?'

'Away from my mind.'

'You need to move on. Consign it to the past, even as you retain memories of the good bits of Afghanistan, of Tom.'

He let go of the spade, flinched when it clattered to the baked earth. 'I *can't* move on.'

'You *have* to and you can. For yourself and for your mum. Can't you see what you're doing to her?'

He shook his head; tears were running down his cheeks.

'You're lucky. You have someone who loves you more than anything in the world, and you're killing her. Many people would give everything they have for what you take for granted.'

'You fucking psychologists. You've never faced any adversity and yet you tell other people how to live, how to think.'

Jessie bit her lip. 'You have no idea what I've faced. You know nothing about me and you know nothing about the life I've lived.'

He gave a harsh half-laugh. 'So perhaps you've had a really shit time and you're just braver than I am.'

'Perhaps bravery is for people who don't have enough to lose,' she had snapped back.

Callan's mobile rang again. Ignoring it, he took a sip of his beer, winked at Jessie over the lip of the bottle. 'Jesus, you were a bitch that day.'

'Did it work?'

'No.' He paused, smiled. 'Maybe a little.' His amber eyes were the colour of honey, warm and alive. 'After you left,

257

I did nothing for days. Then I started thinking a bit, just a bit at a time. I remembered, back then, in Afghanistan, when I was lying on the floor of that police station, how desperate I was to live. How desperate I was not to die, particularly not there, at their hands. I wanted to come out of that nightmare alive and try to get Tom out of it alive too. And then I realized that, though I'd technically lived, I wasn't living at all. I was in some kind of half-life that was utterly pointless, and if I was going to live like that, make my mother live like that, I might as well have died in Afghanistan. You made me realize what I was doing to my mother, at least.' He paused. 'It still took weeks. I went to see Tom's wife and daughter. I hadn't seen them since I got back from Afghanistan, since he died. She was devastated, obviously, but she was OK. Better than I'd expected.' He smiled and shrugged. 'Far better than I was. Tom's little daughter was beautiful and she looked exactly like him. His wife said that even though Tom was no longer there, he'd given her the most amazing gift in Lily. It made me realize that I was giving nothing but shit to the person who loved me most.' Draining the bottle, he put it back on the coffee table. 'So that's me.' Uncrossing his legs, he sat forward, fixed her with a steady gaze. 'I met this psychologist once who said that it's good to talk.' His eyes glinted; they looked almost predatory. 'Tell me the truth, Jessie, because I'm pretty sure that your brother didn't die in a car crash.'

Jessie didn't reply. She pretended to be absorbed in re-arranging the cushions on the sofa behind her, cushions that she had already plumped and laid out with precision.

'For fuck's sake, Jessie, leave them.'

She stopped and her shoulders sagged.

'He killed himself,' she murmured. 'He hung himself from the curtain rail in his bedroom. He was seven years old.'

'Jesus. I'm sorry. I wouldn't have pressed you if I'd known—'

She waved a hand in the air, trying to make light of it, but she could feel hot tears pricking the back of her eyes.

'Why did he do it?' he asked gently.

'I don't know.' She shrugged, paused. 'No, you know what, I do know. But I don't know what the trigger was – why that day. He was born with a heart condition. Restrictive cardiomyopathy, it's called. Basically it's when the muscles of the heart get harder and harder until the heart can't pump any more. The only cure is a heart transplant. We found out when he was two. He was put on the transplant list immediately and then he was constantly in and out of hospital for tests and medication. We couldn't go anywhere. We couldn't go on holiday because a child has to be taken off the transplant list while they're abroad, and my parents would never have forgiven themselves if a heart had come up when we were sunning ourselves on a beach somewhere. The whole family ended up in limbo, our lives about waiting and hoping. Child heart donors are rare, for obvious reasons, so we waited and we hoped. Our father couldn't cope with the stress. Two years after Jamie's diagnosis he met someone else, an agency nurse at the hospital where Jamie was being treated, who was years younger. Years younger and a whole lot happier.' She paused, heard the choppy sound of her own breathing. 'A couple of weeks before Jamie committed suicide, we were told that he would need to go into hospital to be put on an artificial heart. A donor hadn't been found and his heart was failing.' She felt hollow with the telling, overcome by emptiness.

'He seemed to have accepted that news because at least it was progress in some direction and once in hospital, he'd be moved to the top of the transplant list, would have a much better chance of getting one. He seemed happier and more optimistic than he'd been in weeks.' She broke off. Her mouth was bone dry, her skin tingling with tension – the electric suit. She swallowed to help ease the words out. 'I keep wracking my brains for the trigger, why then, why that day. The only thing I keep coming back to is that he felt abandoned. Abandoned and alone – because *I* left him alone.'

Reaching across the table, Callan laid a hand on her arm. 'Hey, come on, you can't blame yourself.'

'Why not? I was supposed to be looking after him, and I was out snogging my boyfriend on the common instead.' She choked, the electric suit constricting her throat. 'I let him be dropped home from school by someone else's mum, to an empty house, on his own. And that was when he killed himself.' Tears were running down her face now; she didn't reach up to wipe them away.

'It wasn't your fault.'

'How the fuck do you know? You weren't there.'

Stepping over the coffee table, Callan sat down next to her on the sofa. 'You have to let it go.'

She shook her head mutely. He was sitting uncomfortably close. She tried to shift away, but she was at the end of the sofa. Folding her legs to her chest, she wrapped her arms around her knees, curling herself into a defensive ball.

'You have to, Jessie.'

'Jesus Christ, you sound like me.'

'Sometimes – occasionally – you talk sense,' he said softly.

'Oh God.' She shivered. 'I'm so tired, so sick of living

like this.' Her eyes grazed around the room. 'Like some fussy old biddy.'

The electric suit was snapping against her skin, the tension so acute now that she had the almost overwhelming urge to drag her nails down her face, her arms, to scratch away her skin and the feeling with it.

'You were only a child yourself,' Callan said. 'You can't keep shouldering the blame.'

Raising his hand to her cheek, he slid his thumb across her cheekbone, wiping away the trail of tears. Jessie stared at the middle of his chest where the threads of her father's old jumper were stretched too tight across his abs, not meeting his eyes.

The sudden, shrill ring of a mobile.

'Fuck, not again,' he muttered, dropping his hand. Tugging his phone from his trouser pocket, he glanced at the name flashing on its screen. He paused, thumb hovering over the answer button, weighing up options. Finally, a terse 'Callan'. His fingers tapped a tense, impatient rhythm on his knee as he listened. 'Sure. I'll come right now.' Jamming his mobile back into his pocket, he sighed and pushed himself to his feet. 'I'm sorry, Jessie, but I have to go. Marilyn needs my help.'

Jessie stood too. 'Sorry, who?' she asked.

A preoccupied half-smile. 'Marilyn. You know, blonde, big tits.'

'Lucky you.'

'I felt pretty lucky here,' he murmured, so quietly that she almost didn't hear him. 'But I do have to get back to Wendy Chubb's crime scene.'

Jessie nodded, dropping her gaze, breaking eye contact. She felt unbalanced, caught off guard, by the sudden lurch from affinity to business.

'Your shirt will still be wet.'

'Can I keep your dad's jumper?'

'Sure, if you want to look like a dick in front of Marilyn.'

'Believe me, Marilyn will look far worse than I do.'

They walked together to the front door, Callan reaching for his coat, Jessie fumbling with the door lock, neither catching the other's eye.

'I'll see you tomorrow morning. I'll pick you up at eight and we'll go back and see Jackson's wife,' Callan said.

'Fine. I'll see you then.' She held the door open for him.

On the doorstep, he turned back and their eyes met. Jessie felt her cheeks redden.

'I'm sorry—' He broke off with a shrug.

She smiled, a fleeting smile that she didn't feel anywhere but on her face. 'You better get going. I'll see you tomorrow.'

He raised a hand. 'Goodnight, then.'

'Goodnight, Callan.'

She watched him walk back down her garden path to his Golf. Shutting the door, she tilted forward and laid her forehead against the hard wood.

44

The luminous green dial on Jessie's watch told her that it was 2 a.m. She could – should – go to bed and try to sleep, but she felt a buzzing, nervous energy that was partly the fallout from Callan's visit, and partly the knowledge that virtually half of the forty-eight hours Gideon had given her had passed and she'd made little progress. It was an energy that she needed to channel into something positive.

Jumping off the sofa, she slipped her trainers on and went outside to her car, remembered halfway down the path that she'd left it at the pub. Back inside, she kicked off her trainers by the doormat. She bent to line them up on the shoe rack, then stopped, deliberately stopped herself, straightening, biting her lip, staring down at the tangle of laces and white leather. She took a step back, felt the suit hiss, took another step, felt the hiss intensify, the claustro-phobic electricity humming over her skin. But even as she consciously forced herself to back further away, the tension, the visceral need for order and control, didn't rise to a level that she couldn't bearably ignore.

She found a second *Ordnance Survey Atlas of Great Britain* in her desk drawer, aware, as she pulled it out that she was probably the only person in Great Britain under the age of fifty who used one. Grabbing her laptop from the bookshelf, she curled back on the sofa with the atlas and her computer in her lap.

A town near the south coast, Miss Appleby had said, reached via a single-lane road, not a dual carriageway. A road with the number eight in it.

Flicking to the atlas's index, she found the page that listed A-roads. The list covered pages and pages, hundreds of A and B roads, scores of them with the number eight in the name – a hopeless task to try to find the one road that Miss Appleby had been referring to by scanning this index.

Laying the atlas on the coffee table, Jessie sat back, casting her gaze to the ceiling, thinking. She knew a bit about homes for severely disabled children from her year as an NHS psychologist before she had joined the Army, knew that spaces in these homes were limited and that parents often had to take a place for their child wherever it was offered, several hours' drive from their own family homes. But Nooria's daughter would have been in the care home for eight or nine years by now, enough time to wait on lists, hassle the NHS, get her moved closer to home. Nooria had tried hard to keep her daughter, Miss Appleby had said. *But she was on her own, and still only seventeen when the baby was born. She couldn't cope.* But she would keep fighting for her daughter, surely, even after relinquishing her everyday care?

Picking up the atlas, Jessie found the double-page spread that covered Surrey, found Aldershot, and then tracked a centimetre left to the narrow country lane on which the

264

Scotts lived. There was a spider's web of A-roads spreading in all directions from Aldershot, a depressing havoc of tarmac coating the countryside. Jessie squinted at the tiny road names going south, towards the coast. The A3, the dual carriageway that she and Callan had taken to and from Wandsworth – not the one – the A281, A283, the A285.

She paused, finger in mid-air, hovering above Godalming. There – the A286. *The A-something-eight-something. Funny the kinds of things that stick in your mind.*

The A286 would fit. From Crookham, Nooria would be able to cut straight down Charles Hill, cross the A3 and pick up the A286 at Godalming. Jessie traced her finger down the A-road, imagining its meandering journey through the undulating West Sussex countryside. Picture-perfect England, the chocolate box towns of Haslemere and Midhurst, a magnet for retirees on weekend trips. *She used to complain that she got stuck behind old people out for their Sunday drive.*

The A286. Ending up in Chichester.

A town on the south coast.

45

The cul-de-sac was less busy now, only Marilyn's battered black BMW Z3, an antique he called it – a piece of junk, more like, Callan had always thought – a marked police car and a transit, and the white panelled van of the forensics team remaining. The Army vehicles had pulled out, Colonel Holden-Hough, agreeing with Marilyn that it was a civilian killing, and that Surrey and Sussex Major Crime team should take the lead, with Callan as military liaison because of the link with Major Scott.

Cutting his engine, Callan sat for a moment, collecting his thoughts, fighting the impulse to turn the car around, drive straight back to Jessie's cottage. Opening the door, he climbed out, the flood of freezing air that enveloped him having the same effect as the proverbial bucket of cold water. Reaching back to grab his jacket from the passenger seat, he shrugged it on. Whatever Marilyn wanted, it had better be good.

Before he had even reached the end of the sandy trail that led from Birch Close to the Sandhurst training area, he saw the glow from the police arc lights, like a super-bright low-slung moon. The track that hugged the boundary fence was still cordoned off, would be for a few more days to preserve the scene until it had been mercilessly combed for clues. The forensic tent was also in place and Callan could see two shadows moving around inside. But it would be empty of Wendy Chubb's body, by now transferred to the pathologist's dissecting table.

A uniformed policeman was standing in front of the cordon, hands in his pockets, staring listlessly into the darkness. He looked cold and bored. There could be few duller jobs than maintaining the integrity of the crime scene for the night, while most of your colleagues were mainlining coffee and sharing bad jokes back in the office.

Beyond him, Callan could see the distinctive battered biker jacket, the ragged face above it. He jogged over.

'Marilyn.'

'Ah, Callan, thanks for coming.'

They shook hands.

'I won't say it's a pleasure.'

Marilyn smiled, his eyes level with Callan's chest. 'At least I know that I didn't drag you away from a beautiful girl – not wearing that jumper.'

Callan laughed, 'You have no idea how beautiful. And isn't that termed "the pot calling the kettle black", criticizing my fashion sense?' Glancing at his watch, he saw that it was a quarter past two. Would Jessie be asleep by now? He doubted it. She would, most likely, be awake, eking every moment from the twenty-four hours she had left before Gideon Duursema handed Sami Scott's case to his Special Investigation Branch colleagues.

Marilyn clicked his fingers in front of Callan's face. 'So you *were* with a beautiful girl, Captain.'

'What?' Callan refocused, caught the amused glint in Marilyn's eye.

'You're looking all dreamy, son.'

Callan smiled. 'Get lost, Detective Inspector.' Zipping up his jacket over the moth-eaten jumper, he stretched. 'Now, what do you need from me?'

'I need someone with a brain to mull things over with.' They walked, side by side, towards the tent. 'Because I have more than a nagging suspicion that this was not a random attack. But I am at a loss for motive, which means that I'm at a loss for pretty much anything more than that.'

Callan nodded. He suspected the same, but asked the question anyway:

'Why do you think it wasn't random? What does the evidence say?'

'The evidence says not much. We've spoken to the handful of friends listed in her address book, all her near neighbours, and everyone else in Birch and Saddleback Closes, bar three who weren't at home today or this evening. She was a quiet woman, considerate neighbour, didn't go out much, few friends, although those friends she did have thought very highly of her. No boyfriend or significant other. She wasn't an alcoholic or a drug user, she didn't gamble, she wasn't in debt and had no enemies as far as any of her friends knew. Your typical everyday, common or garden dull middle-aged woman.'

'Steady.'

Marilyn threw up his hands. 'Well, for God's sake.' His gaze rolled up to the black sky above them. 'Give me something.'

'What about shoe prints?'

'Tons. Most of them washed to unidentifiable indents from the rain. None from which we could take a cast.'

'Even around the body?'

Marilyn shook his head. 'Your friendly Lieutenant Gold ensured that the area surrounding Wendy Chubb's body had a good soaking before he let us erect the tent.'

Callan nodded. He wasn't about to criticize a fellow officer in front of Marilyn, but he shared the frustration he could feel oozing from Marilyn's every pore.

'What about the Sandhurst training area?'

'What about it?'

'How far in did you go?'

'Ten metres in past the body, a hundred metres either side along the boundary fence.'

'Why not further in?'

'Because I'm pretty sure that the murderer would have reached her via the path we're currently standing on. We have one witness, an elderly man, who says that he heard a car drive to the end of Birch Close and park at around midnight. Half an hour later, give or take, he heard the engine start again and drive off.'

'The same engine?'

'He says it was a diesel. Distinctive rumble.'

'What was he doing?'

'Lying in bed trying to sleep. He has a prostrate problem, which he says gives him insomnia. His bedroom is at the front of the house. He lives directly opposite Pauline Lewis, Wendy Chubb's friend. Theirs are the two houses right at the end of the cul-de-sac.'

'He didn't look out of his window?'

'No.'

'Why not?'

'Because he's an old guy, he was already tucked up and it was only a car,' Marilyn snapped.

They had reached the section of the fence by the forensic tent; voices from inside, talking shop, CSIs.

'Did anyone else hear the car?'

'No.'

'Could it have been a resident?'

'None of the neighbours on Birch Close or Saddleback Close were out driving their cars at that time – we have statements from virtually all of them.'

'Virtually all.'

Marilyn sighed like a man close to the limit of his patience. He looked tired. Callan wasn't surprised. He'd probably been awake for close to twenty-four hours straight with no let-up in sight.

'We still need to speak to three households. Households of old people or families, because that's basically it on this particular housing estate.' Marilyn rolled his eyes. 'It was cold, windy, the perfect night for sitting by the fire and watching TV or cuddling up under the duvet, which seems to be what most of the residents were doing at the time of Wendy Chubb's murder.'

'And it's not a through road,' Callan murmured. 'And not well known.'

'Not a place for cottagers, teenagers making out, drug dealers, none of that.'

Callan cast his gaze down the track, past Marilyn's shoulder. What would he do if he wanted to kill someone? Would he park his car in some cul-de-sac? A housing estate like this one, made up of small semi-detached houses on the outskirts of Aldershot, was, as Marilyn had said, full of families with young children, and old people. Families with little kids who rose at 6 a.m. full of beans, who had better things to do than look out of the window at midnight on a week night because someone had parked a car. Old people who, once in bed, would be unlikely to climb back out just at the sound of an engine. A risk, sure, but a calculated one. Wendy's murder smelt of opportunity. Her killer would need to be close, to spot the opportunity. He nodded.

'So our murderer parks at the end of Birch Close . . .' Hefting himself over the boundary fence, he dropped to the other side, landing silently on a bed of damp, sandy earth and pine needles.

'There was a piece of her jacket on the fence. Here.' Marilyn pointed. 'A section from her sleeve.'

Callan stood, bouncing on the balls of his feet, next to the tent.

'Right, so she's about here. Maybe the dog ran off into the trees, wouldn't come back. Why the hell else would she have climbed over the fence in the first place?' He took a few steps into the trees and turned back to face Marilyn. 'So the killer approaches her from the trees.'

Marilyn frowned. 'I'm not with you, Callan. If her killer parked in the cul-de-sac, the quickest, easiest way is down this path. My theory is that she climbed into Sandhurst to try to hide, tore her jacket on the way over.'

Callan shook his head. 'It doesn't make sense. The nail is angled down and it's only slightly raised from the wood.'

Slipping his jacket off, Callan dragged the sleeve of Jessie's dad's jumper down over the nail, aping the motion of someone climbing over the fence. It caught, dragging out a loop of wool. Marilyn raised his eyebrows, gave a small, smug smile, but didn't say anything.

'The jumper's saggy, loose wool,' Callan snapped. 'It's going to catch on anything. You said she was wearing a black Puffa, slippery material. Here, give me your jacket.'

271

'Fuck off, Captain.'

Callan smiled. 'It is a murder investigation, Detective Inspector. Take it seriously.'

'Fuck off all the same. I'll get one of the uniforms to test it.'

Callan did, with his own waterproof jacket. The material slid right over the nail, three, four, five times. He cocked an eyebrow at Marilyn.

'OK, so she's a what . . . a fifty-five-year-old woman, overweight, unfit,' he continued. 'The houses are that way.' He pointed over Marilyn's shoulder. 'Why climb away from them? Midnight, Wednesday night–Thursday morning, most people are in bed, many asleep. It's winter, a cold, clear night. Sound travels much better in the winter.'

'Windy.'

'The wind was coming from which direction?' He looked into the trees. 'North to south that night, blowing towards the houses, carrying sound.'

Marilyn crossed his arms over his chest, tipped back on his heels. 'Go on.'

'If she'd seen someone coming down this path from the end of Birch Close cul-de-sac, late at night, a woman alone, it would have made sense for her to walk or run that way – along the path that backs on to the houses, and scream if she was frightened. She certainly wouldn't have ended up here. And if she screamed, someone probably would have heard her.'

'And yet she ended up here and no one heard a thing.' Marilyn sighed. 'What if she thought it was a jogger?'

Stifling a yawn with the back of his hand, Callan shook his head. 'Middle of the night, cold and windy. Would you?'

'Me? Jog? To the bar, maybe.' Marilyn pulled a face.

'OK, maybe you have a point. So what if she knew the person?'

'She was stabbed?'

'Yes.'

'Front, back or side?'

'The left side. A single stab wound, entry point just below her ribcage. The tip of the knife must have found her heart.'

'Defensive wounds?'

'The autopsy is continuing in the morning but preliminary results show no obvious defensive wounds.'

'She was surprised. Quick, easy.' Callan grinned. 'If you have your head shoved up your arse, Detective Inspector, four out of your five senses aren't working.'

'I forgot for a moment why I hate you Army twats, but I've just remembered.' Marilyn stifled a yawn. 'So how would you do it, Callan, if you were going to top some old lady out for a midnight stroll with her pooch.'

Callan looked towards the trees. Which way would a killer have come? The mouth of the track cutting up from the end of Birch Close was a hundred metres or so to his left. If the killer had stopped his or her car at the end of Birch Close, he or she would have cut straight up the sandy track that ran from the end of the cul-de-sac to the boundary fence. What then?

He'd trained at Sandhurst, spent months yomping through these woods, crawling around on his belly in the dark waiting until dawn to launch an attack. Great cover, silent approach, footsteps muffled by damp ground and leaf mulch, shadows of trees moving, constantly moving. You'd get within centimetres of someone, particularly a civvy at night out here, without them even realizing they were no longer alone.

'I'd climb the boundary fence a hundred metres down, cut in a semicircle through the trees on the Sandhurst side to where she was standing. Cover of sight and movement until the last moment. Her murderer would be right on top of her before she knew.'

Marilyn pulled a face. 'Jesus, you trained killers.'

Callan looked hard at him. 'You think the murderer's Army, don't you?'

Marilyn shrugged. 'I think we both agree that it's unlikely to be random. And having talked to her neighbours and friends, I'm struggling for a motive. I think you need to fill me in on Wendy's employer, Major Scott. We haven't interviewed him or his wife yet, but we'll need to. You said earlier that he's involved in a suspicious death.'

Callan nodded, but didn't reply. He thought of Scott, the car crash that his life had become; thought of Jackson's wife sitting at her kitchen table, sobbing for her dead husband; thought of Starkey, flashing his sharp-toothed grin – *the truth never set anyone free, Captain Callan.*

Marilyn sighed. 'I worked on a case last year. A woman of Wendy Chubb's age, similar profile, who was house-sitting for a friend over Christmas. She was knifed to death in her bed in the middle of the night, her sister, brother-in-law and elderly mother also in the house, and none of them heard a thing. Turned out that the owner of the house was a swinger – married, of course – and he'd made too many promises to the wrong woman, promises he couldn't keep because he already had a wife.' Marilyn's telephone went. Pulling it from his pocket, he glanced at the screen. 'Dr Ghoshal, the pathologist.' Turning, he stepped away. 'Families, Callan,' he called back over his shoulder. 'They're complex, messy things. Best avoided, I'd say.'

46

Laying the map to one side, Jessie pulled her laptop on to her knee. Her tummy gurgled and she suddenly realized that she was starving. Apart from some grapes cunningly disguised as Sauvignon, nothing had passed her lips since her tea and biscuits with Miss Appleby, nine hours earlier. She reached for a slice of buttered toast, curled at the edges now and of cardboard consistency, but at least it was calories and she couldn't be bothered to trog to the kitchen and make herself something decent. She had picked up a scent, needed to track it to its end, without interruption.

Switching on her computer, she navigated to Google. It took her ten minutes of searching, using different combinations of keywords, to find the right website: a list of National Health Service funded homes for severely physically and mentally disabled children. The list probably wasn't exhaustive. The NHS had a habit of delivering half-arsed information, something that had driven her mad when she worked for them, the struggle for funding anything but essential services something the Army now shared, but hopefully the list would be comprehensive enough for her purposes.

There was only one home listed in Chichester. Scribbling down the number, she picked up her mobile. As she started to dial, she caught the time on the phone's face – 2.45 a.m. What the hell was she thinking? Tossing the mobile back on the coffee table, she ground her fists into her eye sockets. What could she do now? Nothing, she realized. Nothing useful until morning. The frustration at being able to make no more progress, when every minute that ticked past was a minute closer to losing Sami's case, felt physical, as if there was nothing but air and electricity between her neck and pelvis.

What now? Sleep? She might as well try to get some, so that she would, at least, be able to fire on all cylinders tomorrow. Setting the alarm on her phone for half-past six, enough time for a shower and a quick breakfast before calling the home at seven, she lay down on the sofa, reaching for the white wool blanket she kept folded over one of its arms. Pulling the blanket up to her chin, she closed her eyes and her thoughts drifted to Callan.

47

When Marilyn had walked away, Callan moved further into the trees, away from the flood of light from the electric arcs. He stood for a while, listening, letting his vision adjust to the darkness, his senses to the nuances of the dense undergrowth, as he had been taught to do on night patrols. It wasn't as windy as last night, but a breeze shifted the branches around him, the air dead cold, the sky above him black paint.

He started to walk, slowly, slightly northwest, squatting every few paces. The bushes here were broken, a few pale brown hairs caught at the end of a sharp twig. *The dog.* He had been right. The dog had torn through here.

Standing, he moved forward again, angling left as he walked, calculating in his mind the trajectory a killer might have taken from where he or she climbed the boundary fence a hundred metres down.

Silence. Intense, almost unnatural silence. Then from somewhere behind him, murmured voices, his name being called. *Marilyn.* He didn't reply, kept moving forward, eyes searching the ground as he walked.

A sudden glint, a tiny reflection of light that didn't belong in the middle of this dense wood. He moved closer, lost the glint for a second – shifted back, trying to re-find his bearings. The glint again: a fragment of silver, coated in mud. Crouching down, he saw immediately what it was. A silver dog-tag key ring, with two door keys attached. The dog-tag was engraved; he could just make out the uneven ridges carved into its surface, but not the words written there. Pulling the sleeve of his jacket down over his hand, his fingers closed around the keys and he slid them into his coat pocket. It was an Army training area – things were forever falling from new recruits' pockets and backpacks. Dropped keys probably meant nothing. But they might.

Pushing himself silently to his feet, he started to walk again, tracking the semicircle in his mind. An owl, which must have been close by, hooted, a single too-wit-too-woo. His name, again – Marilyn calling, clear as a bell in the silence.

Jesus.

He ducked, his heart leapt. The owl had darted right past his face, so close that he felt its feathers brush against his cheek.

Slowly, he breathed out.

He was about to stand when he experienced a sudden, strong sense that he was no longer alone in the trees. Staying low, he scanned the darkness around him for movement, a colour, different from the rest, a reflection of light, anything.

But there was nothing. He could see nothing out of place. Only the straight lines of the tree trunks, slightly blacker than the spaces between, bushes clogging the ground lower down. He listened. He couldn't hear anything, only the sound of his own breathing, rhythmic, controlled, his pulse,

278

slightly raised. The darkness so complete that even the trees threw no shadows.

Moving slowly sideways at a crouch, sidestepping one foot over the other, laying each sole softly so as not to make a sound, he reached the closest tree, stood slowly, pressing himself against the trunk, covering his back.

A shrill noise cut through the silence. His phone. *Christ, not now.* Fumbling it from his pocket, he pressed cancel.

A click right next to his ear.

His mind computed instantly.

A safety.

'Put your hands where I can see them.'

Callan left his hands hanging by his sides. 'You can see them where they are.'

He started to turn.

'Don't move.' A voice that broke with tension.

'I presume that you want the keys?' he replied calmly.

'I do.'

'They're in my left-hand coat pocket.'

'Take them out and throw them on the ground behind you. *Slowly.* Do it slowly or I'll shoot you.'

He moved – slowly – fishing the keys from his pocket, tossing them behind him, evaluating his options as he did so.

None. He had none. Only to play along, for the moment, at least.

'And now I want you to get on your knees, Captain.'

No way. He wasn't about to do that for anyone. Not now. Not ever again. He had made that mistake in Afghanistan, played along, tried to buy some time and some mercy for himself and Tom. It had bought him nothing but shame and self-hatred.

'Fuck you,' he said.

The hand holding the gun shook. Callan's, hanging loosely down by his sides, didn't.

'I'm sorry,' the voice said.

'I doubt that.'

He had no options. But he wasn't giving in so easily, not this time. Taking all his weight on to his left leg, he kicked out backwards, suddenly, fast and hard, with his right. The jarring impact in his right foot, the ooff of expelled air and the groan of pain told him he had connected with muscle and bone.

Not hard enough.

A crack. Milliseconds later, an agonizing burn in his back as the bullet tore into him.

The only thing he thought of before he lost consciousness was that he should have stayed at Jessie's to see where the evening led. That he would never now get the chance.

48

'Callan,' Jessie murmured, sitting up suddenly.

Her sense of him was almost as if he'd stepped back into the room. She looked around, her vision struggling to adjust to the darkness, picking out bulky black shapes in the room but nothing yet resolving into recognizable forms. She was confused, her head cloudy from lack of sleep and food.

'Callan?' she called out.

Had he come back from Wendy Chubb's murder scene? Climbing off the sofa, she padded to the window, pulled back the curtain. It was as dark outside as in, just a sliver of moon and a scatter of stars. She squinted hard through the glass, but there was no Golf outside, no Callan. Only an empty country lane.

I'm going mad.

Reaching for her mobile, she checked the screen. She had no missed calls or texts. Tossing her phone back on to the coffee table, she lay down, pulling the blanket up to her chin and closing her eyes again.

*   *   *

Sounds from a long way off. Voices. Words he couldn't recognize. A rhythmic clatter. *Helicopter blades.* He'd recognize the sound, that clatter, would recognize it anywhere.

He felt hot and cold. Hot in his chest and cold as ice in his bones. He tried to move, to open his eyes, but his lids felt heavy, like lead.

Where was he? He was aware of darkness, but a shifting darkness, shades of darkness flickering and moving above his head.

Then sudden light, right in his face. Blinding light. He moaned, tried to turn his head, felt hands holding him, a face hanging over him, the skin folded and pale.

Death.

Was it death? Had death come for him? He tried to raise his hands, to fight, but couldn't move. He was tired, his body heavy, heavy as lead and icy cold, and he couldn't fight any more. Surrendering to the hands, the voices, he let them pull at his clothing, go through his pockets, talking to each other all the time. *Tom? Where's Tom? Is he already dead?* Talking, shouting, a field radio, he recognized that too, the distorted voices, the crackle, the rhythmic clatter of the helicopter blades.

He felt weightless now, as if his mind had left his body. He drifted, leaving it all: the hands, the voices, the radio's crackle, the clatter of blades. Joining Tom. Leaving it all behind.

49

Jessie felt as if it was the middle of the night when her alarm woke her, as though she'd barely been asleep for five minutes. Her legs were stiff from being bent all night and her shoulder ached from lying on it for hours in the same position, unable to turn on the narrow sofa. She'd slept fitfully, aware in the recesses of her semi-conscious mind that she was uncomfortable, but lacking the motivation to drag herself from under the warm blanket and negotiate the cold, dark stairs to her bedroom.

Swinging her legs to the floor, she sat up groggily, reaching for her phone to shut off the alarm. Its ring was cutting straight through to some soft, fuzzy part of her brain that wasn't yet ready to face the day. Particularly today, her last day before Gideon handed Sami and his family to the Special Investigation Branch.

Pulling the blanket around her shoulders, she padded into the kitchen. Standing on one foot on the cold tiles while the kettle boiled, she stared through the patio doors to the garden and the fields beyond. Sheep were huddled in groups, their dirty cotton-wool coats backlit a deep red from the glow of the rising sun, the sky above a depthless blue-black – still more night than day.

Coffee in hand, she went upstairs, rested her cup on the soap rack while she showered. She took a moment in front of her wardrobe, considering her choices, before she pulled out some clothes. She didn't want to turn up to the Jacksons' house looking too smart, when Rachel would be even more desolate, more wrecked, than she had been two days ago. Then, she was ratcheted to breaking point. Today probably wouldn't have brought any release. She'd just be ratcheted two days' tighter. But at the same time, Jessie wanted to look professional, to inspire confidence, even as she felt none herself. Eventually, she chose navy-blue trousers and a blue-and-white striped Breton jumper, tied her hair back in a high ponytail with a navy-blue scrunchie.

Back downstairs she glanced at her watch. Five past seven, time to make the telephone call she'd been waiting all night to make. Finding the piece of paper bearing the scribbled children's home number, she laid it on her knee and picked up her mobile. A second later, she laid them both back on the coffee table. What the hell was she going to say? Her brain, clouded from lack of sleep, the caffeine not yet kicked in, fumbled for a viable option. She could claim to be an NHS psychologist asking after Nooria's daughter's welfare, but that was tenuous at best. Once children had been placed in a home, their needs were catered for by the home, and perhaps also by a social services caseworker, who would be well known to both the home and the child's parents. There was no reason for a random psychologist to call out of the blue, asking questions. And Jessie didn't even know the child's name.

Had Nooria taken the father's surname, kept her maiden name – not that Jessie had any idea what that was – or given the child her new husband's name, Scott? Her mind went full circle again, grasping at possibilities, discarding them, came up with only one option.

And though she hated to lie, particularly so blatantly to people who didn't deserve to be lied to, she realized that she had absolutely no choice.

Opening the back door, holding her mobile out in front of her, she walked to the end of the garden. Full reception, wherever she stood. Climbing over the fence into the farmer's field, she walked clockwise, skirting around the field's perimeter, stopping only when the reception icon on her phone had reduced from five bars to two. She was a couple of hundred metres from where her back garden adjoined the field, standing in a slight depression where a twisted tangle of stunted trees, leafless and skeletal against the lightening sky, grew from the boggy ground. Steeling herself, she dialled the number she'd written on the scrap of paper.

A ringtone. She waited, scuffing the soles of her trainers in the damp soil, feeling the cold air cut straight through to her bones, wishing now that she'd put a coat on. She could imagine the telephone ringing in some small office, the staff too busy to bother to answer it.

After a full two minutes of ringing, when she was debating cutting off the call to trudge back to her cottage and hug a radiator to defrost herself, the dial tone was replaced by a woman's voice, clipped and efficient.

'Brooklands. How can I help you?'

'Hello. It's uh, it's Nooria Scott.'

'Pardon? Sorry, I can't hear you too well.'

Jessie raised her voice against the interference she had

deliberately engineered to disguise her voice. 'It's Nooria. Nooria Scott.'

'I can't hea . . . keep cutting out.'

'It's Nooria Scott,' Jessie repeated, louder. She tried to mimic Nooria's elongated vowels, her faint East End accent. 'I'm on my mobile. The reception's not great.' She had received no recognition from the woman, no sign that she was calling the right children's home.

'Mrs Scott.'

'Yes.'

'Are you OK? You don't soun . . .' The woman's voice broke up.

Shit. Jessie was shivering with cold. A sneeze was working its way up into her nose – she let it come. 'I've got a cold. I'm fine. How is . . .' She wished that she had a name. 'How is my daughter?'

A moment of silence. She waited, hardly daring to breathe. If this woman had spoken to Nooria a number of times, there was no way that Jessie's poor attempt at her accent would be convincing.

'Is there a problem, Mrs Scott?'

'No. No problem. I haven't seen her for a couple of weeks.' She hoped it was true, knew that the more information she gave, the more chance she had of tripping herself up. 'I was just checking in.'

'Well, she's fi . . .' The woman's voice fading to an unintelligible jumble of noise. '. . . breakfast, so I can't take the phone to her.'

'No, of course not.'

'Her dad came to see her yesterday.'

'Her dad?' Jessie was too startled to hide her surprise. *She said that he didn't care about the baby at all. He told*

286

her that they should drown it. 'That's what we'd do in my country,' he said. 'Her dad came to see her?'

'Yes.' A wariness in the woman's tone. 'He was here for an hour. Lovely he is with Soraya. Really lovely.' *Soraya. Her dad.* A pause. 'I do need to go and help with breakfast now, Mrs Scott, but I'll tell Susie Wingrove that you called, ask her to call you back after breakfast.'

'Hold on. I, uh—'

'—llo. HELLO.'

'Yes,' Jessie shouted. 'I'm here.' She couldn't afford to lose the woman now, risk Susie Wingrove, whoever the hell she was, calling Nooria back on her own mobile.

'Mrs Scott?'

'Yes.' She was virtually yelling now, turning as she did, scanning the field around her for the nearest patch of higher ground. Clutching the phone to her ear, she started to run – run and talk. 'You don't need to ask Susie to call me back. I know that she's extremely busy. I'm planning to come down this Sunday anyway, so I'm sure I'll see her then.' Breathing hard, she held her hand over the mouthpiece, to muffle the sound.

'I'm sure it won't be a problem for her to call.'

'OK, but I lost my mobile. I've got a temporary number,' Jessie shouted.

'Now I really do have to go.'

'It's 07720 287712. Ask her to call me on that.'

Jessie heard the click, stared at the blank phone in her hand. Had the woman registered her number? She had no idea.

50

Standing, looking down at the glistening pool of scarlet blood at his feet, Marilyn felt a deep fury building inside him. Responsibility had already settled, an elephantine weight on his shoulders and in the pit of his stomach, and now he wanted answers.

Answers and a result. Payback.

Why the hell had he rung Callan's mobile when Callan hadn't responded to his shouts? Called him and turned him into a living, breathing target.

He was well aware that killers often came back to the scene of the crime, but he hadn't expected this one to: not now, at least, in the dark, the air mind-numbingly cold, nothing left to gloat over, Wendy Chubb's body now gracing one of Dr Ghoshal's dissecting tables. The killer had wrong-footed him and Callan had paid.

He turned at the sound of a voice. His lead Crime Scene Investigator, Tony Burrows, was standing outside the *Police! Do Not Cross!* tape that Marilyn had had strung up in a thirty-metre circumference around where he'd found Callan.

Dragged out of bed, an hour after he'd finally managed to get into it – twenty-five hours after he had first arrived at Wendy Chubb's crime scene, which he and his team had been scouring for clues, without a break – Burrows' moon face looked blotchy under the arc lights, his eyes wide and red veined from lack of sleep. Marilyn was gratified to see that he had dressed hastily: his shirt was buttoned in the wrong holes and the cardigan he had pulled over it was stained with various foodstuffs.

'You'll be getting a bill for overtime, Marilyn,' he muttered, as he shrugged into his Tyvek overalls.

'How about I write off the hundred quid that you owe me and we can call it quits,' Marilyn said.

Burrows ducked under the tape. 'The amount of time I've put in this past twenty-four hours, that wouldn't even scratch the minimum wage threshold.'

Marilyn chuckled obligingly, though he still felt nothing but cold anger.

'You earn more than minimum wage? Clearly I need to have a word with payroll.'

With a silent roll of his eyes, Burrows pulled on pair of latex gloves, snapping the wrist of each over the sleeve of his overalls. 'What do we have?'

Dawn was finally beginning to lighten the sky above them, which would make the forensic team's job fraction-ally easier.

'Bloodstain here.' Marilyn pointed a metre to his left. 'Boot prints here. Both from Callan. And another set of boot prints—' he swung his arm a metre to the right – 'here. Men's, for sure, from the size of the prints, unless we're dealing with a female bigfoot or a clown, though the even-ness of the prints tells me that the shoe fit the boot.'

'From the perpetrator?'

Marilyn nodded. 'Given where I found Callan, and where Callan was standing.' He took a step sideways, laying his feet carefully to avoid stepping anywhere critical, and squatted down. 'The second set of boot prints are approximately a metre directly behind Callan's. Hip width apart, the right, a quarter of a metre behind the left, with the toe of the print angled forty-five degrees outwards.'

'Right-handed shooter's stance,' Burrows said.

'Absolutely.'

'Careless, leaving such clear prints.'

'Rushed.' Marilyn straightened, rubbing a hand across his eyes. He was knackered, the adrenalin that had kept him going for the past twenty-four hours, adrenalin intensified with outrage on finding Callan bleeding his life into the mud and leaf mulch of this shitty wood, had now evaporated, leaving him feeling shattered and morose. 'I heard the shot. I'd gone off to answer a call from the station. I'd just come back, was standing on the track by the Sandhurst boundary fence, shouting to Callan. When he didn't answer, I called his mobile.' He met Burrows' jaded gaze, shaking his head. 'I heard the fucking ring. He didn't answer – now I know why. A few moments later, the shot.'

'He's a cop, Marilyn. It's his job.'

'It's my fucking job too,' Marilyn snapped. 'And I was on the phone chatting about shift patterns while he was out here doing his properly.'

He usually kept his emotions bottled up at work, cork shoved in firmly, hated unprofessionalism in any form. The inevitable build up of stress was dissipated instead through too many late nights in grotty clubs, overdoses of vodka, dates with women young enough to be his daughter and material enough not to care, as long as he paid.

'I shouted, vaulted the fence and charged like a bloody rhino on heat through the wood. Still got here too late.' He sighed. 'Callan was right. The killer must have cut in a semicircle through the trees to surprise Wendy Chubb.' *Cover of sight and movement until the last moment.* 'Callan must have found something important, some evidence. I can't think of any other reason for the killer to revisit the crime scene in the middle of the bloody night. He must have dropped something. But there was nothing on Callan when I found him. I checked his pockets while the air ambulance trauma team were trying to stabilize him.' Hauling the collar of his jacket up around his neck, he looked despondently down at the patch of blood. 'Get a cast of those prints and then search every centimetre of the woods within this perimeter, Burrows. Every damn centimetre. However long it takes.'

Scratching a latex-clad hand over his bald patch, Burrows nodded. 'Leave it to me, Marilyn. If there is more evidence here, I will find it.'

Marilyn laid a hand on his arm. 'Thanks, Tony.'

Ducking under the crime scene tape, he joined DS Workman, who was briefing a team of constables, setting out search parameters. Back to the house-to-house. Asking more questions. Had anyone been woken by the sound of a car at around 3 a.m.? If yes, did they get a look at it? Was it a stranger's car? A car they hadn't seen before? Or perhaps a car that rang bells from the night before? A diesel engine that sounded familiar?

'Workman, get on to Colonel Holden-Hough now. I want to know everything there is to know about an Army bloke called . . .' He tugged his notebook from his pocket, found the relevant page. 'Scott. Major Nicholas Scott.'

Jesus, you trained killers. A trained killer, to shoot a trained killer?

'Wendy Chubb's employer, sir?'

'Right. Wendy Chubb's employer. Callan said that he was working on a suspicious death involving Scott.'

'It could be a coincidence.'

'Coincidences, smincidences, my arse. I'm going to St George's Hospital to see how Callan is and then I'm off to visit this Major Scott character. Give me a call when you've spoken with Holden-Hough.'

Marilyn navigated his way back through the trees and hauled himself over the Sandhurst boundary fence, for what felt, to his weary bones, like the hundredth time. As he walked back down the narrow track that led to Birch Close where his precious BMW Z3 was parked, a mobile rang in his pocket. Not a ringtone he recognized. Callan's mobile then. He had found it when he had searched Callan's pockets, hadn't wanted it to get damaged or lost in the air-ambulance or in the hospital. He had Callan's wallet in his other pocket, for the same reason. *Small tokens. The least he could do.* Pulling the mobile from his pocket, he looked down at the name flashing on its screen.

Jessie Flynn.

His thumb found 'answer'. 'Detective Inspector Bobby Simmons.'

A pause. He could hear light breathing at the end of the line. Then a young woman's tentative voice. 'Ben? Is that you?'

'No. No, it's not. My name is Detective Inspector Bobby Simmons.'

'Oh, hi. I, uh, I wanted to speak to Ben Callan. I must have dialled wrong. Sorry—'

'Wait,' Marilyn cut in.

At least I know that I didn't drag you away from a beautiful girl, not wearing that jumper.

You have no idea how beautiful.

And now he had to tell that beautiful girl that Callan had been airlifted to hospital with a bullet lodged in his abdomen, was unlikely to see the day out. At times like this, he hated his job with a passion, could think of no logical reason on earth why he hadn't become an accountant like his old man. No logical bloody reason at all.

51

The little girl sat alone on the floor. Pale yellow curtains studded with dainty white daisies framed the window in front of her, softening the flat winter sunlight that cut through the glass. She stared, with tilted head, into nothingness, not seeing the broad sweep of lawn that ran away from the back of the house to join a field of grazing horses – horses that most ten-year-old girls would be captivated by. At the far end of the room the sound of CBeebies filled the silence, other children lolling on chairs or lying on the carpet, watching the cartoon figures charge around the screen.

The little girl was oblivious to the television and to the other children.

The man who had come to visit her didn't notice them either, so focused was he on her. He thought again, as he always did when he came here, how cruel it was that such a beautiful child would never lead a normal life, never experience everything that life had to offer. Lowering himself on to the carpet beside her, he reached for her hand, pulled it on to his knee.

'Soraya.'

She gave no response; continued to look at the window, as if transfixed by the beauty of the view beyond the glass. Unsure if she had registered his presence, he moved in front of her so as to obscure her line of sight to the window. Placing a hand gently under her chin, he lifted it so that he could look straight into her eyes.

'Soraya, it's Daddy.'

Slowly, her eyes focused on his face, and she smiled up at him.

'I have a present for you, sweetheart.'

Pulling the pale yellow teddy bear from his coat pocket, he pressed it into her hands. She held it lightly, smiling again, but he couldn't be sure whether she was smiling at the feel of the soft fur in her hands or something else entirely.

He sat with her for an hour, cradling her in his arms and talking to her: about the horses in the field, the birds in the trees, how in the summer he'd take her to West Wittering Beach and build sandcastles with her. He sang her a song, the words whispered quietly into her ear. He could feel her body rock as he sang, knew from her reaction that she was hearing, processing the tune at least, somewhere deep inside her brain.

He glanced at his watch; an hour had gone by. He had to get back before he was missed. Giving her a kiss on the forehead, tucking the teddy bear, which had fallen into her lap, back into her arms, he stood. Her head drifted to the side and her face returned to emptiness. But her arm remained clutched tight around the pale yellow teddy bear.

Looking at her, he felt a deep upset. When he was younger he had believed in fate, believed that everything happened for a reason, a reason that would, in time, lead to good. Now, he believed none of that shit. He knew that life was tough and unfair, that terrible things happened to good people, and that was all there was to it.

He sensed, rather than heard someone approach. Turning around, he smiled at the young red-headed nurse.

'How are you, Miss Greene?'

He knew that she fancied him – not that he was going to do anything about it.

'It's mid-morning snack time. Do you want to stay, while we feed Soraya her morning snack?'

'I'm sorry. I need to get back to work.'

'Will we be seeing you next week?'

'I hope so.'

'Your daughter will miss you if you don't come, Mr Starkey.'

He smiled a sad smile. 'I doubt that. But I'll try my hardest to visit.'

52

The Jacksons' road looked narrower, dirtier than it had coated in darkness when she and Callan had visited two days ago. Black city grime dusted the cream house next door, and the air smelled tight and claustrophobic against the country air she was used to. The newsagent's was open, a stack of newspapers in plastic containers outside, the containers grimy with fingerprints. An e-fit of a man's face looked out from the front page of the *Daily Mail* and the *Daily Express*, a full-colour shot of a riot in progress in some unnamed country on the cover of *The Times*, but Jessie didn't stop to read the headlines. Her stomach constricted with nerves as she walked up the garden path, her wedge heels clicking on the tiles.

She still felt sick from her conversation with Detective Inspector Simmons, a sick ache that had settled hard in her stomach and in her chest, keeping pace with her while she retrieved her car from outside the pub and drove up the A3 to Wandsworth; felt as if she would burst into tears if anyone looked sideways at her. She clenched her hands so hard that her fingernails bit into her palm. *Not here, not now.*

Rachel Jackson opened the door. At first glance, she looked better than she had two days ago, wearing a crisp white shirt and skinny jeans, her hair newly washed. But when Jessie met her dull, red-rimmed gaze, she realized that the impression was only window dressing. Her eyes were flat, their light extinguished.

'Do you remember me, Rachel?'

Pursing pale lips, she nodded. 'The psychologist.'

'Jessie Flynn.'

She didn't smile. 'What do you want?'

'I'm sorry to come back, particularly without an appointment. But I have a few more questions about Andy.'

'Where's the policeman?'

Jessie swallowed to ease the words out around the choking lump in her throat. 'This isn't a formal visit. I just have a few more questions. Captain Callan didn't need to be here.'

Rachel didn't move.

'Can I come in, please?'

A dull nod. She stood back, pulling the door open.

Jessie followed her down the narrow corridor and into the kitchen. As if following some strange ritual, they gravitated to the same chairs that they had sat in before, facing each other across the kitchen table. Jessie almost expected to hear Steve Jackson's voice – *Of course I'm bloody sure. He was my son. He didn't have any medical problems* – Callan's measured replies. But the house was silent, felt almost peaceful around them. Jessie knew that she would shatter that repose with what she was about to ask.

'Did your husband have any medical problems, Rachel?'

A tiny pause, and then Rachel shook her head. 'No. None. He wouldn't have been in the Army if he had done, would he?'

'Are you sure about that?'

Though Rachel stared back resolutely, her hand moved to finger her lips. 'Positive.'

'You can't lie to me,' Jessie said. 'It's too important.'

'I'm not lying.' Her voice quivered.

Listening to her, Jessie suddenly felt immensely sad: not only for Rachel and her children, but also for Sami, for Callan, for herself, for this whole damn mess.

'Rachel, I know that Andy was an opium addict.'

Her face twisted with anger. 'How dare you.'

'The autopsy confirmed it. Captain Callan has the results and he said that Andy was addicted to opiate-based pain-killers for months, years probably, and opium – pure opium – for weeks before he died.'

Rachel groaned. 'Oh, Jesus.'

'Callan won't do anything with the results. He'll keep them hidden – if he can – but you need to help me.'

Silence. Rachel's gaze remained fixed on the same invisible spot in the middle of the kitchen table as before.

'Callan is lying in hospital with a bullet wound in his abdomen . . .' Jessie paused, took a breath to stop her voice from breaking on the words. 'He lost a ton of blood before they got him to hospital and it's doubtful that he will live.'

Rachel gave a tiny shrug, and that one movement made Jessie want to lean across the table and slap her face.

'He was shot investigating Andy's case,' Jessie snapped. 'So you need to be straight with me, Rachel. Lies won't do.'

She covered her face with her hands. 'I'm not lying.'

'Half-truths won't do either.'

Jessie heard a sudden noise behind her. She turned. Andy Jackson's mother was standing on the kitchen threshold, cradling Rachel's baby son.

'I've heard every word and I want you to leave my house. Now.'

Meeting her gaze, Jessie saw nothing but her own mother, shrunken with grief after Jamie's death. But she couldn't let her own memories cloud her judgement.

'I'm sorry, Mrs Jackson, really I am. But I'm not leaving until I get what I came for. Truth. That's all I want. I just want some truth.' She held up her hand, thumb and index finger a millimetre apart. 'Just a grain of truth.' She felt as if she was going to burst into tears herself; dug the nails of her left hand hard into her palm again to stop herself. 'I can have you arrested for impeding a police investigation, Rachel.'

It was a cheap shot, but the words hit home. Rachel's tear-filled eyes widened.

'You wouldn't.'

Was that even true? Jessie had no idea where the Military Police jurisdiction ended, but suspected that it was far short of spouses – ex-spouses – living in civilian accommodation.

'Could you be any more cruel?' Mrs Jackson said in a voice that shook with fury. 'Could you be? I'm calling my husband. He'll come back from work. He'll come back now and force you to leave.'

Mrs Jackson turned and Jessie heard her footsteps receding down the tiled hall. She sat forward.

'I need you to help me, Rachel.' She was aware that she was almost pleading.

Rachel squeezed her eyes closed 'I don't want his memory ruined,' she said. 'He was a good soldier. He *was*.'

'This goes no further. You have my word.'

Silence. Jessie laid a hand on Rachel's arm. 'Not to the Military Police, not to the Intelligence Corps. Rachel, please look at me.' Jessie waited until Rachel's red, swollen eyes met hers. 'No further. *You have my word.*'

Rachel drew in a long, quivering breath. 'My husband broke his leg on a training exercise in Norway, three years ago. It never healed properly.'

The drawing of Andy Jackson clutching his leg, the huge box that said 'PAN'. Pain. Of course. Obvious now.

'But he pretended that it had?' Jessie asked.

'He couldn't leave the Army, it was his life. It was all he ever wanted to do since he was tiny.'

'So he took prescription painkillers?'

'Steve . . . his father got them for him. He has a bad back. It wasn't much of a stretch for the GP to hand out painkillers to him. They hand them out like sweeties to old people. Anything to get them out of the door, stop them sucking up surgery time.'

'But Andy got addicted?'

'It wasn't about addiction. He *needed* them. He couldn't do his job without them.'

'And then he was sent to Afghanistan.'

Rachel nodded. 'For six months. Steve couldn't get enough painkillers to last Andy that long.'

'So Andy plugged into the local drug dealers?'

'It wasn't like that. *He* wasn't like that.'

'Opium. It's a Class A drug, Rachel.'

'He told me that he was getting the opium from an Afghan that he worked with. One of their Intelligence Corps contacts – not some scummy drug dealer.'

'Who was this man?'

Rachel lifted her shoulders in a weary shrug. 'I don't know. Andy didn't tell me his name.'

'Think. What did Andy say about him? Anything. Any detail you can remember.'

'Has this got something to do with my husband's murder?'

Jessie looked down at her hands. *It wasn't murder*, she wanted to scream across the table. 'Yes. Yes, it could do.'

Rachel sighed; her body slumped. She looked as if the last vestiges of her will had been sucked out of her.

'He was a government official, something to do with water. Andy said that the coalition was funding a dam for the Helmand River, so that the farmers had access to water for their crops. The Intelligence Corps made the contact, managed it.'

Water. Where the hell had she heard that before? Jessie raised her hands to her head, pressing her fingers against her skull, as if she could physically reach into her mind and drag up the memory.

Farmers not fighters. But of course, the money never gets used for what it's supposed to. Sergeant Colin Starkey.

She dropped her hands to the tabletop. 'Water?'

'Yes.'

'You're sure?'

A strangled, 'Yes.'

'What else, Rachel?'

Rachel turned tear-filled eyes to the window, shook her head. 'Nothing else.'

'Think, please, anything. *Anything*.'

She flinched at the tone of Jessie's voice, at the command.

'All I remember is that he used to joke that the man was like a bad dream.'

Hurried footsteps approaching: Mrs Jackson. 'Steve's left work. He'll be here in ten minutes—'

Jessie stood, holding out her hands to halt Mrs Jackson's flow. 'Mrs Jackson, I'm leaving. I'm leaving now.' She turned back to Rachel. 'A bad dream? What do you mean?'

Rachel was picking at the skin around her thumb, drawing blood. She didn't respond.

'A bad dream? A . . . a nightmare? You mean he was a nightmare? To work with? Is that what he meant? Rachel. *Rachel*.'

With a sob, Rachel shook her head. 'No. A nightmare.' She wiped her sleeve across her nose, streaking snot across the white cotton. 'He said that the man's name meant "Nightmare" in Dari. We laughed about it.' Her head fell to her hands. 'We laughed so hard back then.'

53

Back on the pavement outside the Jacksons' house, Jessie breathed in the silty city air.

Nightmare.

Nightmare to work with?

No. He said that the man's name meant 'Nightmare' in Dari.

Her mind sought out Miss Appleby, perched primly on the cream linen sofa in that huge, panelled library at Bearwood School, a place, a moment in time that felt so far from here, from now, that it could have been in some parallel universe. *I can't remember how to pronounce his name but Nooria said that it meant 'Nightmare'.*

What the hell was going on? She had no idea, but whatever it was, she sensed that Nooria was the link. And now that she had more pieces to the puzzle – not that she felt any of them were actually slotting together – she wondered if Gideon Duursema was going to be proved right. *You need to give the child the benefit of the doubt.* The child, not the parents.

She had given Nooria and Scott the benefit of the doubt. Had she put Sami at risk by doing so? Had she consigned him to living in terror of the Shadowman, whoever that was, for longer than he needed to, purely out of professional pride – out of determination to get to the bottom of his psychological problems – herself. *Jesus*, she would never forgive herself if that was true.

And what about Scott? Where did he fit? *The Shadowman? Surely the Shadowman is me.*

Colin Starkey had been driving him to a rendezvous with an Afghan government official when they were flagged down in a street in Kandahar, Scott was doused in petrol and set alight. Who was that governmental official?

She glanced at her watch. She was in Wandsworth. Ten minutes' drive and she'd be in Battersea, at the Royal College of Art, Dyson building. Nooria's exhibition started tomorrow – she was bound to be there.

As Jessie reached her car, her telephone rang. For a self-delusional millisecond before she pulled it out of her bag, she thought that it might be Callan. Then reality kicked in and she felt the familiar lump that had settled in her stomach since DI Simmons had called sink lower, so heavy that she felt as if she might crack through the paving stones under her feet with its weight. She didn't recognize the number. It wasn't DI Simmons or Gideon Duursema.

'Yes,' she snapped.

'Oh, uh, Mrs Scott, it's Susie Wingrove.'

Fuck. She had consigned her phone call to Soraya's children's home to the back of her mind. Readying herself for a return call from Susie Wingrove hadn't been anywhere on her radar.

Pinching the end of her nose with her fingers, so that her

voice was muffled, full of cold, she said, 'I'm sorry if I sound muffled. I have the worst cold.'

'Mrs Jamieson mentioned that you were sneezing.'

'It's so freezing at the moment. I always get sick in the winter.'

She felt ridiculous, standing on the pavement clutching her nose – playing a trick that belonged in primary school – sure that Susie Wingrove would see straight through it.

'Mrs Jamieson mentioned that you might come down on Sunday. Shall we expect you at the usual time?'

The usual time.

'Yes,' Jessie replied lamely. A pause. Now that Susie Wingrove was on the phone, she needed to use the opportunity to get as much information as she could. 'Mrs Jamieson also said that Soraya's dad might come down again on Sunday.'

'Yes. He was here earlier today and said that he would try to visit again on Sunday afternoon. Is that a problem?' Susie Wingrove's voice was tentative.

'No. I was just wondering what time he was planning to come.'

'Mr Starkey said around two p.m.'

The phone almost slid from Jessie's hand; she tightened her freezing fingers around it.

'Excuse me?'

'Around two p.m., he said,' she repeated, raising her voice.

'Right,' Jessie managed.

Starkey? She must be losing something in the translation. Soraya's father couldn't be Colin Starkey. A door slammed, stiletto heels clicking on paving stones, and a woman in tight black jeans and black jacket tottered past, a small, fluffy white dog clutched in the crook of her arm.

'Mrs Scott?'

'Yes. I'm here.' Jessie held her breath, willing Susie Wingrove to continue.

'I know you're not together any more, so I just wanted to let you know what time he's coming to see Soraya, in case you didn't want to bump into him.'

'Bump into Mr Starkey?'

'Yes.' Susie Wingrove's voice had a nervous lilt, as if she was wondering whether she'd overstepped the mark, strayed too far into personal territory. 'Yes,' she repeated.

Mr Starkey, not Sergeant. Jessie had never met another Starkey, but that didn't mean that the name was uncommon. You could hardly spit in Ireland without hitting a Flynn, she remembered her father telling her, and yet she'd never met anyone who shared her surname, despite a significant proportion of Irish youth decamping to England for work. It couldn't be Colin Starkey, surely? That would make no sense. She forced herself to smile, hoped the smile conveyed itself to her voice.

'Thank you for the consideration, but Colin and I get on well, even though we're not together any more.'

Colin.

She waited. Waited for the correction.

It didn't come.

Colin Starkey was Soraya's father? It wasn't possible.

'He's a lovely man, Mr Starkey, and so good with Soraya. Anyway, take care, Mrs Scott. Stay warm and get better and we'll look forward to seeing you on Sunday at the usual time.'

307

54

The Royal College of Art was buzzy, students cutting through the foyer, jogging up the stairs clutching folios, chatting to each other, shouting into mobiles. In the cavernous space, with this confident swirl of activity around her, Jessie felt caged in loneliness. She hadn't heard any more from DI Simmons, who had promised to keep her abreast of Callan's condition. Pulling her phone from her pocket, she checked that the volume was on high and slid it back into her bag.

Ignoring the woman standing behind the reception desk, Jessie bought two takeaway coffees from the shop, a double-shot latte for herself – liquid adrenalin – and a straight black for Nooria. Clutching the coffees, she crossed to the stairs, walking as if she belonged, not as an outsider. Her clothes didn't fit, but her attitude could.

Jogging up the first flight of stairs to Level 1, she stopped at the top and turned to a young man in black Levis and a black shirt who had followed her up.

'I'm looking for Nooria Scott.'

The young man shook his head. 'Sorry, I don't know her.'

'She's on the Fine Art master's. She's putting final touches to her exhibition.'

'Fine Art studios, top floor.'

On the top floor, Jessie found someone else to ask and was directed along a steel-and-glass walkway that hung over the foyer a hundred feet below. The suspended corridor ended in a steel door, which opened into a vaulted industrial-looking space two storeys high, flooded with light from huge glass panels set into the pitched roof. Big metal tulip lights that looked as if they belonged in a World War II bunker hung at intervals from beams that supported the sloping glass-and-steel roof. There was something incredibly dramatic about the space, and Jessie could understand how it would inspire people to paint.

Her eyes grazed across the eight students dotted at intervals around the studio. She found Nooria at the far end, standing in front of a huge painting, four metres tall and a half again wide. She was clutching a paintbrush in her hand, but didn't seem to be painting, just standing, staring at the enormous canvas looming over her. It was a nightmarish image: thick streaks of oil paint in black, white and shades of grey. A man pinning a woman to the floor, the woman's mouth torn and bleeding as she screamed. The man's face was visible, but his features were indistinct, as if the observer was looking at his face through frosted glass. There was a little shape curled in the bottom left-hand corner of the canvas. It took Jessie a moment to realize that the shape was a cowering child, eyes clamped shut, hands pressed over his or her ears.

Looking at the canvas, one word filled Jessie's mind.

The Shadowman.

Nooria had painted the Shadowman.

Slowly, she crossed the wooden floor, her gaze fixed on the canvas. It cast a spectre over the whole gallery, like a stormy grey sky.

The Shadowman. Whispering, whispering. Make Mummy sad.

Nooria didn't realize she was there until Jessie was almost close enough to touch her. She suddenly spun around, eyes wide and frightened. For a second, there was no recognition.

'Nooria, it's Jessie Flynn.'

Her gaze focused. It took a few moments longer for her to formulate words. 'I have nothing to say to you, Dr Flynn.'

Jessie held out the coffee.

'What's that?' Nooria asked warily.

'Straight black,' Jessie said. 'Otherwise known as a cheap bribe.'

Unsmiling, Nooria took the coffee. 'If I had any pride, I'd throw it in the bin, but I could really do with the caffeine hit.' A pause, then a grudging, 'Thank you.' Looking down at the cup in her hand, she added, 'But I still have nothing to say to you.'

She looked as if she had lost half her bodyweight and all of her spirit in the twenty-four hours since Jessie had last seen her at Bradley Court, feet planted wide apart in her sky-blue combat trousers, humming with manic energy and paranoia. Her movements now were slow, uncoordinated, as if each move of her arm, each tilt of her head took an enormous surge of willpower.

'Can we go somewhere to talk in private, Nooria?'

'I already said that I don't want to talk to you.'

Jessie sighed. 'We're beyond that, Nooria. You have no

310

choice. Not unless you want the Military Police Special Investigation Branch all over your family like a bad smell.'

Nooria's eyes widened. 'Jesus. We really opened Pandora's Box when we referred Sami to you, didn't we?'

'I have no choice either, Nooria. I have to do my job, and my job is to make sure that Sami is mentally and physically safe and well. At the moment, I have no confidence that he is either of those things.'

Nooria didn't respond.

'We need to talk, Nooria. Let's go somewhere quiet.'

Nooria gave a dispirited nod. 'The art storeroom,' she murmured. Raising a listless arm, she pointed to a door set into the wall a few feet from where they were standing.

Jessie waited, watching Nooria's clumsily anguished movements as she put her brushes back in their pots, straightened her stool, rubbed her paint-streaked hands down her tunic, activities that looked more designed to delay the inevitable than essential. Walking over to the storeroom, Jessie held the door open.

'Nooria. Come on.'

Another dispirited nod. 'Yes.'

The art storeroom was a quarter the size of the main studio, half its height, filtered light from a Roman-blind-covered window casting stripes of light and shade across the artwork stacked against the walls. It only took a moment for Jessie to find Nooria's stack of canvases, their absence of colour stark against the other artwork, drawing her eye immediately.

The first picture in the stack was a small canvas of a young child – Sami – unmistakably Sami, with his wild black hair and huge dark eyes. The child, Sami, was cringing in the corner of a room, staring at something – something out of frame – his face frozen in terror. *The Shadowman is here*. The painting, a visual record of Sami's tormented trips to hell.

Jessie bowed her head, feeling hot tears flood her eyes. She couldn't cry now, not in front of Nooria – had to keep it together for Sami's sake, if not for her own pride. She heard the click as Nooria pulled the door to the storeroom closed behind them, wiped her sleeve quickly across her eyes. Twisting around, she went straight for the throat.

'Your daughter didn't die, did she, Nooria?'

For a fraction of a second Nooria hesitated, then her face found an expression approximating shock. 'Of course she did, years ago now. She was only a few months old.' A hard light flashed in her eyes. 'Anyway, what the hell has my dead daughter got to do with you? That part of my life is my business. *My private business.*'

'I spoke to Susie Wingrove about an hour ago. Nice woman. She said that Soraya is looking forward to seeing you on Sunday.'

Nooria's hand flew to her mouth. 'Oh my God. How dare you! How fucking *dare* you!'

'I dare to do anything, Nooria, *anything* to ensure Sami's safety.'

'His safety,' Nooria hissed. 'His *safety*. I'm his mother. He's safe with me.'

'Safe? Don't make me laugh. And don't bullshit me either, because I know far more than you realize.' It wasn't true. She had a fistful of random jigsaw pieces that didn't slot together. A fistful of jigsaw pieces, and bluff.

Nooria's hand remained pressed to her mouth. 'What right do you have to go snooping around behind my back?'

'You refused to tell me the truth. You left me with no choice.'

'You were supposed to treat Sami. Just Sami.'

'What did you expect?' Jessie asked incredulously. 'That I would be able to treat Sami with no understanding of where his condition came from and with no likelihood that I would unearth any of the other skeletons that are hidden in your closet?' Turning to the stack of paintings, she pointed to the first. 'He's looking at his father here, is he? The Shadowman. Major Scott?'

The Shadowman. Surely the Shadowman is me?

'That's right, isn't it?' Jessie continued. 'That's what you both told me.'

Nooria's breath sucked in on a sob; she didn't reply. Lifting the painting of the cowering Sami, Jessie laid it carefully to one side. Underneath was a canvas of the same size, a close-up of the Shadowman's face, Jessie presumed. Except that the features again were blurry, as if out of focus. The impression was hideous, of a ghastly, faceless tormenter.

'Your husband again?' Jessie's voice was full of scorn.

She moved that one aside, saw the one underneath, the silhouette of a child crouching on a beach, the beam of his torch illuminating a rough black sea.

'Be careful of them . . . my exhibition,' Nooria whimpered.

Jessie spun back to face her. 'Fuck your exhibition,' she snapped.

She felt like slamming her fist through each of the paintings in turn, except that even she could see that they had been painted by an exceptional talent. And because it would be an insult to Sami, to what he had been through.

'Shall I tell you what else Susie Wingrove told me? She told me that Colin Starkey is Soraya's father. That he comes to visit her frequently.'

'Oh God,' Nooria said weakly.

'Except, I don't get it. Because he's not, is he? He can't be.' She indicated the picture behind her. 'This man is Soraya's father, isn't he? The man who still comes and torments you and Sami. The man Sami calls "Shadowman". The man that you call "Nightmare".'

At the mention of 'Nightmare', a tiny sob erupted from Nooria's lips.

'And this man – the Shadowman – Nightmare – it isn't Colin Starkey.'

Nooria's shoulders shook. She looked as if something inside her was going to burst, had already burst. Jessie went over and laid a hand on her arm.

'Tell me, Nooria. Then perhaps I can help you.'

A single tear spilled from her eye, wound its way down her cheek. 'Nobody can help me.'

Seeing the torment that had twisted Nooria's features out of shape, thinking back, a light came on suddenly in Jessie's brain. Jigsaw pieces clunking together, slotting into place.

'You thought Scott could help you. Protect you.'

Nooria covered her face with her hands.

'Take me back to the beginning,' Jessie said gently. 'Right right back. How did you meet Nightmare?'

'I met him in a restaurant,' Nooria murmured.

'Where?'

'In the West End. London. I was sixteen, doing my A-levels.'

'Were you living at home?'

314

She shook her head. 'I was in a bedsit, working as a waitress to pay my way through the rest of school.'

'Why weren't you living at home?'

'I fell out with my mother.'

'What about?'

'Oh, for Christ's sake,' Nooria said wearily. 'Does it matter?' A heavy sigh. 'She didn't like my choices, that's all.'

Jessie waited for her to continue, watching her, the pain written into her features.

'Kheial, he was called,' Nooria muttered. 'It means "Nightmare" in Dari and, yes, he lived up to his name. He was an Afghan diplomat. I fell pregnant within six months of meeting him, an accident. I had Soraya when I was seventeen.'

'And she was born severely disabled?'

Nooria nodded. 'After I had Soraya, Kheial left me. I didn't see him that much anyway, as he lives between Afghanistan and England. He couldn't stand the thought of having a disabled daughter. A daughter is nothing to many Afghan men – meaningless, an irrelevance. A severely disabled daughter . . .' She shook her bowed head. 'Beneath contempt. He suggested that we drown her. He had diplomatic immunity, of course. He was happy to do it himself.'

'I'm so sorry,' Jessie said, the words meaningless in the face of what Nooria had told her. Whatever she said, empty, not enough.

Nooria lifted her shoulders. 'My fault.'

'You were sixteen.'

She gave a bitter half-laugh. 'Sixteen and stupid.'

They stood watching each other across the space, the zebra stripes of dark and light from the window casting an almost physical barrier between them on the floor.

315

'Colin Starkey helped you, didn't he? Why?'

'Because his mother was in the same situation as I was twenty-seven years ago. She had a severely disabled child, Colin's younger sister. The dad ran – of course – and she was left with nothing. No money, no support. No one to help her. Colin was only five when his sister was born – half-sister, actually – and he grew up with that impact every day. And a fury that his mother had to cope with all that alone. One of the reasons he joined the Army was to have a stable job so that he could support his mother and sister.'

'How did you meet him?'

'At an art gallery in Guildford, seven or eight years ago now. We got chatting—' a rueful shrug – 'arguing, actually, over some paintings. He loves fine art too. We ended up going for a coffee and stayed in touch. I didn't even realize that he was in the Army at first.'

'Why didn't you marry him?'

Nooria looked down at her hands and sighed. 'I loved Colin. I still do.'

The door to the storeroom opened and a woman of about their age came in clutching a watercolour of Albert Bridge. She must have felt the charged atmosphere in the room, because she hesitated, her hand on the door handle.

Nooria forced a smile. 'We're just chatting, Tracy. Do come in.'

Head down, eyes lowered, Tracy hurried to her stack of paintings, laid the watercolour gently against the others and left as she had come, silently, eyes cast to the floor.

'I didn't marry Colin because Colin is gay,' Nooria said, looking up and meeting Jessie's gaze.

'Gay?' Jessie thought of Colin Starkey in the interview – *the truth will set you free*. The overt sexual aggression he had displayed towards her in that room and later, in the car park. An act to destabilize her, she realized now. Clever.

'He offered to marry me, but I couldn't make him live that lie. He's done enough for me, continues to do so much. I couldn't destroy his life too.'

'He still sees Soraya?'

'He visits her when he can. He treats her like his own daughter. He's an incredible man. Incredibly caring, incredibly kind, incredibly loyal.'

'So you moved on to Scott?'

A sob, muffled under her hand. 'Jesus, you make me sound so horrible.'

'Is it a coincidence that Scott and Starkey are both in the Intelligence Corps?'

Nooria shook her head. 'I went with Colin to an Intelligence Corps function and first met Nick there.'

'And then you met him again at Bearwood?'

She nodded. 'Lots of Army officers send their children to Bearwood.'

'Why?' Jessie asked. 'Why Army men? Why the Intelligence Corps?'

'Because I thought they could protect me. And I thought that they could sort him out.'

'Him? Nightmare? Kheial?'

She nodded. 'But I was wrong. All I did was put Nick in danger. It's my fault that he was burn—' A pain appeared to shoot through her, cutting off the end of her sentence. She took a breath, a heaving, sucking breath. 'It's my fault that Nick was burnt.'

Jessie waited a moment. 'And Colin knew everything,' she asked gently. 'But Nick didn't?'

'Nick and Colin are very different characters.' She spoke slowly, as if every word was an effort. 'Colin grew up deprived. He had shit all day every day.'

Jessie nodded. A tough, deprived childhood could drive children in one of two directions – towards good or bad. Perhaps seeing his mother struggle with his sister that had made the difference for Colin, given him the will to make life better for others.

'Colin is so principled.'

'And Nick?'

'Nick had a comfortable upper middle class upbringing: boarding school, ponies, cricket on the lawn. He's never faced real adversity. Never had to stick his neck out as Colin has done and say, "This is what I believe in. This is what I'm going to fight for."'

'So what happened to Sami?'

Nooria rubbed a hand across her eyes, wiping away the tears. 'Kheial left me alone for a couple of years after I married Nick. I thought that I'd got rid of him permanently, that marrying Nick had worked. Kheial was back in Afghanistan.'

'Working with the Coalition. Negotiating with the Coalition to dam the Helmand River,' Jessie said.

Nooria's eyes widened. 'He's a civil engineer by training.'

Farmers not fighters. Jigsaw pieces slotting into place. *But the money never gets used for what it's meant to . . . The farmers grow opium.*

'Negotiating with the Intelligence Corps,' Jessie said.

Colin Starkey. Andy Jackson. Nicholas Scott.

So Andy Jackson's death probably was manslaughter after all. Colin Starkey must have found out that Jackson had set Scott up to pay off Nightmare for his opium and for his silence. Run him into the desert at gunpoint to try to get him to talk. Run him until he turned and fought back in desperation, and his heart gave out. Maybe Starkey had pulled the trigger too, for good measure. *Jesus*, she thought. *The truth will set you free.* No wonder Colin Starkey hadn't had any intention of telling the truth.

'What happened then?'

'He turned up again when Nick went to Afghanistan on his first tour of duty. Sami was two.' Tears were flowing freely down her cheeks now. 'The way he turned up – just arrived at our house – was like something out of a horror film. As if he was always watching me, knew exactly what I . . . what we were doing, when Nick was going to be away. He raped me and then he went upstairs. Sami was asleep in his cot. I begged him to leave Sami alone, but he reached into his cot and picked him up. I was crying and pleading with him to put Sami down. He smiled at me and said, "Whatever you want, Nooria," and he dropped Sami. Just opened his hands and let Sami fall on to the floor. Then he walked out.' Nooria's face was drained white with the memory. 'I rushed Sami to Accident and Emergency, and told them that he'd fallen down the stairs. They kept us in overnight for observation, but Sami was OK.'

'Tell me about Nick's last tour.'

Her face was grey, her eyes dull and desperate: a trapped animal. 'He came back again, a few weeks after Nick had left. He was raping me on the kitchen floor. I turned and I saw Sami standing in the doorway. He had tears streaming down his face. I shouted at him to go back to bed. I was telling him that he was bad, that he had to go back to bed, stay in bed. I didn't want him to see me like that and I

319

didn't want Kheial to get angry with him. Not after what he had done to him when he was a toddler.'

Go back to bed. Stay in bed. You're bad, Sami.

'Kheial said, "I own you, Nooria," very softly, like a caress. Then he stood up, went over to Sami and kicked him, kicked him like he was a dog, and then he left. Left me lying there on the floor bleeding, Sami huddled in the corner crying.'

Jessie felt her own eyes fill with tears. 'The girl. That's why you pretended that Sami was a girl, wasn't it? Because you wanted to keep him safe from Kheial?'

Nooria nodded. 'He would have been furious if he thought I'd had a boy with another man. But a girl—' She broke off with a tiny, dispirited lift of her shoulders.

'Why didn't you tell Nick?'

'I was trapped. I felt as if Kheial could destroy my life if he wanted to. That my situation was hopeless.' Burying her face in her hands, she started to sob. 'And I was right. He did. He destroyed my life and he destroyed Nick's too. Sami's. All our lives.'

'And now?'

Face buried in her hands, she hunched her shoulders. 'He's done everything to me. There is nothing left. Nothing left that he can do.'

'Do you have any idea where Kheial is now?'

'No. But I hope to God that he's in hell.'

55

Marilyn's phone rang. He was standing next to a large sign bearing the black schematic of a mobile, a red line drawn through it, the words *Do Not Use Mobile Phones* written in unavoidably accusing capitals below.

Smothering the ringing hand grenade against his shirt, he jogged down the corridor, casting a quick, guilty smile at the pretty blonde nurse manning the intensive care ward's reception, who he'd tried to chat up earlier, in a feeble bid to divert his attention from the shit-show that Wendy Chubb's murder investigation had become, with paltry success. His smile was rewarded with a frown.

The double doors to the ward were locked. It took him another few seconds of scanning the walls either side of the door to find the lock-release button. Slamming it with his palm, he shoved through the doors and into the corridor.

'DI Simmons,' he snapped into the phone.

'Detective Inspector, I was about to give up on you.'

'I was in intensive care.'

'Really.' Dr Ghoshal didn't sound overly interested. 'The smoking and drinking have finally got to you,' he added, in his trademark monotone. 'I can't say that I'm surprised.'

Very funny. Marilyn wasn't in the mood to rise to the pathologist's bait. Dr Ghoshal was not renowned for his sense of humour and Marilyn found that they got on best when banter was kept to a minimum.

'What can I do you for, Dr Ghoshal?'

'The flesh.'

'Yes.'

'When you collected the autopsy report on your male cadaver on Wednesday, I told you that I believed the flesh didn't look quite right.'

'You did.'

'I have results back from toxicology.'

Marilyn waited in silence, tapping his foot impatiently.

'Vegetable oil.'

'What?'

'Vegetable oil.' A pause. 'Commonly used in cooking,' Dr Ghoshal continued and Marilyn saw his earnest face in the words, no room for irony in the pedantic mind behind it.

'Yes, thank you, Dr Ghoshal, I got that far myself. But how did it get on my murder victim?'

'We found traces in a spatter pattern, mainly on the face and upper torso. To be honest, given the state of your victim, we were lucky to do that.' Another pause. 'It was hot.'

A woman's voice suddenly from behind Marilyn. 'Excuse me.'

He turned. An old woman was pushing a wheelchair down the corridor, its passenger even older, her body twisted like a wind-bent tree. *Granny pushing granny*. Christ, how he hated hospitals, probably because they made him feel that, at forty-nine and with his lifestyle, he wasn't so far away from one himself. He stepped aside.

'The door,' the old lady pushing muttered.

'Oh. It's a buzz-in,' he said, clutching the phone to his ear, hearing Dr Ghoshal's voice, but not catching the words. 'Press the speaker and the nurses will buzz you in.'

A pause.

'Excuse me!'

'What now?' he growled and immediately felt guilty. Stepping forward he jammed his finger on the buzzer. 'Two old la— DI Simmons. Open the door please.'

He held the door open while they trundled through.

'Detective Inspector. Did you hear what I said?' Dr Ghoshal's voice was laced with impatience.

'No, sorry.'

A heavy sigh. 'I'll repeat: the vegetable oil was hot – boiling hot – when it came in contact with your murder victim. Given the density, the location, face and upper torso and the splatter pattern, I'd say that someone threw a pot of boiling oil in your murder victim's face.'

'Jesus.'

'It would have hurt, most certainly.'

Master of the understatement.

'So he was burnt?'

'Yes. Burnt with boiling vegetable oil. And then killed with several blunt blows to the head.'

'Right. OK.' He needed to think, get some clarity. Wendy Chubb's murder, followed by Callan's attempted murder, had sideswiped him, taken all his attention. He'd almost forgotten about the molten pile of flesh on Dr Ghoshal's dissecting table. 'Thank you, Dr Ghoshal.'

'My pleasure. I'm starting Wendy Chubb's autopsy now. I'll be in touch. Have a nice day, Detective Inspector.'

The phone went dead in Marilyn's hand. *Burnt? His Chichester Harbour murder victim had been burnt*. He hadn't expected that.

56

Out of nowhere the tears came, fuzzing Jessie's vision as she drove. She found herself clutching the steering wheel as if it was a lifebelt and crying for everything. Jamie. Her mother and father who Jamie had effectively taken with him. Her normal childhood – *before*. And Ben Callan.

Pulling into the petrol station on West Hill, she tucked her Mini into a corner and cut the engine. Slumping forward, she buried her head in the crook of her bent elbow and sobbed.

She was at the end, wasn't she – had proven that Sami wasn't the victim of abuse, by his parents at least – so why didn't she feel even a tiny nugget of relief? She could walk into Gideon's office when she got back to Bradley Court and tell him to call off the Redcaps' Special Investigation Branch. The diagnosis that Scott had made – post-traumatic stress disorder – had been correct all along, only the cause needing to be uncovered, which she had done, the treatment plan developed – still to do. So why the hell did she feel as if her insides had been torn out, an icy vacuum installed in their place? She knew that a huge part of the feeling was due to Callan's condition, and another part to do with what Nooria had told her, the trauma that she and Sami had suffered. But there was something else too. An emptiness in her head as well as in her heart, a lingering doubt that made her feel as if she had missed something.

A sudden knock on the window. Face stained with tears, she looked up.

'Are you OK?' the petrol attendant mouthed through the glass.

She nodded, couldn't yet form words, was grateful when he stepped away.

Flipping down the rear-view mirror, she looked at the reflected sliver of her face: pale and puffy, streaks where the tears had cut wet tracks through the film of city grime on her cheeks. Rubbing her sleeve across her face, she smeared the tear tracks into the rest of the dirt.

Head down to avoid eye contact with the couple of other customers filling their cars, she crossed over to the shop, shivering in the cold wind cutting across the forecourt. She was hungry, realized that in the past twenty-four hours she'd eaten barely more than a biscuit and a couple of slices of toast.

Lined up outside the shop was a row of plastic flip-lidded newspaper containers, identical to those she had seen outside the newsagent's by the Jacksons' house. As she passed, her eye was once again drawn to the e-fit staring out from the front page of the *Daily Mail*. The man's face – his features – blurry, so indistinct that it could have been an out-of-focus photograph that she was looking at. Bending down, she lifted the clear plastic cover and pulled out the newspaper, flicking to page five as instructed under the photograph, hurriedly skimming the words written there. Tossing the newspaper back into the holder she sprinted back to her Mini, yanking her mobile from her pocket as she ran.

57

A woman's voice from behind Marilyn, businesslike, prepared to brook no dissent: 'The trauma surgeon would like to speak with you, Detective Inspector.'

He turned. The blonde nurse was holding the door to the intensive care ward open for him. As he stepped forward, her arm shot out, blocking his way.

'That phone needs to be off, sir.'

'I'm expecting some important calls.'

'I'm sorry. Hospital rules.' A frown twisted her pretty features out of shape. 'Right now. No exceptions, I'm afraid.'

Feeling like a five-year-old boy caught nicking sweets, Marilyn switched off his mobile, slid it into his pocket and dutifully followed the nurse back through the double doors. The waiting room was deserted. He cast her a questioning look.

'I've moved Mrs Callan to the intensive care family room, so that you can have your conversation with the surgeon in private,' she said. 'She'll be more comfortable in there anyway. The doctor will update her on her son's progress after he's spoken with you. He'll be down in five minutes. He's just cleaning himself up.'

Marilyn nodded. Her words made him feel slightly nauseous. *Cleaning himself up.* A bland euphemism for scrubbing his hands, his arms, his clothing, of Callan's blood. He was pleased, though, that Mrs Callan was no longer here to listen, had singularly failed to offer her any meaningful comfort in the four hours since she'd arrived in intensive care, to be greeted by the news that, for the second time in a year, her son had a life-threatening bullet wound. Marilyn's heart had gone out to the woman, standing alone in this clinical space, trying to hold it together in front of him. Offering commiseration wasn't one of his strengths and he usually left the breaking of bad news and the succour required after to DS Workman. He had felt adrift in a small boat, watching a tidal wave accelerate towards him, in the face of Mrs Callan's grief.

Slumping down on one of the plastic-covered chairs in the waiting room, he pulled out his mobile and looked hard at the blank screen, as if the intensity of his gaze might miraculously cause it to show signs of life. Shoving it despondently back in his pocket, he glanced over at the television screen on the wall – BBC News 24 – an unremitting stream of the violent and depressing acts that humankind could perpetrate on one another, acts he saw quite enough of in his day-to-day job without feasting on more. Tilting back in the seat, he closed his eyes, was asleep before the news anchor had moved on to the next story.

Twenty minutes later, he woke with a start. A doctor of about his own age, wearing pressed navy-blue scrubs, his salt-and-pepper hair covered by a pale blue cloth hat like an old-lady's rain bonnet, was sitting opposite. He looked as grey-faced and frayed around the edges as Marilyn felt.

'Tough day, Detective Inspector?'

Marilyn yawned into his sleeve. His eyes felt as if they had been taken out, rubbed in salt and jammed back in their sockets.

'Tough night-day-night.' Marilyn held out a hand. 'Bobby Simmons. Surrey and Sussex Major Crimes.'

'Simon Baines, Consultant Surgeon in trauma/emergency surgery.'

'You've been operating on Captain Callan?'

Baines nodded.

'How is he doing?' Marilyn asked, craving information but at the same time dreading what he might be about to hear.

'I'm afraid that we're not out of the woods by a long shot.'

Baines spoke quickly, in a soft, sing-song voice, which Marilyn recognized. It was the same tone he used to speak with the relatives of victims of crime. He steeled himself.

'Captain Callan arrived with extensive internal injuries and haemorrhaging, and severe damage to his right lung and liver. He had also lost over half of his blood volume,' Baines said. 'We have successfully removed the bullet from his abdomen and sewn up his lung. At the moment, we're working to repair the damage to his liver.'

'No drinking then,' Marilyn muttered.

'Huh.' Baines raised an eyebrow.

'No. Nothing. Sorry.' *Jesus*, what was wrong with him? Too used, he realized, to anaesthetizing stress with inappropriate behaviour. 'Continue, please, Doctor.'

'If it hadn't been for the air-ambulance bringing him in,

I'd be telling you that he was dead. Another five minutes getting here – less, even – and he would not have made it this far. That's how close it was. But he is alive now, and my team will continue to do all we can to keep it that way. We have a very experienced major trauma team here at St George's Hospital. One of the best in the UK.'

'Thank you, Doctor.'

'It's my job.' He gave a weary smile. 'And one that I am very privileged to do.'

Marilyn couldn't muster a return smile. Not even a poor imitation of one. *Just as it's my job to catch the bastard who did this.*

Baines extended an open right hand and Marilyn looked down at the gold round nestling in his bare palm. The bullet was unmistakably a 9 mm, standard at first glance, no visible modifications. Plenty of them out in the criminal network, but 9 mm was also Army handgun ammunition, an abundance of which he knew went missing from MoD armouries every year.

'The bullet was clean – didn't fragment, at least,' Baines said. 'Pretty lucky, considering.'

'I'm going to need your fingerprints, Doctor.'

Baines gave a weary nod. 'Sorry. I didn't think.' He yawned. 'God, I must be more tired than I thought.'

'Don't try napping on these chairs. They're crucifying for the lower back.'

Taking an evidence bag from his pocket, Marilyn slid his hand in, picked up the bullet, reversed the bag, sealed and pocketed it.

Baines rose. 'I need to speak with Mrs Callan and then I must get back to the operating theatre.'

'Thanks again, Doctor,' Marilyn said. 'I need to get going

now too, but I'll leave my mobile number with reception so you can call when you have more news. I'll send someone in to fingerprint you later today too, if that's OK.'

Baines nodded. 'I'll be here all day. They may have to wait if I'm in surgery.'

They stood and shook hands. Baines headed to the family room, Marilyn to the exit. The moment that the intensive care ward's double doors clicked shut behind him, he pulled his phone from his pocket and switched it on.

Four beeps in quick succession. A missed call from DS Workman and three other missed calls – all from the same number, he noted – a number that he didn't recognize.

Who the hell was trying to get hold of him so urgently?

58

Sergeant Colin Starkey pushed open the door to the Non-Commissioned Officers' Mess at Intelligence Corps headquarters, Chicksands. Navigating through the empty chairs, in the deserted room, he made his way up to the bar.

'Whisky, sir?' the Catering Corps private behind the bar asked, as Starkey settled himself on to one of the stools.

'I clearly need to stop drinking during the day,' he sighed. 'It's becoming a nasty habit.'

The barman glanced at his watch. 'It's nearly four, sir. Not obscenely early.'

Starkey gave the barman a rueful smile. Four p.m. on a weekday, everyone else gainfully employed. It was only him, it seemed, who had fuck-all to do but hang out in the bar and drink. Drink and wait for his judgement to be handed down. Not that he had any regrets. Given the same situation, the same options he had been faced with in Afghanistan ten days ago, he would make the same choices.

'When are you back on the job, sir?'

Starkey shrugged. 'Soon, I hope.'

'And the investigation?'

'I'll be acquitted.'

'Glad to hear that, sir.' The barman smiled. 'Though you'll miss this life of leisure when you're back.'

Starkey shook his head. Leisure gave him too much time to think, and he didn't like to think too much. His thoughts always turned bad: to Nooria, to Soraya, to his mother and sister living out their lives in the council house in Fulham that he had grown up in, every day a wearisome struggle, despite the money that he sent them monthly.

No. He wanted to get back to it. Couldn't wait.

Pushing himself up from the bar-stool, he went over to the window, where he swivelled an empty chair so that it was facing out, relaxed into it, putting his feet on the windowsill. The sky was leaden, heavy black storm clouds layering to the south, darkness falling fast. He took a sip of whisky, savouring the taste. Another. Closing his eyes, he took a large slug, felt the burn course down his throat, fire spreading into his chest. The darkness in his mind's eye flickered, yellow, gold, and he was back in Afghanistan.

I'll be acquitted.

He'd had no idea at the time that Andy Jackson had suffered a heart attack. Everything had happened too quickly. They'd been down in the dirt, brawling. Andy Jackson had been a big lad too, strong and vicious, with the purpose and focus of a trapped animal fighting for its life.

He had felt no satisfaction when he had pulled the trigger. Just blind fury and a profound need to re-address the balance, according to his own rules and morality. Salvage a tiny bit of right from wrong.

His eyes snapped open. The bar was still deserted. Darkness of the late afternoon closing in. And even now, back in England, sitting here with a drink in his hand and the dirt of Afghanistan long since washed from his body, he felt no regrets, no remorse. Andy Jackson had deserved everything that he had got.

Starkey knew that he was in the clear. Forensic examination of his gun had given the Redcap nothing and he would find no other evidence, however hard he looked. There had been no witnesses and the only person left alive had no intention of ever talking. *The truth never set anyone free, Captain. Only the fucking stupid believe that.*

Raising his glass, he gave a silent toast – to Nooria and Major Scott, to the little boy, and to Soraya. He hoped that their lives would work out, had tried hard to make sure that they would. But he knew that the chances were slim. They had already been through too much, done too much, were probably too far gone now for salvation.

59

'Dr Flynn.'

'Major Scott.'

He was sitting in the same chair she had found him in the first time she'd been here, in front of the window, but facing into the room this time, a shadow framed in the dim light of the table lamp and the darkness of the winter afternoon, closed in now, cold and dense.

They held each other's gaze across the room, the tension between them an almost physical presence. Jessie's gaze flicked down from Scott's face for an instant: she noticed the bottle of whisky on the chair beside him, empty, a thin gold string running down the leather from the mouth of the bottle; a millisecond later the snub-nosed Browning cradled in his lap. His hand resting lightly on its butt, index finger tapping out a musical note on its trigger.

He watched her eyes move, the flicker of recognition – the fear – and his face broke into a smile, the burnt skin on his cheek cracking like drying mud.

'I've come to see Sami, Major Scott. Is he in his room?'

Her voice infuriated her, thin and reedy, like a nervous little girl.

He smiled. 'Are you frightened, Dr Flynn?'

She shook her head, the movement so weak it almost wasn't there. 'Why should I be?'

'You're a terrible liar.'

Suddenly, he was moving, reaching for the arm of the chair, hauling himself up, bearing down on her across the room with the force of a collapsing building, the Browning clutched tight in his swinging hand. Stepping back, Jessie came hard up against the wall. Left or right – was the door to the sitting room left or right? – she wasn't sure, had lost her orientation in the dimness of the room, the disturbing force of his presence.

His face was so close to hers that his breath stirred her hair. She recognized that rabid look in his eye, a look she had seen before in the most damaged of her patients, smelled the whisky, rancid on his breath. The Browning hung by his side, gripped lightly in his right hand. Jessie forced herself not to look at it, not to acknowledge its presence.

She cleared her throat. 'Is Sami upstairs in his room?' The politeness in her tone felt almost comical.

'You leave Sami alone.' His voice hissed from his mouth like poisoned gas.

The urge to turn and run from his claustrophobic proximity was almost overwhelming. But she had come here for a reason: to see Sami. She stood her ground.

'I've just seen Nooria. She told me everything. The truth.'

'The truth?' He gave a harsh, half-laugh. 'Nooria told you the truth, did she? It was more than she did to me.' His voice, strangled with pain, rose and cracked. 'The truth will set you free, Dr Flynn. One of my sergeants in Afghanistan, the one who tried to save me from all this—' he raised his hand to his burnt face – 'used to say that.'

Starkey.

'It's bullshit.' His face was so close that she felt as if she would drown in the red liquid of his naked eye socket. 'The truth, if you really want to know it, Dr Flynn, is that I'm a murderer. A double murderer.'

'Murderer?' Her voice was strangled.

'Wendy.' He tilted forward until his mouth was kissing her ear. 'I stabbed Wendy Chubb.'

Jessie recoiled. Twisting her head, she searched left and right for the door. It was right, barely two metres away. She could dodge through quickly, dart to the front door, escape. His fingers snapped closed around her wrist like a trap. Had he read her mind?

'I'm sorry.'

'Sorry?' Jessie croaked. 'For Wendy?' Her heart was slamming in her chest.

'I had no choice.'

'We always have choices.' As she spoke the words, she felt the heavy weight of his hand tight around her wrist. Why the hell was she challenging him when all she wanted to do was get out of here alive? But she couldn't help herself. Challenging was part of her job, in her nature, her DNA.

'I'm sorry about Captain Callan too,' he muttered.

Callan?

It took her a moment.

Jesus Christ.

'You shot Callan?' She felt blood rush to her brain, anger flare, hot and furious. She tried to yank her arm from his

338

grip, but the muscular fingers tightened with a strength that frightened her. 'You fucker,' she said, right into his face. She couldn't help herself. 'You shot him in the back. You shot him in the back, you cowardly fucker.'

Major Scott twisted her arm so hard it almost popped from the shoulder joint. She gasped, clenched her teeth against the pain. She didn't care now. Couldn't give a shit.

'You're a fucking coward,' she sneered.

'Do you think a third will make any difference to me or to them? The Army? The police?'

'Callan is alive.'

Was he? She didn't know. DI Simmons' phone had gone straight to voicemail. It was as if Scott hadn't heard her.

'It's your fault,' he growled. 'We were fine before you.'

'Nothing was fine. You and Nooria just buried your heads in the sand.'

Sliding her free hand to her coat pocket, she pulled out her mobile, glanced down quickly. No signal. *Shit.* No bloody signal. She held it up to his face, conscious that the words on the screen were blurred with the trembling of her hand.

'The Detective Inspector running the Wendy Chubb murder case knows I'm here.'

Scott chuckled. 'Nobody knows you're here. That's why you're shaking.'

'I called him before I came.'

'Bullshit.'

It wasn't bullshit. She had called him from the petrol station on West Hill, another two times while speeding, one-handed, down the A3, left three messages on his voice-mail. He clearly hadn't listened to them yet. She was on her own.

Tilting her head, she fixed on the door two metres away, Scott's bulk blocking her escape to it. But if she *could* get there, run through. The stairs would be straight ahead, the door to the outside and escape to her right. Which way? Should she go to Sami, or should she run?

Then it hit her.

The acute memory of pushing open the door to Jamie's room, seeing the shape of him hanging in front of the curtain. *It was your fault. You were supposed to be looking after him.* Buried self-hatred snaked into her mind like molten lava through a fissure.

'I just want to see Sami and then I'll leave. I want to say goodbye.'

Relaxing her arm – the one he was grasping – she let it flop freely, so that his hand was supporting a dead weight. No tension. No resistance. *Take the aggression out of the situation.* Playing the psychology.

A second. Two.

She heard Scott sigh, felt the rigidness in his body relax fractionally. His fingers around her wrist loosen. Fractionally.

'I let them both down,' he murmured. 'I left them here to be his victims.'

'You had a job to do,' she said gently. 'You had no choice.'

Snatching her arm free, she ducked sideways, darted through the door, and sprinted for the stairs. She had a second's head start, while his brain struggled to adjust from compassion to escape.

Suddenly he was behind her, snatching at her leg as she started up the stairs, yanking it from under her. Staggering, she cycled frantically, trying to stay upright on her other leg, but momentum was propelling her forward and she slammed down prone. The edge of a stair caught her under

340

the ribcage, knocking the breath from her lungs. She lay for a moment, winded and shocked.

'You fucking bitch,' Scott snarled.

Kicking out hard with her free foot, she caught him under the chin, saw his head snap back, his torso follow. His hand fell from her ankle. She scrabbled up the first few stairs, her hands slippery on the polished wood, found her feet, charged up the rest. At the top of the steps, she stumbled. The darkness on the landing was denser than in the hallway; for a few seconds she was blind. Scott was at the bottom of the stairs, a crouching, groaning shadow framed in the dim hallway. He was on his knees clutching his jaw in agony. Had she broken it? She hoped so.

Careering down the corridor, she found the door to Sami's room, burst through without knocking. Slamming the door closed behind her, she searched for the lock.

No lock. Fuck. Turning, she scanned the bare room.

The bed.

The chest of drawers.

Plastic play buckets.

Sami, a motionless statue in the corner, his dark eyes huge with fright.

'Sami, it's Jessie Flynn.'

No reaction. No obvious recognition. Just the familiar look of frozen, wide-eyed terror. And a bruise, blooming purple and blue on his cheek.

Putting her weight behind the chest of drawers, she bumped it across the carpet to the door, hauling one end, running to the other, bumping that end, heaving, dragging it across the room like a giant crab. It was heavy old oak, full of clothes, weighed a ton. She stopped, panting, catching her breath.

Footsteps.

Her heart was in her mouth, watching as the door handle twisted.

'Open the door, Dr Flynn.' His voice full of threat.

He had the gun. Would he shoot through the closed door? Surely not. Not when his only son was on the other side.

'Call the police and when I hear them arrive, I'll open it.'

A thud as he threw his weight against the door. Spinning away, she ran over to Sami, was momentarily blinded. The torch. Sami pressing himself into the corner of the room, shining the torch beam straight in her face.

'The torch will keep the Shadowman away. The torch will keep the Shadowman away.' Chanting under his breath, eyes jammed closed.

Squatting in front of him, she put her hands lightly on his shoulders. He cringed away.

'Look at me, Sami. Look at me,' she urged. 'Open your eyes and look at me.'

He met her gaze through cracked lids, his dark eyes brimming with tears. She touched her fingers lightly to the bruise.

'What happened to your cheek, Sami?'

'Daddy angry,' he whimpered. 'Daddy angry with the girl . . .' he stuttered. '. . . with . . . with the boy.'

Jesus. Looking at him now, the bruise, the utter terror, the depth of psychological damage in one tiny, four-year-old boy, she felt furious.

'You have my son in there. Open the fucking door.'

'Call the police now,' she shouted back, her voice cracking with tension. Tension and rage. This was all wrong. This was so badly, madly wrong. She turned back to Sami.

342

'Remember that you're safe with me, Sami. The boy is safe with the woman.'

Tears ran down his cheeks.

'The boy is safe with the woman, Sami. Say it. Say it, Sami. The boy is safe with the woman.'

A choking sob. 'The boy is safe with the woman,' he repeated – a mechanical toy – hugging the torch to his chest. 'The boy is safe with the woman.'

'Open the fucking door now, or I will kick it open.'

Lifting him gently by the upper arms, Jessie brought him to his feet and guided him over to the window. Yanking the curtains open, holding tight to his trembling hand, she slid the sash window up. Freezing air billowed into the room, watering her eyes, swirling around them. An electric storm muttered in the distance, thunder, a flash of sudden lightning. With a cry, Sami cowered away. Jessie pulled him to her, hugged him tight.

A thud. The chest of drawers swayed, slammed back against the door again.

She looked right into his tear-drowned eyes. 'The boy is safe with the woman, Sami. Remember, the boy is safe with me.'

Pulling him on to her knee, sitting herself on the window ledge, she swung one leg and then the other out of the window. Clutching the frame with one hand, the other arm wrapped tight around Sami's chest, she shuffled forward, felt the window ledge shift to the edge of her bottom, tensed her bicep ready to take the strain. She gave one last push against the crumbling brick with her feet. Their bodies swung – out and back – she slammed sideways against the wall, her shoulder and hip taking the impact, bicep burning with the effort of

343

holding them both. They were hanging fifteen feet above the ground.

A crash in the room. *The chest of drawers.*

She closed her eyes. Took a breath. Opened them, and let go.

Her feet hit the frozen earth, her knees buckled, she rolled sideways as she'd been taught when parachuting, transferring the energy from the impact into motion. Her knees and ankles felt as if they'd been cracked with a sledgehammer. Sami was silent. Silent and still and pale as a corpse in her arms, too frightened to move or scream.

Grabbing the torch, which had rolled away from them, carrying Sami in her arms, she sprinted across the grass to her Mini, clicked the locks and shoved him in through the driver's door, following in one fluid motion as Scott rounded the corner of the house.

'I love that boy and I love his mother,' he screamed.

Tyres screeched on gravel as Jessie put her foot down, spun the Mini across the drive and on to the road, leaving him, running, screaming in her wake.

60

He was standing in the middle of the lane, staring straight down it towards her, in the gathering darkness. Slowing to a stop, she cut the engine. He raised his arm to shield his eyes from the glare of the headlights and their gazes locked through the windscreen.

She sat for a moment longer, fighting the tide of nausea that had threatened to overwhelm her, ever since Doctor Flynn had come to her studio and seen her artwork. She had known then that her time and grace had run out. Even as the psychologist's eyes filled with tears, Nooria had seen the shadows of doubt in them, the reflection of her brain computing as she studied the paintings. There had been too many loose ends in her own explanation; loose ends that would now hang her.

She felt sick with exhaustion. Exhaustion and defeat. And the knowledge that whatever she had done, however hard she had fought to change the predetermination that had mapped out her life from birth, she had still lost. She had been born to be used and to lose, and she

345

had lost. And in losing, she had taken Nick and Sami down with her.

Swinging open the driver's door, feeling the chill wind cutting across the fields, straight through her thin black cotton dress, Nooria walked slowly towards her husband.

'She's taken him, hasn't she?'

He nodded.

'When?'

'Ten minutes ago.'

'Where? Where did she take him?' But even as she asked, she already suspected. The final painting Dr Flynn had seen, of the little boy crouched on a beach, his torch lighting the rough black sea, hadn't been explained. *Waves on the pond.*

'I'm sorry that I couldn't stop her.'

He looked hollowed out, a husk of the man she had first met six years ago, every gram of vitality, of fight, gone.

'No. It wasn't your fault. None of this is your fault. I shouldn't have told you about Wendy, about the keys.' A sob rose up in her throat, straining her vocal cords. 'I shouldn't have involved you in *any* of this.'

'I failed you,' he murmured.

'I was asking the impossible.'

He gave a dull, defeated nod. 'So what now, Nooria?'

'I'm going to get Sami back.'

'And then?'

'And then I don't know.' Tears welled in her eyes. 'We've reached the end of the road, Nick. You, me. Us together. Us apart. All I know is that I want to be with my son.'

'Your son.' His bitter laugh met the dense, cold night.

Nooria bowed her head and felt hot tears streaming down her face. 'And you? What are you going to do, Nick?'

'If I was more of a man, I'd put the barrel of this Browning in my mouth and pull the trigger. But of course I won't, because I've never been man enough, have I? So I'll wait here and they'll come for me.' He swallowed, fighting back his own tears. 'Did you ever love me, Nooria, or did you just need me?'

Nooria hunched her shoulders. In truth, she didn't know. She could lie to him now, but she had already told him enough lies to last a lifetime. Stepping forward, she took the Browning from his slack hand, lifted her other and stroked it down the damaged, ravaged skin of his cheek, feeling the rough knots and grooves against the soft, cold skin of her palm.

'I'm sorry, Nick. I'm sorry for everything.'

61

Jessie showed her pass and waited while the gate guards ran a mirror under her car, shone a torch through the windows, pausing for a second when the beam found Sami, curled on the back seat, twitching and whimpering as he slept.

'My son,' Jessie lied, with a smile.

'That's fine, Dr Flynn.'

Night had fallen – pitch black. A cold wind was flattening the grasses either side of the narrow tarmac road, the storm that Jessie had heard from the Scotts' house roaring over the ocean now, a few miles south.

'Which way to the sea?'

The guard looked surprised.

'I want to have a look while Sami's asleep, before I go to the Officers' Mess. I sailed here this summer.' Another lie. 'It was beautiful. I can't remember the way in the dark.'

He gave her directions, raised the barrier. Starting the engine, she followed the ribbon of tarmac that stretched in front of her through the darkness, the lights of the guardhouse fading behind her as she drove.

Baker Barracks was on Thorney, a tiny island separated from the British mainland by a narrow channel called the Great Deep. The island was typical coastal plain: skeletal trees, branches uniformly twisted and bent away from the wind that cut in from the ocean; coarse grasses; pale, sandy soil which had lapped over the edge of the tarmac road, blown there by the wind.

She passed the accommodation blocks and houses to her right, looming square shapes even blacker than the sky, the Officers' Mess, off to her left, lights blazing from its windows. The buildings petered out as she drove on towards the sea, the road swinging from south to southeast, the trees and shrubs thinning, then finishing abruptly, replaced by scrappy grass and sand, the road tailing to nothing.

Cutting the engine, Jessie stared through the windscreen at the inky expanse in front of her, sky and sea almost indistinguishable, just a faint undulating line where the deep blue-black of the sky transitioned to the cold black swell of the sea. A couple of yachts bucked at anchor fifty metres offshore; lightning streaked over the ocean beyond the harbour mouth; the wind whipped eddies of sand up around her car.

Sami was awake now, blinking, disorientated from sleep. Reaching over the back seat, Jessie found the switch of his torch, clicked it on for him. She stroked a hand over his cheek.

'Sami, we're here.'

Clutching the torch to his chest, he pressed his nose to the window.

'Dark,' he murmured.

'Yes, it's dark. It's nighttime now. But I wanted to bring you here, to see if you remember,' she said gently.

She had used exposure therapy like this with adult patients suffering from post-traumatic stress disorder, but never with a child, knew that she was risking both her job and her reputation by bringing him here. But time had run out. She had to find out what had happened to him, what was going on, once and for all – bring those terrifying, repressed memories to the fore now, before he was taken away from her and she lost the chance to help him forever.

She held the car door open with her hip, feeling the strength of the wind as it pushed the door against her leg, reached back and hauled Sami into her arms. Taking off her coat, she wrapped it around him and carried him towards the sea. As they got closer, the moon lit the waves and she felt Sami stiffen in her arms. He looked up at her and his eyes were hollowed out with fear.

'Waves on the pond,' his voice, so quiet, was almost lost in the sound of breaking water.

'Have you been here before, Sami? At nighttime? Did you come here before when it was dark? With Mummy? Did she give you the torch to make you feel safe in the dark?'

'Waves on the pond.' He was breathing in great, shuddery gasps, his torch clutched tight in his hand. 'Where is the man?'

'The man isn't here any more, Sami. He's gone.'

He whimpered, eyes casting around him in terror.

'You're safe now, Sami. The man is never coming back. But is this where you brought him? Is this where you and Mummy brought the Shadowman? Did Mummy put the Shadowman into the sea?'

'The Shadowman,' he wailed. 'The Shadowman is here. Mummy brought Shadowman here.' He began to struggle, powerful in his terror. Slamming his fist against Jessie's chest, he screamed and writhed. She held him tight.

'The Shadowman has gone, Sami. He's never coming back.'

With a cry of frustration and fear, Sami yanked his arm back and swung the torch at her head. She ducked, just in time, felt the heavy metal Maglite whip past her temple and slam into her shoulder. Pain exploded in the joint. Falling to her knees, biting back the pain, she held on to him while he screamed and kicked, scratched at her face with his fingers, struggled to free the hand holding the torch from her grip.

'The Shadowman has gone. *Listen to me, Sami.* You'll never see him again. *Never*, Sami . . . You're safe now. Listen to me, Sami. *You're safe.*'

62

Jessie heard the car engine from a long way off. At first the sound barely penetrated the noise of the wind and waves. Quietening Sami, she listened.

The sound manifest now, and then headlights cut through the night, making black skeletons of the bare trees and bushes that lined the single-track road to the shore. A Land Rover Defender, two hundred metres away, unmistakable now. Approaching fast.

Her blood ran cold.

Quickly, she scanned the area around them. Only the shingle beach, ankle-high grass flattened by the wind, the bright moon washing them in a halo of light, the nearest cover fifty metres away. Her Mini, parked like a bright yellow Belisha beacon where the road ran out. There was nowhere to run, no hiding place.

The Defender pulled up twenty metres away from her and Sami. Trapped in the glare of its headlights, Jessie could see nothing beyond the vehicle's black bulk. The driver's door opened and Nooria climbed out. She was holding something in her right hand, black and shiny, and Jessie didn't need to look twice to know that it was Scott's service Browning.

'Mummy,' Sami shouted.

Pulling himself from Jessie's grip, he ran towards Nooria.

'Sami, no,' Jessie screamed. She charged after him, whipped him off his feet.

'I want my son,' Nooria shouted. She held the pistol out to the side briefly, making sure that Jessie had seen it without Sami also catching sight of it. Then she shoved it into her coat pocket. 'I want my son back *now*.'

'Nooria, I know,' Jessie shouted.

'Know what?'

'About Kheial.'

'Of course you know about him. If you recall, I told you only three or four hours ago.'

Jessie shook her head. 'You know that's not what I mean.'

'I have no idea what you're taking about.'

'The Shadowman. Waves on the pond. The man in the pond.'

'You're sounding crazy, Dr Flynn.' She laughed, high and brittle. 'You should get yourself referred to a psychologist. I'd like my son back now.' Dropping to one knee, she beckoned to Sami. 'Come here, darling. Mummy's here now.'

Jessie clung to Sami's shoulders, felt him straining against her grip. The pull of his mother too hard for a four-year-old boy to resist.

'Stay with me, Sami, just for a moment,' Jessie whispered. 'Hold your torch tight and stay with me while I talk to your mummy.' Pressing her hands over his ears, she shouted. 'I know that you killed Kheial, Nooria. It's in the newspapers – the e-fit. The body washed up in Chichester Harbour that Surrey and Sussex Major Crimes are trying to identify. It's him, isn't it?'

'I've never been to Chichester Harbour.'

'Major Scott was stationed here at Thorney Island for six months three years ago. You lived together on this base.'

Nooria shook her head, but there was no commitment in the denial.

'Don't lie to me, Nooria. I've heard enough lies to last me a lifetime. The truth now. Only the truth. Please.'

Nooria's eyes blazed. 'I told you everything when you came to see me at the Royal College of Art. Kheial raped me and threatened me, and now he's gone. Gone to hell.'

'Helped on his way by you, because you killed him.'

Nooria yanked the pistol back out of her pocket. 'You're crazy—'

'Enough!' Jessie yelled. '*Enough now.*'

Silence.

Just the beat of the wind, the crash of breaking waves. Nooria, shocked and pale-faced, staring at Jessie across the expanse of sandy grassland. Sami twisting and shrugging Jessie's hands from his ears. A howl as the light from his torch found the gun in his mother's hand.

'I couldn't go on,' Nooria shouted, her voice rising and breaking. 'I couldn't go on fearing him, fearing for Sami's life, fearing everything. Sooner or later he was going to find out that Sami was a boy and then he would kill him or take him. He couldn't have stood me having a son with another man. And then when he arranged to have Nick attacked in Afghanistan – that was it. That was when I knew that I'd never be free of him, not while he lived.' She raised the Browning. 'I can shoot you now, Dr Flynn, and you'll just be another one on my list.'

Jessie ran her tongue around her palate. She knew that it was fear, adrenalin that had dried out her mouth.

'No one will blame you for Kheial. It was self-defence. You won't go to prison.'

Nooria drew in a long, quivering breath. 'Wendy.' Her words so quiet that for a second Jessie was unsure that she had heard right. 'I murdered Wendy.'

'Your husband murdered Wendy. He told me.' But even as she said the words, doubt rose in her mind. Why would Scott stab Wendy, risk getting covered in blood from killing someone at such close quarters, and then shoot Callan? He had an unlicensed pistol, one of the hundreds that were spirited from Army armouries each year, untraceable to him. Shooting both would have made sense. 'He was lying, wasn't he?' she said, as the realization dawned. 'He was lying, taking the blame, to protect you.' As he had shot Callan to protect her. Protection that had come too late for all of them. 'So Wendy knew about Kheial.'

'She forgot her keys one evening. Drove all the way home and then had to turn around and come back. He was with me when she arrived, taunting me, slapping me around, threatening to hurt Sami. The next day, Wendy saw me covered in bruises, saw how frightened Sami was—'

'And the kitchen?' Jessie asked, glancing down at Sami, squirming in her grasp, pulling towards his mother. Was that the night your kitchen was burnt?'

I got my thumb jammed in one of Nooria's kitchen cabinets. Some of them were damaged. She wanted to replace them, make it nice for when Major Scott got back from Afghanistan.

'I said that I'd had a chip-pan fire. But she wasn't stupid. And when the e-fit was published in the papers, I knew that it was only a matter of time before she saw it and worked out the truth. And she was such a bloody talker.'

Suddenly Sami wrenched himself free and charged across the sandy ground. Nooria ducked down and he flung himself into her arms. Sobbing, she pressed her face into his hair. Jessie started forward, but Nooria swung the Browning so that it was pointed straight at her heart.

'Don't come any closer, Dr Flynn. I *will* shoot you.'

Jessie stopped, breathed slowly, in, out. In again, out again, trying to calm the swollen knocking of her own heart.

'I'll stay right here, but listen, please. We can work this out. Let's go back to Aldershot, Nooria, and we can work this out.'

'There is nothing to work out.' Hugging Sami, she kissed his face. 'They'll put me in prison for years and then what will happen to Sami?'

'There are so many mitigating circumstances, Nooria.'

'Nothing has worked out for me before, why should it now?'

Jessie bit her lip. *Why should it now?* Why the hell should it?

'Because Kheial is dead. You have Nicholas and Sami. You have a family that loves you.'

'Nick and I have no future – together or apart.'

'So look after his son. You owe him that at least.'

'You still don't see it, do you?' Nooria laughed, harsh and sad. 'The evidence has been right in front of your nose all along and you still don't see it.' Gently, she turned Sami to face Jessie. 'Look at Sami. *Look at him.* Does he look like a blond man's child?'

Astonished comprehension overtook Jessie.

'Kheial is his father. Sami is the product of my rape – Sami and his sister, Soraya,' Nooria cried. 'It went on for years. The torment, the rapes, and both my children are a product of that.'

Looking at Nooria and Sami clutching each other, Jessie felt a freezing numbness spread through her body. It made all her senses acute. She could smell the sharp seaweed and salt carried on the cold wind, sense the lightning flashing over the ocean in the distance behind her, feel the cold air pricking across her skin. She was aware that she was ice cold, her body numb, but her mind was clear. For the first time, it was completely clear. *Sami and his sister Soraya, the disabled child. Why was she born disabled? Was it just bad luck?*

'Who was he, Nooria? Who was Kheial? He wasn't only a boyfriend, was he?'

Nooria made a guttural noise. 'It's not important.'

'Tell me.'

The sound suddenly of sirens in the distance, the flash of red-and-blue lights arching up to the black sky.

Fuck.

The realization that this situation was spiralling way out of control. That DI Simmons must finally have listened to his voicemails.

'He was my half-brother. Kheial was my half-brother. My father was an Afghan engineer, my mother was his secretary. He worked between Afghanistan and England and when he married my mother he already had another wife in Afghanistan. Kheial is his oldest son by his Afghan wife. My father died ten years ago, but as a woman I am owned by my father and, when he dies, I am owned by my oldest brother, until I marry.'

But she had married an infidel.

A howl of pain. 'As a woman, I am nothing. I am only property. I am owned.'

357

63

Pointing the gun at Jessie's heart, clutching Sami in her arms, Nooria backed down the shingle beach towards the sea.

'Nooria, run,' Jessie shouted. 'Take Sami and go somewhere else. Move to France, to Spain. I've got some money, I'll give you money. Enough to survive until you get yourself sorted.'

'I'm a murderer, Jessie. They'll find me. Wherever I go, they'll find me.' Her voice broke on a sob. 'It's too late. I'm tired. I can't fight any more, I can't hide any more.' Dipping her head to Sami's neck, she spoke softly, 'Sami, Mummy's here for you now. I'll never let anyone hurt you again. We'll be together, always. Together and safe.'

She took a step back, the shingle crunching under her shoes.

Another.

Cold realization overtook Jessie. 'Nooria, no.'

'I can't let them take my son away from me, Jessie. You'll understand one day, when you're a mother. You'll understand.'

Another step backwards and the black water swallowed her shoes.

'*No!*' Jessie yelled.

Nooria pointed the gun. '*Stay back.*'

Jessie saw her flinch as the freezing seawater lapped around her ankles.

A third step. A fourth.

The black water to her thighs now. Her gaze resolute. Tears running down her cheeks. Sami clinging to her; Nooria clinging to him, stroking his hair, talking to him all the time, words that Jessie couldn't hear.

She started to run towards the water, not caring about the gun, seeing only Jamie hanging from his curtain rail, the terror in Sami's face the first time she had seen him, inching into her office clutching his torch, the trust in his face now as he looked at his mother, the utter and total trust. The love.

The boy is safe with the woman.

'*Get back*,' Nooria screamed. 'You can't stop me. I can't lose Sami.'

Jessie kept running.

Sirens, closer. Headlights.

She heard the crack of the gun, Sami's scream, milliseconds before she felt the bullet tear into her leg, dived, a delayed reaction – *too late* – slammed into the sandy ground, hot daggers stabbing her thigh. Scrabbling to her feet, she stumbled, fell again, biting down the scream of pain, feeling blood running through her fingers, boiling hot against the frozen chill of her skin. Gritting her teeth, she pushed herself up again, balancing on her good leg. Dragging the other behind her, she hobbled down the beach and into the water, the pain in her thigh blinding.

The icy sea hit her like a wall. She gasped with shock, faltered.

'Nooria, no,' she yelled. 'Please, *no*.'

Nooria was up to her waist now. Turning away from Jessie, from the shore, she pushed forward through the waves and over her shoulder Jessie saw the pale moon of Sami's face, the trusting smile. His huge dark eyes met hers.

'*Sami*,' she screamed, reeling forward. Her injured leg snagged on something beneath the waves and she fell. Freezing water swallowed her whole – the shock of the cold and the sudden blackness so profound that her breath was knocked from her lungs. She was caught by a wave, turned over and over, salt water filling her mouth. Scrabbling for purchase on the slippery stones with her good leg, swimming upwards, she found her footing, broke the surface, disorientated, numb with cold, rubbing her stinging, blind eyes, coughing salt water from her lungs.

'Sami?'

She was shaking so hard that her teeth were chattering.

'*Nooria. Sami*,' she screamed.

Where were they?

The salt spray clouded her vision as she staggered forward against the force of the waves, screaming for Sami, scanning the water, seeing nothing but the unbroken swell, black water, the shapes of two yachts bobbing at anchor, another flash of lightning over the ocean, the unbroken swell, black water.

Nothing but black water.

64

Black water, the shapes of two yachts bobbing at anchor, another flash of lightning out over the ocean – lighting the stream of tide around the buoys anchoring the yachts.

Out. The tide was going out. The force of millions of tons of water moving towards the harbour entrance, dragging everything with it.

Sucking a balloon of air into her lungs, Jessie dived again, swimming hard and fast, eyes and mouth clamped shut against the freezing, salty water breaking over her head. She was swimming blind, cutting away from the beach and the red-and-blue flashing lights of the police vehicles, the torches, the shouts and screams, swimming with the tide, feeling its irresistible pull out into the blackness of the harbour. Her head was throbbing, pain pulsing in her injured leg, and she felt faint from the cold and the blood loss, her sodden clothes dragging her down, stripping her arms and good leg of energy. How easy it would be to stop – stop swimming – let the cold and the darkness take her.

Drowning was a pleasant way to die. *Who had told her*

that? She couldn't remember, couldn't think. Someone who hadn't drowned, she realized in the recesses of her mind.

A sudden bright light above her. Lightning?

No.

A hot yellow disc of light and the water around her churning with white horses. Looking up, she saw the heavy red-and-white underbelly of a helicopter hovering above her, recognized the hammer of the rotor blades now over the rush of water in her ears. A man, dressed in an orange survival suit, was hanging from the helicopter's open doorway. He was shouting something. Shouting and gesturing.

She couldn't hear.

Paddling her arms and kicking to stay afloat, she looked hard in the direction that he was pointing. Nothing. There was nothing out there. She couldn't *see* anything. Only white horses close by, black water beyond.

The circle of light moved away, and she was plunged into darkness again, just her retina shining bright white from the shock of the sudden brightness, its aftermath. Kicking hard again, she swam after the helicopter's beam. She couldn't feel her limbs at all, her teeth were chattering uncontrollably, her brain throbbing with the cold. *Give up.* She had to give up. Give up and sink.

With the last vestiges of her will, she reached the circle of light, stopped again, paddling frantically to keep her head above the waves, scanned the area of water lit by the helicopter's beam.

And saw it.

Something floating on the surface a few metres ahead of her. A tiny bundle of sodden clothes.

One stroke. Two. A third, and she was reaching out,

closing her fingers around the bundle, dragging it towards her, flailing with her free arm to keep herself afloat.

The pale moon of a face. Huge dark eyes. Unblinking eyes, staring without recognition.

Sami.

Wrapping her arm tight around him, she tilted his face clear of the water, kicked and flailed, watching the orange man swinging on the end of the wire, closing the distance between them.

The boy is safe with the woman, she whispered into Sami's hair, cold tears mixing with the salty spray on her face. *Say it, Sami.* Please, *say it. The boy is safe with the woman. The boy is safe with me.*

65

Eight days after Sami and Jessie had been airlifted to Southampton General Hospital and Nooria's body had been pulled from the sea, Jessie was discharged, her leg healing well. Sami had left the day before, fully recovered from the hypothermia that had slowed his heart rate and, perversely, kept him alive in the water. He was released into the care of Major Scott's sister, who had two young daughters of her own.

Marilyn collected Jessie from Southampton General himself in the dilapidated BMW Z3 that was his pride and joy, drove her the fifty miles home. Callan was in intensive care at St George's Hospital, he told her. The surgery to repair the extensive trauma to his internal organs caused by the bullet from Scott's gun had lasted twenty-two hours, and required three separate blood transfusions. It was only yesterday, a full week after the operation, that the surgeons were able to say for sure that he would live.

Ahmose was at his window, watching for Jessie's arrival. He had tidied her garden, cleaned her cottage from top to bottom though it hadn't needed cleaning, put a vase with fresh flowers in every room, made tea and a homemade chocolate cake to welcome her home. He had tears in his eyes when he hugged her.

The following day, Jessie drove her Mini to the tiny Hampshire church near to where Major Scott had been born, where Nooria was to be buried. The church was filled with men in uniform, their wives in black suits and dresses, a flock of sleek crows, showing solidarity with a fellow officer, even after disgrace. Jessie, wearing civvies and keeping her head down so that she wasn't recognized, took a seat at the end of the last row, by the wall. In the front pew, Major Scott, flanked on either side by a uniformed police officer, sat dry-eyed and silent, too stunned to cry. Jessie remembered that feeling: staring at Jamie's coffin, her brain and body numb with shock and grief.

As they left the church to line the path and a pay a final tribute to Nooria as her coffin was carried to the car that would take her to the crematorium, Jessie felt a hand on her arm. Turning, she saw a middle-aged woman, Scott's features laid out plainly on her pale face.

'Dr Flynn?'

'Yes.'

'I'm Pamela Taylor, Nick Scott's sister.'

Jessie shook the extended, black-gloved hand.

'How is Sami?' she asked.

'Better than I would have expected, given what he's been through.' She paused. 'But he keeps asking to see you.' Her tone was strained. 'I don't think it's a good idea, but he is very, very insistent. Will you come to my house tomorrow to see him?'

Jessie hated the word closure. It was used in too many pop-psychology books and television chat shows to make it sound anything other than pretentious and trite. However, the sentiment behind the word was solid. The last time she and Sami had seen each other was when their eyes had met as Nooria carried him into that freezing sea. It would help him to see her again on neutral territory, not at his old home or in her office. To see her, to chat and to play, as a normal child with an adult friend.

'Yes, of course, I'll come.'

Pamela Taylor's house was in a quiet, pleasant suburb of Farnborough, one of a horseshoe of pretty semi-detached houses ringing a green, the grass a haze of silver in the morning frost. It was clear from the expression on her face when she opened the door to Jessie that she still doubted the wisdom of allowing this visit.

'He's upstairs in his room, playing with his toys,' she said. 'Shall I get him to come down?'

'If he's happy and settled playing upstairs, it would be better if I go up. It makes it less formal, less of an occasion,' Jessie replied.

The door opposite the top of the stairs was ajar, and Jessie stood in the shadows on the landing for a moment, watching Sami through the opening. He was playing with cars and a three-storey garage – new toys. The room had been hastily decorated, clearly an office in its previous incarnation, as the notice board was pinned above a slightly darker, rectangular shadow on the white wall where a desk had stood. But navy-blue dinosaur curtains hung from a blue wooden curtain rail and the duvet on the bed was covered with a matching dinosaur cover. His plastic toy buckets had been replanted here, but Jessie could see no sign of his dolls – only Baby Isabel in her pink sleep-suit, lying on Sami's bed, her head resting on a stegosaurus on his pillow. She was pleased that Scott's sister had had the sense to keep Baby Isabel, that at least something Sami loved deeply was still with him. The doll would give him security, help speed his adjustment.

Her heart was in her mouth as she slowly pushed the door open, waiting in the doorway until he had registered the movement behind him and turned. She had been worried about his reaction on seeing her again, but she needn't have been. Leaping up, he charged across the room and clamped his arms around her thighs. Dumping the farm box, which she had brought with her, on to the carpet, Jessie knelt, pulled him into her arms and hugged him tight.

'I brought you a present, Sami,' she said, after a moment, gently levering him away.

'The farm,' he cried.

Jessie smiled, relaxing into the moment, as he sat down in front of the heavy-duty printed vinyl box, a huge grin spreading across his face. She had taken a calculated risk in bringing the farm with her, even though she had removed the black donkey, but had desperately wanted him to have it. It was the farm that had allowed her to find the first chink in his protective psychological armour.

'Go ahead,' she said, echoing the words that she had used the first time she had showed it to him, back in her office. 'Open it.'

They played for an hour, setting the animals in the fields, rearranging them, conducting fictional animal conversations, pretending to plough the fields with the tractor, sewing crops, harvesting them. When he reached to place the ducks in the pond, Jessie tensed, waiting for a reference to waves. But to her relief it didn't come.

When she finally stood to leave, he started gathering the animals together, putting them back into the centre of the vinyl box, zipping up the sides.

'No, Sami. The farm is yours now. I want you to keep it.'

She gave him a final hug, wrapping one arm around his torso, the other around his legs, lifting him off his feet and cuddling the whole of him, feeling the warmth of his little body, sucking in his smell one last time.

'Remember you can always ask your aunt to call me and I'll come. Whenever you want to see me, I'll come.'

Her last view, as she pulled the door to his bedroom closed, was of him lying on his stomach in a pool of cool winter sunlight, bouncing the tractor over the cobbled bricks of the farmyard, making 'vroom, vroom' noises – just another typical four-year-old boy. A four-year-old boy who had experienced far too much trauma already in his short life, but who in time, she believed, would be okay.

After seeing Sami, she hit the A3, drove fast through the rolling Surrey Hills and London satellite villages to Tooting. St George's Hospital was huge and rambling, a mini-town of grey concrete blocks sprawled over ten acres. It took her over half an hour to find the right intensive care ward, where she was told by the pretty blonde reception desk nurse that Callan was groggy with sedation.

'Are you family?'

Jessie shook her head.

'Girlfriend?'

'No.'

'Pity.' The nurse laughed brightly. 'He's gorgeous, even with all the tubes.'

368

Jessie felt her cheeks colour. 'I'm a work colleague.'

'Oh. Well, I'm sorry, but only immediate family are allowed to visit. There's a very significant risk of infection.'

Jessie nodded. 'Thanks for your help,' she murmured. Turning, she headed towards the exit doors.

'There's a newsagent's in the main foyer. You could get him a card,' the nurse called after her.

In the hospital foyer, she stood in front of the newsagent's, staring at the racks of 'Get Well' cards – a few birthdays on the bottom row in case any of the patients were unfortunate enough to celebrate their birthday while incarcerated – dithering. *It's only a card, for God's sake.* Eventually, she chose the only one not embossed with pastel flowers or bandaged teddy bears, and spent the next fifteen minutes, back in the intensive care waiting room, flipping between the sorrowful puppy with the bleeding paw on the front and blank white paper inside, no idea what to write. Finally, she scribbled a bland, *Get well, Ben. Love from Jessie*, and handed the card to the nurse.

By the time she arrived at her mother's house in Wimbledon, the day had slipped to evening, the winter darkness falling fast and solid as a curtain dropping at the end of a play. The little cul-de-sac she had grown up in was ablaze with electric lights. She parked right outside the house this time, walked straight down the path without hesitation.

She hadn't been inside her childhood home for six months, but it still felt like home. Her mother, however, was different. She looked younger, healthier. Her skin had lost the grey pallor it had possessed since Jamie's death, the look she'd had of living a half-life – half-human, half-ghost.

'I came down to see you. Did Ahmose tell you?'

Jessie nodded. 'I didn't have time to come before. I've been working on a case.' Tensing at the verbal attack she expected to follow.

It didn't come. Instead, her mum lifted a hand to stroke her arm, sliding it down to her hand, squeezing Jessie's cold fingers in her own soft, warm ones.

'It's fine, sweetheart, but I've missed you and you look exhausted.'

Jessie bit back the tears.

'Tell me, Jessie.'

She shook her head. 'I'm fine.'

'I'm your mother.'

Jessie dipped her head, a single tear rolling down her cheek. 'You told me fifteen years ago that I was too old to need a mother.'

Her mother's eyes hung closed for a moment. 'I'm ashamed of myself, Jessie. I'm ashamed at what I said and I am ashamed at the way I've treated you. I can recognize that now – fifteen years later than I should have done. I wanted . . .' A catch in her voice. 'I *needed* someone to blame. You were the only one here. I'm sorry, darling, more sorry than I can ever say, than I can ever make up to you.'

'But if I hadn't left him alone.'

'He would have found another way. Another time.' She pulled Jessie into her arms. 'We both need to let it go now, sweetheart, to move on. We both need to live our own lives. We've spent long enough grieving, atoning.'

Back outside, Jessie stopped halfway to the gate. A tiny yellow flower, just one, was blooming on the winter jasmine by the side of the path. She looked at it, astonished, as if a flower was the last thing she expected to see brightening the sludgy brown earth in her childhood garden. A signal of new growth. New beginnings. She stood looking down at it for a long time.

And Jessie realized that her mother was right. Here she was: twenty-nine years old. Twenty-nine and she hadn't lived. Instead, she had sat looking over her shoulder, back to the past, trying to make amends while her life played itself out without her. She could let it go on, continue to feed the guilt, to punish herself. Or—

New growth. New beginnings.

Acknowledgements

As always, huge thanks to my amazing agent, Will Francis, who is endlessly supportive and without whose help I would never have been able to embark on this amazing and fun journey. Thanks also to the rest of the fabulous team at Janklow and Nesbit (UK).

I would also like to thank Julia Wisdom my Editor at Harper Collins, who lives up to her surname (I'm sure she has heard that many times before!). I am delighted to have the opportunity to work with you. Also thank you to Kate Stephenson, Assistant Editor, who is not only hugely professional, but also great fun to spend an evening at the bar with. Thanks also to Felicity Denham, Alex Allden, Hannah Gamon and Sarah Benton for all your hard work on *Fire Damage*.

I was fortunate to have Mo Hayder as my mentor early in the writing of my debut thriller, *White Crocodile*, and all that she has taught me was invaluable in the writing of *Fire Damage*.

Love and thanks, always, to my mother, Pamela Taylor, Maggie Knottenbelt, and Jo Medina. I also wanted to mention: Bettina and Sean, Nancy Le Roux for your much appreciated support, my book club (Tor, Radhika, Liz, Bronte, Rebecca, Tonia, Bettina), Eleanor Whitehead, Laura Wood, Dylan King (now your classmates will believe you!), Ian, Jane, Izzy and Lottie Middleton for filling in my Army blanks, Paul and Katie Creffield for your friendship and your police and SOCO knowledge and my Godson, Will.

Huge thanks also to Chris and Michael Brice and Matt Higgins for all their help with the Royal Military Police and 'Hello' to Max Higgins.

I wanted to mention a very brave little boy, James Lewis, who had restrictive cardiomyopathy and, thankfully, found a new heart. Live a full and happy life, little James.

In loving memory of my late father, Derek Taylor, who I miss every day.

Most of all, love and thanks to Anthony, Isabel (the inspiration for Baby Isabel) Anna and Alexander.

Note: The literal translation of the name Kheial is phantom/hallucination.

Read on for an exclusive extract from the new
Jessie Flynn novel:

SCARED TO DEATH

1

Eleven Years Ago

The eighteen-year-old boy in the smart uniform made his way along the path that skirted the woods bordering the school's extensive playing fields. He walked quickly, one hand in his pocket, the other holding the handle of the cricket bat that rested over his shoulder, like the umbrella of some city gent. Gene Kelly in *Singin' in the Rain*. For the first time in a very long time he felt nimble and light on his feet, as if he could dance. And he felt even lighter in his heart, as though the weight that had saddled him for five long years was finally lifting. Light, but at the same time keyed-up and jittery with anticipation. Thoughts of what was to come drove the corners of his mouth to twitch upwards.

He used to smile all the time when he was younger, but he had almost forgotten how. All the fun in his life, the beauty that he had seen in the world, had been destroyed five years ago. Destroyed once, and then again and again, until he no longer saw joyfulness in anything. He had thought that, in time, his hatred and anger would recede.

But instead it had festered and grown black and rabid inside him, the only thing that held any substance or meaning for him.

He had reached the hole in the fence. By the time they moved into the sixth form, boys from the school were routinely slipping through the boundary fence to jog into the local village to buy cigarettes and alcohol, and the rusty nails holding the bottom of the vertical wooden slats had been eased out years before, the slats held in place only at their tops, easy to slide apart. Nye was small for his age and slipped through the gap without leaving splinters or a trace of lichen on his grey woollen trousers or bottle green blazer, or threads of his clothing on the fence.

The hut he reached a few minutes later was small and dilapidated, a corrugated iron roof and weathered plank walls. It used to be a woodman's shed, Nye had been told, and it still held stacks of dried logs in one corner. Sixth formers were the only ones who used it now, to meet up and smoke; the odd one who'd got lucky with one of the girls from the day school down the road used it for sex.

Nye had detoured here first thing this morning before class to clean it out, slipping on his leather winter gloves to pick up the couple of used condoms and toss them into the woods. *Disgusting*. He hadn't worried about his footprints – there would be nothing left of the hut by the time this day was over.

Now, he sprayed a circular trail of lighter fuel around the inside edge of the hut, scattered more on the pile of dry logs and woodchips in the corner, ran a dripping line around the door frame and another around the one small wire-mesh-covered window. Tossing the bottle of lighter fuel on to the stack of logs, he moved quietly into a dark corner of the shed where he would be shielded from immediate view by the door when it opened, and waited. He was patient. He had learned patience the hard way and today his patience would pay off.

Footsteps outside suddenly, footsteps whose pattern, regularity and weight were seared into his brain. Squeezing himself into the corner, Nye held his breath as the rickety wooden door creaked open. The man who stepped into the hut closed the door behind him, pressing it tightly into its frame as Nye knew he would. He stood for a moment, letting his vision adjust to the dimness before he looked around. Nye saw the man's eyes widen in surprise when he noticed him standing in the shadows, when he saw that it wasn't the person he had been expecting to meet. His face twisted in anger – an anger Nye knew well.

Swinging the bat in a swift, neat arc as his sports masters had taught him, Nye connected the bat's flat face, dented from contact with countless cricket balls on the school's pitches, with the man's temple. A sickening crunch, wood on bone, and the man dropped to his knees. Blood pulsed from split skin and reddened the side of his face. Nye was tempted to hit him again. Beat him until his head was pulp, but he restrained himself. The first strike had done its job and he wanted the man conscious, wanted him sentient for what was to come.

Dropping the cricket bat on to the floor next to the crumpled man, Nye pulled open the shed door. Stepping into the dusk of the woods outside, he closed it behind him. There was a rusty latch on the gnarled door frame, the padlock long since disappeared. Flipping the latch over the metal loop on the door, he stooped and collected the thick stick he'd tested for size and left there earlier, and jammed it through the loop.

Moving around to the window, too small for the man to fit through – he'd checked that too; he'd checked and double-checked everything – he struck a match and pushed his fingers through the wire. He caught sight of the man's pale face looking up at him, legs like those of a newborn calf as he tried to struggle to his feet. His eyes were huge and very black in the darkness of the shed. Nye held the man's gaze, his mouth twisting into a smile. He saw the man's eyes flick from his face to the lit match in his fingers, recognized that moment where the nugget of hope segued into doubt and then into naked fear. He had experienced that moment himself so many times.

He let the lit match fall from his fingers.

Stepping away from the window, melting a few metres into the woods, Nye stood and watched the glow build inside the hut, listened to the man's screams, his pleas for help as he himself had pleaded, also in vain, watched and listened until he was sure that the fire had caught a vicious hold. Then he turned and made his way back through the woods, walking quickly, staying off the paths.

It was 13 July, his last day in this godforsaken shithole.

He had waited five long years for this moment.

Thirteen. Unlucky for some, but not for me. Not any more.